ADVERSARY

"A blood-drenched battle of wits and will . . . McMahon's story and prose are fired straight from the hip . . . Slam-bang!" (*Revolution No. 9*)
Philadelphia Inquirer

"Like John Grisham and James Patterson, McMahon excels at moving his plot along . . . *Blood Double* is all about movement–the only thing stationary is the reader, likely for the entire length of the book."
BookPage

"Intelligent, well-crafted entertainment . . . (with) deft characterizations . . . horrors and more await us in *To The Bone.*"
Washington Post Book World

"*Revolution No. 9* spins the thrills and twists like a Tilt-a-Whirl–it's equal parts Stephen King and John Sandford, with a dash of ER thrown in for good measure."
Tim Dorsey

"McMahon . . . delivers his finest achievement to date with this beautifully written stand-alone set in contemporary Montana." (*Lone Creek*)
Publishers Weekly

ADVERSARY

Neil McMahon

Quinotaur Press

Missoula, Montana

Cover design by Jason Neal

Author photo by Kim Anderson

ISBN 978-0-9847750-1-9

AUTHOR'S NOTE
November, 2011

Almost thirty years ago, an aspiring author who'd had some minor literary success decided to try his hand at a horror novel. He'd never written a full-length book before, he only had a murky idea of how to go about it, and a lot of what he thought he knew turned out to be wrong. There was also another major wrinkle– the pesky need to make a living by some other means, which in his case took the form of swinging a hammer on construction jobs, trading that work for time to write.

As he got into the novel crafting process, he started comparing it to hiking in the mountains. You can stand on a peak and see a clearly marked trail leading down into the forested canyon below, then emerging on the other side and up to the next peak. At first, it looks like a straight shot from here to there. But what you can't see are the hazards hidden in those thick woods between the vista points–a bewildering network of false trails that branch off to nowhere, rockslides and brush-choked gullies, impassable deadfalls and rushing streams.

That labyrinthine trek through the prose wilderness ended up lasting several years and a couple of thousand discarded pages. Along the way, he adopted the pseudonym Daniel Rhodes, for reasons that seemed good at the time and seem better now.

Eventually, in 1987, the book was published as *Next, After Lucifer* (St. Martin's Press). A sequel, *Adversary*, followed in 1988, and a third horror novel, *Cast Angels Down To Hell* (originally titled *Kiss Of Death*) in 1990.

And then, quite suddenly, it was over. Daniel Rhodes was through with publishing (or more accurately, vice versa), those three books faded from print, and he faded with them.

Another decade passed before that writer re-surfaced as Neil McMahon (his/my real name) with a medical thriller titled *Twice Dying* (HarperCollins, 2000). My luck has been much better the second time around, with several more mainstream thrillers published to date. Writing them has kept me busy, and I haven't ventured into horror again (yet, anyway).

But those first three books, and the hope of getting them back in print, were never far from my mind.

The wait turned out to be a long one—roughly one-third of my life—but finally, thanks to a lot of help from terrific people, here they are.

"Look upon them again, I dare not," Sir Walter Scott said of his own earlier works—words that ring so true. As I've gone through mine this time, I've seen countless things I wish I'd done better. (It's a somewhat eerie experience, by the way—like meeting the ghost of who you were many years ago, and getting glimmers, or outright jolts, of how you thought and felt when you were that much younger.) I was sorely tempted to revise, but somehow, it just seemed right to leave them as they were. Except for very minor changes to improve formatting appearance, these are the original texts.

All in all, despite their flaws, I think they still hold up pretty well, and that there's more to them than might meet the eye—elements of religious thought, history, and perhaps most of all, a sense of how the supernatural is tied to human longing, promising the things we all desire but are unreachable to us by ordinary means.

In terms of what these books aim to do and how they go about it, I don't know of anything else quite like them.

I'll close by saying that I believe the story behind all this might be intriguing to readers interested in the writing process. So we've set up a website that's mainly devoted to discussing it in more detail—how the idea for the books first came, the thinking that underlies them (read: method to my madness), how they fared with reviews and the publishing world, my use of a pseudonym, and related issues such as this basic question about the horror genre: Why do so many millions of people love to be scared by stories like these?

Please visit us there at:

EvilAwakens.com

And also on Facebook at:

facebook.com/neilmcmahonbooks

PROLOGUE

*Be sober, be vigilant; because your adversary
the devil, as a roaring lion, walketh about,
seeking whom he may devour.*

St. Peter

When Joey Figureido opened his eyes, the world was
dark. He lay rigid, breath stopped in his throat, gaze
flicking from side to side, searching for the shadowed
face that had torn him from sleep. It was gone.

Above, the full moon was just topping a row of cliffs,
illuminating with a faint phosphorescence the endless
drifting lines of surf on the night-black Pacific, casting a
ghostly, glowing funnel to the horizon. The boom of the
breakers and the long, sucking swirls of the dark water
whispered of things cold, dripping, forever hungry for
warmth. He shivered violently, and as if the motion had
broken the spell in which he lay, the scene clicked into
familiar focus.

The place was a protected cove on the beach near
Tunitas; he and his buddies had discovered it as kids,

bicycling down from Half Moon Bay to prowl the cliffs, building forts and holding wars in the brush, and spying on the nudists and gays at San Gregorio, just south. This afternoon he had come here with his girlfriend Layla. After several lazy hours of beer drinking and sunbathing and fucking, they had fallen asleep under a blanket. The warmth across his legs was Layla's thigh; his hand moved automatically to touch her. But then the dream that had awakened him flashed back into his mind.

The face itself had been bad enough: half hidden in shadow, the other half dominated by a hard, pitiless eye that stared at Joey with unmistakably evil intent. And the face was impossibly vivid, as if the man really had been there, not an arm's length away, leaning over him. Trapped in his dream, unable even to twitch, Joey had stared back, terror rising within him.

Then the lips had curved into a cruel, knowing smile, and an unbelievably bright red stream of blood spilled from the corner of the mouth. Joey's fear surged so terrifically that it tore him free, plunging him into a dark, waking awareness of the moon and echoing surf. The memory of the face hovered and for a few seconds, fear mastered him again. But he fought back in the way he had since childhood, forming his own face into an ex-aggerated snarling mask of his older brother Cedro's. Cedro was so tough he did not have to snarl.

Layla stirred suddenly in her sleep, murmuring in rising protest about something only she could see. Her blond hair was dark in the moonlight, spilling across Joey's chest. He touched her shoulder with his callused hand, but then understood that he was really trying to reassure himself. This angered him. Layla was twitching now, making little yelping sounds.

"Gotcha!" he whispered sharply, and grabbed her ass hard. She came awake thrashing, eyes wild with fright. Joey grinned, feeling better, her fear giving him confidence over his own. Her fine high breasts bounced as she sat up, the dark nipples puckering taut in the cool night air. He could see the goosebumps, almost taste the hard buds softening under his tongue, and with some surprise, felt his cock stir. He had already come four times that afternoon, pretty good even for him, and it felt for all the world like number five was on the way. With the face in the dream fading quickly to the edges of his memory, he slid his fingers up Layla's thigh.

She caught his hand and held it. "I'm scared," she whispered. Her head was moving quickly from side to side, wide eyes straining to see. Joey watched her, realizing with growing astonishment that it was her fear that was arousing him, acting on him like a warm tongue.

"Nothing to be afraid of," he said thickly, putting her hand on him.

She pulled away, roughly this time. "I dreamed there was somebody after us."

"Yeah?" Joey said sarcastically. "Where are they, in the water?" The tide was coming in, making the cove the size of a small yard; the eighty-foot cliffs were smooth and sheer. The only access was by wading around from the main beach to the north.

She shook her head, gaze still roving. "I was being chased," she said, "by this thing." Her voice wavered. "It was . . . like . . . short, and had these stubby little arms, and it was coming after me."

"Uh-huh," he said, pulling her down beside him.

"Please, baby, don't. I'm not kidding. Besides, I'm sore."

This time it was Joey who sat up, pissed. "You're scared, you're sore," he mimicked with an exaggerated whine. "Okay, I get it."

He stood, jerked open the cooler lid, pulled a beer from the half-melted ice, and stalked to stand ankle-deep in the sea. The early summer water was cold, and the soft sand sucked at his feet.

Broads, man, he thought unhappily. Cedro was right. Let them get started, and they'd run every kind of number there was on you. She should be thanking her stars just to get a look at his cock–him, Joey Figureido, last year's hottest halfback on the high school team, making more money as Cedro's deckhand than some of the skippers in town, sure to have his own salmon boat by the time he was twenty-five. He flexed the thick muscles in his arms and shoulders and rubbed the mat of curly black hair on his chest. It pissed him mightily, but it made him feel somehow desperate, too. He liked Layla. He'd told her things he'd never told any other girl, believing he could trust her. Hell, he'd been thinking about marrying her. He waited with his back turned, giving her one more chance to touch him and beg forgiveness.

Instead, she called hoarsely, "Joey, let's go home." Her voice told him that she was still back at the blanket and still scared and that she meant it. He turned, his mouth bitterly forming the words, *You can forget about any wedding, man,* when he noticed something glinting on the cliffs above.

A man was standing there, clearly outlined in the bright moonlight, gazing down on them.

Joey blinked, shook his head, looked again.

The man was gone.

His heart suddenly pounding like a jackhammer, Joey forced a shaky smile. Whoa, buddy, he thought. Cool out. You're seeing things. Feeling the icy weight of the beer in his hand, he popped the top and took a long drink, his eyes still searching the cliffs. It was that dream, together with Layla's fear, working on him. That was all.

But if he was imagining things, he sure was doing it in style. The man had looked eight feet tall. And the thing that was glimmering—son of a bitch if it hadn't looked like a *sword.* Not any little machete, either. It was wide as his hand and tall as his chest. The dude had been, like, leaning on it. Joey swallowed the beer slowly, not tasting it. His smile was gone. He was remembering that the San Francisco Bay was one of the world's prime areas for weirdos. There were probably more mass murderers than accountants on the streets, more bodies buried in the woods than at Arlington. If it was just some creep up there who thought maybe he could spy on them fucking, that was one thing. Joey could handle that—he'd run the guy down, kick his balls up into his throat.

But a creep with a sword?

He was not sure that even Cedro would know what to do.

Layla was dressing; he noticed with distracted lust that she pulled on her jeans and sweatshirt with nothing underneath. He was sure she had not seen the man, but she moved quickly, impatiently, throwing things into a beach bag and wadding up the blanket.

A fucking *sword?*

A faint sickness touched his stomach. He looked at the beer in his hand, then sidearmed it into the surf. When he got to his clothes, he was hurrying too. He had started thinking about how there was only one way out of here: wading around the cliffs to the main beach, then climbing those easier bluffs to where his pickup truck was parked, in a turnout off Highway 1.

Not far from where the man had been standing. Suppose—just suppose—the fucker put it together and hid by the truck?

"Maybe," he said to Layla. His voice sounded weak. Clearing his throat, he tried again. "Maybe we should just leave this stuff. Come back tomorrow." Her face was pale and frightened, and he hated himself for saying it, but he could not hold it back. "I thought I saw a guy up on the cliffs. A weirdo." He bit off the words *with a sword,* and was glad of it, because she looked like she was about to faint.

When she spoke, her voice was so tiny he could hardly hear her. "Maybe we should just stay here."

But, Joey thought, suppose the guy was climbing down to the main beach right this second, knowing they were trapped in this little cove?

Like a light bulb in a comic strip, the answer popped up in his mind. Haul ass to the main beach now, before anybody could possibly get down from where the man had been. If they saw him coming, they could outrun him, go into the ocean if they had to, or lose him in the brushy cliff terrain Joey knew well. Find a house, get on the phone, and call the Surf club, where Cedro and Frank Schmidt and Big Mike Lisbon would be drinking, tell them to get their guns and gaffs and come on down for a wild pig hunt. Only it was going to be *long* pig. The fury that rose in him when he imagined what he was going to do to the asshole who had dared to frighten him was so intense it blinded him and stopped his breath.

Layla was watching him fearfully. "Okay," he said, in charge again. "We're going up the beach. If you see any-body, run as fast as you can. Go into the water if you have to." She nodded, eyes round and solemn as a child's, and he took her hand and stepped into the chilly waves.

It took them three or four minutes to make their way through the knee-deep surf around the sheer cliffs. As the main beach came into sight, Joey put a finger to Layla's lips and waded quietly ahead. He crouched behind the last shoulder of rock, scanning the beach and the bluffs with an intensity so fierce he felt he could see in the dark, hear footsteps a thousand yards away, *smell* an ap-proaching enemy. The numbness in his feet from the water belonged to someone else. Maybe this was what war was like, he thought. Maybe this was Rambo. The moon was so fat it seemed to drip light. Nothing moved except the surf. He had almost started to enjoy the whole thing when an entirely new aspect flashed into his mind: the rough, disbelieving laughter of Cedro and his friends. *A sword, you say, Joey? No shit? You should have kept*

7

the cooler with you, my man, you could have used the lid for a shield.

It was for Layla, he thought, bristling. *I* wasn't scared of the creep, I just couldn't take any chances with her. But as he hovered there, he wondered unhappily if he had really seen the man at all, or if the whole thing had somehow stemmed from Layla's bad dream. *You haven't been eating those cowshit mushrooms, have you, Joey?*

"Okay," he whispered to her. "All clear." She came forward, eagerly grasping his hand. They started walking, moving to the firm, packed sand above the surf line. He remembered with shame that only a couple of minutes before he'd been planning to hit this stretch running, to take the next mile at an all-out sprint.

The surf boomed and slapped; their footsteps made light crunching sounds. Far to the north he could see the lights of Pillar Point. The whitish strip of beach ahead thinned in a long crescent to merge with the black ocean to the left and bluffs to the right. At intervals a squat, heavy rock thrust up out of the sand. Joey's eyes stayed busy just in case, scanning the diminishing cliffs, the widening stretch of beach behind.

After a quarter of a mile he decided to head for the truck. This was definitely bullshit. An easy trail up to the highway lay just opposite. He changed direction suddenly, tugging Layla a little roughly. He was starting to remember that not only was it her fault he had acted like a fool, but she had shut him down.

"Listen," he said harshly. "What I said back there about thinking I'd seen a guy–I don't want you to tell anybody about it. I didn't really see nothing. I knew you were scared, and I was trying to make you feel better."

She nodded timidly and, for the first time, smiled. "I *was* scared," she whispered. "But I'm okay now." She squeezed his hand and his anger softened, but he scowled and pulled free.

"Don't be mad at me, Joey," she said. "Please. I love you. I do." She stopped, watching him imploringly.

"You got a funny way of showing it," he muttered.

Suddenly she was kissing him, her mouth hot and wet, and then her fingers were unzipping his jeans and she was sliding to her knees. He stared down at her, not quite believing what was happening. His fingers twisted in her hair, the delicious pressure building quickly. His eyes closed, his back arched, his knees began to shake, and then lights seemed to burst behind his eyelids. As he sagged, he was dimly aware of a sound in the distance that seemed to echo his own groan: a faint, mournful whistle—some seabird, maybe, though he had never heard one like it.

Slowly, lingering, Layla drew back, her dark, adoring eyes fixed on his. His own gaze caressed her face.

Then a motion on the beach made him look up fast.

Perhaps a hundred yards ahead stood a rock he did not think had been there before. It was a little bigger than a fire hydrant, shaped about the same, and black. With his hand frozen on Layla's nape, Joey stared.

The rock moved, a sudden, bizarre scurrying toward the water, then back inland toward the cliffs. It had short stubby arms—or at least limbs where arms usually were—that stretched before it. There was something eager about the way they were held.

Abruptly, the creature paused, straightening and casting its head about, as if searching the wind for a scent. It seemed to be muffled head to foot in a thick, hooded garment. And while there was something about its motion that made Joey think of a weasel or a snake, he understood with absolute certainty, deep in his guts, that this was no animal—that it was not any kind of being he had ever imagined.

With the same ferocious quickness and stealth, it crouched again and continued its gliding search, making another traverse of the beach. Toward them.

"Do you love me?" Layla whispered, her eyes still searching his face.

He yanked her to her feet and started to run for the cliffs, frantically stuffing his cock back into his pants with his free band, dimly aware of her angry yelps as she struggled to break free of his grip.

". . . the hell you think you're doing . . ," she panted.

At last Joey found his voice and screamed, "Run!" and she whirled to look behind. A shivering moan broke from her lips.

To the base of the cliffs they raced along side by side, until Layla's foot came down on a half-concealed rock and she fell, plunging forward in a spray of sand. She was up in a second, but limping.

"I can't," she gasped, and Joey, cursing, threw her over his shoulder. As he did, he caught a glimpse of the dark shape. It was coming straight after them now, stubby limbs outstretched as if to embrace. Joey seemed to feel its thoughts forcing their way into his mind: a hot, crawling lust, a desperate thirst to destroy. Though he had always prided himself on his strength, he had never known anything like the power that coursed through him as he raced up the cliff. The trail switched back and forth for the first steep eighty yards, then dropped into a gully choked with deadfall. He pounded across the fallen logs in huge, grunting leaps, branches whipping his face, his breath coming in shrieks. The voice in his mind was growing louder, its desperation rising. An element of coaxing had entered in, a plea for Joey to sink to his knees, give up, rest–forever.

He surged on, electrified by fear. Layla was a weight he could hardly feel, a child, a kitten clinging to his neck. Fifty yards more, a final, steep, scrambling stretch of agony, and he burst over the top of the cliff and onto the solid roadside of Highway 1. The pavement was endlessly dark in both directions, the terrain nothing but vast fields of ice plant, without so much as the lights of a distant farm. There was only his truck, silhouetted a quarter mile away. Joey put his head down and sprinted.

He arrived with lungs on fire and body vibrating as if it would explode. Layla's feet slid to the ground but she kept her arms tight around him, whispering "Hurry hurry hurry–" He tore the contents from his pockets. A knife and coins, bright in the moonlight, rang as they spilled to the ground. At last he had the keys, his shaking fingers separating them and shoving one into the lock. A quick glance behind showed nothing moving, but there were shadows everywhere. He jerked open the door, his arm around her to sling her into the cab–

And shrieked when the dark, muffled shape rose from the floor, its grotesque limbs reaching, its silent shriek of triumph tearing through his mind.

Layla slumped to the ground. He tried to lift her up again, but his strength was gone. Hopelessly, with a hot mist deepening across his vision, he ran across the highway and into the fields, no longer sprinting, but plodding. The crisp juicy ice plant split under his feet, making him slip.

When he fell, he saw that the creature was moving toward him. But it was no longer hurrying.

In the shadows of the brush along the clifftop, the tall man stood waiting. When he heard the screaming begin, he nodded with satisfaction and stepped forth. The hungry mouths of the servants would be fed. All was well for another moon.

He walked to the truck, where the girl still lay in shock, barely conscious. For a moment he stood contemplating her, leaning on his great broadsword. Then he set the sword aside. It was no longer strictly necessary—he carried a smaller and more convenient implement—but it brought back pleasant memories of seven centuries before, when the man he had been at that time rode through Europe and Asia with such a sword in his hand, in the service of the Knights of the Temple. Until he had turned from that service to another, infinitely more powerful and profound.

He gathered her in his arms and petted her hair, commanding her to consciousness with his will. Her eyes fluttered, then opened fully, and he watched with pleasure as she became aware that the face looking down at her, with its bleared dead eye, was not the one she had expected. Smiling at her struggles, her strangled cries, he carried her to the edge of a sheer bluff. Far below, the waves crashed against the rocks of a deep pool, throwing sprays of mist like rainbows in the moonlight.

When he spoke, it was in a language that only a few had ever known, most of them dead for a thousand years. What he addressed could not be spoken of in human concepts of sex or nature. Given the limitations of language, he preferred the term *Adversary*. He held the panting, squirming girl tightly as he murmured. It did not take long. Then his hand moved to her throat and made a sudden, sure motion. Her cries stopped.

Although the blood was only a symbol of the true underlying power, it was necessary. That was the way of things. When he had drunk, he gazed into her dimming eyes and smiled once more, this time gently. She was a pretty child. It was almost sad.

"I have spared you the pain of a long life," he whispered.

With one hand in the small of her back, he raised her effortlessly above his head and held her there while he watched the dark fins he had summoned slice in agitation through the surf below. Then he hurled her far out into the maelstrom. The frenzied shapes rose and fell in the bleak, booming waves.

When all was finished, he sounded once more the eerie whistle, sending his pet back to the place, found on no map, whence it had come. There he had courted and won the favor of powers only dimly imagined by most humans: where he had become something more than a man.

Six hundred and eighty years before, he had fallen, punished for his arrogance, and had lain as a prisoner through the dark centuries. But he had risen again at last, and after a time of acclimating himself to this bizarre modem world, he was ready to resume the work he had long ago bound himself to do. If one danced to the music, he thought grimly, one must pay the piper. It was the oldest rule, and one of the few he perforce obeyed.

He wiped the blood from his twisted mouth and returned to the shadows, where his own vehicle lay waiting.

PART ONE

The devil can cite Scripture for his purpose.

Shakespeare

ONE

The rain began as Nicole crossed California Street, sprinkling the pavement with soft fat drops, filling the San Francisco evening with a warm, musty smell that hinted of decay. Although it was Friday, there were few pedestrians and not many more cars; she had worked until after six, missing the financial district's cocktail hour rush, the frantic pairing off that preceded each weekend as if it were the last of all time. A flurry of drops spattered her face, and she squinted up into the heavy gray fog that rolled between the buildings, trying to gauge the storm. She had not brought an umbrella. Summer was here; the last few days had been hot; this was a final, defiant gasp of spring, to be enjoyed rather than evaded. She tucked her hair into the collar of her jacket and slowed her step.

And why not join the game? she thought, watching a man leap out of a double-parked Volvo to buy a bouquet of flowers from the kiosk on the corner. It would be easy enough. She was certain to know people in any of several popular watering holes. She could count on being welcomed into a witty group flushed with cocktails and Friday afternoon cheer, and on being appraised by men with eighty-dollar haircuts, thousand-dollar suits, and wedding bands in their pockets. She hadn't really needed to work late and was in no real hurry to get home. Nicole Partrick, Girl-at-Law: a name you could trust for dedication, integrity, boredom.

As she turned toward Montgomery Street, she glanced at the sculpture that squatted like a boulder of glazed obsidian in the Bank of America plaza–a mass of fluid, polished surfaces, the size of a car, shaped something like a rounded wedge. Known in the financial district as the "Banker's Heart," it was hard and cold as diamond and absolutely black. The plaza was deserted except for a single man standing beside the sculpture, motionless, hands in the pockets of an expensive overcoat. Nicole realized, with a little jolt, that he was watching her.

There should have been nothing disturbing about that. Men's attention was something she took for granted, and besides, she reminded herself wryly, she was the only person moving on the street. But there was an element to his bearing–an intensity, a forcefulness that came across even while he stood at rest–that held her attention. He was tall–over six feet, she guessed–and strongly built, with thick, graying hair, a face that seemed reasonably handsome but not striking, and, oddly, sunglasses. Then she realized that her interest stemmed mainly from her sense that she had seen him before.

It came back then: she'd lunched this afternoon at Le Charcuterie with her friend Heather Bryant. The man's dark glasses, inside the restaurant, were what triggered the memory; they had seemed out of place, an affectation that did not fit the circumstances. She thought too that he had been wearing gloves, but could not remember for sure.

In any case, that man had had no coat, and he'd been sitting off to the side where she had gotten only glimpses of him. And now this man was at least fifty yards away with his hands in his pockets; it was raining and misty and impossible to tell; and it's a hell of a reflection on your state, Nicole, she told herself sternly, when you notice a man at lunch and have him stalking you through the city later that afternoon.

But the memory of lunch brought back the conversation that had gone with it. She winced a little, lowered her head, and hurried again, hearing in her mind Heather's confident, slightly shrill voice:

"Nicole, honey, I could see you carrying a torch for that Jesse guy if he was rich or brilliant, or even if he was just crazy about you. But the way you tell it, he's a goddamned carpenter, and a drunk, and he couldn't care less if you ever take another breath. This is the eighties, doll. If you're gonna burn that candle, you'd better make sure it's shining on something bright."

Heather was twenty-nine, three years younger than Nicole, and was, Nicole supposed, her best friend, although theirs was not a relationship of much emotional intimacy. They worked in the same building and had finally seen each other enough times in elevators and the lobby to get acquainted. Heather was an investment counselor and stockbroker, with an MBA from Berkeley and a husband who regularly made more money trading real estate in a month than Nicole's father ever had at his factory job in a year. The Bryants had a houseboat in Sausalito, an apartment on Russian Hill, and a condo at Heavenly Valley–all profitably rented when they were not using them–and they moved in a circle of people who considered themselves to be the up-and-coming lions of power and finance in the Bay Area. Heather was forever trying to fix Nicole up with some rising star. Nicole would agree from time to time, doing her best to join in what seemed to her a slightly desperate search for amusement.

But the men ended up seeming much alike: somehow, sexlessly like Heather. They were attractive, charming, and intelligent, but lacking another quality she couldn't define–as if they were not even aware that any less material facets of life might exist. In short, the whole scene bored her.

So was that what was really going on with her attraction to this neighbor of hers named Jesse Treves? Was she using him as a shield against the offered society she found so depressing, simply because he was impossible? Everything Heather pointed out was true. Although he'd gone to college, he made his living as a rough carpenter, not even contracting on his own, but working for wages. He was a self-proclaimed alcoholic, without the slightest remorse or intention to change his ways. And while he was unfailingly polite to her, he had shown no interest in her as a woman and had ignored–skillfully, or through honest lack of awareness?–the subdued but unmistakable overtures she had made.

She could hear Heather's voice again, at a party a few weeks before, strident after too many drinks and angry at Nicole for leaning glumly in a comer while the cocaine-backed hilarity passed her by.

"You're a sucker for losers, Nikki. It's the oldest riff in the book. Okay, he got blown up in Vietnam. So did a lot of other guys. The point is he's going to ride that the rest of his life, and you want to fly in on silver wings and be his fairy princess and his mamma all rolled into one. That shit went out with paisley, babe. These days it's every girl for herself."

Hovering behind those words were the ones that even Heather wasn't insensitive enough to say: You might be nice-looking and smart and have a great job, but at thirty two, you'd better move fast.

Especially with an eleven-year-old son.

She had reached the end of the block. Remembering the man in the dark glasses. she allowed herself a quick look back, an exaggerated turning of her head as she crossed Montgomery. But she could no longer see the sculpture. Irritated, she realized she was blushing. What was all this hype about men, anyway, everybody looking at you as if not having one around meant you were some kind of pariah? She had in fact had a number of them with varying degrees of seriousness for varying lengths of time, and more often than not they were a hell of a lot more trouble than they were worth.

But then she exhaled and put her hands in her pockets and stopped, gazing up into the soft rain. He got to her somehow, that Jesse. It was just that simple. She supposed it had to do with chemistry, or whatever you wanted to call it. And no matter what Heather thought, no matter how little rational sense it made, it was there, at least from her side.

The first time she'd seen him was an evening last fall, a week or so after she and her son had moved into the apartment in the Sunset. She'd come home late, as usual, gotten off the streetcar at Twentieth Avenue, and started up the hill—then seen from half a block away that Tom Junior was playing catch with someone in the vacant lot across the street. At first she was pleased that he'd found a friend, but then immediately concerned because the friend looked to be a grown man.

But Jesse had introduced himself as the neighbor in the apartment upstairs. She had recognized him then from the glimpses of him she'd gotten the couple of times she'd peeked out her window at dawn, still in her nightgown and half-irritated, to see who the hell was not only awake but starting a truck in the garage below her and leaving for work at six A.M.

Not a bad-looking man, she admitted when she got her first good look: lean and wiry, with sunburnt skin and kinky black hair and a deeply lined face that carried a network of poorly concealed scars.

And then she'd seen the deep stains of sweat on his clothes, the sawdust still in his hair, the streak of dried blood on the back of one hand, the general weariness in his shoulders—and remembered how physically beaten her father had always been when he came home from his day on the assembly line. She learned later that Jesse had found Tom Junior sitting forlornly on the steps with his baseball glove, and offered to go root out his own old mitt from the closet and play a game of catch.

She'd wondered, of course, if maybe Jesse had noticed her and was trying to make a move by means of her son, so she'd waited, wary, unsure about whether or not she was interested. Nothing happened, except that every few days she'd come home and find them throwing or batting a ball, until being ignored finally started to irritate her. She was certain he was not gay. It did not help that Tom Junior mentioned Jesse's name an average of fifty times a night, until she had mentally started to preface it with "Saint."

And then one weekend night they'd met on the stairs, she on her way out to one of Heather's parties, wearing a new white linen dress; he still in work clothes, returning to his place with a greasy paper sack of some kind of food from the delis down on Irving Street; and she'd realized he was absolutely shitfaced drunk. Though she'd heard him lurching up the winding staircase below her, he'd caught himself when he saw her, held the banister to keep steady, and said with pained enunciation:

"A vision in white." Then he grinned, and while the comers of his eyes crinkled as always, this time there was an awareness far back in them, black, endless, unwavering–an understanding of life and a coming to terms with it, cold, calm, unbitter yet unforgiving–that was unlike anything she had ever encountered.

She had blurted something silly and tried to laugh, feeling like an idiot, a twittering bird, and had hurried on down the stairs while he held himself upright with stern dignity. But at the bottom she had paused, listening to the steady, lurching footsteps begin again, and to the ringing of keys being dropped on the floor and then fumbled with for what seemed like minutes, until sound faded behind the quiet closing of his door.

The party, for her, had not been a success.

A fat raindrop landing squarely on the tip of her nose brought her back to the present. She shrugged and kept on walking. The dark stretch of Montgomery was like an aisle in a cathedral, lined with solemn stone buildings of self-evident importance. From any sensible standpoint, Heather was of course right. The attraction lay in the forbidden fruit. Aside from being neighbors, they had nothing in common. And the last thing she and her son needed in their lives was a man with an alcohol problem—even though she was privately convinced that it could be cured by a more attractive alternative.

If only her heart would obey her mind, she thought bleakly, she'd have it made. Grab off a hot young banker, move someplace like Mill Valley, and start to consolidate. That seemed to be the thrust of the decade: grasp money, emotions, life itself, until you held them all in your tightly closed fist.

Or was the truth that she was just feeling sour because she was alone on yet another Friday night?

A glance at her watch told her it was approaching seven o'clock. Tom Junior would have snacked by now, on a TV dinner or hot dogs, and probably would be settled in with his Atari and video games. Much as she disliked leaving him home alone, there was really no choice; and from infancy he had been an astonishingly responsible boy, as if he'd sensed it would be necessary.

And for young, single, should-be swinging Nicole? A light dinner, a lingering bath, a few glasses of wine, and perhaps a novel: a good, mushy romance, say, where she could almost forget the empty room she sat in—and the man who sat one floor above her, quietly drinking himself into some form of happiness, she supposed—and enter a world of make-believe, where characters always found the passion and adventure they longed for and where things always made sense in the end.

The man in the dark glasses watched her go, perceiving her thoughts. He had first noticed her in the restaurant, where he followed her conversation with her friend, as he had followed hundreds of others during the past days. Then he had trailed her to her place of work and waited for her to come out, in order to see further into her mind. She had surprised him by almost recognizing him; most people were oblivious to such things. But that was a trifling matter easily handled. The important thing was that she would do, nicely. There was something she wanted very much, but thought herself helpless to get.

And the son was just the right age.

He stepped out from behind the so-called sculpture, waiting for her to disappear from sight, and gazed up at the buildings that surrounded him. They were for the most part monstrous, shapeless, without character: fitting for this age in which he had awakened to find himself. All had been sacrificed to comfort, to a leveling of station and ability—to mediocrity. When he had ridden with his brother Templars, there had been no such contemptible leveling, no system of laws to protect the cringing weak. The strong had been lords of the earth, taking what they wanted and in return, dealing out punishment and fear.

Men had grown no wiser in the past centuries. Though they understood better the physical nature of the prison in which they were chained, only a few sensed dimly that it was, in truth, a prison. They were like a society of insects, busily and efficiently performing their life-sustaining tasks without the slightest glimmer as to why.

More than ever, they pursued the specter god of money, not understanding that the true currency of life was death: who caused it and who suffered it, who lost and who gained. A man who knew how to harness the power that death released–there was no limit to what he could do. There had only ever been a few such, and he, once called Guilhem Saint-Luc Marie de Brissac et Courdeval, Master of the Temple, had stood among the greatest. He wondered briefly if others had arisen in the centuries since, and if any of the old ones had, like himself, survived. He would learn in time; for time, and everything it contained, was henceforth his.

He began to walk in the direction Nicole Partrick had taken. She was two block ahead now and, he knew, had forgotten him. Still, he stayed unobtrusively near the buildings. When she reached Market Street and went down the flight of stairs to the streetcar station, he stopped again, his mind filled with loathing. He had ridden such trains, of necessity, a time or two in the past months; they were cattle wagons for peasants.

In the sheltered entrance of a building, he summoned a minor servant, one invisible to humans. His dead left eye monitored its obsequious approach. Curtly and silently, he willed it to perform the required task. There was of course a chance that the Partrick woman would not respond. In this delicate enterprise he could not force, but only suggest.

And if she did come to him? First, an adjustment to his appearance. Artifice and muscle control could achieve a slight lengthening of the nose, and a hollowing of the checks and jaw that she would not associate with a man she had perceived as thickset. His hair must be colored, his dress more flamboyant. Makeup would cover the Adversary's mark on his hand, concealed now with gloves. Most important, though, was his eyes. The tinted spectacles would have to go, leaving the left one cold and dead. A patch, then. If necessary, it would be a simple matter to add a little fogging of her mind.

As for a name, the one he had chosen to appear on necessary identification papers—a reminder of the once-mighty lineage of Guilhem de Courdeval—would serve well enough: Guy-Luc Valcourt.

He wheeled and strode north again, in search of one of the automobiles for hire that prowled the streets. His own vehicle was stabled—*parked,* he reminded himself—at a garage not far away, but he had learned that in cities, especially, it was far easier to let others drive. It spared one much aggravation and hugely reduced the chances of a collision, which would bring precisely the petty sort of trouble he wished to avoid. When one was concerned with great work, one could not afford such distractions. He still was amazed that, like firearms, such vehicles were carelessly given into the hands of the otherwise powerless in this world, who missed no opportunity to use these instruments in mean-spirited attempts to make the lives of their fellows as miserable as their own.

A cruising cab of deep blue color answered his hail. The wet, darkening sky signaled the early advent of night. Guy-Luc Valcourt slid onto the seat and said, with the slight accent he cultivated, "North Beach."

Perhaps a dozen other passengers joined Nicole on the N-Judah streetcar, nothing like the rush hour crowds. She sank with relief into a seat. The car moved noisily but smoothly through the tunnel beneath Market Street, heading west toward the avenues. Several people got off; few got on. It was not like the New York subway, demanding constant vigilance. She let the rocking of the train lull thought from her mind, and stared out the window. In a moment the tunnel's darkness turned her gaze to the row of advertisements above the seats. It was the usual array—women in black gowns caressing liquor bottles, cigarettes that were fun rather than dangerous, theater shows—except for the sign directly across from her. A name was printed in heavy, black, Gothic script, with several smaller lines of writing above. Unable to quite read any of it, she turned away in disinterest.

But a moment later she found herself looking at it again. It was unusual just in the fact that there was no illustration. A public notice? Was the streetcar line about to be shut down for repairs, perhaps? She glanced around the car. Only five passengers were left, none of them paying any attention to her. She rose and moved across the aisle.

Destiny controls the wistful, said the first line. *The wise control destiny. Why not grasp what is yours by right? Only the worthy. No charge.* The name in larger print read, *M. Guy-Luc Valcourt.* A telephone number followed.

Nicole smiled, partly at the pitch to the oldest human instinct in the book, partly at her own inquisitiveness. She was intrigued, she admitted, in spite of herself. No charge. No doubt–at first. The rest of the wording was clever, too: *wise . . . destiny . . . yours by right . . . worthy.*

Probably it was another of the endless pop psychology scams that invariably surfaced strongly in San Francisco, assuring you that they held the means to mend all the fences in your life–and promoted by a sophisticated advertising campaign designed to hook you with oblique, tantalizing information. In fact, the ad was annoying precisely because some part of her responded–because it followed so closely on the heels of what had been on her mind all afternoon, since her talk with Heather at lunch. The letters seemed almost to be *in* the plastic rather than printed on a poster beneath. *Why not grasp what is yours by right?* Well, to want someone to care for you hardly seemed to be a right. But there didn't seem to be anything wrong with it, either.

The streetcar emerged from the tunnel into the deepening evening, thick with wet mist as they approached the ocean. Several passengers boarded at the medical center on Parnassus Heights. They rattled past the darkened ghost of Kezar Stadium, then started down the hill to Nineteenth Avenue.

She got off at Twentieth, glancing once more at the sign before stepping down onto the street.

TWO

The Club Tropicana was what Spencer Epps called a splash palace—black Naugahyde, chrome, fake plush—but it was a splash palace with a very interesting additional element, as the sign out front announced: LIVE NUDE GIRLS. Although Spencer had walked past the advertisement almost daily for several weeks, tonight, for the first time, it struck him as curiously worded. He supposed the owners wanted to make things clear. Dead nude girls would hardly be good for business. The place was rarely crowded this early in the evening, and except for the stage, it was very dark, which suited Spencer fine. He neither wanted to be recognized there himself nor liked watching other men's eyes on Tina as she danced.

But at the same time, he would glance around covertly, taking in the hands that slowly raised drinks to lips and the stares that never left Tina's swaying form, and he would feel an entirely different emotion, one that was hard for him to identify: pride, maybe, or even gloating, or both of those and several more all mixed together. All of those men could only imagine, but he *knew.* It was weird, mixed up with the excitement of Tina herself, and he was not sure he liked it, but he could not seem to make it stop.

Her three-song set was near an end, and so was her clothing. The hidden speakers played a tape Spencer had heard hundreds of times: heavy rhythm, crooning voices, repetitive, meaningless lyrics–the musical equivalent of velour. As the second song died away, Tina wriggled out of a scarlet bottom cut high above her hips to reveal an even briefer G-string. Dutiful applause and whistles rose from the audience; a few men came forward to tuck dollar bills into her remaining scrap of cloth, most of them trying to cop a quick feel in the process, although anyone who spent much time in the Tropicana knew that a pair of large and unfriendly bouncers watched narrowly from the shadows, hoping for a chance to beat the shit out of a drunk and maybe break a couple of offending fingers in the process.

The final song began. Spencer watched with lust, pride, and hatred of those around him as she teased her way out of the G-string. The whistles had some heat in them this time, and she smiled graciously as she pranced around in her high heels for the last seconds, her curly auburn hair cascading down her back, the perfect globes of her surgically rebuilt breasts shaking tantalizingly. As the music died, she stooped to gather up her pile of clothes and dollar bills, then stalked elegantly back to the dressing room.

The interval before the next girl appeared was calculated to be just long enough for customers to order another drink. Spencer twisted in his seat, looking for a cocktail waitress. The nearby tables were empty except for one man wearing dark glasses and gloves. Dipshit, Spencer thought, annoyed at the guy's proximity; you don't want to be recognized, okay, but you attract more attention *with* a getup like that than without. He caught a waitress's eye, ordered a Chivas for himself and a Black Russian for Tina, and decided there was just time for a line. He rose and hurried to the head.

A greasy-looking man in an iridescent greenish leisure suit and a shirt with collar points that seemed eight inches long was standing at the urinal. He glanced around knowingly as Spencer locked himself into the stall. There Spencer sat, waiting impatiently while the dude finished pissing, washed his hands, and lovingly adjusted his appearance, crooning a song under his breath. At last the door swung closed, and Spencer's poised hands pulled the vial from his sport coat pocket, unscrewed the cap, and dipped in the gold spoon that hung on the chain around his neck. Two good shots to each nostril and he was on his feet again, flushing the toilet in case anyone walked in. He glanced quickly in the mirror to make sure none of the powder had clung to his mustache, smoothed back his carefully razor-cut hair, adjusted the collar of his navy blue silk shirt, and, with the sweet, vibrant flare of the coke swelling in his brain, reached the table just as Tina emerged from the dressing room. She was wearing a fluffy hot pink robe that came just past her hips, and the men in the bar turned, watching the flash of her long legs. When she sat beside Spencer, gazes lingered. Then the music began, a hard-driving bass line, and China Doll high-stepped onto the stage in a short black kimono emblazoned with a red dragon, calling the shadowed faces to herself. Her smile looked glazed, and there was something weary about the way her fingers fumbled with the kimono's strings.

Tina was watching him coyly, one hand on his knee. He leaned forward and kissed her, half hoping the other men were still watching.

"You look great tonight, baby," he said.

She smiled and tossed her head, fingers moving in little circles on his thigh. Conversation was not her strong suit, but what the fuck, Spencer thought. You could get conversation in any bar in town.

"I brought you something," he said. Her eyes turned expectant, sparkling, but he waited until they began to plead, until her fingers were moving with an excitement of their own, before his hand pressed the packet into hers. It was a thrill to watch her catch her breath as she peered under the table and saw a hundred-dollar bill folded around a gram of cocaine.

"I'm gonna get you good for this," she breathed, and then her long fingernails were stroking him through his slacks and her voice was whispering just exactly what she was going to do to him later. A hard little knot that kept him from swallowing rose in the back of Spencer's throat.

"I have to go home tonight," he said thickly.

Her hand and voice both paused.

"Yvonne's getting pissy," he said.

"Fuck her," Tina said harshly. "I don't care what she thinks."

She had spoken loudly, and he glanced around. There was only the man in the dark glasses a table away, his gaze fixed on China Doll, who was mechanically un-hooking a black lace bra. The pop Spencer had done in the bathroom was fading.

"I can come to your place for a while," he said.

Tina's lips twisted into a pout. "I hate it when you get up and leave. It makes me feel like a whore."

"Tina, I love you, you know I do. We just have to be careful a little longer."

"How much longer? You've been saying that for-ever."

Forever amounted to roughly three months. Spen-cer clamped down on the swell of uncertainty that was rising in the wake of the coke. It had not been enough.

"I've got to go to the john," he said. Tina smirked as he hurried away. Standing at the urinal, he tried to calm himself.

He'd been frequenting the strip joints in North Beach and the Tenderloin for some time, increasingly unhappy with his wife and with the bar and restaurant they owned—or, more accurately, that she owned and he managed—and hungry for something different. The endless display of good-looking women taking off their clothes on stage served mainly to make him miserable, but he couldn't seem to stay away.

Then one night he happened into the Club Trop and watched Tina dance, and he was so knocked out by her sheer raw beauty that he was unable to think about anything else. For weeks he haunted the place, re-straining himself to tip her only once a set or so. That close to her, he wanted to drop to his knees and scream that she was the most wonderful thing he'd ever seen.

Finally, as he slipped a five into her G-string, she looked into his eyes and smiled with recognition. He went straight to the can and packed his nose until he was buzzing with power, timed his exit as she was walking back to the dressing room, and said, with a coolness that amazed him, especially because she was standing there naked:

"Hey, could I buy you a drink?" and nearly fell right on his ass when she smiled again and said, "Sure."

Two nights later, after telling his wife he had to go to Marin on business and he'd probably stay over, he took Tina to dinner at the Top of the Mark. They drank Mumm's champagne and each made several giggling trips to the restrooms with his vial and spoon. They spent the night in a suite at the Fairmont, doing most of the eighth-ounce of coke he had, a substantial portion of which she rubbed into his cock and then ingested into her own body in a number of ways, all of which were astonishing and a couple of which were altogether new to Spencer Epps. He came away from that night understanding that his world had changed radically and fundamentally: that from then on, everything else was insignificant.

There was only one not-so-small problem.

He had told Tina that he was married but that he was wild to divorce his wife and marry her. Both of these things were true. What he had not told her was that the thriving bar and restaurant, which were supposedly the source of his money, were neither thriving nor his—that both, like the condominium he lived in and even the car he drove, were set up unalterably in his wife's name by her rich and canny father, who had known perfectly well that he was providing a dowry for an only, and not very attractive, daughter. On top of all that, the money Spencer had been using to entertain his new love came from a loan of approximately twenty thousand dollars he had taken out for business improvements on the res-taurant–remodeling and equipment–which had never materialized.

Twenty grand. It had seemed like all the money in the world–seemed that a few hundred, and then a few thousand, off the top would hardly make a dent, and that when things settled down, the remodeling would go on as planned. But after three months it was nearly gone. As Spencer stood at the urinal, a worst-case voice began to rise in him, a hard little whisper that was becoming in-creasingly familiar. Tina had no idea of the true situation. Like most of the young strippers, she maintained that she was dancing only temporarily, on her way to a modeling or acting career. The little voice prodded Spencer with a reminder that he had promised to take her to Hollywood and support her while she got her start.

His panic turned suddenly to rage. Was it his fault he hadn't been born rich, that he had no mind for college or business? He was good-looking, witty, likable, the kind of guy who deserved a break. But his fucking father-in-law had it all set up so that he was Yvonne's fucking employ-ee. So she fucking *owned* him.

The bathroom was still empty, the crowd of men outside absorbed in the approaching critical moments of China Doll's dance. Spencer put the coke up his nose right there at the urinal. It kicked in behind his eyes with heatless electricity, lifting him toward that coveted point where his power was absolute, where problems shrank to distant abstracts, minor matters to be attended to by another self at a future time. Twenty grand was nothing. Fucking chump change.

He strode back to the table, the music's bass line booming through him like a crest he could ride. Things were okay again. He was in control. Tina was watching China Doll with cool, appraising eyes; the Asian girl was down to a G-string now, her golden skin rippling under the slowly revolving lights. As Spencer sat, the man in the dark glasses stood and moved toward the door. Good riddance, Spencer thought, and slipped his hand under Tina's robe to give one of her silicone-enhanced breasts a squeeze.

She smiled automatically, her fingers finding his thigh.

"I didn't mean to get heavy with you, Spence," she said. "It just drives me crazy to have to share you." Together they watched China Doll step out of the G-string, cock her hips to one side, and twirl it around her finger. Her pubis was naked as a child's.

"Not for long," Spencer said. "I promise." He glanced at his watch. Tina was working the early shift; another hour and she would be up for her last set. "I'm going to go check on the car, make sure it's all right. Back in ten minutes." She looked properly disappointed, but her gaze flicked to the dressing room, where, he knew, she would go immediately to powder her own nose.

He stepped out onto Columbus. Twilight was deep, and the street was a stream of lights from the bars, restaurants, and traffic. His Porsche was parked five blocks away, toward the Embarcadero, and while it was true that he felt almost as possessive about it as he did about Tina, there was also the fact that the car would be a convenient place to do a quick line. You could only go to the john so many times.

He shrugged off a bouncer with a top hat and leering smile who was trying to hook him into one of the live sex joints, and turned from the heavy traffic on Broadway toward the relative quiet of Green Street. Abruptly, the panic touched him again at the thought of that twenty thousand dollars that had just disappeared, gone up their noses and down their throats and into clothes and perfume and all the other things he so desperately needed to give Tina. Twenty grand. It was only a number, a figure on paper, nothing to a big-time operator. But what if he had to pay it back? The restaurant had been losing money steadily the past months, and while he stubbornly refused to relate cause and effect, there was no denying that he no longer spent much time there running it. He swallowed and walked faster.

The Porsche's shape was there, silvery and comforting under the streetlight. It was a pristine new 944, and he had paid almost fifty thousand dollars for it—or rather, he thought, wincing, Yvonne's father had.

Then he saw a note on the windshield. His instant rage turned quickly to fear. If he had taken a parking space someone considered theirs, he might have slashed tires or scored paint along with a warning. The nearby garages charged two bucks every twenty minutes; like an asshole, he had tried to save a little money. He tore the paper out from under the windshield wiper and stared at it.

Events control the weak, it read. *The strong control events. Why not take what you desire? Only the determined. No charge.*

Spencer's lips tightened. He crumpled the paper and threw it viciously into the gutter. Some dipshit self-help group, with the nerve to touch his car. A quick walk around it assured him that all was well; a glance up and down the street, that he was alone. He slid into the driver's seat, and with shaking hands, took out the vial and spoon. The powder rose to his brain like a hard white line of bliss.

There was a way out of this, he found himself thinking, a way that a smart man, a strong man, would find. His brain formed a sudden image of Tina bent over him, cooing, his cock cradled between her breasts. It made him dizzy with lust. *Why not take what you desire?* He had taken it, all right. The problem was going to be keeping it.

As he stepped back out of the car, the crumpled ball of paper caught his eye. *The strong control events . . . No charge.* There was a name and phone number he had not bothered to read. He hesitated, looked around, then quickly picked it up and smoothed out the wrinkles. It did not seem like the standard come-on of some hippie-dippie religion or yuppie positive-thinking outfit. There was actually something intriguing about it, perhaps the authority of the tone—or perhaps because it seemed to speak to exactly what had been on his mind.

The name was Guy-Luc Valcourt, a single individual. It was obviously foreign, which struck Spencer as exotic.

He wondered if other nearby cars had been peppered with these notices, but as he looked up, headlights turned onto the street, their glare catching him full in the eyes. Flustered, he shoved the paper into his coat pocket and headed back to the Tropicana.

Tom Junior's dinner had consisted of hot dogs and potato chips, Nicole saw when she walked into the kitchen. She sighed, guilty; but she worked late an average of three nights a week, and she could hardly let him starve, waiting for her to come home. Well, at least she fed him well on the other nights, and saw to it that he ate breakfast and took a good lunch to school, just as she made sure that video and TV time were strictly limited and dependent on good grades and finished homework. It was a necessary tyranny, and he had hardly ever complained–another facet of the almost adult sensibility he had shown ever since he started talking.

In eight days, she was going to drive him to southern California, to spend the remainder of the summer with his father in Burbank. It was a part of the divorce agreement she didn't much care for, but she admitted that the exposure to a different environment was probably good for him.

She knew from experience that his absence was going to leave a big hole in her life.

Down the hall, his bedroom door was ajar. She pushed it open and leaned into the room, smiling at the intensity of his slender shoulders hunched over the

41

controls of the Atari. He appeared to be saving earth from the latest attack of hostile aliens; the screen was a kaleidoscope of flashing lights, with ships being blasted from the sky by the outnumbered but fearless terrestrial fleet.

"Hey, tiger," she said, ruffling the mop of once-blond hair that kept darkening every year.

"Hi, Mom." His eyes never left the screen. It was nothing personal; Nicole understood that moms were pretty small cheese when the future of all humankind was at stake. Then she noticed an aluminum baseball bat leaning inside the door, his glove on the floor beside it.

"Were you playing ball with Jesse?" she said, surprised. The rain had ceased by the time she got home, but the streets were still damp.

"We were gonna," TJ said, "but they started building a house in that lot. It's all dug up. They've got it roped off, with signs and stuff."

She wheeled and walked swiftly back down the hall to the front windows. The vacant lot across the street, the only open space for blocks, was cordoned off with ropes, flags, and sawhorses. Some sort of digging machine sat amidst trenches and large mounds of dirt.

"Well, you didn't waste any fucking time," she said quietly. Perhaps there had been preparations she hadn't noticed, but she would have sworn that as of yesterday the lot had been untouched. She turned from the window, arms crossed, thinking. There was a park, but it was six blocks away, with bigger, rougher kids hanging around–and for all she knew, peddling dope. Tom Junior's school and playground were almost a mile away.

And the apartment building's backyard was a patch the size of a garage.

The refrigerator held two chilled bottles of Carmenet Vineyard Sauvignon Blanc. She opened one, thinking about her visit to that winery, with Heather and her husband, earlier this spring. Heather had some sort of investment connection, and they had traded on that as an excuse to take a tour, driving across the Golden Gate Bridge to Sonoma on increasingly smaller highways until turning off the pavement altogether and traveling up a dirt road into the mountains.

At last they had passed through a gate, and the vista opened up into sunny slopes of picture-perfect vineyards. There were no buildings in sight except those of the winery–no urban sprawl and no streets, with the only sound the warm, easy wind. The staff were friendly, relaxed, lacking the brittle edge she had come to expect in the city. And why shouldn't they be? The place was a small paradise. She had gazed at the hills, picturing Tom Junior racing up and down like a little deer, growing strong and brown and learning about life at its roots instead of spending too many hours cooped up in a room, with his eyes glued to some screen. She had come home late that evening with a case of fine wine and a sharpened longing for a life where the priorities close to her heart could be realized.

And now her son's only neighborhood refuge, his last place to be a boy, was gone.

She poured a glass of the golden wine, recorkcd the bottle, and put it back in the refrigerator. Ritualistically, she savored the first sip as she had been taught, swirling it in her mouth, sucking air through it, then spitting it into the sink. The second taste was so good it made her close her eyes. She walked to the couch in front of the windows and sat, staring west over the miles of rooftops sloping down to the invisible ocean.

The apartment itself, like city life in general, was fine for her: two good-sized bedrooms, hardwood floors, a nice view. It was quiet and safe, relatively inexpensive, and close to the streetcar line—a twenty-five-minute commute. For another three or four hundred a month she could trade up, to the Marina, say, where Tom Junior would at least have some room to run around. Even Marin, across the Golden Gate, or south to the peninsula were not out of the question. They would cost more, but she was making nearly thirty thousand now, and that would almost certainly double in the next several years.

Then why not just do it?

Her eyelids lowered. The primary reason was walking around in the apartment upstairs right now—she could hear Jesse's footsteps. Again she remembered Heather's words, and again she rebelled at their coldness, their implication that life was nothing but a giant marketing game, where you treated yourself as just another commodity and tried to use your assets to command the best price.

But the no-longer-vacant lot brought home the point that there was not just herself to think about, and she admitted again that Heather had been right about this much: if Jesse cared for her in other than a neighborly way, he certainly had given no sign of it.

So, was it time to end the fantasy, the deep-secret dream of him and her and Tom Junior moving away to some sprawling house in the country, where Jesse could quit the work that drained him visibly more each month—and the even more deadly liquor that sucked out what was left—and perhaps move into low-key, part-time contracting; while she could give up her budding career of ambulance chasing and learn the practice of small-town law, becoming the protectress of simple but honest folk, paid in chickens and potatoes, and perhaps nurturing another fat baby or three?

Night had come; the mist on the windows streaked the lights of the city. She was still not hungry, but knew she would be, and Tom Junior could probably be induced to snack later, more healthily than he already had. She flipped on the TV, just to have another voice in the room. Then she started water boiling for rice, and lathered chicken breasts with mayonnaise to bake, thinking resignedly of the calories. But it was a quick and easy meal, and this was, after all, Friday.

As she worked, she listened with half an ear to the end of a sitcom featuring several improbable teenagers who came to improbably wise conclusions about their hugely improbable experiences, followed by a string of imbecilic commercials. She washed the dishes she had used and was pouring another glass of wine when she caught the tail end of a news brief.

". . . mutilated body discovered in a field near San Gregorio beach has been identified as nineteen-year-old Joseph Figureido of Half Moon Bay. Police are still searching for his girlfriend, eighteen-year-old Layla

Christensen. Anyone with any information . . ." The screen flashed a photo of the girl's pretty smiling face as the announcer droned on with professional concern.

Great, Nicole thought, another psycho on the loose. Why did they all seem to move here? The announcer's voice lifted–the vital moments of a baseball game had come on–and she snapped off the set.

She checked on Tom Junior, still absorbed in intergalactic warfare; demanded and received a promise to eat a piece of chicken and salad in an hour; stood in the living room for a minute or two, rejecting television, reading, and writing overdue letters; and finally put on a tape of cello music, turned off all of the lights but one, and returned to the window. A decision was rising on the horizon, a major one; this was as good a time as any to try to think it through.

In her third year of college, she had married Tom Senior and dropped out of school to support him, against her father's stern advice. Soon she had found herself pregnant; she would never be sure whether it really was accidental or because of her desire for a child. Though her husband had pressed for an abortion, promising a family when they were settled and secure, she had refused to even consider it.

Her father had turned out to be right. The increased pressure on the marriage quickly made it intolerable. The separation, not much more than a year after Tom Junior's birth, was a relief. Tom Senior moved back to southern California, dutifully rendering minimal child support. While the situation was far from ideal, it was workable–at first.

46

A year and a half later, he filed for divorce. Nicole learned that he was living with a woman. She realized now that she could have forced a more favorable settlement for herself, but she had been hurt far more by the actuality of the divorce than she had imagined, and she only wanted to end it. Soon after, she began to come to terms with the position her pride and naïveté had gotten her into. Once an A student, she was now almost twenty-four, with an infant child, no husband, and no income except for the pittance of child support–worth less with each month of rising inflation–and the small amount she earned as a waitress, much of which went to babysitters. Worst, she was losing what she craved most: to spend all of her time and attention raising her son.

After months of agonizing, she took the most humiliating step of her life: went home with her child to her parents in San Diego. For nearly three years she worked in a title office, saving her money, while her mother took care of her son. The September that Tom Junior entered kindergarten, Nicole reenrolled at San Diego State, taking twenty-four units a quarter. The following year she was accepted at San Francisco's Hastings School of Law, and on graduation–Law Review, top ten in her class–walked into her present job. The firm was fast-growing and prestigious–*aggressive* was the term the men used–and within ten years, if she stayed, she was virtually certain to be a partner.

Although the bitterness of the failed marriage had faded, Nicole still had never imagined that she would desire a full time man in her life again. There had been a number of applicants, and she had engaged in a fair amount of exploration, both sexual and emotional, gaining the range of experience the early marriage had not allowed. But always, before everything else, there had remained the steadfast priority fur her and her son to be on their own, beholden to no one; and the men had gone as she had decreed, some angry, some hurt, one or two understanding. Now she had it made: the job, the security, the promise of modest wealth, and, most of all, the independence that she had craved. But during those years when all of her time and energy were taken up by the struggle itself, she had never foreseen the loneliness that would come to her upon the attainment of her goals. She should have, she thought cynically. How many songs and stories celebrated precisely this? Still, to know it with the mind was one thing. Not until you experienced it did it pierce, with that terrible intensity; to the heart. And even that pain remained comparatively dull until it found an object: until you fell in love.

Her glass was empty again; she decided to allow herself one more. The footsteps upstairs had ceased. She could picture Jesse clearly, sitting in front of his own darkened windows and staring out, just as she was. But in his hand would be a glass of whiskey, the bottle by his side; and Friday meant only that there was no five A.M. alarm tomorrow, so he could drink all night if he chose. Though she had never so much as heard him say the word Vietnam, she knew he had been there because Tom Junior had ingenuously asked him about his scarred face. But more than once, she had awakened suddenly in darkness to hear him stumble from his bed in the room above hers. She was almost sure that what dragged her from her own sleep on those occasions were cries.

She thought of calling him, and began to phrase an invitation in her mind: cooked too much chicken, have a bottle of great wine, why don't you swing by? But she could see that darkness that would come into his eyes and hear his hesitation as he tried to find an excuse that would spare her feelings, that would cover the fact that he preferred being alone with his whiskey. She shook her head and went back to the kitchen.

After turning the chicken, she decided there was just time for a bath before dinner. She took the wine with her and ran the water, adding one of the scented packets of powder she bought in Chinatown. With relief, she rid herself of heavy tweed skirt, slip, and stockings, and let down the heavy dark hair she refused to cut short, in spite of prevailing fashions. Then she stood in the mirror for the obligatory self-examination.

With alarm, she saw that she had gained yet more weight, and she sighed with frustration. She was naturally big-boned, and in spite of the hateful calisthenics she forced herself through three mornings a week, calories went on with the speed of thought and came off only with starvation, a trend that was growing more pronounced every year. Reubenesque, she thought defensively. It helped that her hands and ankles were slender. Her breasts, too, were softening imperceptibly with the years, but they were still full and symmetrical. She felt them carefully for lumps, and as she pronounced herself healthy, decided they had not been touched by any hands but her own in far too long. Then she leaned forward to examine her face: good skin; fine, slightly arched nose; deep blue eyes that showed a hint of violet in certain light; cheeks that would hollow charmingly if she could lose those extra pounds.

Would that make the difference? She did not think Jesse was that shallow, but perhaps it would give her confidence. Her hands went to her hips while her face pouted, mocking herself. Throw on a robe, march up-stairs, and when he answers your knock, let it fall to the floor–

She lay back in the steaming tub, feeling sweat beginning to bead her forehead. Her eyes were closed, and as she sipped the cool, delicious wine, she realized that the image her mind held was the odd advertisement she had seen in the streetcar, complete with the tele-phone number.

The man who called himself Guy-Luc Valcourt walked into the Harlan Brothers parking garage, hands in the pockets of his Burberry overcoat, satisfaction on his face. It had been an excellent day. He was confident that both Spencer Epps and Nicole Partrick would con-tact him shortly. Servants would keep his message in the forefront of their minds.

The automobile he had purchased was a deep gray Mercedes, handsome, inconspicuous, and suggestive of wealth–a combination which went a long way toward establishing credibility and forestalling petty trouble. He started the vehicle, taking pleasure in its fine engin-eering. The Teutons had always been good craftsmen. He had once commissioned a suit of armor from a smith from Bamburg, importing the man to his fortress of Montsévrain, in the south of France, for the purpose. The steel plates had been tempered in human blood.

He drove carefully to the exit, allowing the reflexes of the body he occupied to take over. The garage was uncrowded; his vehicle was the only one moving. Inside the booth, the attendant, a young man with slick black hair and olive skin, was talking on a telephone, his back turned. A radio played a loud, particularly unpleasant form of music, which Valcourt had learned was termed *salsa*. He waited patiently until it became clear that the attendant was deliberately ignoring him. Then he considered simply driving on through the flimsy gate, perhaps after taking a moment to snap the young man's spine. But that would be certain to bring down precisely the sort of trouble he was anxious to avoid. He settled back in the seat and sighed. What a world this had become! The powerful were harried by the weak at every turn. And punishments were so mild as to be almost non-existent: reprimands, or a few years in prisons more luxurious than most living quarters of his time, or, at worst, painless executions.

No, there was no such thing as discipline anymore. In his day, such insolence would have been simply unthinkable. As Guilhem de Courdeval, he had first witnessed what would now be called an atrocity when he was eight years old. A group of bourgeois in one of his father's villages had taken airs about their importance, declaring themselves free men, and handled a tax collector roughly. The tax man had arrived at the fortress beaten and bleeding. After hearing the story, the Sieur de Courdeval immediately summoned his nearest vassals.

That night, the young Guilhem rode with the knights to the rebellious village. At dawn, they burst down doors, pulled the half-dozen leading citizens from their beds, threw them to the ground, and castrated them before the eyes of the assembled populace. There was no more trouble from that village or any other, and Guilhem had learned a lesson in practical wisdom from his father. To have slaughtered the peasants would have injured productivity.

But now, even if he were free to punish such trivial insolence as that which confronted him tonight, it was so widespread that he would have no time for anything else. He contented himself by reflecting on a massacre of Spanish pilgrims, perhaps including distant ancestors of the parking attendant, that he had conducted not far from Santiago de Compostela in the year 1293. The Spaniards' screams had gone on long into the night, and all the hungry mouths had been well fed for that moon.

When at last the young man turned, his gaze was cool and impudent. Valcourt handed him a piece of paper currency of a large denomination. Even before he received his change, he understood that it would be one dollar short. He accepted it with a smile, not counting it, and drove quietly out to the street. There he paused, considering. To retaliate would be a waste of energy he could ill afford and a futile gesture to boot, like a spear thrown into an ocean of petty insults.

But where was the pleasure in living impotently, like those wretched, castrated peasants?

52

He closed his eye and concentrated. The servant required was more powerful than those he had used earlier that evening, and the effort of imposing his will upon it cost him. Afterward, he rested a moment before beginning the thirty-mile drive to his new home. For an instant, anxiety touched him. It had been a foolish yielding to pride, something that had caused him much trouble in the past. He was not as strong as he had once been, not nearly, and he was declining rather than gaining.

Soon, he thought, all will be well again. Hardening his will, he began to drive. At this hour, traffic was comparatively light. He would be home before long, and there he could rest—with the pleasant anticipation of the surprise that was waiting for the young parking attendant when the clock struck midnight.

As he drove, he monitored the competent actions of the body that had come within his grasp. It was admirable for his purposes: healthy, attractive, but not so striking as to leave a lasting casual impression. It had once belonged to a man named John McTell, who had forfeited control of it through weakness and lust. The seduction of McTell had been a masterful performance, a *tour de force* that had earned Guilhem de Courdeval the right to walk the earth again.

Six hundred and eighty interminable years in a watery prison! Years of silence, darkness, and rage!—of punishment for allowing his own desire for revenge to take precedence over his master's work.

But he thrust the remaining bitterness from him. To dwell on the past was profitable only as a means of education; it served well as a reminder of what lay in store for him should he fail again. While he had long since driven any tremor of human fear from his heart–faced death in battle a thousand times, felt flames consume the living flesh from his bones as he stood chained to a stake–the thought of what awaited him in the event of another downfall made his grip tighten on the car's steering wheel.

Away! he thought again. There would be no more failure. In all, his new circumstances were excellent. The mind of John McTell served him as well as the body: a scholar's storehouse of most useful information. He had learned much in the eight months since the magnificent night when at last he had won his freedom, both picking McTell's mind and forming his own impressions of the life to which he must outwardly conform. Most important, he discovered that he was no longer free to simply take from the peasants, striking down any who opposed him. Instead, his procuring of goods, identification papers, and currency had required great effort and subtlety. This new world purported to be governed by an immensely complex and troublesome system of laws. In fact, it was fueled, as it always had been, by greed and corruption. But now there were organizations of enforcement, modes of transportation and communication, and weapons undreamed of in his time. The most trifling mistake could begin a chain of questioning and investigation that would bring no end of tumult. The watchword had been, and must remain, caution.

Europe had become tiny and crammed, Asia even more of a violent wasteland than in his own day. His old alliances were gone like dust, even the names of the great princes no longer remembered; and everywhere lurked the hideous urge to equalize, to bring down the great and exalt the timid until all were condemned to the same deadly stew of mediocrity, boredom, and the unseen chains of comfort. He had made his way westward, until he stood on a bluff overlooking an ocean that as Courdeval he had never seen, that he had heard of only as the sea beyond the fabled land of Cathay. In the city named for Francis of Assisi, whose earthly life span had nearly overlapped his own, he understood that he had found the proper place to begin. It was large enough for anonymity, small enough to be manageable; there were cool air and fog, as on the Norman coast of his childhood, and yet an almost Mediterranean flavor; and the people were not suspicious and hostile as in the eastern cities. On the contrary, he had been amazed at their eagerness to believe anything that smacked of the mystical.

And now that he was settled—the layout of the city committed to memory, a suitable house let, a cover identity established to expedite dealings for necessary services and supplies—the time was at hand.

Clear of the snarl of traffic just south of the city, the drive was pleasant. The countryside reminded him of parts of the southern coast of France—inasmuch as he could imagine these hills denuded of the thousands upon thousands of grotesque dwellings that covered them like scabs. The house he had taken was a much finer structure, large and private, set well back from the road. The broker, impressed by his careless lavishness with money, had seen to furnishing it with sturdy antiques, heavy drapes, and rugs; and he had since accumulated certain *objets d'art* to cater to his own tastes. He had learned with contempt that wealth itself was not even necessary to acquire such things. It was only necessary to make people believe that one possessed wealth, and this they were pitiably eager to do.

An unseen servant opened the black iron gate for him and placed in his hand a single piece of mail, then closed the gate behind him as the Mercedes moved quietly down the long drive to the house. Valcourt climbed the porch steps wearily, ignoring the black cat that waited at the door, and walked into the spacious parlor. He poured a glass of cognac from a crystal decanter; distilling had been unknown in his time, and he was forced to admit that it was one innovation of which he approved. The hour was nearing ten. He smiled faintly, thinking again of the surprise the new day would bring to the parking lot attendant.

He turned his attention to the envelope the servant had given him. It was a mailgram from Le Havre, in response to his own dispatch of three days before. He opened it, read the single line, nodded with satisfaction, and placed it on the mantel beside the centerpiece: a glass case displaying a dark leather-bound book with a strange looping design, traced in rust-colored ink, on the cover. He spoke a word. The lock on the case sprang open, and the cover lifted.

As he touched the book—the grimoire written in his own hand seven centuries before, and bound in the skin of a heretic flayed alive—he felt its power course through him. It was the tangible proof of what had transpired: of his journey from this world to the next, across an abyss inhabited by beings frightful beyond human imagination. Quite a number of men had tried it. Very few had survived. Several of the grimoire's pages were charred at one comer, a result of the time he had been forced to risk it. That had been a critical moment, when the man McTell had touched a flame to it in a last, desperate attempt to escape the snare Courdeval had set. An ounce more of courage–

He would see that such a risk did not arise again.

He leaned forward and gazed into a dark gilt-framed mirror.

"Our little love will soon be with us," he said softly, indicating the mailgram he had received. Then he raised his left hand, palm out, so that the deep, red mark on it–identical to the design on the cover of the book–was reflected.

And he smiled again at the terror he saw in his own right eye when he allowed it to light, just for an instant, with the consciousness of John McTell.

Sitting in his booth in the Harlan Brothers Garage, Hector Rivera was getting pissed. The time, kept exactly by an electronic punch clock, was nine minutes to midnight, and his replacement should have been there at a quarter till. It was an unwritten policy on the switch from swing to graveyard shifts, when none of the bosses and only occasional customers were around, that the guys would spend a few minutes bullshitting and getting high, cheering each other up for the long, solitary stretch of time behind or ahead. And tonight it was his replacement, Eugene's, turn to bring the dope.

But it was more than that. He was restless. Something had had him on edge for a while now, a growing sense that some kind of bad shit was coming down. He glanced uneasily around the booth. Usually it felt like his castle, the place from which he ran the show. Tonight it seemed like a cage. Though it was not particularly warm, he had started to sweat.

All in all, he liked this setup fine. You couldn't ask for an easier job. As long as you stayed high, the boredom didn't get too bad. The weird hours on swing took some getting used to, but they had their advantages: no bosses around to stop you from playing the radio and talking on the phone; when you got home, your buddies were just gearing up to go out; and you didn't have to get out of bed until noon.

And if the wages weren't for shit, there was a sweetener: you could take in thirty or forty bucks tax-free pretty much every night, and double that on weekends, simply by holding back a dollar from people's change. You had to be careful who you did it to—no regular customers, although there weren't many of those at night; nobody who looked tough or suspicious; nobody who paid with small bills. But it was amazing how many *rico* chumps, down here near Union Square, would hand you a twenty and not pay any attention to what you handed back. At two bucks per twenty minutes, it was too tricky to figure the exact cost. If they looked like they were about to hassle you, you just gave them that cool, heavy-lidded Latino stare—especially if you'd fucked with their heads a little, made them wait, let them know who was in charge—and they'd give you back that sickly liberal bullshit smile, tuck away the money, and drive off. For the one in a hundred who actually bitched, you took plenty of time recounting the change, and you shrugged and said, "Sorry, man," together with that contemptuous stare—like, I can dig you really need that buck, asshole—and handed them the dollar. If you did it right, it was even better than getting the money; they'd be squirming in their Saabs. And if they never came back to the garage, you'd won all the way around.

Five minutes to twelve. Something must have happened to Eugene. He was a pretty good dude, and he was a real hardass about being on time—bucking for manager. On the other hand, he was coming from Hunter's Point. Any fucking thing could go down between there and here. Hector fooled around with the radio a minute, thinking about the coke Eugene was supposed to be bringing. He had some angel dust in his own pocket and considered doing a quick bowl, just to take his mind off his nervousness. Usually the guys waited until there were two of them together to do PCP so they could take turns, because if somebody came along when the top of your head was off, there was no telling what might happen. You could mess around plenty here, but you had to keep a lid on it or you risked blowing the whole sweet scene. There seemed to be nothing on the box but country-western or easy listening, neither of which he could stand. He switched it back to salsa.

Well, what the fuck. Nobody had come into the garage in fifteen minutes, and even if someone did, he could get high and be back in charge by the time they got their car and brought it to the booth. One thing about angel dust: you went up like a fucking rocket, but you were back on earth, or at least most of you was, within a minute or two. This much was for sure: It would take his mind off whatever was bugging him. He took out his hash pipe, filled the bowl halfway with sinsemilla bud, and carefully sprinkled a pinch of the powdered PCP on top. He glanced around once more. Still no customers and no sign of Eugene. He shrugged, irritated at his own edginess. As he tore a match from a book, the time clock hit twelve.

At that instant, before his hands could strike the match, Hector Rivera understood that he was not alone in the booth.

He whirled, elbow knocking the phone off its hook. There was nobody, nothing except his own reflection, in the glass. But as he stared at his image–seeing the tight-stretched grin of terror on his face, his eyes opened so wide that the whites were visible all around–unseen tentacles seemed to snake around his body, loathesome, clinging. Sweat pouring from his forehead, he struggled and tried to scream. But his voice stayed trapped in his throat.

Horrified, he watched his hand open to drop the pipe on the floor. Then it began to move, with agonizing slowness, up to his face. Bit by bit, the invisible power pried open his jaws.

The radio launched into a spirited rundown of the up-to-the-minute news, in Spanish.

Eugene Gates wheeled his Buick into the garage and jumped out, trotting to the booth. His face was pinched with unhappiness. He had never before been late for work. While he had no objection to doing some dope when nothing was shaking, he took his job seriously and had his eye on a managers slot. Inside the booth, Hector's back was turned. Eugene figured he was probably too pissed to say hello, and did not blame him. The clock said four minutes after twelve.

"Hey, shit, man," he said, tapping on the glass. "I'm sorry, baby. That damn car of mine stalled when I come off the freeway, I could not get that bitch to start."

When Hector did not turn around, Eugene's face creased further.

"Hey, come on, man, lemme in. I got some shit to put up our nose, cheer your ass right up."

Then, suddenly, he noticed two things. Hector's shoulders were sagging, his whole body slumped in the chair, as if he had passed out sitting up. And the telephone was hanging at the end of its cord.

Eugene's fingers shook as he shoved his key into the door. Opening, it hit Hector's pipe, sending it across the floor with a clatter. He quickly put two and two together.

"Say, fool," he said, angry now. A single wrinkle like this could fuck it up for all of them. "What kind of bullshit you pullin' here? Man, don't you know–" He gripped Hector's shoulder and spun him around.

His words stopped.

Hector Rivera's eyes were as round as quarters and glazed with fear, and his shirt and chin were smeared with blood. This was not the first bloodied man Eugene

Gates had ever seen; he braced himself instantly, searching for the wound. Face and teeth seemed intact, throat was not visibly marked. He scanned downward with increasing puzzlement—until he came to Hector's hands, which were resting in his lap.

As if on cue, Hector leaned slowly forward and vomited an evil pool of greenish bile and dark blood. It included an object readily identifiable, in spite of its surroundings, as a thumb.

Hector slumped forward to his knees. As the second thumb emerged to join its mate, Eugene felt himself whirling in slow motion, clawing for the door. He clung to the jamb and let his own dinner gush out of his throat, while his mind insisted, with odd clarity, *No more angel dust, baby. Not ever again.*

THREE

Saturday was the one day of the week Nicole nearly always managed to spend with Tom Junior, taking him shopping with her, going on an outing, or just staying home and being together. Time with him was especially important this weekend; he was leaving for his father's the next.

Yesterday's storm had passed on, the morning was clear, and he had requested the beach; she had sensed his child's impatience for summer to truly begin. Her first thought had been of the television news brief of the night before, about the murder/disappearance of the young couple at San Gregorio, and she had contrived to fuel his interest toward visiting Point Reyes, many miles and a long bridge to the north.

Though she had feared he would be disappointed by the coastal fog that so often set in even on clear days inland, their luck held. The temperature lingered in the mid-seventies, the sky was a crisp, dear blue, and the traffic seemed unusually benign, perhaps in shared relief at the reprieve from the rain. Once across the Golden

Gate, they chose the steep, winding road that climbed Mt. Tamalpais, breathing the scent of pine and eucalyptus as they passed through shadowed glades, craning their necks to see the tops of the towering redwoods. In spite of the beauty—or because of it—Nicole was touched by a longing, almost a melancholy: the wish that she could live in a place like this, instead of just driving through it every few months—

And the wish that there were someone in addition to her son to share it with. She had thought of asking Jesse to join them, but the idea had quickly died, swept away by the wearyingly familiar flood of reasons not to.

The ocean looked rough, with hundreds of shifting white lines of surf. Perhaps a half-mile out, the pale jade color of the water changed sharply to a deep blue that stretched to the horizon. When they stopped at a deli and bought hoagies thick with salami and provolone, sodas, and potato salad, she decided on Sir Francis Drake Bay, where the pirate was thought to have landed and claimed the coast for Queen Elizabeth in 1579, only to decide there was nothing in the area worth returning for.

Though the ocean was too cold for comfortable swimming, the tide had formed a little inlet of clear, tepid water, and into this Tom Junior plunged gleefully. Nicole had not planned to swim, but had worn a suit under a denim skirt and loose cotton blouse. The beach was not crowded; most of the dozen or so people were surf fishing. She found a sheltered spot against the foot of a dune, stripped to her suit, and stretched out on a blanket. Then, after a glance around, she unhooked her top and, feeling pleasantly scandalous, let the sun warm her breasts.

Through half-closed eyes she watched her son jump and splash, rushing out of the inlet to sculpt a sand fort, then as quickly losing interest and dashing back to do battle with an imaginary aquatic enemy. He was a beautiful child, even given a mother's bias: his skin clear and smooth, if paler than she would have liked; his bones beginning to lengthen with adolescent awkwardness, but cleanly and firmly muscled; and, more than anything else, his eyes, dreamy, trusting, easily hurt. It was impossible for him to hide what he was feeling, and she knew this was going to cost him on his journey through adolescence—that he would have to develop a tougher second skin in order to survive, and that in the process, he would lose some of what made him so precious to her.

But much of it would remain, and in any case, a too-sensitive nature was infinitely preferable to a hard or manipulative one. While she was pleased that he had inherited his father's physique, she was thankful that he did not have Tom Senior's self-centered heart. Again she wondered if there would be other children before nature, in its inexorable cruelty, dosed that particular door.

Destiny controls the wistful, whispered a voice in her mind. *The wise control destiny. Why not grasp what is yours by right?* She realized that the strange sign on the streetcar last night had been stirring in her subconscious like a great fish twisting just beneath the surface of the water—and with surprise, that she even remembered the telephone number. It *was* intriguing: the quietly authoritative tone, the absence of hype. She tried to think of

65

other such claims she had encountered, wondering if this might be an oblique front for some organization that had fallen into disrepute and was trying to re-group.

Abruptly a shrill cry came from the direction of the inlet, a child's near-scream. She was up and moving before it stopped sounding in her ears, her bare feet digging into the sand, sending sprays behind her. Tom Junior was waist-deep in the water and thrashing toward shore, his mouth contorted with fear. Nicole stretched out her arms and ran as she had not run since girlhood, oblivious to the sharp stones and shells cutting into her feet.

They met at the water line, and she scooped him into her arms and held him tight against her, trying to calm her own breath enough to speak.

"What?" she managed to gasp.

"There's a shark!" he blurted, and craned to look fearfully over his shoulder. Nicole straightened, with a rising suspicion that his imagination, fueled by too many movies, had supplied to a game an image that did not exist. She walked forward a few feet, Tom Junior clinging to her hand. Thirty seconds of intense scanning of the football-field-size inlet showed nothing but the rippling surface. She was about to phrase a gentle suggestion that perhaps he had seen a submerged log or even a seal, when he tugged at her arm and his hand flew up to point.

"There!"

She stared in disbelief at the unmistakable triangular fin that sliced the surface and the shadowy shape twisting lazily beneath, and felt her stomach contract, her quieting heart beginning to pound again.

"You folks okay?" said a voice behind her. Startled, she was already turning before she remembered her bare breasts. She crossed them with one arm. The speaker was a man in his forties, wearing shorts, T-shirt, and cap, and holding a fishing pole. Nicole noticed that several of the other people on the beach were watching them, and she was suddenly aware of how she must have looked, racing across the sand naked except for what amounted to brief turquoise panties.

"My son saw a shark," she said. Tom Junior pointed again to where the fin obligingly remained above the surface.

The man grinned. "Little sand shark," he said. "Lots of them around. They get trapped in these pools by the tide. Nothing to worry about, they don't eat anything but trash fish and garbage."

"Oh," she said. "Well. Thank you. I think we'll leave it to him, all the same."

"Where you from?" the man said. He had not moved. His smile had changed subtly, and she was suddenly aware of the smell of beer on his breath and his heavy belly beneath the sweat-stained T-shirt. His eyes pried like crowbars at the arm that hid her breasts.

"Santa Rosa," she said.

"I been fishing here twenty years," he said. "I could tell you all about this place. Bet you didn't know the Japs tried to land here in World War II."

"No," she said. "I didn't."

"I could show you where. It's about a half-mile up." He nodded toward the deserted stretch of coastline to the north. The shore disappeared around a point perhaps a

67

hundred yards farther. Tom Junior had walked timidly a little closer to the shark and was watching it, entranced. "That's my sister and brother-in-law over there," the guy said, nodding his head toward an expressionless couple sitting on lounge chairs beside an enormous cooler. "They could watch your kid."

"I'd love to, I really would," Nicole said, "but if I don't get back to the clubhouse in time to give Poison Jack his tattoo, my old man will beat the shit out of me." She smiled prettily as his face changed, then, for the hell of it, dropped her arm just a little as she turned away, giving him a peek at one rosy nipple. "Come on, Tommy," she called. As they walked back to the blanket, she waved at the stony-faced sister.

It was after one o'clock; the sandwiches remained in the cooler.

"You hungry?" she said, hooking her top back in place. Tom Junior shook his head. "I'm not either, but I bet we both will be pretty soon. Tell you what: let's drive bade up to the top of Mount Tam and have a picnic. I've had enough beach." They quickly dressed and packed up. As they started back to the car, she felt the man's gaze on her, and resisted the urge to flip him off.

"Mom?" Tom Junior said, after glancing at the man. "Did you mean it when you said somebody was going to beat you up?"

He looked solemn, worried. She smiled, but winced inwardly at her carelessness; she had thought he was not close enough to hear.

"I was teasing, honey. He didn't seem like a very nice man, and I wanted to get rid of him."

"Me and Jesse'd take care of him," Tom Junior declared.

"Nobody's going to hurt either of us," Nicole said firmly. In her mind she added: But you sure don't have to put up with nearly as much hassle if there's a man with you.

She was quite sure the Japanese had never done any such thing as land near Drake's Bay.

The traffic was heavier now, the heat less pleasant. Her head had begun to ache slightly. She asked Tom Junior to open her a diet cola, and she concentrated on driving.

It was almost nine by the time Tom Junior was in his room reading. Nicole poured herself a glass of wine and collapsed into a chair. They had caught the Saturday afternoon traffic across the bridge and down Nineteenth Avenue, and it had taken forty minutes of stiffing heat, exhaust fumes, and loutish behavior from other drivers to travel less than ten miles. Then she'd had to walk down to Irving Street to shop for dinner. She stared vacantly out the window, realizing that she was doing precisely the same thing as the previous night, except that then she had merely been tired. Now she was exhausted. She would spend tomorrow, like most Sundays, going over her cases in preparation for Monday.

Some existence, she thought. Work your tail off five days a week, steal a few hours with your kid on the sixth, spend the seventh getting ready for the first five to start over again, and in the spare hours rush around trying to keep up with all the necessities of life maintenance:

shopping, cooking, laundry, chauffeuring Tom Junior to friends' houses and school activities–the endless list of errands that cropped up no matter how efficient you were.

Yet it would all be infinitely more bearable-even enjoyable-with someone to share it.

Why not grasp what is yours by right?

Was that what lay behind this unusual line of thought, this dissatisfaction with what she had worked for so long, this sudden, surprising streak of rebellion? *Yours by right.* The words seemed to imply that people deserved to get what they wanted. It was entirely contrary to the ethic she had grown up with, that you'd damned well better take what came and keep your mouth shut, because it could always get worse.

Why not–?

"Well, and why the hell not?" she said aloud, surprising herself. What could a phone call hurt? No one would be there on Saturday night anyway; doubtless she would get a slick-sounding recorded message that might at least give her some clue to the nature of this game.

The voices in her mind immediately leaped into battle. She was letting herself in for contact with who knew what kind of creeps; but then, what could they do to her? If nothing else, she stood to learn something. Around and around the argument went, the wearying, all-too-familiar cycle.

Suddenly angry, she said, "Christ, Nikki, for once, just do it." She reached for the phone, her movements quickened by irritation. If it did seem to be some sort of con, she would not hesitate to let this Monsieur Valcourt know that she was an attorney and that she was ready and willing to make trouble for him.

It was an excellent rationale, almost sufficient to mask her feelings of foolishness. After a final hesitation, she punched the buttons of the phone.

To her surprise, a man answered: a deep-voiced, pleasant "Hello?" She wondered if she had remembered the number correctly.

"I'm trying to reach a Monsieur Valcourt," she said.

"Yes, this is he." The voice seemed good-humored, a little hesitant, with just a trace of an accent: not at all the sort of smooth patter she had expected.

Thrown off balance, she introduced herself, adding, "I hope I'm not calling too late."

"On the contrary. I sleep little, I live alone, and I am somewhat of a stranger to your area. I am quite grateful for company after sunset."

"Did I pronounce your name right?" she said, stalling, trying to get a feel for the man. She had rhymed it with "ball-court."

"It's actually Val-*coor*, and more properly still, De Valcourt. But I have grown accustomed to the Americanization." His voice held resigned amusement, and she had a sudden intuition as to why: though she spoke no French, she knew that the "De" often signified nobility. "Your own name would be of Danish extraction?" he said.

"Yes," she said, surprised. It was not something many people caught.

"Then perhaps we share Norman blood."

Her conviction that he was a fraud was wavering.

"I saw your advertisement on a streetcar," she said. "I found it—very intriguing. Would you tell me more about . . . the nature of your services?"

Valcourt remained silent, and Nicole had the odd sense that it was not because he was trying to gauge his words, but because he was deciding whether or not to proceed—that it was her worthiness that was, in some mysterious manner, being judged. With that came the realization that this had hardly started, and already the tables were being turned on her. It was amusing, distressing, and startling.

"Very well," he said. "I will tell you without pretense or false modesty that I possess great psychic gifts. I have spent many years developing them. You may be aware, Miss Partrick—it is 'Miss,' is it not?"

"Yes," she said, surprised again. A lucky guess, she decided.

"Miss Partrick. That in any spiritually related discipline, one feels in time the duty to communicate one's understanding for the benefit of others. I have developed my own peculiar system of going about this. It involves contacting potential candidates for instruction in ways which are sometimes rather unorthodox."

"Then you give lessons in"—she groped for a word, but none came—"being psychic?"

"One might put it that way. I prefer to think in terms of unlocking abilities latent within others, rather than teaching, per se."

Trying to keep suspicion from her voice, she asked, "And at what point do you begin charging?"

He laughed, a deep, good sound. "You will find, Miss Partrick, should we meet, that money is not of much consequence to me. There is no charge at any time. I require only faithful and conscientious effort from my participants. But I should make it immediately clear that I do not by any means accept everyone who contacts me."

Her confusion deepened, intrigue warring with common sense. Her whole adult life seemed to have been one long lesson in the truth of the cliché, *There's no such thing as a free lunch,* not even from–especially not from–spiritually oriented institutions. But the man sounded so sure of himself. The sense that he was trying to impress her, to sell her something, was completely lacking. She decided to circle, a well-learned courtroom tactic.

"I may have missed something," she said, "but I'm not quite sure as a participant in what."

Valcourt was silent again. Then he said, "I hesitate to speak in these terms; one runs the risk of sounding like certain magazine advertisements, or popular cults. But let me say that there is a way of perceiving, hidden to most minds, which can greatly enrich one's own life, and ultimately the life of everyone with whom one comes in contact. This ability is latent in all of us, although like any other, stronger in some. But it requires to be unlocked."

She noted the slip in his otherwise flawless grammar. "Do you have a name for this knowledge?"

"It has been called by many names over the centuries, Miss Partrick. Different adepts have interpreted and presented it differently, according to their own degree of understanding and to the circumstances of time and culture. The principle remains the same. I believe that I can offer most convincing evidence that my own method of imparting it is extremely effective and comparatively swift. Of course if you should decide otherwise, you would have no obligation to continue."

Nicole paused to assess, another carefully developed professional habit.

"You're telling me, then, that if you were to accept me as a participant, you would try to teach me a form of esoteric knowledge that could materially improve my life and the lives of others, and you would do this for no money or other obligation?"

"I would say 'help you discover this ability within yourself,' rather than 'teach,' but yes—that is, in essence, correct."

She hardened herself, all business again. "I hope you won't mind my asking what's in it for you."

"I would consider you foolish if you did not. As I said, there is an inherent duty to pass on this knowledge, a duty which cannot be ignored by those who possess it. This is in the nature of things. In itself, that is incentive enough, just as the pleasure of doing so, of helping, is reward enough. It's difficult to explain; one simply comes to understand it as one proceeds along this path—as you yourself may do one day."

She laughed suddenly, not quite sure why. "Forgive me again. I'm afraid I'm not used to anybody doing anything for nothing."

"That," Valcourt said quietly, "has ever been the way of the world."

There was a pause. Then, hardly believing she was even considering this, Nicole said:

"Well, if I were to decide I was interested, how would I go about getting accepted?"

The good humor returned to his voice. "We would have to determine that by meeting. It must be, after all, as much your decision as my own. But I assure you, if I had not sensed your potential, our conversation tonight would not have gone beyond an exchange of greetings."

"You can tell that over the phone?"

"That and much more. For now, I will say only that I am coming to sense the nature of the wish that prompted you to call me. It is a good wish, a worthy one, and you are right to hold to it. Many lives would be improved by its fulfillment."

She tensed, suspicious again of the con. But Valcourt laughed.

"I admire your skepticism," he said. "That too is healthy. Very well, I will tell you just a little more of what comes to me. This man you are concerned with: his name begins with a J. He lives quite near you. He is a good man, but sad, wounded in his heart. This is much of what you love in him, but it is your enemy, too: it keeps him aloof from you, from all the world. He nurtures it with drink."

She stared at the phone, holding it away from her.

"I did not mean to frighten you, Miss Partrick," she heard him say.

"That's quite . . . remarkable," she said dizzily.

"Shall we meet, then?"

The dizziness washed away in a wave of excitement. She nodded, then said, "Yes."

"Would it be convenient for you to come to my home, let us say, tomorrow?"

"Yes," she said again, abandoning her plans to work.

"It is some distance outside the city."

"That's all right. I have a car."

She copied the directions he gave, surprised yet again at the Woodside address, which seemed to bolster his claim of disinterest in money.

"I look forward to meeting you, Miss Partrick. I have a strong sense that we will get along famously."

She thanked him and hung up. As the swell of emotion ebbed, she tried to understand what had just happened. Had he really said those things, picked them out of her mind from thirty miles away, over a telephone? Could he have known them in some other way, or simply been guessing?

Neither was possible, she decided immediately. The information was far too detailed for guesswork, and she had provided no dues, at least none of the sort she knew so-called psychics often worked from. As for the chance that he had done clandestine research in order to work a scam, well, if he had contacted her, she might consider it. But the fact was that she was just one of hundreds or even thousands of people who might have seen the ad on the streetcar. Besides, with no money involved, why would he go to such trouble?

She poured one more glass of wine, turned out the lights, and sat again before the window. At the thought of Jesse, something like guilt touched her. That he was at the heart of this–this *madness* of hers–she could not deny. It was almost as if she was scheming.

But she told herself firmly that her interest in exploring this possibility, thin though it might be, lay in the chance of improving the lives of herself and Tom Junior. And whatever happened, it was exciting. It was action, it was change–it was *something*. Of course, the possibility of the hidden catch remained; she would be on the alert.

She finished the wine and checked on Tom Junior. His book, a novelized *Indiana Jones,* was collapsed on his chest, his head fallen to the side in sleep. She set the book on the table, kissed his check, and turned out the light.

Then she put herself to bed, trying not to think about how long it had been since there had been a pair of arms waiting to reach out and welcome her.

FOUR

And so, Sunday afternoon Nicole found herself on her way to a meeting with a man who was certainly eccentric and might turn out to be insane. As she drove, she alternated between speculation as to exactly what she was getting into and amazement mat she was getting into it at all. She had begun to wonder if she was being lured into something bizarre, even dangerous. Feeling a little ashamed, she had jotted down a brief note of explanation, containing Valcourt's address and phone, and left it on the table by her bed. If anything happened to her, it would be found.

But she did not think she was in danger. She had been cautious in her approach, and her instincts told her she was in for an experience that at worst would be interesting and unusual, a good story to be repeated with rueful laughter among friends, and at best—

But at that point she forced her imagination to stop. She wanted to walk into this with her mind open. The weather was like yesterday's, warm and clear, and she was a pretty girl in a blue dress, alone in her bright yellow Celica, her hair blowing in the wind.

She did not get down the peninsula much—there was little reason to—and as she passed through the thick cluster of houses and apartments and condominiums that lined the steep hillsides along Interstate 280, she tried to imagine herself and Tom Junior in one of them. But she found herself shaking her head: they did not fit. It would just be exchanging one set of problems for another, with no substantial gain.

The houses thinned after she passed the airport and increased her distance from San Francisco. On her right, the great reservoir that lay in the belly of the San Andreas Fault shimmered clear and blue. It was attractive from a distance, but she knew that it was surrounded by fences and patrolled against trespassers. That was the trouble with the Bay Area: too many people and not enough room. There was no space, no real freedom, no areas that were not spoken for.

Valcourt's directions were clear and precise. When she turned on Green Mountain Road, she checked her odometer. The house, he had said, was not quite two miles from the freeway. The road was narrow, a series of steep rises and hairpin turns, but she maneuvered it with skill and pleasure, shifting and downshifting the way Tom Senior had taught her during the good times—before she had married him. For a few minutes, she paid less attention to her surroundings. Then she realized that the driveways were no longer dirt, but paved roads with pillared gates and carefully trimmed hedges, sweeping off into unseen grandeur. They were also several hundred yards apart.

A tarnished brass plaque with the numbers 2713 hung on a black iron gate suspended from brick columns on either side of the drive. The right-hand gate was open. Nicole turned in slowly, almost fearfully, not quite believing she was in the right place. The road continued for perhaps eighty yards, lined at precise intervals with eucalyptus trees that must have been a hundred feet tall. To the right she caught glimpses of grassy meadows and a pond; to the left, a thick wood of madrone, bay, and oak.

She came forth from the shaded lane into a burst of sunlight, and her mouth opened in astonishment. The drive circled around a fountain that looked for all the world like real marble. Clean, faintly blue water bubbled from jets hidden in a Roman-style statue of a nude with winged heels and an elegant pose–perhaps Mercury. Up a tier of stone stairs stood the house: a monumental three-story structure of faded red brick, with half a dozen many-paned bay windows on the first floor and as many gable dormers on the third. The roof was slate tiles of a deeper red, sloping down into an elaborately symmetrical design of hips and valleys. It was topped by an octagonal cupola complete with weather vane.

As she stared, the oversized front door opened and a man stepped out. The sight of him gave her an instant, eerie sense of déjà vu; it lingered while she added his appearance to her list of surprises. She had formed no clear mental image of him, but now realized that in spite of his deep voice, she had expected someone a bit foppish. But her instant impression now of Guy-Luc Valcourt—for she knew instinctively that it was he—could hardly have been more contrary.

He stood over six feet tall, and the black monastic robe he wore did not conceal the physical power of his body. Sandaled feet and short, curling, rusty brown hair that could almost have been tonsured completed the picture of a medieval monk—except for the patch that covered his left eye. That was black, too. His hands, clasped before him, were thick and strong; his feet firmly apart; his face, with the mouth a set line, looked stern and gaunt. Nicole's déjà vu gave way to a sudden, cold twist of discomfort. Her fingers tightened on the steering wheel and her foot moved to hover over the accelerator.

But then his face broke into a smile, and he bowed, gesturing that she should park around to the right. Her nervousness subsided, though it did not vanish; as she climbed out of the car, her own smile felt timid.

"Miss Partrick?" he said. She nodded, feeling like a schoolgirl. He moved toward her down the stairs, his walk stately and deliberate, and extended his hand: the gesture of a noble greeting a favorite. The third finger wore a heavy ring of onyx, his only adornment. His face was handsomer at close range, the harsh features somehow softened; the hidden eye added to this, perhaps because it suggested suffering. As their fingers touched, she imagined a faint tingle of current.

"Welcome to my house," he said.

He was probably used to women falling apart in his presence, she thought. She straightened her shoulders.

"Thank you. It's . . . magnificent." He inclined his head, graciously offering his arm. Taking it, she climbed the steps beside him and entered the grand old mansion.

"Will you take some tea?"

"That would be nice."

"I am but recently arrived here. Soon I shall have a housekeeper, but for the present, I must fend for myself. You will forgive me if I leave you for a moment?"

"Of course."

"Talking is more relaxed over refreshment, I think. Please make yourself at home. Examine anything you find of interest." He exited through a large, sunlit dining room and a pair of swinging doors.

The coved ceilings must have been nearly twelve feet high, the walls were wainscoted with foot-wide paneling that looked like walnut, and the floors, of intricately patterned hardwood, were thrown with thick Oriental rugs that she could tell at a glance were genuine. The furniture was sparse but tasteful: a heavy couch and matching chairs of dark wood and purple velvet, which she judged to be European and at least a century old, and a six-foot-long coffee table that appeared to have been carved from a single slab of ebony.

She turned slowly, taking in the other wonders that lined the walls and nooks of the room: an instrument that might have been an astrolabe; a shelf of massive, ponderous books, some modern, some with cracked leather bindings and gold lettering; several vases that looked Eastern, ancient, and, like everything else, expensive and genuine. The single painting was an impressionist work of deep greens and blues, apparently of a black-clad figure strolling in a forest glade at dusk.

But the object that attracted Nicole was on the mantel: a glass case closed with a silver hasp and lock, upon which were engraved symbols that looked Arabic. Inside the case, upright on a stand, was a book. The cover was of dark, fine grained skin, worn with age and handling. On it was a very strange symbol etched in a deep rust color. The ink was faded and the room dim, but it seemed to consist largely of loops. She had never seen anything like it. Then she noticed that several of the pages appeared to be charred–as if someone had once tried to burn the book. She stepped back, feeling uneasy, and inhaled sharply when she noticed Valcourt standing in the doorway to the dining room, a silver tray in his hands.

"I beg your pardon," he murmured. "I should have announced myself."

She managed a smile. "It's a bit much–this house, all these beautiful things."

Valcourt walked forward and set the tray on the coffee table.

"An advantage of coming from an old and wealthy family. I would be quite lost without my treasures." He nodded at the book she had been examining. "Like that."

"Is it a Bible?"

His hands, pouring, hesitated. "No," he said.

She waited, but he offered no more information. "It must be very old."

"Very old indeed, Miss Partrick. Its value is beyond measuring in money. As you can see, someone was once careless with it; that is why I keep it enclosed." He paused again, then added, "Long ago, it was the property of a most interesting man. Perhaps one day I shall tell you about him."

His charm began to relax her again. She sat on the couch, and as he handed her a cup of tea, her eye caught a blur of what she was sure was makeup on his palm. Perhaps to cover a birthmark, or a scar from the same accident that had blinded him? It was not the sort of thing one asked.

"So," Valcourt said, sitting on one of the heavy chairs opposite her. "May I ask which of my notices attracted your attention?"

For the first time Nicole had a flashing vision of hundreds of eager hands dialing Valcourt's phone number–bag ladies, soap opera addicts, tabloid subscribers, the whole subculture of those desperate to believe that wishes could come true–and felt a twinge of shame.

"On a streetcar," she said. "Funny, I never thought of it, but you must have gotten lots of responses."

"Oh, quite a few." He watched her with grave amusement. "Most of them–I perceived enough of their thoughts over the telephone to realize they would be unsuitable, and was able to persuade them that they had misunderstood my intentions. Three or four remain." His single eye held her, steady, benign. "I should explain that my advertising efforts do not involve any sort of widespread canvassing. As I told you, money is not an object to me. I was born very rich." He swept his hand at the splendor around him, a silent, eloquent gesture. "My family has many holdings in Europe, dating back to long

84

before the French Revolution. These bring me more income than I could spend without going to a great deal of trouble, and high living does not interest me.

"What does interest me is cultivating the ability of which I spoke, in those whom I sense possess it to a large degree. I devoted the early part of my life to the development of my own; and while I of course continue this, for the past two decades I have felt it incumbent on me to share the knowledge I have acquired.

"I began with a small group in Paris. My students—to use a term that is more convenient than strictly accurate—were excellent, and the experience was most rewarding. But in time I realized that they had reached a point beyond which I could not take them—that from there, they must proceed on their own. I realized too that I had begun to grow stagnant, staying in one city; I have ever been a great traveler, and my heart yearned for new places, new minds.

"And so, a little at a time, I developed a system that has served me well. When I feel that I have done as much for a group of students as I can, I close up shop, as it were, and journey to someplace new. When I am settled, I recruit a new group by a variety of means; frankly, these are often quite whimsical on my part. The streetcar advertisement you saw was the only one of its kind, and remained in place only twenty-four hours. Very few responded to it—a tribute to your sharp eyes. Or perhaps there is more to it than that. Perhaps your eyes were directed." He paused. Uncertain of what he meant, she said nothing.

"I also distributed a handful of leaflets in various ways. From these, I received quite a few calls. I rarely use newspapers, as the response tends to be overwhelming and tiresome. And on occasion, by chance I meet someone who I sense is gifted, and invite them to join me.

"It is, as you say in America, a sort of potluck; but if one accepts, as I do, that there is a great design to all events, one can take pleasure in being its instrument on even the humblest of levels."

Nicole reached for her tea, shaking off the trance. Whether it was the hinted mysticism of the ideas he voiced so casually, or the force of his personality, or the power of his voice itself, she could not tell, but she continued to feel slightly stunned. Valcourt remained composed, watching her kindly.

Well, there was every reason to assume that he was on the level—so far. It seemed clear enough that he did not want or need her money. There was no sign of a sexual advance—none of that *feel* to the situation.

The next question, then: How real was what he purported to offer? And if it was real, how capable was she of making use of it?

"The way you read my thoughts over the phone was very impressive," she said. "And I have to admit, a little disturbing."

"Forgive me if I intruded on your privacy. In general, when a person wishes his or her thoughts to remain secret, this is clear to me, and I refuse to press further. Again, there are reasons for this—restraints which are in the nature of this power—which you may one day come to understand.

"But in your case, I was able to see your thoughts clearly because: you do not really wish them to be secret. In fact, they remain rather obvious, probably even to a person devoid of psychic ability. You have shared them with others, have you not?"

She nodded, thinking of Heather.

"And, I must confess, I wished to impress you with the seriousness of this enterprise. But you may rest assured that any thoughts you wish to hold genuinely private will remain so," He leaned forward. "Shall we go one step further?" She tensed, but nodded again. He smiled reassuringly, patted her wrist, and rose.

"Come." He led her to the mirror above the mantel, beside the glassed-in book, and positioned her in front of it. "Tell me," he said, stepping back. "This woman you see: Is she beautiful?"

Flustered, she immediately said, "No."

She could see his reflection, behind her and to the left. "Imagine that this is the mirror of your heart," he said, with a note of reproof. "When you gaze into it, you must abandon all conceit, even false modesty. Look again."

She looked and finally admitted, "Well, not bad." Then, laughing nervously, "She could stand to lose a little weight."

"Ah, yes, the women these days, they crave to be thin. It was not always so." He paused, then said, "And why has she come here? Truly?"

Her smile turned rueful. "She's in love," she said quietly, adding, "and not having much luck."

"Yes," he murmured. "Then tell me one more thing: Is she worthy of this man's love?"

Again she looked long. Finally she said, "Yes. I think she is."

"I believe you are right. Whether *he* is worthy of *her* is another matter, one we will not yet touch on. For now, I will tell you that you fight with yourself over this. That is good and necessary, a mark of character. But I think you will soon see that what I offer is also good. It is not by any means a simple matter of attaining things you desire; that is only an aspect. Of far more importance is developing this very special potential within you and learning to use it for the benefit of all. And for that, it is helpful to be settled, happy in one's mind and life. The idea that one need be tormented in order to become spiritually powerful is a myth. You will come to see that your own happiness is conducive to the common good.

"Now—repeat these words."

He leaned forward and spoke into her ear, quietly and slowly, perhaps ten syllables. They were sibilant, flowing, unlike any language she had ever heard. They might have been Eastern; they might have been nonsense. She could feel his warm breath, pleasantly scented with sesame, and wondered dizzily if this was it, if after all the buildup he would bring it crashing down by caressing her; and if he did, whether she would be angry or, in spite of herself, respond. She could see him in the mirror, his single eye fixed on her reflected face. Except for his lips, he was absolutely motionless. The sounds were a blur; she was too confused to attempt them. He repeated them, gently, patiently. Stumbling, she began to follow. After a half-dozen tries, she succeeded on her own.

"Excellent," he said, and stepped back. "Let us sit again."

There seemed to be a great hollowness inside her head. Meekly, she returned to her place on the couch and sat upright, hands in her lap. Valcourt remained standing, and as he began to speak, he paced. His demeanor was very serious.

"So, Miss Partrick, your education begins. When you have heard what I have to tell you this afternoon, you must take some days to think about it. I, too, will consider. Then we will talk again, and decide whether you are to continue.

"The words you have just learned comprise a sort of prayer, or mantra, of a very special nature. It originated in Persia, near the beginnings of mankind. In those times, humans understood clearly that there is another world–'dimension of being' might be a better term– which is ordinarily invisible to us but whose affairs are intertwined with our lives, every instant of every day. Men realized, too, their helplessness in the face of such infinitely more powerful forces, and sought ways to control–and failing that, to propitiate–those forces. This is the origin of all religion. Most of what has since arisen is window-dressing heaped upon it.

"Nowadays, this understanding is for the most part a thin remnant of belief, an empty shell without content. With our science, we have learned much about the physical nature of our world, but we have lost contact with the forces that shape our destiny and we have come to trust false gods. We have lost, too, the understanding of what we ourselves, in reality, are.

"Here, then, is the secret that lies at the heart of the knowledge I offer, the first all-important thing you must seek to understand. What you have always thought of as *you*–the conscious part of your mind that takes charge of your daily life–is in large part an illusion. In fact, the consciousness that is 'you' is like a tiny seed that is surrounded by, and under tremendous pressure from, innumerable other sources–call them 'intelligences,' or 'entities'–which exist in that other dimension of which I spoke.

"It is very much in the interest of these entities for you to behave in certain ways, to perform certain actions and not perform others. In fact, there is no exaggeration in saying that their very existence depends on it. Further, different entities have entirely different aims; and not knowing fatigue, like humans, they battle unendingly among themselves in seeking to persuade you to act as they would wish.

"Thus, the 'you' which believes it is in control of its life, actions, and destiny, is really like a dreamer–most of the time being pushed and pulled by forces of whose very existence it is not even aware."

His voice had dropped, become gravelly, the accent more pronounced, and she listened with parted lips, not quite believing what she was hearing.

"By becoming aware of these intelligences, you can first put an end to their control over you, and then begin to exercise control over them. This is the proper order of things. At one time, wise men understood well enough

90

how to do this, but alas! Barbarians destroyed the works of wisdom and drove underground those who dared to seek it. The proponents of orthodox religions, sad to say, were among the worst. Fear, ignorance, and superstition have ever been great enemies of knowledge; these things, you see, are weapons employed by the entities which wish to keep us in bondage. They are hugely, pitiably, successful. Even the most powerful men of this earth are for the most part pawns of the intelligences, used to purposes beyond their ken.

"Little enough knowledge has survived, and only a few have had the means to seek it. Through a combination of fortuitous circumstances–possession of the natural gift in large measure, access to those who could give me a rudimentary education in its use, and wealth to uncover and assemble resources long hidden throughout the world–I have come to a high level of understanding. One of the convictions I have reached is that students are best served by coming immediately into contact with the entitles which surround them, since your degree of attainment in this endeavor will ultimately rest on your awareness, and control, of them.

"So, as a first step to true knowledge, you must remember these words I have taught you. You must repeat them to yourself three times each evening before you retire–in privacy and, preferably, unclothed, although this is not necessary if circumstances do not allow. The words themselves comprise the name of a particular intelligence. Names hold much more significance than we are generally aware of. By repeating this name, you signify to the intelligence that you are aware of it and that you are ending its power over you—that you, who have spent your life serving it, now demand that it begin to serve you. If you do this properly, it must obey—it has no choice. This is in the nature of things.

"In no long time, your control will increase and also expand to a greater number of these entities. Besides offering you wisdom, they will help you attain things that you desire. The name you have learned, for instance, includes among its powers a certain control over human metabolism. You have expressed a wish to be more slender. Concentrate on that each night as you speak this name." Suddenly Valcourt smiled. "If you are not most pleasantly surprised within, let us say, a week, I will expect never to hear from you again, and I will carry to my grave the shame of your believing that I am deceitful. If, however, we succeed, then we will discuss moving on to more important matters."

His smile broke her trance. She reached automatically for her hardly touched cup of tea. To her amazement, it was still hot. Had her sense of time gone awry? Or was this another exhibition of Valcourt's power? His face was impassive again.

"I've never heard anything like it," she said weakly. "Trying to control those things almost seems like . . . witchcraft, or something."

Valcourt made a gesture that suggested irritation, but his face was quickly composed again.

"Did you not grow up praying to saints and angels?"

"Well, sort of. I mean, we were Presbyterians, not Catholics."

"And what do you think that practice is, if not a primitive form of trying to influence such entities as those of which I speak? What you call witchcraft was only an equally primitive effort to influence a different spectrum of such intelligences. Usually, it was just as effective–that is to say, not at all.

"No, I am talking about something quite different: not a superstitious attempt to propitiate powers one does not understand, in the impotent hope that they will grant one's wishes, but rather a thoroughly scientific method of acquiring a particular kind of knowledge–which, like all knowledge, culminates in power. To be sure, it can be used wrongly. That is why I first satisfied myself that you were a worthy recipient, and then required you to satisfy yourself that you were worthy of the object of your desire. When the time comes, I will teach you safeguards against the potential misuse of your gift. But you are a long way from having to worry about such things."

She managed a smile. "I'm still a little nervous about the idea of summoning some sort of entity. I suppose I've seen too many spooky movies."

"That is precisely where you must readjust your way of thinking. You are not summoning–on the contrary. This intelligence is one of many that has been with you since your birth, a voice that has been persuading you to do its bidding for many years. You will come to recognize it clearly as a part of the incessant background noise of your mind, once you learn to pick it out. Do you not think it is time to turn that around? To cause it to serve you, instead of your serving it?"

"Of course," she said. "I mean, that makes perfect sense . . ." Her voice faltered and trailed off.

"Perhaps it will reassure you if I add that the entity in question is entirely benign and not very powerful. It cannot, for instance, change your height or sex-fixed attributes—nor can it exert any influence to speak of on other humans. But it can influence things within you that are changeable in themselves—your metabolism, for instance, as I said. More important, it, and others like it, can become extremely useful allies in maintaining your psychic well-being."

"Sort of like a guardian angel?"

"A very apt analogy."

"And there are other kinds?" she asked suddenly, not sure where the thought had come from—a competing entity, maybe. "More powerful, and not so benign?"

His eyebrows rose pensively. "That is a matter we will discuss in time," he finally said. "For now, I will answer yes. The truly powerful entities themselves only interfere directly in human affairs by invitation—in fact, coercion might be a better word—and that is business of an altogether different order. But it does not concern us directly, and I advise you to keep it from your mind as much as possible. You are entering a vulnerable stage, and while there is nothing that can actually harm you, there are influences which could prove . . . troublesome. Should any such difficulties arise, you need only tell me, and I will deal with them swiftly and surely."

He smiled, and as if on cue, an absolutely black cat stalked into the room. It went straight to Valcourt, rubbed once against his ankle, and sat at his feet, gazing at Nicole with languid intelligence in eyes of a startlingly deep green.

She laughed aloud; it was like comic relief. "What timing," she said.

"My friend Lamashtu," Valcourt said. "Named after a spirit held in much regard by the Babylonians. When I was younger, I did not care for cats." He stooped to scratch Lamashtu's ears. "But I find she provides much company in this large and somewhat lonely house. She was wild in the woods outside for some time, until she won my respect and prevailed upon me to begin feeding her. After that, of course, it was but a short time until she moved in; and now I think it is she who suffers me to live here."

He rose again, extending his hand. Nicole took it— warm, strong, hard—and stood, too.

"I realize this was a great deal to put before you in the space of an hour," he said. "Nothing less than a completely new way of viewing life. But within a few days, you will begin to decide whether there is something to what I tell you, or whether I am simply mad. Let us leave it there. Either I will hear from you soon, or I will not."

They stepped out onto the sunlit porch, where Nicole drank in the fresh-aired beauty, the quiet, the grandeur that spoke of a lost time—a better time—of which Valcourt somehow seemed a stalwart, even saintly, relic.

"I have mentioned that others contacted me," he said. 'We are still in the early stages; my plans have not yet coalesced. But it is my custom to gather a group of perhaps a half-dozen—never more—and meet together once a month, on an evening convenient for everyone.

This is beneficial in many ways: less demanding on my time, and I have found that students learn as much from each other as from me. If we should agree to continue this relationship, would you be willing to participate?"

"I'd be willing to try it," she said hesitantly.

"Excellent. I must also request that you keep the nature of our work to yourself for the present. Misunderstanding or jealousy, even on the part of those close to you, can be very damaging to your progress until you are on firmer ground." She nodded, a little disappointed. She had planned to tell Heather every detail at lunch tomorrow.

"There is one more small matter. I have given you a name of power. In return, I ask to be permitted to use your given name."

"Nicole?" she said, puzzled.

"May I call you that henceforth?"

"Of course," she said, laughing. She had assumed he stood on the formality because of his upbringing.

"Nicole," he said, giving the *l* a slight French roll. His face changed slightly, with what she thought was satisfaction. "It is a lovely name. I thank you." He raised her hand to his lips. "Now, my dear Nicole, I wish you a safe journey home, and I will hope with all my heart to hear from you again."

"Not summon an entity to make sure of it?" she teased.

His face remained grave. "In certain matters of personal freedom, one must never interfere. There are laws; you will learn them."

She was opening the car door when he called, "Nicole: once more-the entity's name."

She repeated it perfectly, realizing that it had a rhythm that demanded proper enunciation.

"Very good," Valcourt said. "You must never, never let anyone else hear it-unless the day should come when you, too, will pass this knowledge on."

As she drove away, she looked in the rearview mirror and was again touched by the sense of déjà vu: that she had seen somewhere else the man who stood with arms folded, watching her. Hesitantly, she waved, and she saw him raise one hand slowly, as in a gesture of benediction.

Valcourt watched the little yellow car drive away like a bright bird, returning Nicole's wave as she drove from the circle onto the main drive. Her hair fluttered in the wind, and a gold ring on her finger flashed in the sunlight.

Charming.

The hook was firmly set. There was not the slightest doubt that she would call again, especially after she came to believe that her "guardian angel" did indeed have the power to make her more slender. In truth, there was only one way to acquire such favor: to tender something more precious in return.

A second candidate, the Epps man, was due to arrive within the hour. If that interview went as well as this one had-and he would see to it that it did-then only two more remained to be found: a man and a woman, to preserve the semblance of sexual balance.

For now, a few. Next year, another ten. In a decade, thousands: a vast human pyramid sowing the seeds of evil, with himself at the top, reaping the fruits.

He turned to the cat Lamashtu, cleaning its paws in the sunshine. Its presence was calculated for precisely the effect it had produced on Nicole Partrick: to add an air of ingenuousness, warmth, even humor. Though it was not, of course, the great being of that name, the servant that controlled it was similar in nature–one might say, a little sister. He smiled ferociously at the thought of what would happen should his visitors glimpse it in its true aspect.

"Alert me to Epps's arrival," he said, and went back into the house to prepare his thoughts. The cat yawned, then leaped onto a windowsill with a view of the drive.

In the front room, Valcourt poured a glass of red wine and sat in a heavy chair of dark leather. What he had told her was true enough–to a point. Her questions had proved to be more perceptive than he had anticipated–there was no doubt of her intelligence. But she was almost devoid of psychic ability. If she possessed any, he would not be able to use her. It was a requirement that in that sense his "students" be *tabulae rasae*: blank slates.

In any case, he knew well that they cared little about the whys and hows of their gains, but only about the whats–until it was too late. The supremely important thing was to give them enough information to allow them to choose of their own free will, but not so much that they would see how they were digging themselves in–to tempt, but never to coerce–until they had gone so far that desire to keep what they had gained outweighed the fear of what might lie ahead.

To avoid planting the faintest seed of suspicion, he had not mentioned her son.

In the centuries since his imprisonment, he had come to learn, there had been men who had killed millions, who had made even the great Genghis Khan himself look puny. But killing, in itself, accomplished nothing, and in the end it had dragged those men down—as it must any who did not understand how to harness it. Death was the most common thing on earth: the sacrifice of life, the economy on which all existence depended. But to squan-der it ignorantly was like destroying a crop instead of harvesting it. Eventually, one was bound to starve. His own work was not, and never had been, merely to slaugh-ter. Any fool could do that.

No, the object was to harness the power that was exchanged: to direct the minds of others toward destruction and then reap the rewards. The lesser beings, the hungry mouths, could be appeased with blood. In return, they would serve the hand that fed them—as long as that hand retained its power. Many men had succeeded in this endeavor to a greater or lesser extent, sometimes consciously, sometimes not, and rarely for long.

But only a few had ever understood the ultimate truth—those few who had possessed the knowledge, the patience, and the unshakable courage to tread the path that he had trod, to court the great dragon that fed on the hearts of men. To the Adversary, death itself was a trifle. Only one offering was acceptable, that most precious of all commodities: free will—or rather, the corruption of it in the human soul, until that human became the victim of his own crimes and lusts. The epitome lay in inducing someone to destroy the one dearest to him.

Or to her. Again he thought of Nicole Partrick and her son, and his mouth tightened in anticipation.

There was no feast as rich as that of betrayed love.

The single greatest secret that he had not told, and would never tell, Nicole or any of the others, was this: all humans were slaves, all but the few real saints who had journeyed beyond the entities' grasp—who had enjoyed the power *not* to choose. Valcourt glanced down at his monastic garb, and his lips twisted at the irony. That was the path that Courdeval, as a young man, had truly craved.

But his violent nature had proved ungovernable, and no holy men had appeared to guide him. He had seen only the emptiness and corruption of the religion of his day, the futility of man's cries to God, the suffering of life. The arcane mysteries of the Templars, empty, too, of content by his time, served only to whet his thirst. At last he had encountered wisdom in the East, which pointed out that the middling existence of the mass of men was the most contemptible thing imaginable to a nature like his own. It was infinitely preferable to rage and war against the tyrant in so-called heaven—against the creator who engendered helpless human beings, only to mock and destroy them as if they were puppets—than to join the groveling ranks of servitors, adoring that creator mindlessly and unquestioningly in spite of the endless

100

misery he inflicted. To be utterly powerless was the worst fate of all; and since Courdeval's nature had not allowed him to pursue the path of sanctity that might have led to true freedom—since he, too, must serve—he had chosen to serve a master who both protected him and gave him strength.

And if there had been moments of something like regret when he looked back on the anguish he had caused and was sworn to cause again—if he wished in his heart of hearts that he might have turned his great strength toward that other path of righteousness, or simply bowed his head in the face of his own pride and accepted himself as only a man, neither all good nor all bad, and had lived his natural life as best he could—

But such thoughts were too dangerous even to entertain. He had made his decision in the distant past; he was committed, and the slightest notion of betrayal, of turning back, would bring down final wrath upon him. He must keep his side of the bargain, and keep it well. In return, he would be granted anything he desired.

Anything except rest.

He turned at a slight noise. Lamashtu sat in the middle of the floor, tail curled around its feet. Valcourt finished his wine, rose, and walked to a window. A sleek, expensive car of a silvery color—they were called Porsches, he had learned, and there was a sort of cult about them, as there had been about the relics of certain saints in Courdeval's time—was pulling into the circle before the house. He gazed into the shaded windshield, making out the driver's expensive hairstyle and clothing, the hundred-dollar pair of sunglasses—and the reddened, nervous eyes behind them. Here was a man of little will and morality, who could be bent to any purpose: a useful soldier. Valcourt watched him take a small glass vial from his pocket and, with a tiny spoon that hung from a chain around his neck, quickly inhale a quantity of white powder into each nostril.

"Excellent," Valcourt said to the cat. "Let us welcome Mister Spencer Epps."

He strode to the grimoire on the mantel and stood silently before it for several seconds. Then he bowed, a deep, solemn gesture of obeisance. Turning away, he caught sight of his own face in the mirror.

"Guardian angel," he said aloud. He laughed, a short, harsh sound, and went to greet his guest.

Nicole merged back onto I-280, uncertain about which was more of a dream: the whizzing traffic and modern homes that surrounded her, the thousands of ordinary people going about their ordinary business, or the hour she had just spent with a man who spoke offhandedly of spirit servants and magical charms, who read her thoughts as if she wore them printed on a T-shirt. This morning she would have laughed aloud at the ideas he had voiced. Yet in his presence, anything seemed possible. He spoke with such authority, such utter confidence–such *power*. Silently, she mouthed the syllables he had taught her, and tried to imagine what a guardian angel might look like. Shimmering white robe? Wings? Halo?

Were you *supposed* to be able to order them around?

There was something unsettling about the whole business, the sense that she was going against the grain of the way things were meant to be. But she could imagine Valcourt's quiet question, almost hear his voice: *And how, in your opinion, are things meant to be?*

She realized that she had no answer, no firm convictions. It was not something she had ever thought much about. She had abandoned churchgoing as a teenager, after her mother admitted that she had only wanted to raise Nicole in some church, any church, to give her a basic religious sense. Since then Nicole had been far too concerned with the problems of her own life to worry about the moral order of the universe.

These days, almost everyone she knew either was or had been involved in some sort of modern, positively oriented philosophy: creative visualization, self-actualization, even chanting. All of these seemed to be somewhat weaker-kneed, pseudoscientific versions of the same thing Valcourt was suggesting: your life was yours to command, and by learning to control some form of psychic energy, you could see to it that you got the things you wanted. What could be wrong with that?

Why could she not quite shake the feeling of being like a peasant girl in a fairy tale, sneaking off to the old witch in the forest for a love charm?

The important thing, she decided, was whether or not it worked. There was no denying that Valcourt had given her a fair, no-strings offer: a one-week free trial, as with a hand lotion or a newspaper subscription. If nothing happened, that was the end of it.

She envisioned herself stripping naked in her darkened bedroom, with perhaps a candle and some incense, and solemnly repeating the name of the spirit who was meant to be her helper, just to let that entity know she was hip to its game, that things were being turned around on it, that it could start by trimming her down into the svelte shape of a blue jeans model.

She blushed, laughed aloud, and stomped on the gas pedal to swing around a pokey old van.

FIVE

Five days later, Friday afternoon, Nicole at last finished going through a series of witness statements and
wearily began to straighten her desk. The case was a
negligence suit against a slumlord in the Mission District, who in his miserliness had refused to repair a
collapsing railing along an outside staircase, thus
occasioning the fall and brain injury of a three-year-old
child. Typically, the man carried no insurance, and he
had already made several blustery phone calls to
her—stopping just short of threats—to the effect that he
had no intentions of paying any damages and nothing to
pay them with.

But she had discovered that he in fact owned several
million dollars worth of poorly maintained slum rentals,
many of them in his wife's name or in the names of half
a dozen front corporations. She had not yet told him this,
and was awaiting the moment with grim satisfaction. She
would demand, and was sure she would get, an out-
of-court settlement of several hundred thousand. One

poor family, at least, was finally going to get a piece of the American dream.

When she finished putting everything in order for Monday morning, she walked to the window of her cubicle and stood overlooking the streets of the financial district, nine stories below. It was almost six; everyone else in the office had left an hour or more ago. She felt a twinge of self-pity; she was becoming the firm's girl scout. It just seemed that there was always more to do than time to do it in.

At any rate, the week was over, and after fixing Tom Junior's dinner tonight—lasagne, his favorite—she faced the bittersweet task tomorrow of driving him to his father's, with the attendant strain of seeing her ex's kindly but overanxious wife, and, of course, Tom Senior himself.

Coming back alone Sunday, she had a decision to make.

Whether the charm Valcourt had given her was in fact working or something altogether different was going on, she could not say. But this much was undeniable: without any effort whatever, without a shred of noticeable change in her diet or daily habits, she had lost eight pounds since her meeting with him. They had simply disappeared, melted. She looked and felt better than she had since she was a teenager—since bearing her child.

More: each night, as she stood in her darkened bedroom and whispered the secret syllables, the sense of summoning a presence had increased. Perhaps she was only reacting subconsciously to Valcourt's suggestion, but her feeling was that the presence was in fact becoming obedient–that it even yearned to serve her.

It was, in a word, thrilling.

It was also unnerving–perhaps because, as Valcourt had said, the voice, or intelligence, or whatever it was, *did* seem to be one that had always been there in the shadows of her mind.

Perhaps she was frightened of the truth.

Whatever it was, she had decided that the drive back would be a good time to sort it all out. She would take it slow and easy, stop along the way, treat herself to lunch. And that night she would call Valcourt to tell him either that she wanted to continue on the path of his promised knowledge or that she did not. Losing weight, of course, was a silly thing, a trifle; but had he not made it clear that this was only a beginning?

And was that not precisely where the gray area, filled with her own doubts as to the *rightness* of this, began?

The sound of the main office door opening surprised her. Probably one of her colleagues had forgotten a coat or a bit of weekend work. But a tap came at her cubicle and a stocky man of about forty, with a receding hairline and sharp blue eyes, leaned in.

"What's the best-looking broad in town doing up here alone on a Friday night?" Then he blinked. "Jesus, where'd you get those cheekbones?"

"Came in the mail," she said, surprised and pleased. Cameron Wilkes was the firm's private detective of choice. Besides criminal investigations, he spent an unenviable amount of time at the bread and butter work of substantiating accident claims: interviewing victims who'd been crippled and their distraught spouses, photographing crushed vehicles and deadly machinery, and often engaging in risky subterfuge to wring evidence from hostile witnesses. He was absolutely the most cynical human being Nicole had ever met. Any mention of an incident where someone had seemingly performed an act of generosity would be met by a knowing, almost malevolent look from Wilkes's steely eyes; he would then casually drop an alternative suggestion as to what the benefactor's underlying, self-serving motive might have been. He was usually right; and while at first she had found his grim, street-smart humor irritating, she had come to appreciate it. It made most conversation seem insipid by comparison.

"I got the photos of that kid who offed himself in the San Leone jail," he said, tossing an envelope on the desk. "The cops were not interested in turning them loose. Had to call in a favor."

A little reluctantly, she opened the envelope and spread the half-dozen photos on the desk. They showed a slender, scruffy-looking young man hanging by the neck from the bars of a jail cell by a sort of thick white rope. It was, she knew, a pair of tied-together tube socks: his own. His bare feet still rested on the floor. Wilkes lit a cigarette and walked to the window.

"Have a swell weekend," he said.

The young man, whose name was Rutledge, had a long record of petty and not-so-petty crime, including rape, and had been apprehended for the last time after a desperate chase in a stolen car. Nicole swallowed.

"He tied his socks around his neck and just . . . lay down?"

"The cops beat the shit out of him," Wilkes answered flatly. "The coroner found several interesting bruises. I've got his statement on tape. After they got the kid in the jail, they put him in a cell by himself, at the end of a long corridor, and left him unsupervised for most of an hour. Curious procedure, considering he kept threatening to kill himself while they were bringing him in. Guess they were just trying to be accommodating. Of course, nobody heard him say anything about suicide except the cops who booked him. No tape, no video." He paused and blew a series of smoke rings. "Funny thing about it is another little piece I picked up from the coroner. The kid's the third poor schmuck to hang himself in that jail in a little over eight months."

Their eyes met.

"That was another thing the gendarmes weren't interested in talking about," he said.

The suit was being filed against San Leone County by Rutledge's parents, sad, weary farmers, old before their time, torn between shame at the criminal they had raised and anger at the correctional system that had allowed him to die.

Or was allowed the right word?

"You think, like, somebody leaned on him?" she said quietly.

Wilkes shrugged, lips tight. "I think we can get his folks two hundred grand right this second, without ever walking into a courtroom. Straight negligence. You want to start turning over rocks and looking under them–" He shrugged again and stubbed out his cigarette.

Nicole sighed. "I'll think it over." Slowly, she gathered up the photos and returned them to the envelope.

"Let me buy you a drink," he said. "We can gloom each other out."

"I'd love to, Cam, I really would. But moms don't belong to themselves. Tommy's leaving for the summer tomorrow, and I promised I'd make him lasagne tonight, and I'm already late."

"I bow to the better man. Tell that kid to keep his nose clean, or he'll end up like me."

She smiled. To Tom Junior, Cameron Wilkes, a real live detective who carried a real live gun, was a hero of mythic proportions.

"I'll tell him," she said.

He paused at the door. "Maybe it's okay he's going to be gone a while. Not to alarm, but the word is, there's another serial loose. They don't want to put it out yet, but that Figureido kid who got tom up down at San Gregorio last week matches up with two other incidents in the past couple months, and they've got psycho written all over them. One in Marin, near Sausalito; one down in Los Gatos. All on the night of the full moon, and all pretty young."

"You're a mother hen, Cameron. There's a million kids between Sausalito and Los Gatos."

"Yeah," he said. "A million minus three." He closed the door, leaving her feeling vaguely ashamed, as if she had said, It's okay as long as it's not *my* son.

A few minutes later she locked the office, rode the elevator down, and began her familiar, solitary walk through the emptying streets. What a world–murders and suicides, psychotic killers and brutal police. Everybody too concerned about themselves to worry until it happened to them. And why shouldn't they be? Things were tough enough without walking around under an umbrella of apprehension. You tried to exercise reasonable care and you waded on ahead. What else could you do?

Except call up your guardian angel . . .

The weather was warming, promising full summer. A sign in a tavern window, bright and alluring, offered fellowship and laughter. The sight put an edge on her disappointment at having to turn down Cam's offer of a drink. She felt nothing for him like she did for Jesse, but she did find him attractive, and had more than once toyed with the notion of what he would be like in bed. In any case, an hour or two of entertaining talk over cocktails would have been a pleasant interlude. Normal people did that sort of thing all the time. She wondered if he had intended the offer in a more than friendly way. Did she look that much better? But she doubted it. While she sensed that his private life involved several or even many women, he kept it strictly apart from his professional one. Their flirtation was without substance.

What is it about you, Nikki? she thought dryly. Take a shine to a man, get treated like a sister.

The streetcar, as usual on a Friday evening, was uncrowded. She glanced at the space where she had first seen Valcourt's sign, one week ago. A glowingly healthy young couple lounged on the shore of a mountain lake, smoking cigarettes and smiling into each other's eyes.

It was probably not the same streetcar anyway.

A little before five PM, Jesse Treves heard Grover's ritual yell:

"This chickenshit outfit ever go home?" and slowly, with dull pain, straightened from his crouch. Skilsaw in hand, eyes filled with sweat and sawdust, he paused to survey his surroundings, as he did every afternoon, to try to get some sense of how things might be different at the end of this day than they had been at the beginning. It was a ritual of his own.

The roof upon which he stood was one of a dozen, nearly identical, in the cluster of houses going up. At this stage they were only bare rafters of slick new lumber or sheeted with plywood, soon to be covered with asphalt shingles. More foundations lined the newly paved streets, with stubs of black ABS plumbing pipes sprouting up like obscene, atomic age tubers. Farther yet, toward the green of the East Bay hills, acres had been bulldozed level, and fluorescent orange tape fluttered listlessly from engineer stakes in the faint, hot breeze. For the next weeks and months, as the hills turned brown, he and Grover and Pellegrini would follow those stakes, throwing up the frame skeletons of your basic California starter home: model A, B, C, or D, low down payment, easy terms, half of your salary for the next thirty years, unless you did well, bought up, and unloaded the place on some other poor son of a bitch desperate to have at least a yard for his kids–or you went the other way and the bank foreclosed, and it was back to Roach City. The framers called these tracts "the slums of the future." All Jesse could say was that it beat the hell out of building precious, custom, New Age shit for the ricos in Marin. That place gave him the creeps.

As for his day, he had cut a roof and stacked it with Pellegrini, and then covered most of it with ply. This was not a new experience. He'd framed maybe three hundred roofs over the past fifteen years–or maybe it was closer to five hundred–not to mention the other parts of the house you more or less had to put up in order to get to the top. He liked roof work best, maybe just because of the height. Maybe because that chance of taking a dive, slender though it was, put a tiny edge on a day that otherwise was pretty much like every other. He took a wrap of the heavy extension cord around his saw's bevel gauge, so as not to put strain on the terminals, and lowered it to the deck below. Then he climbed onto the ceiling joists and swung himself down. He hit with a jolt, more fatigued than he had realized. Bright gold-green vinyl-coated nails, jarred loose from the leather pouches on his belt, went ringing across the plywood deck.

He joined Grover and Pellegrini on the ground floor, where they rolled up the cords, separated out their own tools, and loaded them into their trucks. They worked silently and without haste, but methodically, precisely, each man knowing exactly what to do with each object. They were not a young crew, all in their forties–old, very old, for framers–but that had its advantages. There was no hotdogging, no racing, no macho displays that caused mistakes and wasted energy. The work was simply too hard; it required everything. With fair regularity, Grover would subcontract a dozen houses in a tract, and they'd find themselves across the street from a bunch of young guys, starting about the same time. The young guys would be whooping and hollering and ordering each other around and, while not exactly razzing Grover's crew, maybe dropping a few loud remarks about wheelchair ramps and such.

Until the end of the week, when the young guys would be halfway into their second house and still doing pickup on the first one, and Grover's crew would be starting the third, with the first two clean and square and plumb, not a single loose end left behind. That's when the young guys would start dropping by with donuts in the morning and beer at quitting time, trying to figure out just what was going on with these graying, leathery dudes who never seemed to hurry and didn't talk much and went through lumber like thin shit through a tall Swede.

It wasn't enough, not nearly; but it was something.

So–Friday afternoon. Jesse remembered a time when elation had accompanied the thought. Now there was only a certain relief. He squinted through the shimmering haze of dust toward the freeway, trying to gauge how bad the traffic would be over the Bay Bridge. Then he shrugged; he was in no hurry to get anyplace. He took three iced cans of Pabst from the cooler inside his pickup and carried them to his partners. Then he and Pellegrini leaned on the hood of Grover's Ford while Grover sat in the cab, one foot on the ground through the open door, and wrote out paychecks: another ritual.

"So, Jess, you gonna go get you some safe sex this weekend?" Grover said without looking up, mumbling through the Camel between his teeth.

Jesse nodded. "Bought me a full-body condom, Jack."

Pellegrini squinted at him suspiciously. "How you put one of them on?"

"Just like any other rubber, except you start at your feet. Closes at the back of your neck with velcro."

"Yeah? Well, how do you breathe?"

"Special receptacle at the mouthpiece, my man."

Pellegrini grunted, turning away. "Safe sex. Kiss my ass and call me Howdy."

Grover murmured agreement, and Jesse took a long drink of beer, so cold it hurt his teeth. They had worked together almost ten years; he wondered often how much longer it would be before something took one of them out. Pellegrini was powerfully built, with a wolfish profile and ponytail of gleaming black hair. His walnut brown shoulder bore the 1% tattoo of the outlaw biker, and while he no longer rode with a club, from time to time he would still leave his tools in one of the other's trucks and bring his Fat Bob to work. Though he would not admit it, arthritis was beginning to cripple him. Grover was half again as big, a thick, burrheaded Okie who could lift a beam it took any other two men to carry; but his bulk and light skin were giving him increasing trouble in the sun.

Jesse knew that his own problem was in his head, although he was betting on his liver to go first.

They finished the beers, watching the parade of pickups and cars as the job sites emptied, waving to men they knew, then said their laconic good-byes. Jesse climbed into his truck, jeans stiff with sweat, fingers aching from being wrapped around a hammer or saw all day, pitch stuck to his arms and chest, making him hiss when it pulled at hairs. Fifteen minutes later he was on Interstate 80 heading toward San Francisco. Traffic was moving slowly, but it was moving, and he had three cold beers. Wary of the highway patrol, he popped a top and raised the can to his lips.

The rest of the drive took a little over half an hour, not bad, and he was just finishing the last beer when he pulled the truck into the garage on the building's ground floor, right next to Nicole Partrick's yellow Toyota. Upstairs, he locked the door behind him and went straight to the kitchen. He filled a glass with ice, then with Jim Beam, and drank it down. The burning took his breath away and doubled him over. When it let up, he filled the glass again and walked with it down the hall to the shower.

After he came back, he began the game he always played with the bottle, at first returning it to the cabinet after each drink and carrying the glass alone to his chair at the window. Soon, though, the bottle would come with him.

"To Mister Beam," he announced, raising the glass, "the Chevy of bourbons." Blackwall tires and no radio, but it got you where you wanted to go. He sank into the chair.

What you've got to do here, Jess, is break the cycle, he thought. Dry out. Get straight. Put something out there to go after, and go after it.

He shrugged, refilled the glass, and cracked a beer to cut the whiskey. There was just one little problem with getting straight, and that was that this was the part of the day he lived for: the hour or two when he felt pretty good, when he'd showered and shaved and changed into clean clothes and the juice kicked in and made him smart and funny—pretty much on top of this life he'd somehow ended up in. For a while, things would be line. He never bored himself when he was like this.

Then at some point, he'd lift his head and realize night had fallen and he'd nodded off, and maybe the glass had dropped out of his hand. He'd stand, clenching his teeth against the ache in his back, and get a clean glass and fresh ice and pour one more, trying to hang on to that faded good feel. But there was no way to get it back except to go through the motions of the next twenty-four hours. It had occurred to him that that was really why he bothered going to work at all.

So he'd limp into the kitchen and fry up a hamburger, not really hungry but knowing he had to eat, or maybe walk the two blocks down to Irving Street and buy a piroshki, chewing it slowly with one last beer. And then finally he'd give in and lie down, hands clasped behind his head, savoring his own weariness before yielding to his body's greedy craving for sleep.

Put something out there, he thought again, and go after it. Doesn't matter what. Climb a mountain, take a trip to Botswana, start building model cars. Read the Durants' *History of Civilization*. Something to break the cycle. In the closet, the beautiful Martin D-28 that he'd bought when he came back from Nam was buried under a pile of winter clothes and seldom-used tools. The last time he'd touched the guitar, maybe five years ago, he was so appalled at the ineptness of his fingers that his eyes went damp. There was a time when he'd gotten around that fingerboard pretty good, done all kinds of fancy picking–Mississippi John Hurt, Doc Watson, even a little free-form stuff of his own.

So he quit whiskey for a couple of months then, limiting himself to a few slow beers after work, buying books and reading them, taking walks, thinking about all the things he could and doubtless should make of himself. He toned up his guitar playing, and as the old songs started to come back, he took pleasure in their rediscovery.

At first.

Until he realized that none of it had any whack anymore. That he was bored out of his fucking skull. That no matter how he looked at it, he was in a cage, and whether it had gold bars or iron ones, it was a cage all the same. He forced it a while longer, trying to tell himself it was a phase. Finally, in desperation, he bought a TV and stayed glued to the screen each evening until it was time to sleep.

And then one Friday night, after starting one of his solitary walks, he stepped into a liquor store and bought a fifth of Bushmill's and took it home and drank it. For the first time in sixty long days, he escaped for a few hours the agonizing weight, the intolerable loneliness–the *apartness*–of a life that made no sense. There was a verse that had stuck with him from his college days: "a tale told by an idiot, full of sound and fury, signifying nothing." The biography of Jesse Treves.

Sound and fury. He'd been there just under a year; it was near the end of his tour. They were on a routine mission, bringing a Huey into a landing zone that was supposed to be secure, and he jumped out of the chopper and was moving on out when there was this amazing flash of light, together with an explosion that seemed more inside his head than out. He woke up in a hospital bed with the right side of his face essentially dissolved, and found out that it was two days later and he was on Guam.

After that he spent a fair amount of time in VA hospitals. The docs did a pretty good reconstruction job, wiring all the bones back together, setting his eyeball on a piece of plastic, and getting it more or less at the same height as the other one; they even tried to hide most of the scars in folds of skin. It worked pretty well except in certain kinds of light when he was really shitfaced. Then he looked like the Frankenstein monster.

But in Nam, that was good luck. Bad luck was what had happened to many of the other men in his company–blinded, missing limbs or balls, or just plain fucking dead. Those eleven months had changed his way of looking at the world more radically than he ever could have dreamed. He had gone into the whole thing believing people could settle disputes reasonably, and came out of it understanding that the concept of "reasonable" was ultimately a thin fiction. He simply had never imagined that people could behave that way toward one

119

another–had never imagined that he could learn to behave that way himself.

After he'd gotten home and healed up, he spent some years trying to do right: went back to college, joined vets against the war, did a lot of backpacking and fishing, and eventually started taking his studies seriously. He got married and fathered two girls and spent five years teaching high school history and coaching baseball.

When he thought about all of that now, it was like it had happened to somebody else. At some point in there, things had just started to fade. First he didn't understand what was going on. When he began to, he tried to fight it. But the trouble was, there was nothing to fight. It was just something inside him that seemed to be disappearing: a growing collection of absences.

But Vietnam had taught him that ugly things did not require reasons, and he was pretty sure by now that what had happened to him–the bottom falling out–would have happened anyway: that it was something he had unknowingly carried inside himself all his life, like the spores of a rare disease that only reached a critical stage when time and circumstances were right. The worst part was that nobody who did not have the disease could understand it. Most people were uncomfortable, even fearful, when they sensed it, as if it were a sort of mental AIDS that might rock them from complacency.

He lost interest in teaching, and while he tried to push it for a while, it wasn't fair to his students. So he quit and went to work for a contractor friend, which pissed his wife off mightily; and while the construction work and its comparative freedom agreed with him, that was the beginning of the end of the marriage. His girls were nearly grown now, one in college, one about to start. He still sent them a check every month and managed to see them a couple of times a year, and they seemed to like him in spite of his ex-wife's heavy propaganda campaign that he was a shitbum and a drunk–which, he had to admit, was at least partly true. All in all, he could not say he had done terrifically well; but, too, there were lots of ways he could have done worse.

On his next trip to the kitchen, the bottle stayed in his hand. Fuck it, this was Friday. He stood in the bay of his window, watching the N-Judah streetcar pause at the comer. Three or four people got off and hurried in different directions–Asians, mainly, there were a lot of them in the Sunset. But one woman was walking up the street toward the apartment, and in a moment he recognized Nicole. She looked good–in fact, she looked great, wearing a brightly colored peasant skirt and high boots, her thick, dark hair bouncing down her back. Her stride was brisk and confident, and it caught his attention. Usually she seemed preoccupied, weighed down by work and responsibility. He felt happy for her.

When she was almost directly below, she glanced up. He smiled and raised his glass. Nicole put her hands on her hips, shaking her head in a parody of exasperation, then disappeared into the building.

Jesse shrugged. He knew she disapproved of his juicing; she had made it clear enough times that he was wasting his life, that he had too much to offer to throw it away, that there were so many better ways he could spend that energy. Between the lines, the message came across loud and clear. He'd been nice to the kid; maybe that was where she'd gotten the wrong idea. But hell, he liked kids, missed his girls, even missed coaching. Tom Junior was a good boy, the way he'd have wanted a son of his own to turn out.

The problem wasn't Nicole herself. She was a genuinely good-hearted woman, smart, pretty, and capable of pulling her own weight. No, it came right back down to the same thing: he knew, finally, once and for all, that he was on his own. That was the culmination of the inner war of attrition he'd been fighting for fifteen years. He supposed he could have tried to tell her, as he'd tried to tell others once he'd come to understand it himself: that he could already see the end, that he knew what she wanted and he knew what he needed and the two things were universes apart. Nothing could ever bring them together.

But it was impossible to say without sounding either noble or like a country and western song, and so, as with more and more aspects of his life, he'd learned to just leave it alone. It would take care of itself. When she got on his case nowadays, he just smiled, nodded, and said, "No doubt," knowing that sooner or later the interest would burn out, she'd find somebody else to get concerned about, and one more wrinkle would be smoothed out of his existence. Sure, it would be nice to have a warm body to curl up next to, the company and comfort of another presence. He liked all of that as much as anybody, missed it more than he let on even to himself.

But it simply couldn't be done without all the rest of the baggage, and one thing he was sure of by now was that you did not fuck your neighbor unless you were prepared for unending drama. When the need became overwhelming, he'd hang out in the bars until he ran into a tumble for a night or maybe several. But he wouldn't let it go past a certain point, so that he could walk with a reasonably clear conscience. Or at least a minimum of hassle. And between the juice and age, it was a need that was becoming less and less frequent.

If the price was that his life had a big hole in it, and if it was a hole he tried to fill with whiskey, at least he was toe-to-toe with it, looking at it in his own red eyes in the mirror every morning, cursing it methodically while he laced up his boots, laughing at it when he leaned over the edge of a roof thirty feet in the air and dared the rafter-tail he stood on to break. It wasn't much, but it was something: clean and dear, just him and it. Whatever the fuck it was. The work kept him in good shape—a remnant of perverse physical vanity—and maintained a precarious balance with the drinking, a dynamic equilibrium of alcohol intake and perspiration output. If the wire in his face did not rust out, the way it sometimes felt like it was doing in wet weather, he might be good for another fifteen or twenty years.

But probably not. It came down to that business of not being able to bullshit himself, that AIDS of the mind that undercut everything else. The vise was tightening. He'd run out of things to laugh about and things to say, stopped seeing old friends one by one and stopped trying to make new ones, stopped caring what went on in the world around him. He knew that the juice was his enemy—but it was also the only thing that kept him going.

The problem, finally, was not that he was incapable of going out and getting things he wanted—it was that he did not want anything. He had no fantasies left.

In short, he was dying, and there was not a thing in the world anybody could do about it—least of all, especially, himself.

Then why not help it out, Jess? he thought. The Golden Gate's an easy walk. Pretend you're in a chopper, coming in on one last assault. Suck up your balls, clamp your teeth together, and jump. Hit that water, cold and black and wet, and it's good night, sweet prince. Or pull that .38 Airweight out from under the pillow, take a drive to the woods—someplace pretty . . . Mendocino, say—and bite the barrel.

So why not?

Like the sickness itself, the reason hid from him, refusing to come dearly into the light; or maybe he just did not care to look hard enough. But it had something to do with quitting. He had quit too many things already: quit college and gotten drafted, quit his teaching career and his marriage and his kids. It didn't matter how good his reasons for all of those things were, he'd still quit. This one he was going to stick out with his eyes open until his last breath, and if that hidden enemy finally showed itself, he was going to use that breath to rage in its face.

The phone rang, startling him. He listened to it, twice, three times, certain it was Nicole inviting him to dinner. His mouth twisted in wry indecision. He could hardly not answer, since she knew he was home; but an evening of trying to be cheerful was more than he could face. It pained him to hurt her feelings, but he had no ready excuse. Plead fatigue? Simply say no? Unhappily, he picked it up.

"Meester Treefs?" It was a female voice with a heavy Hispanic accent. The line crackled with long-distance static.

Cautiously, Jesse said, "Yes?" He did not owe any money that he could remember.

"My nem is"–the combination of the static and mumbling blotted it out–"and we like to ask you some questions for the 'Mercan Sociation of Funeral Directors who are located in Chicago, Illinoise. Hokay?"

Jesse stared through the window, down over the twilit city. Friday fucking night, he thought. There is a god after all. It's just that he's nobody I want to know.

". . . prefer to be berred in a coffin or cremated?"

"It don't make a good goddamn to me, lady," he said, "just as long as I'm dead before it happens." Quietly, he put down the receiver and went to the kitchen for more ice.

The sheer amount of food on the table was already unbelievable, and Yvonne was going back to the kitchen for more. *Rich* food: a green pasta salad with Parmesan cheese, spinach soufflés, baked potatoes drenched in sour cream, fat-marbled New York steaks, and about a gallon of béarnaise sauce staying warm in a crock pot. Spencer knew it had been like this for quite a while, but he had not been eating at home much lately and it got to him every time he did. Yvonne came back into the dining room carrying a bushel-sized basket of golden popovers dripping with butter. She had taken to wearing enormous, caftanlike dresses.

"You be sure and save room for dessert, now," she said, beaming at him like a mother. "It's chocolate cream pie." Apparently satisfied that starvation could be held at bay for the next minutes, she sat with a surprising grace, the almost mincing delicacy of a much smaller person, and watched Spencer with affection and anxiety, waiting for his approval. Her checks were literally like apples; her hairdo, cut fashionably close around her neck and ears and culminating in a vaguely orange-colored shock on top, brought back his boyhood perusals of National Geographic.

"This is great, honey," he mumbled. "Terrific." He nibbled at the soufflé while Yvonne ladled béarnaise onto her steak, then excused himself to go to the bathroom.

He laid two quick lines on the imitation marble vanity, and afterward rinsed his nostrils and mustache. The thought of returning to all that food made him a little sick. He stopped in the living room and stared out over the Marina. Couples walking dogs, Frisbee players, and joggers crowded the large green expanses of lawn that stretched to the harbor. A fleet of yachts rocked gently at their moorings with the ocean's swell, while dozens more drifted in from their afternoon on the bay. Everybody looked clean, healthy, dressed in the latest recreational apparel. Even Alcatraz looked more like a park than a prison. The condo was in one of the city's prime locations; with two bedrooms and a choice view, it had gone for a cool three hundred and twenty thou. And like nearly everything else in Spencer's life, it had been paid for by

126

his father-in-law, Langdon Winslowe–the name said it all–and was owned by Yvonne.

The distance to San Jose, where Spencer had grown up, was not much over forty miles; but what an immense forty miles.

A working-class kid who was unexceptional at everything, Spencer had barely finished high school and had ended up working as a bartender at a middle-class cocktail lounge. He hated the job and its lifelong certainty of wage slavery–but he happened to be good-looking and knew how to turn on the charm. One afternoon a party of horsey rich folks from Saratoga happened in, on their way home from a nearby wedding. He read the situation instantly, seeing his chance in Yvonne's ringless finger and wistful eyes; and his street-smart instincts assured him that it was the only chance he was ever going to get. By the end of half an hour, he and she were flirting;

Her father had seen through Spencer clearly, and had taken pains to let him know it. But at that time, Yvonne was twenty-seven–two years older than he was–with nobody on the horizon, and time not being kind to her. Except for wealth, she was as unexceptional as he. Langdon Winslowe saw his chance, too, and the two men entered an unspoken, if one-sided, alliance.

Even Spencer had been surprised at how quickly he had taken to easy living and expensive tastes.

Since he had no education or business skills to speak of, Langdon Winslowe had decided, with thinly veiled contempt, that the simplest thing to do was buy them a bar of their own. Although Spencer hated the business more than ever, it beat the hell out of the way his life had been before. For five years, he kept his act very clean.

Then he met Tina, and the whole thing started to come apart.

Yvonne was halfway through her loaded plate when he returned. She ate with the manners of money–small, delicate bites, unhurried chewing, expert manipulation of knife and fork–but with the nonstop efficiency of a high-powered machine. He swallowed and sat down, dutifully cutting into his steak.

"*Gone with the Wind* is on HBO tonight," she announced invitingly.

Food and TV, he thought. Guilt flared suddenly. How much was he responsible for what she had become? In her heart of hearts, she had to know–not about Tina, but that he had married her for her father's money. He had not made love to her in weeks–could hardly bear to touch her–and even through the buzzing of the coke in his brain, through irrational anger at her that smoldered just below the guilt, he understood that the situation was terrible in its unfairness. Yvonne was, fundamentally, a good person. It was not her fault that she was obese. She deserved better treatment. She was generous and warm, and, goddamn it, she loved him.

He stared down at his plate, fork clenched in his motionless fingers, while emotions spun furiously in him. He would go straight, kick the cocaine, break off with Tina: become a hardworking, loyal husband. In the warmth of his new affection, Yvonne would diet, shrink miraculously, and maybe have one of those lipoid surgeries, until she looked as svelte as the dancers at the

Tropicana. He would confess about Tina and the money he had squandered, and they would weep together but it would strengthen the bond of their love. She would forgive him, and the rest of their lives would be a hand-in-hand march into bliss.

"I better get down to the bar," he said. And then, lamely, at her look of disappointment, "Friday night, hon. You know."

She lowered her gaze, and they ate in silence for a minute or two. Then she said:

"Spence, all the time you spend down there. What do you do?"

When his eyes met hers again, he saw something of her father in her: smart, hard, and, above all, aware exactly of the power of money, knowing just how much it would buy and having no compunctions whatever about spending it–or withdrawing it–in order to ensure that her life went on as a pleasant dream. Spencer's anger surged, but with it came instinctive, feral caution. He laughed, charm coming to his rescue; but the sound fell shrilly on his own ears.

"I run a business–what do you think? I keep the books, I order the food and liquor, I tend the bar–"

"I thought you paid people to do all that."

"Yvonne," he said with false weariness, "you've never had to work. You don't know anything about it. Yeah, I hire people to do some of that. But half the time they don't do it right, and somebody's always calling in sick, so when I'm not doing my own work I'm babysitting and putting out fires."

"Maybe I should start coming down to help."

Carefully, he speared a bite of steak and lifted it to his mouth. It tasted like soybean curd.

"Honey," he said, "I don't want to sound mean, but you don't know how to do anything."

"I could learn. You could teach me to tend bar."

The image of Yvonne behind the bar of the Jasper Tubbs made the bite of steak pause uncertainly on its journey to his stomach.

"We could be together more then," she said. "I've hardly seen you the last few months, Spence. I feel like a widow."

Perhaps four minutes had passed since his trip to the john. There was no reasonable excuse for leaving the table. Cool, Spence, he told himself. You are very cool.

"Yvonne," he said, "I have been working my tail off trying to get this business off the ground so that we can be secure from here on out. Okay? That's the way it is with any business—you bust your ass for the first few years, and then you get to start taking things a little easier. We are just now getting to that point. But I'm going to have to keep on putting in these kinds of hours for a while longer. And then, I promise you, I'll be laying around the house so much you'll want to kick me out the door."

She smiled, then giggled, and he smiled back warmly, amazed at his own ability to hide the insane whirl behind his eyes.

"I can't wait," she said, and he saw with relief that her gaze roved to the béarnaise and lingered there. "If you need more help, though, I'll tell Daddy. He'll arrange it so you can hire people."

130

"Yvonne," he said, with what he hoped sounded like patience, "I don't want to go running to your father for every little thing. I'm a grown man. I can handle this myself. It's very important to me to prove that to your father."

She made a noncommittal sound, her attention back on her plate. Spencer realized that he had been walking into a danger zone: something that genuinely bothered him had started to come out.

"I do it for you, Yvonne," he said. "You know that, don't you?"

She looked up, ladle poised in her plump hand, and smiled with such a softness, such an eagerness to believe, that she looked almost pretty.

Hating himself, he glanced at his watch and said, "Jesus, it's after six. I've got to run." He rose quickly, patting his mouth with his napkin, and hurried around the table to kiss her cheek. "Why don't you record *Gone with the Wind,* and we'll watch it maybe Sunday, huh?"

In the garage, he started the Porsche with a roar, and while it warmed up got a couple of good shots from the vial up his nose. Things began to clear out. He had done fine. He had allayed her suspicions, bought more time. The crisis was over.

For now.

The Jasper Tubbs was on a relatively quiet stretch of Washington Street, which was part of the problem: too far from the nightlife centers of Ghirardelli, the Wharf, North Beach, and Clement Street. Spencer pulled into the alley behind it, ignoring the No Parking signs—he had an ongoing arrangement with the ticket cops that cost him a hundred bucks a month–and automatically took out his vial and spoon. The plane of contentment that had carried him from the house had crumbled on the drive down from the Marina. He had not set foot in his own bar, had not even called to check in, since meeting with that weirdo, Valcourt, last Sunday.

The memory disturbed him further. Somehow, talking to the man made him excruciatingly aware of just how deep a layer of shit he was in, even though he'd said nothing about it. And while Valcourt had laid down a pretty smooth rap about mind power and all that, and had given him a little charm to say three times a night–and Spencer, feeling like a jerk, had done so–it was coming home to him harder and harder that he'd been acting like a kid, reaching desperately for some sort of magical hype to get him out of a tight situation. The man had style, he had to admit, and obviously he had money, which had impressed Spencer enough to try the charm. Who knew? People swore they'd gotten rich by chanting and all kinds of other shit.

But nothing had happened to Spencer Epps except that he'd felt like an asshole, standing naked in a dark room whispering nonsense syllables. That, he decided, was that for Valcourt.

He packed the spoon as full as it would hold, inhaled sharply, then did the same with the other nostril. Better. One more good pop and he'd be able to walk in the door with authority and stare down his main man, Lou Stern, if Lou complained about his not being around. Fuck Lou. It wasn't him that owned the place. Okay, he thought as the coke hit. Everything was okay. Yvonne was under control. The only problem was the twenty thousand.

And the fact that it was pretty much gone. And that he needed more and had no idea of how to get it.

He slumped in the seat, his calm evaporating. Twenty thousand bucks. It seemed like a guy ought to get a break once in a while. It seemed like it was not his fault if the restaurant never quite sold the thirty dinners a night it needed to make the nut, if the bar intake was always stretching over to cover the kitchen, if the business from both had been mediocre to begin with and was fading measurably.

Lou was forever bitching at him, "Look, Spence, if you're not making money, you're losing it. There's no such thing as standing still. We're not making it. We've got to tighten the operation or we're up shit creek." What he meant by tightening the operation was that Spencer paid himself a salary of fifty grand a year, nearly as much as the rest of the payroll combined.

Fuck you, Lou, Spencer thought viciously, unscrewing the cap of the vial. Fifty grand was chickenshit.

But he could hear Lou's answer: Yeah, it's chickenshit if you're in here eighty hours a week busting your tail to make sure this is the hottest spot in town, seeing to it that your help's smiling and kissing ass, supervising the menu, advertising, walking through the tables calling the clients by their first names and clapping them on the back and winding that famous Spencer Epps charm to them—

In short, all the things Spencer let Yvonne assume he was doing. But he had never done much of it to begin with, and now he did almost none, and Lou was putting in those eighty hours a week trying to do it all and also manage the joint, for twenty-two five. It was an exchange that hadn't yet been voiced aloud, but each could see it in the other's eyes, and Spencer knew it would not be long. He knew, too, though he hated to admit it, that if Lou left, the cake would pretty much crumble.

Lou did not yet know about the twenty thousand dollar loan.

Spencer swore under his breath and considered just driving away, as he'd already done twice that week. He'd gone straight to Tina's both times, once making her call in sick to stay in bed with him—something the management of the Club Tropicana took an extremely dim view of. She'd done it—been glad to—but while she hadn't come out and said it, the implication was plain: if she lost her job, she was his to take care of.

She was working tonight. Spencer's mind raced with the power of the drug: Fuck them all, go for broke, he wasn't going to let their chickenshit concerns push him around. He'd pick her up, take her to Tiburon, they'd scream across the Golden Gate in the Porsche, a great-looking guy and girl in a great-looking car, laughing and high, the envy of everybody on the road. So she got the boot at the Trop. It was a scumbag joint, owned by greaseballs and run by ex-con pimps. He wanted her out of there anyway. He'd take care of her. What was another two or three grand a month? He started the car furiously, shoved in the clutch—

Then stopped, switched off the ignition, and forced himself to lean back in the seat. It was time to get a grip on this thing. Maybe he'd bought a little time tonight, but Yvonne was fat, not stupid. The handwriting was on the wall. Lou had covered for him so far, under strict instructions to never call him at home and to field any calls Yvonne might make to the bar, but there was no telling how close his patience was to the edge. What if he blew up, called Yvonne and blurted out the truth, and walked? Or what if she decided she wanted a look at the remodeling that had supposedly been done? Or if her father asked to examine the books, as he had done once already, on the pretext of making sure Spencer wasn't being cheated by his employees? There were a thousand little glitches, the probabilities increasing by the day.

Any one of which would leave Spencer Epps in the extremely untenable position of his wife being alerted to the fact that he had been spending a large portion of his life with people and in places unknown; that he had been lying barefacedly to her about it; that the Jasper Tubbs had not, in fact, been prospering under his steady businesslike hand, but was sinking farther under water every day–

And inevitably, that the twenty thousand dollars he had appropriated from the bank, on her signature, for equipment and improvements, had disappeared into glossy living and a stripper with surgically rebuilt tits.

It was not that he would go to jail. Yvonne's father was a big operator, a man far more concerned about his reputation than about a few thousand dollars. But it would mean that Spencer would have to walk the chalk from then on–either stay under Yvonne's unrelenting suspicion or, if he split, go back to some dumbfuck job and wage slavery, living like a rat while he struggled to pay off the debt that old man Winslowe, out of sheer vindictiveness, would certainly hold him to. It would mean the end of the highrolling, the end of the coke–and, he knew, the end of Tina. He groped for the window switch, fighting the feeling that the car was caving in around him, and thrust his head out to inhale the heavy city air. The shit was endless. What did a guy have to do to get a *break?*

He took one more double hit. When he stepped out of the Porsche, he was ready to stride in the door of the Jasper Tubbs, kick Lou Stern in the ass, and read everybody else the riot act so they'd do their jobs and leave him the fuck alone. Was that so much to ask? Then, soon enough, he'd be rocking and rolling in Tina's arms. He inhaled, pushed open the door, and stepped into the kitchen.

At first he could not quite believe what he saw. The usual scene was Rennie, the cook, whose real name was Harold, listlessly tending the nearly empty stove, while the two Chinese dishwashers sat on the stainless steel counters talking quietly, not bothering to even make a pretense of staying busy.

Tonight Rennie was zooming around like a butterfly in heat, his face pale with shock, and the dishwashers were grimly slinging plates, bowls, glasses, and grails full of silver into the smoking machine. Both waitresses hovered anxiously in the saloon doors to the restaurant, order books clutched in their hands. From behind them came a din of laughter, conversation, and clinking glasses that sounded like a Shriners convention.

Rennie spotted Spencer, drew himself up theatrically, and swept forward, waving his hands wildly at the food-laden counters. Order tags hung in festoons above the stove.

"If you don't get me some help *immediately,* I'm quitting at the end of this shift," he wailed. "I've had to send out *twice* for more pasta!"

Stunned, Spencer pushed past the waitresses and stared at the scene before him. The tables were packed shoulder to shoulder, a sea of flashing teeth and darting forks. Half a dozen couples stood patiently inside the door, waiting to be seated. There was not an empty space at the bar, and hands were thrusting money at Michael, the bartender, and at Lou, who was washing glasses as fast as he could. He glanced up, his gaze catching Spencer's, his forehead gleaming with sweat. He looked like a wounded fish.

"Where the fuck have you been?" he screamed. "It's been like this all week!"

"Spencer, we're almost out of tablecloths. What do you want us to do?" It was Janine, one of the waitresses, shouting to be heard over the noise.

"I'll order some," he said, dazed, and hurried to his office behind the bar.

With numb fingers, he took a bottle of Chivas and a glass from a cupboard and poured a drink. Then he sat at his desk, staring at an untouched pile of bills and memos.

Never–not *ever*–had he seen more than a dozen people in the place at one time.

It was a fluke. Some kind of holiday he'd forgotten about, or a convention at a nearby hotel that had whimsically decided to descend.

It's been like this all week!

He drank the liquor without tasting it, listening to a voice in his mind calculate that the gross tonight would far exceed the take of an average week. At a guess, he'd call it four grand.

Suppose—just suppose—it *wasn't* a fluke. That they were looking at well over a million per year, in a place that had been doing a fraction of that.

And suppose it had something to do, after all, with that little song and dance Valcourt had taught him?

Raises all around, for openers, to keep the ship sailing smoothly, to keep lips tight about the fact that he was never around. There'd be plenty left over for him and Tina to play to their hearts' content, while he quietly repaid the twenty grand.

But why think small? another voice in his mind was whispering. Why not think like a strong man would? It would take people quite a while to catch on—people like Yvonne's father, or the IRS.

Especially if somebody managed to keep the books showing pretty much the same profit as they had all along—in the meantime, quietly salting away the extra income, until the day came when he and Tina were set for the rest of their lives. A warm, friendly climate, say, where they did not extradite rich white men who had plenty of money to spend. The end to old man Winslowe and the shit Spencer had been putting up with since his marriage.

He would have to be smart, smarter than he had ever dreamed of being. But this–this was worth being smart about.

Was that really what was doing it? Valcourt's charm?

He picked up the phone book, flipping to restaurant supplies to see if anyone could provide him with several dozen tablecloths on a Friday night.

Though the room was warm, he suddenly shivered, with the eerie feeling that something that had been looking over his shoulder had just left.

SIX

The used-book section of City Lights was Robbie Kinsella's favorite place in the world: floor-to-ceiling stacks of every conceivable kind of paperback, whole rooms full of them. The selection changed from week to week, and every Saturday afternoon he was there to pick through it, thoroughly, methodically, a shelf at a time, lifting out anything halfway interesting that pertained to the occult. Except maybe for New York or Paris, he doubted there was anyplace in the world where people were into more weird stuff than San Francisco, and the used-book market reflected that. Just last month he had picked up a copy of Aleister Crowley's autobiography for a dollar and a half. That man had been into some very heavy stuff: casting spells, raising demons, the works.

Of course, most of what you found in print was just trash, the sort of learn-to-be-a-witch-in-your-spare-time bullshit that had ridden the crest of the late sixties. But once in a while he ran across a real find, like the Crowley book or the works of Montague Summers. That was like discovering a buried treasure. He would take the book home, set it on his desk, and just walk around it for a while. Then, slowly, savoring every word, he would begin to absorb its contents. Crazy by anybody's standards, he supposed, but he'd long since stopped caring. The occult was the only subject that really interested him. That was all there was to it.

He'd gone to junior college for a couple of years and taken some business courses, with the vague notion of becoming an accountant, and done well enough when he tried. Lack of ability was not the problem. It was just that he could not sustain any interest in his course work or the professional opportunities it offered—or, for that matter, in most facets of modem life in general. He told himself it was because he was pure Irish, a picture-perfect Celt—gaunt features, curly reddish-brown hair, and drooping mustache, one of the faces you saw on two-thousand-year-old coins—and his racial imagination ran in a completely different direction than anything so prosaic as success in business. So he'd dropped out and gotten a job swamping out a North Beach bar. He made enough money to pay for his tiny apartment and drink Guinness and occasionally take a girl out and get laid. Along with his books, that pretty much sufficed.

He was not nearly fool enough to believe in ninety percent of the stuff he encountered—the home witchcraft recipes and shirttail Satanists and tabloid poltergeists. But he knew—*knew*—there was something to the whole thing. He was just a kid during the heydays of the sixties, but he'd tried some psychedelics—blotter acid, mush-rooms. Whether his Irish genes and vivid imagination had anything to do with it, he couldn't say, but he had

141

come away from those experiences certain that there was a whole lot going on around people that they weren't generally aware of—call it other dimensions, astral planes, whatever you wanted.

The problem was that while reading about it was all well and good, it only went so far. He'd long since come to the point where he wanted to *do* something—not necessarily raise any demons or levitate tables, but just get some sense of touching those other planes of being. He had researched and canvassed, even cautiously contacted a couple of organizations that professed to know about such things; but everything he'd succeeded in unearthing had quack written all over it. They wanted your money, or they wanted to get naked and roll around with you, or they just wanted you to stand still and listen to whatever preposterous line of shit they'd cooked up.

Still, he wanted very much to believe that hidden away somewhere in the world there were genuine adepts quietly practicing their art, whether it was black, white, or gray. So far, he had not a shred of evidence. It seemed clear that in the Middle Ages, quite a few people had spent a good deal of time and energy—often at the cost of their lives—trying to touch that other world. But whether any had ever succeeded, or any were still trying, he had no idea. He reminded himself that there remained an excellent chance he was simply crazy. He shrugged. It wasn't his fault he was a mick.

He straightened from his crouched examination of a bottom shelf and bumped into someone he'd noticed a couple of times in the past ten minutes, a man who also seemed to be studying the occult books. He was easy to spot; even in North Beach, you didn't .see many guys with eyepatches and gloves. He smiled and waved his hand nonchalantly when Robbie excused himself, and Robbie got a better look at his face. Maybe it was the single eye, but he gave off an impressive sense of confidence.

They stood a few feet apart for a minute or two, then Robbie spotted a copy of *Isis Unveiled*. He'd read it, and as far as he was concerned it fell pretty much into the bullshit category, but he pulled it off the shelf and leafed through it, noting that it had once been the property of Staci, who dotted her *i* with a circle, had begun making comments in the margins in purple ink, and did not appear to have gotten much past page ten. He didn't blame her.

"Have you read it?" the man with the eyepatch suddenly asked. The voice was deep and cultured, with a trace of accent.

"This?" Robbie said, surprised. He held the book up critically. "Once, a long time ago. I didn't get much out of it."

"Nor I. I found her intention admirable, but so much of the contents are—how do you say?—hard to swallow."

He half-turned away, his attention back on the shelves. Robbie hesitated. Bookstore conversations, except with attractive women, were dangerous. You ran a high risk of being trapped by some boring asshole or even outright madman who would follow you around, spouting off every piece of lunacy that ran through his mind until you fled, and thereafter would lie in wait for you every time you walked in the door.

143

But this guy was different--intriguing. He seemed both intelligent and interested in the occult, not a combination you encountered often. He was a foreigner, probably European, dressed expensively and conservatively in slacks and jacket, with a two thousand dollar Rolex on his wrist. Eccentric, maybe, but not a creep—and Robbie was ninety-nine percent sure he wasn't gay. In fact, there did not seem to be any kind of hustle about him. Maybe, just maybe, he knew something interesting.

Wary, ready to shut the whole thing down in an instant, Robbie phrased a question.

"Are you familiar with, uh, this sort of literature?"

The man seemed not at all surprised. "In general, quite. Although I must say that I much prefer the works of the ancients to those of more modern authors. In the past, there was real knowledge. Over the last few centuries, it has become mainly speculation, mingled with a goodly portion of absurdity. Still, I review the available literature when I have occasion, hoping to be pleasantly surprised."

"Ancients," Robbie said. "You mean, all the way back to Paracelsus—like that?"

The man turned, studying him with what seemed a mixture of amusement and interest.

"I would call Doctor Theophrastus Bombastus a relative newcomer, and his offerings in the field of magic rather pitiable, although he did add to our understanding of the physical sciences. But no, I was thinking chiefly of his lesser-known predecessors. Are you familiar with the *Book of the Toad,* the *Book of Miriam,* the *Turba Philosophorum?* The *Book of the Thirty Words?*"

Robbie shook his head, astonished and sheepish. "I looked through a copy of the *Lesser Clavicle* once."

"A fraud," the man declared curtly. "Some of Solomon's wisdom did survive, but not in that piece of trumpery. The case is similar with the so-called grimoires–like the one falsely attributed to Honorius the Pope, and the distressingly misnamed *Grimoire Verum*. Products of latter-day charlatans, seeking to validate their claims to knowledge which they possessed only shreds of."

"But those other books you mentioned–you think they're for real?"

The man's brows rose judiciously, and the single eye seemed to lose focus and gaze past Robbie.

"They are useful to a greater or lesser extent," he finally conceded. "They might aid in reaching a certain point, after which one must proceed on one's own. And it is essential to be extremely skillful in one's dealings with them."

Pulse quickening, Robbie warned himself, Look for the catch. This was too much to be true.

"Where'd you run across those books? If you don't mind my asking."

"Some are in the great libraries, mainly of Europe, although not available to the general public. One must have a certain . . . influence to be allowed to examine them at leisure. Others are in private collections. I, myself, own copies of several." He paused. "Of course, one must read them in the original form, since even the order of letters in a word can be of such great significance that the very idea of translation is preposterous. This, in turn, requires as a mere beginning a thorough acquaintance with Latin, Greek, and Hebrew. Do you know those tongues?"

Robbie hung his head.

"A pity," the man murmured. He turned away apologetically.

Great, Robbie thought. Fucking terrific. You spend ten years hungering for the chance of a lifetime, and when it comes, you find out you should have been going to night school to learn languages.

"I, uh, don't exactly know how to say this," he mumbled, rubbing his cheek, "but I'm, like, really interested in all that stuff. I mean, I'm not a scholar or anything, but . . . is there any way . . . I mean, would you, like, be willing to tell me a little about it?"

The gaze of the single eye focused intently on him, measuring, gauging, as if his mind were being read. It was not an altogether comfortable feeling.

"Very well," the man said at last. "If you wish to visit me at my home, we will talk further. I perceive that you work nights. Shall we say tomorrow, then, at four in the afternoon?" As he spoke, he took out an expensive fountain pen and leather note case, and quickly scratched out a name and address.

"I promise nothing," he warned with an upraised finger. Abruptly, almost as if he regretted what he had done, he wheeled and walked to the bookshop door.

Almost in a trance, Robbie stared at the note. *I perceive that you work nights.* Had he really said that? The name and address were written in a firm, neat hand on expensive linen paper: Guy-Luc Valcourt, 2713 Green Mountain Road, Woodside.

Robbie turned back to the bookshelves, but his appetite for browsing—for second-hand experience—was gone.

He stepped onto the sidewalk, blinking in the bright sunlight—it was like coming out of a movie theater in the daytime. Now it was his turn to wonder what he had done. Woodside was nearly an hour's drive. What if the guy was a creep, or worse, a phony? What if the address itself was a sham?

Well, what the hell, it wasn't as if he had anything better to do. It would cost him half a tank of gas. If he got down there and it went weird or didn't happen at all, he would turn around and come back—it was that simple. But he had to admit, if the guy really knew what he was talking about and wanted his cock sucked to tell it, that would almost be worth it.

Robbie glanced around the crowded street. As the man had guessed—or known?—his workday would start when the bar closed, in several hours. It was getting toward time for a meal and a nap. He started walking, deciding he'd stop by Speck's for a beer, on the chance he'd encounter a lady who could be persuaded to come back to his hovel for an afternoon of Irish delight.

From the bookshop in North Beach, the man who called himself Guy-Luc Valcourt took a taxi across the city to Golden Gate Park. Here he commenced a stroll which, while outwardly leisurely and amiable, had an object—like everything else he did.

147

The day was lovely, golden and warm, and he inhaled the fragrance of the many plants and trees foreign to him. He found the concept of a park agreeable, if somewhat odd; it reminded him a little of the pleasure gardens of certain Eastern potentates he had visited during his years in Asia, centuries before. Of course, there were significant differences. A commoner found wandering the grounds of one of those gardens, for instance, would have been dismembered with the speed of thought.

All was proceeding with excellent dispatch. Spencer Epps had called that morning, almost frothing in his eagerness to pursue his "studies." His addiction helped, and was to be cultivated; it was a powerful tool in manipulation, and the more that could be done by natural means, the less energy of more potent varieties would be required. Nicole Partrick had not yet come to his fold, but his servants assured him that while she was trying to affect restraint, she was in fact most impressed by the bauble he had thrown her. Women were wonderful, he thought, smiling warmly at a passerby. In the effort to make themselves more attractive, they would quite literally sell their own souls.

The Irish lad he had chanced upon this afternoon, who bore the name of the great house of Kinsale, would make three. Valcourt had followed him into the bookstore after seeing him on the street and sensing his eagerness for precisely this sort of experience, but then he had hesitated in accepting the young man, as he possessed knowledge and intuition that might alert him to the truth.

But that, too, could be used to advantage. A plan had suggested itself even as they spoke. Mister Kinsella's own perspicacity would destine him to prove an object lesson to the others, should they require firm persuasion. And in the process, he would experience firsthand the occult dealings he so craved. It was a pity, in a way; as Courdeval, he had admired the Irish Celts. They were ferocious in battle, worthy opponents of his own Norman cousins, and no limit of treachery was beyond them.

Now he required one more: a woman, and one of particular qualities, very different from Nicole Partrick. This implied wealth–a great deal of it–and the haughty attitude that so often accompanied it. The logical places to search were where the wealthy bourgeoisie gathered in these times–places where, while lip service was paid to the laughable pedigrees which they assigned themselves, consisting of only a few generations, the true hierarchy was one of money. If he failed in his search today, he would have to find a means of gaining access to this class of people, to their gatherings and haunts. This he preferred not to do; the exposure was great, and the need for haste was mounting. But servants had whispered to him of another possibility. It was well worth an afternoon of investigation, and it played on one of his particular strengths: a masterful knowledge of horses. He continued on his way toward the polo field.

He paused beside a fenced court where several couples played at the game called tennis. Except that it might improve the accuracy of one's sword strokes, he could not see much use for it. The women wore next to nothing on their lower bodies, apparently in the belief that their exposed limbs increased their allure. He had been stunned to speechlessness on first encountering modem modes of dress, not to mention the ubiquitous photographic likenesses of barely clothed women that were used to sell commodities of all descriptions. It had been one of his first indications of the barbaric nature of the new world he had entered.

A group of boys kicking a round ball–the game was called *soccer*–distracted him again. He had heard of something like it played by court ladies in Cathay, using the stomach of a eunuch who had been force-fed tea for many days. Other boys raced around on small-wheeled boards, with those astonishing devices called boom-boxes on their shoulders, blaring distressing music. Some of the haircuts reminded him of a tribe of Kurds he had once seen in Aleppo, captured by Arab slavers in the Central Asian steppes and brought to market to be sold. The boys' bare legs flashed as they ran, stirring in him a long-suppressed emotion. He considered bringing his cloaked companion, whom the French peasants had called *celui*–the one–for an outing here when the moon was next full, perhaps having an opportunity to combine pleasure with the crucial business of feeding the hungry mouths. But again, the risk was too great. For the present, he must continue to transact such business in lonely spots. There would be ample time when all was settled. Contenting himself with memories, he watched a few moments longer; then he reminded himself that there was work to do, and walked on until he reached his destination.

For some time, he stood overlooking the polo game in progress, noting points of the players' horsemanship. This was more to his taste: the rush of snorting animals, the simulated combat. Some of the riders were quite accomplished, although he knew that a man's true mettle was not tested until he faced swinging battle-axes and maces. If the stakes of the game had been raised–if it were played as in parts of the East during his time, with the head of the losing side's leader providing the ball for the next game–his interest would have intensified.

He turned his attention to the crowd. There were a number of women whose appearances meshed with his design. But all were accompanied–ideally, he wished to be noticed by no one but the woman herself–and in the swirl of emotion surrounding the game, it was difficult to read individual thoughts. He decided to stroll for a little longer and return during the intermission the clock promised in another few minutes. Then it might be easier to single one out.

He skirted contemptuously a field for golf–he had gone livid with disgust upon first learning that the object of this game, considered a fit sport for grown men, was to pursue a small white ball, on foot, and knock it with a stick into a hole in the ground–and turned down a deserted lane shaded by eucalyptus trees. Before he had walked two minutes, he saw a horse and rider approaching, perhaps half a furlong–one hundred yards, he corrected himself–ahead. His interest quickened at the realization that the rider was female. Quickly, he scanned her outward appearance: breeches, knee-high boots, waistcoat, and silky dark-blond hair tucked up into a peaked cap; haughty features, hard beyond her twenty-some years; beauty that depended largely on artifice. Then, with his left eye, he looked deeper. In her heart he saw black anger. Its object was a man who had recently thrown her over.

She was not many paces away now, the horse moving at a spirited walk, and her bearing suggested that she would enjoy riding him down. Excellent, he thought, and quickly scanned the roadside until his gaze found a dead branch of the proper size. Closing his eye briefly, he issued a harsh command.

The branch began to stir, bending, then writhing; and suddenly it slithered onto the path, head raised, tail buzzing menacingly.

The horse reared, snorting in, terror, and the woman shrieked. In six running strides, Valcourt had hold of the bridle, his gaze fixed sternly on the horse's rolling eyes, his deep voice commanding it to calm. It was a small gelding, perhaps fifteen hands, with none of the power of the Arabian warhorses that had been his joy, but like the woman astride it, it showed evidence of expensive breeding–and like all animals, it obeyed him. When it had settled to a nervous shifting of feet, he released it and stepped back.

The woman leaned over the pommel, breathing fast and deeply. Her face had gone white, the haughtiness, he saw with satisfaction, gone. After a moment, she straightened and stared at him.

"Thank you," she gasped.

Valcourt bowed. "A pleasure to be of your service, mademoiselle." He allowed his accent to sound a trifle thicker than usual.

"I can't believe there was a . . . a *rattlesnake* here in the park."

Inwardly, he grimaced. He had only seen these New World vipers in photographs, had known they were indigenous to this land, and had thought the rattle would be a sure way to attract the horse's attention. It had not occurred to him that in such a city, dangerous snakes would have long since been purged even from a forested area.

"Perhaps it escaped from captivity," he answered smoothly.

"Maybe." Looking fearful, she scanned the ground. "Where did it go?"

The branch lay unmoving and unnoticed by her on the other side of the path.

"I think we may assume the poor beast was far more frightened of us than we of it," Valcourt said.

"Certainly more frightened than you." One of her eyebrows rose in critical admiration. "You must have stepped right over it."

Valcourt shrugged. "In emergencies, one does what is necessary."

"I'm going to make sure somebody hears about this," she declared with sudden heat. "I could have been killed."

For a moment longer he stood, waiting, reading her mood. He watched her eyes take in his casual but elegant attire, the expensive gold wristwatch he had learned to wear, the strange, soft shoes that had no laces or buckles. To such women, appearances were everything.

"Perhaps," he said, "you should take something to settle your nerves. May I offer you a cognac?"

Her head cocked a little to the side, interest battling with caution.

"Thank you, but I'm supposed to meet up with some people."

Valcourt smiled graciously. "In that case, with your assurances that you are well–" He bowed once more and turned away, understanding that to be so easily dismissed would be the one thing she could not bear. He could feel her hesitation, her curiosity, her annoyance.

"*Pardon,*" she called after him. "*Vous étes Francais?*"

He paused and turned back, feigning surprise. "*Mais oui,* mademoiselle."

"Where from? If you don't mind my asking. I've spent quite a bit of time there."

"Most recently, Paris," he said. "But I live from time to time in various places."

"Really? I was in St. Tropez last summer. It was wonderful."

"Ah yes, that is country I know very well. One of my family's estates lies nearby, not far from Grasse."

"What does your family do?"

He smiled, realizing the importance of the question.

"Many things. Among others, we raise horses." He stepped forward again and caressed the gelding's muzzle; it trembled, but stood still. "Arabian stallions, older brothers to this fine little sorrel."

There was another pause. Her gaze swept over him again, and he saw the answer in her eyes. She wanted revenge on her ex-lover, but he was inaccessible. A rich Frenchman would provide a piquant substitute.

"I have to meet some friends," she repeated, "but that's all they are, friends. I could be free in an hour, and that cognac sounds very attractive, Monsieur–?"

He pronounced the name, giving extra fluorish to the *r*, watching the effect of his voice on her.

Minutes later, he was strolling back through the park, with an assignation in one hour's time at a tavern called the Cliff House, with Miss Charity Haverill. As he walked, he offered silent thanks to the Adversary for putting this treasure in his way. She was not only the fourth he required: though as yet unawakened, she was, by nature, an ally.

Yes, it had been an excellent day, and if all had gone according to plan on other fronts, it would end with a most special pleasure awaiting him at home.

In a rented truck, moving south from San Francisco in the early twilight, Frantz Masson was driving and considering, both with great care. In the back of the truck was a plain steamer trunk, not much bigger than a large suitcase and weighing perhaps fifty kilos–relatively easy for a man of his strength to carry. Because of that strength, earned through years of handling freight on the docks of Le Havre, and because as a merchant seaman he had spent considerable time in the United States, becoming familiar with its customs–including the operation of motor vehicles–he had been chosen by Monsieur Claude

Barousse for this very special mission. A Belgian with shipping offices at several points on the Mediterranean and North Atlantic coasts, Barousse was an extremely rich man. Much of the business he did was legitimate. Much of it, including the present enterprise, was not.

Frantz Masson had been called into the office some three weeks before and personally given his instructions by Barousse. The trunk had been stored for some months in one of the warehouses. Frantz was to accompany it by ship from Le Havre to San Francisco, never letting it out of his sight; it would travel in his cabin rather than as cargo. Its importation into that city–uninspected–had been arranged. He was then to drive the trunk to an address approximately fifty kilometers south, deliver it in person to a Monsieur Guy-Luc Valcourt, and return to the San Francisco airport to board a plane for New York and then Paris. For this service he had already received an amount of money equal to half of his usual wages for one year. An equivalent amount would be paid to him upon his return.

And while Monsieur Barousse had not actually said so, it was clear to Frantz Masson that if anything went amiss, he could count the remaining days of his life on his fingers. In the world of such men, trust did not exist; fear and money were the real and potent forces.

During the long days of the voyage, Frantz Masson had given much thought to all of this. A single major implication stood out like a pyramid in a desert: whatever the trunk contained must be of immense value. Further, Barousse must have been paid an immense sum to handle it. The cost of bribing the customs officials alone must have been enormous. Why, then, had Barousse not opened the trunk and appropriated its contents himself?

The answer could only be that he was afraid of this Monsieur Valcourt–even more afraid than Frantz was of Barousse. In fact, he thought Barousse had seemed nervous as he gave the instructions, as if the trunk were something he was both anxious to get rid of and greatly concerned to deliver safely. This was most intriguing. Barousse was known even in the very rough world of shipping for his steely nerves, and more than one man who had crossed him had quietly disappeared.

What, Frantz wondered with a curiosity that had risen near to madness, could be in the box? Drugs? Currency? Nuclear secrets? Many times aboard the ship he had examined it carefully. The heavy padlock was one he could have picked with ease, and once, after a few hours of drinking, the demand to know had overwhelmed him to the point where he had actually started to do it.

But he had stopped, telling himself that Barousse might have set a snare, some sort of identifying trap that would betray Frantz's disloyalty–a spray of paint that would mark the lid when it was opened, say, or even a canister of poison gas.

In any case, the point was that Frantz was now alone with the trunk, safely in the United States, and finished with both customs and any spies Barousse might have planted. There remained only this Valcourt, who had never seen Frantz and would have no idea of how to go about finding him if he did not turn up. Eventually, of course, a search would begin. But days, even a week, of confusion would intervene; and Frantz Masson had not spent the last twenty-five years of his adult life as a merchant seaman without learning numerous ways and places in which a man–especially a rich man–might disappear. He owned several passports from different nations, identifying him by different names and occupations. If the trunk's contents were valuable enough to warrant it, he could vanish in such a way that even Claude Barousse could not find him–false trails, plastic surgery–and live out his remaining years in luxury instead of as a wharf rat in a cold, gray, industrial city in northern France.

The mechanics of how to translate the cargo into cash might or might not be feasible, and the possibility of a trap remained. But Frantz Masson had been waiting a lifetime for such a chance, and he was neither a coward nor a fool. Nothing great came without risk. If it blew up in his face, well, it was still better to have tried than not. His wife was a nag, his children grown and out of the house, his job a wearying bore. In short, he had little to lose.

A glance at his watch told him he was on schedule–he was expected at Valcourt's between eight and nine o'clock. A fifteen-minute delay would go unnoticed. He slowed his speed, scanning the countryside for a place where he might find seclusion. The houses had thinned, and as he topped a rise, he saw below and to the right the northern end of a long reservoir, a shimmering pool of deep blue in the evening light. An exit was approaching; he could see the road wind down to the reservoir and disappear into forest. He judged that he was still several miles from Green Mountain Road and

Valcourt's house. In fifteen minutes he would know whether he would spend the rest of his life as a dock-hand, or as a fugitive from Barousse.

Or as the owner of a luxury villa in a tropical climate, sipping rum beside a pool in which bronze-skinned, bare-breasted young women frolicked.

The exit took him onto a two-lane road toward the reservoir. In a couple of kilometers he came to a large turnout surrounded by trees. There was no other traffic. He swung in and pulled the truck around to face the way he had come, then climbed out and raised the hood. If anyone drove by, he was simply a workman examining his engine. Then he unlocked the back, leaned in, and dragged the trunk to the door. From his tool kit he took the leather case that held his lock picks and selected the proper pair. He inserted them and probed carefully. The tumblers clicked. The lock came open in his hand.

He paused again, excitement building in his chest. There remained the possibility of a trap, but he was more certain than ever that Barousse had not dared to open the trunk. The forest around him was oddly silent, the road deserted. Far to the east, he could see the stream of head-lights on the freeway. He shrugged.

"*On va au bout du monde,*" he said softly and, springing back, threw open the lid.

No explosion. No hissing of gas. No movement of any kind. Cautiously, he stepped forward and peered inside. As he had expected, the cargo was wrapped, in a sort of heavy quilt. It was large, nearly filling the space. If it was drugs or currency, there was a great deal of it.

The evening light was nearly gone. He took a slender flashlight from the tool kit; moving quickly but with extreme care, he searched with its finger-thin beam for the edges of the wrapping. With relief, he discovered they were not sewn shut. He spent a few seconds memorizing their position in case they had been photographed, and then, with infinite caution, began to separate them.

His probing fingers touched something. For an instant he paused, trying to identify the substance. Then his hand jerked back as if it had been burned.

What he had touched felt for all the world like flesh.

Human flesh. Smooth skin. Neither warm nor cold.

Frantz Masson began to feel sick. If that in fact was what the cargo was, there could be only one explanation: at some point within the past forty-eight hours, he had been duped. During one of the rare occasions when he had been forced to leave the trunk for a few minutes, someone had opened it, stolen the cargo he was meant to deliver, and substituted–

A body.

His brain whirled, trying to remember. It would have taken great skill, but it could have been done, while he was taking a meal or answering a call of nature. It was impossible that he had carried a corpse across the ocean, for even if the trunk had been lead-lined, the stench when he opened it would have overpowered him.

Unless it was still alive.

Grimly, he returned to his work. Through the quilt his hand discovered a shoulder, hip, legs: a small person, curled in a fetal position. One hand holding the flashlight, he carefully uncovered the head. He blinked in amazement. The face was that of a young woman, and even in these bizarre circumstances, it was clear that she was quite lovely. She seemed more asleep than dead, her features peaceful, with none of the racked agony of rigor mortis. His grip on the flashlight tightened. Could she be alive? After having been given some powerful drug, perhaps, to slow her metabolism to near zero? Had she been on board the ship all the time, concealed in another part, and put into the trunk at the last minute? Was he, Frantz Masson, being used as a tool in some sort of extraordinary kidnapping scheme? He scowled. He had no compunctions about smuggling, even of drugs. But human beings– Quickly, his fingers moved to the pulse point on her throat.

And touched a ragged edge of flesh.

Frantz Masson swallowed. He did not want to see what his hand told him, but he needed to be sure. He looked, then turned quickly away, awash with pity. Although he was no stranger to violence, the sight of this lovely young woman, hardly more than a child, with her throat sliced completely through, stunned him. That she was dead, there was no doubt–the wound was deep, the severed arteries plainly visible. Nor was there any doubt that she had been killed recently. The edges were still fresh and raw, and her flesh showed no signs of decomposition.

And he, Frantz Masson, had been tricked into carrying this grisly burden in his arms, into delivering it to a man who was doubtless expecting something vastly different. A man of whom even Claude Barousse was afraid. A man who might take out his anger on Frantz.

Had Barousse appropriated the trunk's contents after all, and set up Frantz to take the blame? Was that the true cause of his nervousness?

Angry and confused, he forced himself to calm down and considered his alternatives. To escape without the money he had hoped for would be foolish and probably impossible. He could hardly contact Barousse and admit that he had opened the trunk. Grimly, he decided there was only one possibility: deliver it as planned, and feign ignorance. There would be no sign of his tampering. In all likelihood, Valcourt would not wish to open it in his presence, thus allowing Frantz to be well on his way to San Francisco by the time the contents were discovered. If the situation looked dangerous, he had the remedy: a 7-mm automatic, which the customs officials had also thoughtfully overlooked. Whatever happened, at least he could go back to Barousse and claim innocence, rather than face certain death for having crossed him.

Carefully, he wrapped the quilt around the girl as he had found it, locked the trunk, and wiped everything for fingerprints. Inside the cab, he checked his map once more and, with utmost caution, began driving. He wanted this business over, as quickly and smoothly as possible, with no low-level interference. During the fifteen minutes it took him to reach Green Mountain Road, he practiced his well-developed air of nonchalant conspiracy between two men of the world: even more, between two Frenchmen. In all likelihood he would be back on the road to San Francisco within minutes of making the delivery, there to board the first available flight to New York.

He found 2713 without trouble, an imposing pillared drive with black iron gates. He drove through, hardening his nerves for the show of ignorance he must make. The driveway was long, lined with tall, overhanging trees; the cone of his headlights gave him the sense of moving through a tunnel. He traveled nearly one hundred meters before the road opened into a circle with a fountain. His lips parted slightly. The house was immense, illuminated by ground lights of an eerie softness, almost smoky. This much was immediately clear: Valcourt was indeed a man of means. Most of the many windows were dark, but far back in one of the rooms on the ground floor there appeared to be a candelabra flickering. As he opened the door of the truck, he thought he saw a small, black shape disappear from a windowsill inside.

He was unlocking the back of the truck when a figure stepped onto the porch. Frantz immediately thought of the monks he occasionally saw in France; the man was wearing a black robe that came to sandaled feet, his arms folded in his sleeves. Except that Frantz had never seen a monk with an eyepatch. Nor had he ever seen one who presented, even in the dim, smoky light, such a bearing of sinister power. He realized that he was starting to sweat–a bad sign. Again he steeled his nerves. The shadowed face and single eye made the man seem more formidable than he was. He might be rich, eccentric, even dangerous. But Frantz Masson was no amateur in tight situations. A few friendly words, a brisk departure–and if there was trouble, the Beretta rested against his hip.

"*Bonsoir, mon ami,*" he called, turning his head as he pulled the trunk to the edge of the truck bed. "You are Monsieur Guy-Luc Valcourt?"

The man inclined his head and said in French, "You bring me a present from Claude Barousse?"

"A present, monsieur? That I do not know. I only follow instructions, and they are to see to it that you receive this." He lifted the trunk in his thick arms and started up the steps, holding at bay the awareness of what was in it. Valcourt did not move. The gaze of the one eye rested on Frantz, harsh, knowing; and Frantz felt a cold drop of sweat slide from his armpit down his side.

He set the trunk at Valcourt's feet and straightened.

"Monsieur Barousse informs me that you will give me a token to take back to him."

Valcourt said nothing. The gaze held steady.

"A receipt," Frantz said weakly. "That you and he agreed on."

Slowly, Valcourt's hands came forth from his sleeves. One held a small key in front of Frantz Masson's face.

"Open it," Valcourt said.

Frantz tried to laugh. "Me, monsieur? But I do not wish to pry into your affairs. The less I know of another man's business, the happier I am."

"No doubt that is why you took the trouble to have a look already," Valcourt said quietly.

Frantz's hand edged toward the Beretta. "I do not know what you mean, monsieur," he said, hearing the bluff in his own voice. "But trouble is something I do not like. I have accomplished my job. I ask you for the promised token. If you will not give it to me, I will report that when I return. Only a very unwise man crosses Monsieur Barousse."

"Very well," Valcourt said. "Then I will give you your token."

Tensed, Frantz waited. Abruptly he became aware that something was extremely wrong with his body. His nerve endings quickly located the problem as being in his right buttock, and even as they informed his brain that it seemed to be on fire, the stench of his own burning flesh reached his nostrils. With a shriek, he clutched the pistol, tugging it free, searing his fingers on its red hot barrel, and threw it from him. With his lips stretched into a grin of agony and his left hand squeezing his right, he stared first at his blistered fingers, then up at Valcourt's contemptuous face. There came a sharp metallic crack. Frantz Masson whirled around to look at the trunk.

The padlock had snapped. In disbelief, his pain forgotten, he watched the lock slide by itself off the hasp, the hasp creep open, and the lid of the trunk begin to rise.

For the first time in many years, Frantz Masson realized distantly, he was praying—praying that what his eyes told him was happening, was not. The quilt inside the trunk stirred. A slender hand found its way out and gently separated the edges, like a sleeper leisurely shaking off covers on a warm morning.

The girl rose and turned to face them.

Even in his horror and disbelief, even with his eyes riveted on the deep red slice across her throat, he could not help but note her beauty. She was perhaps seventeen, exquisitely formed, breasts high and small, skin a dark gold in the smoky light, her sex a delicate, shadowed triangle.

"Lovely, is she not?" Valcourt said softly. "You see why I have taken such great trouble to bring her to my side."

Frantz Masson felt his knees sagging. The agony in his buttock and hand was a faraway cry in an unimportant chamber of his mind. Valcourt made a curt, dismissive gesture.

"*Allez, paysan,*" he said. "You will not travel alone."

As if the words broke his trance, Frantz found the strength to move, limping, to the truck. Groping awkwardly, he turned the ignition key with his left hand.

Just before the engine caught, he heard from behind him a high, thin whistle.

Tears streaming down his face, his mind numb with shock, he stamped on the accelerator and left in a spray of gravel. The twisting kilometers of Green Mountain Road were a nightmare of pain and fear, and it was not until he reached the freeway that he remembered Valcourt's parting words: *You will not travel alone.*

As he started to make the turn toward the city, invisible hands of great strength seemed to close over his own on the steering wheel, wringing a howl of pain from him and forcing the truck to continue straight toward the coast along the two-lane road.

Within a few minutes, the lights of houses had become sparse. He drove on, sobbing quietly, his hands and feet guided by the invisible force, until something in the side mirror caught his attention. His weeping stopped.

Perhaps twenty meters behind the truck, he could barely make out a darker shape against the gray of the pavement. It was short and squat, seemingly muffled in a sort of hooded robe that reflected a faint, strange red from the taillights. Though the truck was moving at a high speed, the shape remained close, disappearing on curves and hills, only to appear again in its steady, gliding pursuit.

Through the longest—and yet terribly briefest—minutes of his life, Frantz Masson rode on, staring helplessly at the mirror. At last, the air turned noticeably cooler and he sensed the vast, black void of the sea ahead.

As the shape began to gain perceptibly, he could feel its whimpering anticipation crawling like flames around the edges of his mind.

The man who called himself Guy-Luc Valcourt smiled faintly as he watched the truck race out of the drive. It had not mattered that Frantz Masson had betrayed his trust and examined the trunk's contents: his doom was sealed the moment he agreed to chaperone it across the ocean. But he had provided a most entertaining few minutes. When truck and driver were found many miles away, having plunged off the coastal cliffs, no connection could ever be made to Valcourt. And the news would serve nicely as the token of receipt for the *Flamand,* Claude Barousse.

He turned to the girl, Alysse, whose life had been taken by the hands of John McTell.

"Come, my love," he said, and she stepped from the trunk, moving dreamily to take his extended hand. As he

167

gazed at her, he felt the agonized twisting of McTell's consciousness within him.

"Beautiful indeed," he murmured to McTell. "Was your hour with her worth the price you have paid?" The twisting subsided into the desperate fearfulness Valcourt was accustomed to: McTell's horror at being trapped inside his own body while another consciousness controlled it–a consciousness that had begun by seducing him into destroying what he had loved and would end by destroying him.

Valcourt led Alysse inside. In the parlor, he knotted loosely around her neck one of the several silk scarves he had purchased for this purpose. Then he posed her beside the candelabra and, with a glass of fine cognac, sat back to admire her. Although as Courdeval he had preferred boys, he was a connoisseur of beauty of all forms. It was true that he had gone to a great deal of trouble to keep her; and while ostensibly his reasons were, as always, primarily practical, the simple pleasure of having her to look at had contributed largely. Of course, she was not, strictly speaking, any longer "Alysse": rather, this was her material form, animated by a docile servant that could be replaced by a more powerful one if need be. For now, it suited him; it only had to be called from time to time, and it required little effort on his part to control.

As for the immaterial part that had made her more than a mere body, that was gone to a realm where even he could not reach.

Watching her, his pleasure increased, and he realized that he had never really taken the time to study her. Youth and slimness gave her a certain androgyny. He felt

McTell quail at the possibility that suggested itself, and he smiled again.

The escape from the French village of Saint-Bertrand had been an often tense affair, but the wealth of terror and blood that preceded it had given him great temporary strength. Possessed at last of McTell, he was still largely ignorant of the new world he had entered, so he had forced the man's mind to provide information, while he himself engineered and implemented. He had set Alysse on the road–wearing only a flimsy chemise, obviously in distress–and waited in the shadows. It had only been a matter of minutes before a motor vehicle stopped. The driver was a young man who was returning to Grasse from Cannes.

Some hours later, he walked into the Rhone river, just south of Lyon, and drowned.

The next vehicle to be commandeered belonged to a businessman from Paris; this time, there had been more leisure to choose. Expecting a fling with a pretty hitch-hiker, he had instead relinquished his cash, clothing, identification papers, and eventually, like the young man from Grasse, his life. It had been child's play to alter the businessman's *cartes d'identités,* along with McTell's fingerprint patterns. That was when Guy-Luc Valcourt had come into existence:

But modem France was small and crowded–one could not even rent a chamber for the night without filing a paper that went to a centralized police authority–and McTell, while reasonably at home there, was still a foreigner, thus capable of making a blunder that might have had serious consequences in those vulnerable early days. The new land, America—vast, wide open, and the natural home of McTell—had been the obvious choice.

And so, with regret, Valcourt had traveled to the port of Le Havre, through his native Normandy—passing within miles of the place of his birth, remembering tournaments and battles, châteaux and lords, as he moved across familiar countryside now blighted by the spreading stain of modem "civilization."

As for Alysse, the authorities had been watching keenly for her. Walking by his side, she certainly would have been noticed. Thus, he had placed her in the steamer trunk, deep in a state of what would be called in these times "suspended animation."

But how to transport her? McTell had warned of elaborate customs investigations, including something called X rays—a sort of second sight that gave common men a power once reserved for adepts. To transport it by means of magic was impractical; moving such a bulky item across that great a distance was beyond him even at the height of his powers. Thus, he had decided, with reluctance, to leave the trunk behind and have it shipped after he was settled. This had required the services of a certain kind of man. In Le Havre, he had sent servants on a search. They had led him to Claude Barousse.

For the proper price, the Flamand assured him, the smuggling of such a trunk into the United States presented no problem. But the amount he demanded was enormous, and while Valcourt did not object to this in itself—the money meant literally nothing to him—he was not fool enough to miss the obvious: that if he was willing to pay such a sum, then the contents of the trunk must be more valuable still, and Barousse would not hesitate to examine those contents as soon as the trunk was in his possession. He was a very powerful man; Valcourt was merely wealthy.

Or so he thought.

Thus, Valcourt had taken the trouble to offer Monsieur Barousse an additional inducement to honesty—one that would not reveal his true nature, but would nonetheless make clear his power to deal with deceit. As they spoke, he had scanned the Flamand's mind and had found there, close to the surface, a memory that both excited and troubled Barousse. Some months earlier, a man had cheated him in a business dealing. Barousse had had the man abducted, loaded with chains, and thrown, alive, into the English Channel. He had personally supervised the proceedings, and at the last moment had patted the doomed man's cheek in ironic farewell. The image of the body thrashing through the dark water into eternity had made a lasting impression; though Barousse rightly fancied himself to be a harsh man when the need arose, he had no real stomach for cruelty, and his exercise of it still preyed on him.

When Valcourt arrived to deliver the required sum, he had lifted this image from Barousse's mind and played it in precise detail, like a moving picture, on the office wall. This had given him great pleasure. Centuries had passed since he had seen a man actually turn green.

From that moment, Barousse had been his, never voicing a question, never daring to consider disobeying. The money had been additional insurance, purchasing his willing, as well as his unwilling, allegiance. Such a man might well prove useful in the future.

There remained unfinished business in France.

Valcourt grimaced, drank, and wiped his mouth on his sleeve, forgetful of his facade of gentility. Allowing Mélusine Devarre to escape had been his one serious mistake. She and her husband alone knew the truth of what had happened in Saint-Bertrand. To have finished her then and there would have been a moment's work. But he had wished to extend her terror as an offering to the hungry mouths—had been certain it was safe. The servant he had set upon her was powerfully destructive. How could he have dreamed that she would sense the one means of overcoming it? She was powerful, too, he knew now—or rather, she had powerful allies, whether or not she was even aware of them. Her very ignorance of her own strength added a dangerous edge. She was impossible to quantify; there were too many unknowns. It was conceivable that with her psychic powers she could locate him and be canny enough to mount an unexpected attack. While servants kept him informed of much that transpired, they had to be set to specific tasks; and even he could not be absolutely certain of safety from, say, a bullet fired from a distance, taking him by surprise. While the death of his physical body would not be the end of him, it would leave him vulnerable to those who possessed the knowledge of how to imprison him—

This time, forever.

He could simply wait for Mélusine Devarre and her husband to die; but their natural lives might last three, four, even five more decades—an intolerable length of time to be looking over his shoulder.

Besides, there was the matter of revenge. They had come within an hour of besting him.

He rose and began to pace. Though the possibility existed of finishing them by so-called magic, it was impractical because of the sheer distance, because his power was far from its peak, and because the woman was clearly possessed of considerable power herself. Magical force allowed him to transcend many natural laws to a certain extent, but in most ways the power was like any other, subject to its own rules, weakening with distance and requiring greater effort for greater tasks. Much of it had to do with the nature of things themselves. Objects that had once possessed life, for instance, were easier to animate than those that had not. He could not fly in the air like Simon Magus; he could not render himself invisible or walk through walls. He *could* summon entities of varying degrees of power, and these could be compelled to perform tasks: clouding or reading minds and reporting to him the information they received, transporting small objects for short distances, animating or controlling bodies. To summon his companion *celui*—to make manifest that being from the next world in this one—required great energy and could only be done by night; but each successful hunt replenished him. While he sneered at most ritual magic—it was a stage he had long since passed, a game for charlatans, not for him who had made the journey across the abyss—certain extremely potent and complex ceremonies required the aid of his grimoire, itself a talisman of greatly concentrated power.

173

Ceremonies such as the acquisition of a new body.

In essence, it was the same as any other economy, this set of laws that had been created before time by the forces that fought the eternal great battle. The more energy one expended, the more one must acquire. The more one had in reserve, the safer one was. The more powerful the entity summoned, the more effort required to force it to one's will and the shorter the duration of control. One used natural energy whenever possible, to conserve the more "expensive" arcane.

For now, the balance was ebbing dangerously. His existence since his escape had been precarious, hand- to-mouth, that of a lord reduced to a beggar. Each full moon's hunt yielded him just enough for cautious living until the next, as if he was no better than a feral beast dependent on its belly. In order to regain the strength he had once known, to become fully the man he had been, a very particular sort of offering was required–an offering to the Adversary himself. The anguish must be not merely physical, but spiritual: it must stem from the betrayal of love.

Thus the supreme importance of seducing Nicole Partrick into destroying her son, in order, as she would think, to save herself.

When this was past, she would serve him once more. At the proper time, he would lure the Devarres to him. They would come–they would have no real choice–and would be led to the home of a pleasant, seemingly puzzled woman named Nicole–who would be firmly in the grip of her "guardian angel." While Mélusine might intuit the truth, by then it would be too late. There would be a sudden eruption of violence, a burned building, leaving for the authorities only an inexplicable crime and several charred corpses—

And Guy-Luc Valcourt never again would have anything to fear from mortal man.

The plan was virtually ironclad, with all the advantages on his side. There was only one problem: deep within him, it caused a rebellion of his warrior blood, a touch of self-contempt. To ambush—to overcome enemies by deceit—had never been his way.

Or did the real truth of the matter lie even deeper: that Mélusine Devarre was the first woman who had ever interested him? As Courdeval, he had lived from birth in a world of men—knights and monks—where women were chattels, regarded as items of luxury for the soft. But this one—when he had first become aware of her, still in his disembodied state, he had begun to wage psychic war against her, and had very nearly succeeded in killing her by means of a vision. She had not succumbed, but had instead continued to pursue him, to fight back. He remembered her courage when she had faced him at last, had realized who and what he was and what was certain, they both had thought, to be her end. He had never imagined that a female could display such qualities.

Was that fascination with her, even, perhaps, the truth that lay beneath his failure to make certain of her death that same night?

Dangerous thoughts! She and her husband must die, and this time, there must be no mistake about it. Along with her he would utterly destroy whatever perfidious softening might have sprung up within himself.

So. With his enemies disposed of, he would be at leisure to perform a final task in the old country–one that was more a matter of caprice than necessity. The bones of Courdeval still lay in the stone vault, within the slope of Montsévrain, that had held them for nearly seven hundred years. There was little chance of their discovery. But he felt somehow incomplete without them, and he was determined to have them back. They had served him well for many years, had braced the body that made Guilhem de Courdeval one of the era's most feared warriors. Call it sentimental. He would find a suit of armor, one that had been preserved from that time, dress the bones in it, and stand them in his study: a *memento mori* with teeth, so to speak. While he would hire agents to effect the actual recovery–perhaps through Claude Barousse–he toyed with the idea of visiting Saint-Bertrand in person to supervise the project, with the piquant addition of taking revenge on the descendants of the peasants who had betrayed Courdeval centuries ago, and who had cursed him as he burned.

Then someday decades in the future, when the body of John McTell began to weaken, he would prepare a new one–this time in safety and comfort. He walked to the mirror and leaned close.

"Then," he whispered, "I will cast this carcass aside, and you will go to join those whom you destroyed. Their spirits wait for you in the next world, longing to be with you–forever." He smiled grimly at the terrified twisting inside. There was little enough pity in his heart anyway, and none for a man he considered a coward and a weakling, who had sacrificed what he loved in the hope of saving himself.

He turned again to Alysse, and again considered using her to ease the bodily pressures that had been building within him. A similar sort of practice, with the dying and still-warm dead, had been common enough on the battlefields of his day, particularly in eastern lands.

But no; it would be, simply, ignoble.

Taking Alysse by the hand, he led her upstairs into the chamber he had prepared for her. It was as he imagined a typical young woman's room of this era would be, with pastel walls and bedclothes, posters of certain moving picture and popular music idols, and assorted trinkets on the dresser and shelves. He had done this partly out of whimsy, and partly in case anyone should happen in while he was not present—one of his "students," for instance. There was also an extensive wardrobe, although here, he had indulged his more traditional tastes. Alysse lay obediently on the bed and crossed her hands over her breast; as he dismissed the servant that moved her, her eyes fell shut. For convention's sake, he covered her with a quilt.

Then he returned downstairs, to ponder the precise nature and extent of the services he must offer Robbie Kinsella and Charity Haverill in order to bring them firmly into the fold.

SEVEN

On the evening of the first Thursday in July, Nicole turned from Skyline Drive onto Green Mountain Road, following with some impatience a battered red Volkswagen beetle. The meeting was at eight; she had eaten a light, quick dinner–already lonely without Tom Junior–but still had ended up rushing. A look at her watch reassured her that she would make it with ten minutes to spare, and she dropped back a little from the VW. She could make out the driver as a young man with a shock of curly hair. His car wandered on the curves, as if operating it were far from the foremost thing on his mind, and she was surprised and a little dismayed when he braked at Valcourt's drive–predictably, one of the taillights was out–and swerved in.

But when she saw his face, she liked him immediately: drooping mustache, premature wrinkles beneath kind eyes, and a manner that was hesitant but energetic.

"Robbie Kinsella," he said, holding out his hand. "You here for the Sabbath?"

She smiled and introduced herself. Together, they walked past the sparkling fountain and the other two vehicles parked in the circle, a sleek silver Porsche and a fierce-looking black Jaguar XJ-S.

"Looks like we're the poor folks," Robbie said.

"No kidding." She noted his clothes–baggy khaki pants, wrinkled Hawaiian shirt, and well-worn high-top sneakers–and felt better about her own decision to dress in jeans and a turtleneck. She had lost four more pounds, and the jeans were new. She had not been able to resist. "Have you known Monsieur Valcourt long?"

"Met him last week in a bookstore. You?"

"At about the same time." She hesitated, then said, "He seems to be a very unusual man."

"Unusual," Robbie said, as if testing the word. He grinned.

The heavy door opened silently before they could knock. Nicole's instant impression of the person who faced them was so startling that she inhaled sharply. It was a young woman of seventeen or eighteen, astonishingly pretty. She was slender, with rich chestnut hair done up in a chignon, wearing a floor-length gown of a deep burgundy color and a matching scarf, almost like a collar around her neck. The overall effect was Victorian, even medieval. In the dim light inside the doorway, her eyes were dark, hollow pools, and she was pale as death.

Maybe, Nicole thought, breathing again, that paleness was the reason for her reaction. She stole a glance at Robbie. His grin was gone. Shifting his weight nervously, his hands were now out of his pockets and clasped in

179

front of him. Without a word, the girl turned and led them into Valcourt's sitting room.

It was brightly lit, which surprised Nicole for some reason; overhead recessed fixtures seemed to war with the three candelabras, each of which contained seven red candles. A man and a woman waited in chairs; their clothes matched the vehicles outside, with the woman in a high-fashion suit of white pegged pants and silk blouse, the man in an expensive sport coat and open shirt. He rose, his movements swift and jerky. The woman remained seated, looking them over with a faintly condescending air. Nicole bristled but smiled coolly. The maid, if that was what she was, left the room without a sound or another glance. There was no sign of Valcourt.

For some seconds, no one spoke, and then Robbie Kinsella broke the ice, introducing Nicole and himself. Spencer Epps's hand was sweaty when she took it, and his eyes twitched and shifted. Charity Haverill hardly stirred, offering her hand, heavy with rings, as if it were to be kissed. Another awkward pause followed; Nicole sensed them gauging one another, suspicious and perhaps even a little ashamed to be there.

Then she noticed the black cat Lamashtu, lying on the mantel beside the glass-enclosed book, and watching them with what she imagined to be intelligent boredom. She walked over, grateful for a prop, and the cat suffered its ears to be scratched. What could you say to someone in circumstances like these: Live around here? What do you do? Abruptly, she wished she had not come, had never heard of Guy-Luc Valcourt and his mysterious bag of tricks.

Although there was no denying that she looked terrific in those new jeans, even to herself.

Behind her, Robbie cleared his throat. "You've got to hand it to the man, he knows how to put on a show. Grimoire, zombie maid, red candles–right down to the black cat."

She turned to see Spencer Epps laugh nervously. "I could use a drink," he said, his eyes moving restlessly around the room. It was a syndrome she encountered often in the circles of her profession, and she understood that it was not a drink he needed.

"What was the first thing you said?" she asked Robbie. "A grim-what?"

"*Grimoire,*" he said. "A book of magic. Like the one beside your elbow."

She turned back quickly, staring with suspicion at the ancient black book with the charred pages. Robbie came to stand beside her.

"It's very rare to see an original; most of them are in libraries, locked up tight. But the word is they're all pretty much hocus-pocus, or at least if there are any that aren't, it's kept quiet."

"What about this one?" she said. The cat was watching them impassively.

Robbie shrugged. "No telling. He took it out of the case and showed it to me when I came down here last week. It's all in Latin, and I have enough trouble with English. But it's old, no doubt about that, and that sign on the cover–" He stopped, his gaze moving swiftly, almost guiltily, to the doorway.

Valcourt was standing in it, motionless, silent, wearing his black monk's habit and eyepatch. There was no telling how long he had been there. She felt skewered by his stare, like a child caught at something forbidden.

Then Valcourt smiled. "My friends," he said. "I bid you welcome."

The other door to the room opened and the young woman reappeared, carrying a tray with cups, glasses, the silver tea service, and a crystal decanter of sherry. Nicole watched her covertly. Her movements were like the rest of her, delicate, gentle, and somehow somber: odd for a young beauty who should have been bursting with life. Perhaps there was a hidden story–illness or even madness. The girl was certainly not what Nicole had envisioned when Valcourt had said he was expecting a housekeeper; and she suddenly wondered just what the relationship between them was. She was hardly dressed as a maid–or as a twentieth-century teenager, for that matter.

As if he had sensed her thoughts–and there was a good chance that he did, Nicole realized–Valcourt said:

"My niece, Alysse. She has come from France for a look at your great country. *N'est-ce pas, chérie?*"

The girl gave them a ghostly smile and a curtsy.

"She speaks little English," Valcourt murmured. Nicole realized that Alysse's eyes seemed to have no color except dark, as if they somehow obscured one's own vision or changed with the surroundings.

Perhaps Robbie was right: it was a deliberate effect, like the cat, the grimoire, the apparel, and the stilted language, created by this man who certainly seemed to possess remarkable powers. Or was it all just trickery, a fraud to some hidden end? She had debated all the way back from Burbank last Sunday whether to continue; but when she had finally called him that night, she had the sense that on some unconscious level, both of them had known all along that she would. It was as if something had been set in motion that had taken on a life of its own.

"Refresh yourselves," Valcourt said, sweeping a hand at the tray. "Then pray be seated." Nicole poured herself a glass of sherry she did not really want–just another prop, she thought–and took a chair.

These were arranged in a semicircle. Valcourt remained standing at its center, hands clasped behind his back, the gaze of his single eye seeming to encompass them all. For more than a minute he neither moved nor spoke. Power seemed to emanate from him in a wave that was almost tangible. Even Charity Haverill straightened perceptibly, with her hands, which had been continually toying with her many rings and bracelets, now quiet in her lap. Nicole wondered distantly if this was some form of mass hypnosis, if that was the basis of his seemingly greater-than-natural abilities.

"I trust," he said abruptly, "that you have had opportunity to get acquainted?"

They nodded tentatively.

"Then let us begin. I will tell you first that of the many people who contacted me, only the four of you possess the peculiar combination of factors–natural ability of a very high order, strong character, noble intentions–to become participants. Please bear in mind that there are many who dearly craved this chance.

"Next, I can see that doubt and suspicion remain in all of your hearts–that I am a fraud, that I am seeking money, and so forth. This is natural and right; I assure you that you will understand the truth in no long time. Let us discuss a few points toward that end.

"To each of you I gave a simple exercise toward strengthening yourselves, by means of singling out and courting an intelligence which is prepared to serve you, but which, until now, you have been ignorant of. For each of you this entity is different; as with its name, I wish you to keep the service it performed for you a closely guarded secret. But is there anyone who is not pleased, even astonished, at the results of your little practice–your 'wetting of feet,' so to speak?"

Glances were exchanged; no one spoke. Valcourt smiled faintly.

"Of course. You would not otherwise be here to-night. Then believe me when I tell you"–he leaned forward and spoke with great intensity–"this is only the merest beginning. The potential of what is available to you is beyond your imaginations."

He paused, letting the words take effect. "I will be more specific. The idea of a mental exercise aiding one's personal development is perhaps not so foreign to you. Two of you began to influence entities which affected your own mental or physical being, and this seems not entirely out of line with what we know from natural and psychological sciences.

"But the exercises performed by the other two affected the behavior of persons whom they could not influence directly–indeed, with whom they had no contact or even acquaintance. You wonder, how can this be? It smacks, you think, of magic." Again he paused for dramatic effect, and Nicole thought she detected a hint of amusement in his eye, a sense that he was enjoying his role.

"The answer, my friends, lies in a proper understanding of the universe and the workings of the human mind within the overall frame. We shall come to that in a moment. But first, let us have a minor demonstration.

"Dogs, as we all know, can be trained with relative ease. But much of the attraction of cats lies in their aloofness, their independence, their refusal to behave as we wish. Has any of you ever seen a housecat who would perform according to command?"

Again, no one spoke. Valcourt laughed, clearly enjoying himself now.

"I can see your thoughts: He is about to show us parlor tricks. Very well. Lamashtu!" He spoke sharply, pronouncing the name with a strange, perhaps Eastern inflection. The cat leaped down from the mantel, stalked unhesitatingly forward, and sat at Valcourt's feet, tail curling around its legs.

"So, you are thinking, here is a cat who comes when called. Unusual, but certainly not extraordinary. Again, very well. In deference to the noble nature of Lamashtu, we will spare her the common sorts of paces one puts dogs through, leaping through hoops and the like, and proceed directly to more complex matters. I think it is bright in this room. There is a–how do you say?–a rheostat on the light switch. Lamashtu, be so good as to diminish it, oh, a quarter of a turn."

185

The cat walked to a table beneath the light switch, jumped onto it, then rose on its hind legs, suddenly long and feral looking. With one paw braced against the wall, it hooked the claws of the other carefully into the grooves of the rheostat knob and turned it. The light from the overhead fixtures faded.

Valcourt's laughter boomed through the chamber. "Enough, my little friend," he said. The cat dropped to a crouch on the table, watching them impassively. Nicole stared, then glanced covertly around, seeing her amazement mirrored on the other faces.

"But you arc thinking still, parlor tricks. This man Valcourt has a remarkable way with animals: somehow he has trained this cat. So, let us hear from one of you. Miss Haverill? A simple task, please, for Lamashtu—one that can be performed here, for all of us to observe."

She looked so shaken that Nicole felt a touch of pity for her. Her expression erased any doubt that this might have been prearranged.

"My cigarettes," she said, her voice hardly above a whisper.

Almost before the words had died, the cat leaped to the floor. It trotted straight across the room, jumped to the table where Charity had left her purse, and pawed through the bag. Its head disappeared inside, then emerged with a pack of Benson & Hedges held lightly in its teeth. These it dropped politely in Charity's lap. Then it hopped back down to the floor and sat. Nicole realized that her mouth was open. As in a dream, she heard Valcourt laugh again and say:

"I apologize that she cannot light it; there are, after all, certain limits. Allow me." He stepped forward, holding out a candle. Charity stared at him as if she had never seen a human being before. Slowly, her fingers took a cigarette from the pack and raised it to her lips. With exaggerated courtesy, Valcourt lit it and returned the candle to its place.

"Now, my friends," he said. "I see that your disbelief has changed to near-panic. Take a moment to regroup. Sip your drinks, smoke your cigarettes, relax yourselves, while I provide you an entirely logical explanation of what you have just witnessed." His voice was soothing but edged with command. Numbly, Nicole raised the sherry glass to her lips and watched the others try to recover their sense of normality. She realized that her hand had been clutching her own purse, as if for flight.

"To begin with, while Lamashtu is a most intelligent being, and she understands certain patterns of human speech, she is certainly not capable of fulfilling a request as complex as Miss Haverill's. Rather, it is I who have been commanding her with my thoughts, pointing out to her the objects in question and expressing what she was to do with them.

"But even that does not penetrate to the core of the matter. To recapitulate what I have told each of you individually: What you have been conditioned from birth to think of as your mind, your 'self,' is in fact primarily a capacity for awareness. All the faculties you possess—intelligence in its various facets, emotions, sympathies—lie in realms which are, strictly speaking, outside this 'self.' These are made available to you, to a greater or lesser degree, depending on a number of factors–your nature, your upbringing, things which are determined by your previous existences as well as your present one–by entities which impinge upon you continually. It is these entities which bring you ideas themselves, from the lowliest habits to the greatest creativity. You are all familiar with the theme of an artist being visited by a muse, or a scientist being possessed of genius? Accept this literally. It is your choice to devote your energy to constructive entities, thus strengthening the range and power of your 'self,' or to give in to entities which encourage you to sloth, thus allowing that self to atrophy.

"All of these entities have a tremendous interest in your 'self': it is, quite literally, the substance on which their existence depends. In certain schools of thought– the ancient Gnostics, for instance–the unaware self was considered to be a slave to the entities, in the grip of the 'Powers and Principalities,'whereas the fully informed human turns the tables, as you say, and puts these forces to work. The truly wise man courts, and eventually masters, great intelligences.

"And this is what the uninitiated think of as magic. To the adept, it is a use of knowledge and power no more remarkable than that required to build a house or harvest a crop.

"Here, then, is the matter I wish to stress in our first meeting: that those who are possessed of this gift to any large extent–as all of you are–are bound by a law higher than any made by man, and most made in the name of so-called gods; a law that demands you to develop your precious ability. There is no accident in the universe, my friends, and that includes your presence here tonight. You have reached this point only by many lifetimes of striving, as the great philosopher Pythagoras taught, and to continue on in this most important of all studies must henceforth be your life's true aim.

"So. To bring us back to our starting point, the little demonstration you have just witnessed was simply a matter of communicating my wishes to the entities which inform the small mind of Lamashtu. The difference between myself and all of you is that I have learned to do so in such a way that they must obey me. They are my servants; not I, theirs.

"In a similar way, by performing the small exercises I gave each of you, you have begun already to command certain entities. When you speak their names, you demonstrate awareness of their existence; and this is the first step toward power over them.

"But come! I have lectured enough for one night. I can see many questions burning in your minds, but for now, I must ask your forbearance. These will be largely answered in the course of our next meetings; and when the time is right, I will gladly satisfy your curiosity as to those that remain.

"Now, let us break for a few minutes. Chat among yourselves, deepen your acquaintance. There is a minor matter I must attend to. When I return, we will begin the important business of learning to extend our power to increasingly practical ends."

Nicole watched him stride—almost sweep—from the room, noting the dignity, the grandeur, with which he carried himself. It would have seemed affected in anyone else she had ever met. The others watched him, too—still a little in shock from what they had just seen and heard, she sensed—and when he was gone, there was another awkward moment of facing one another, all uncertain of how to behave. Charity lit another cigarette; Spencer rose and paced nervously, then muttered to no one in particular:

"Left something in my car." He slipped, a little furively, out the door.

Robbie Kinsella was watching Nicole, one eyebrow raised, a bemused smile on his lips.

"Pretty impressive, huh?"

Nicole exhaled. "Either he's the king of the animal tamers or there's something to what he's saying."

As if by signal, both turned to look at Charity. She glared back defiantly.

"If you're thinking that was set up, think again. It scared me nearly to death."

"I didn't think that," Nicole said quickly.

"Never crossed my mind," Robbie agreed.

Charity's face softened. Then she leaned forward, eyes alight with excitement.

"Do you think it's true? That you can learn to make people do whatever you want?"

There was a pause.

"He kept telling me there were rules," Nicole said. Charity did not appear to hear; her gaze had turned inward, and seemed thoughtful, even smug.

Spencer Epps stepped back into the room, moving with more assurance than when he had left.

"What a place, huh?" he said. "Fountain, the works. Man is worth some money."

"Born rich, he told me," Robbie said.

"Some people have all the luck."

Nicole watched Spencer's restless gaze categorizing, quantifying, and pricing the objects in the room. She wasn't sure what she had expected in the way of other participants—people athirst for knowledge to benefit mankind? But then, she admitted, she was not exactly Mother Teresa herself.

When Valcourt reentered, they automatically took their seats, like schoolchildren. He stood before them for a moment, hands folded in his sleeves, gaze moving from face to face. Nicole swallowed, certain that her thoughts were as plain to him as a printed page. But his face was noble, kind, seemingly a little strained with effort.

"Each of you," he began abruptly, "has a particular problem foremost on his or her mind. My custom is to take these problems, one meeting at a time, and as a group, to turn our efforts toward resolving them. Although each of you is powerful alone, the combined energy of five strong wills is far more so.

"Therefore, I propose that we draw lots to see whose case we consider tonight. That person will describe to us briefly the troubling situation. Then, if we agree that action is warranted, we will turn our collective will toward a successful outcome.

"Is this acceptable to everyone?"

They exchanged nervous glances. Absurdly, Nicole felt like giggling. There was something about it that smacked of elementary school. But Valcourt's face was solemn and purposeful.

From a drawer in a heavy, ornate secretary, he took a squat vase that had a mouth just big enough for a hand to fit into. Nicole had seen too much already tonight to be surprised, and she noticed almost absently that the vase was jade and very old, chased with figures that might have been from the Arabian Night. These appeared to be involved in curious pursuits: one turbaned man was prostrating himself before an enormous jinni with folded arms, and another being borne through the air by a winged creature whose features she could not make out.

"It contains four pebbles," Valcourt said, "three white and one black." He shook it three times, the pebbles rattling within, then began at the far end, with Charity. Her bracelets clinked against the jar's lip as she reached in. The stone she withdrew was white; she grimaced, whether in disappointment or relief, Nicole could not tell. Spencer, and then Robbie, also pulled out white stones. Valcourt offered the jar to Nicole. Sure enough, the pebble was black, a hard, glittering stone shaped oddly, she realized, like the sculpture she passed downtown every day, the Banker's Heart. She forced a smile.

"Come now, Nicole," Valcourt said kindly. It was the first time tonight he had called anyone by their first name, and it made her feel a little better. "There is no need for shyness. I know your wish already, and I have assured you it is a worthy one. Share it with our other friends. You will see; we can help."

192

For several seconds, as the others' curious gazes rested on her, she hovered on the edge of standing, saying, I'm sorry, this was a mistake, I wasn't expecting to have to go public–

She sighed, took a sip of sherry, and sat back, trying to relax.

"There's this man," she began.

EIGHT

Nine days later, Saturday evening, Nicole set her table for two. The warm, rich scent of simmering wine sauce filled the apartment; she had decided, somewhat whimsically, on beef bourguignon, realizing that it had to do with the new French influence in her life. She had also bought two bottles of Saint-Emilion, although she was nervous about having too much wine around Jesse. He was due in ten minutes, and she knew that, drunk or sober, he was punctual. Hoping he would be more the second than the first, she walked to the window and stood. There, she at last allowed herself to come face to face with what she was doing, and admitted that she felt sheepish.

The others in the group had listened with interest as she haltingly told them her secret—although a faint smirk on Charity's face angered her. In a way it had seemed ludicrous, a sitcom parody of an encounter group. But Valcourt's presence, grave and stern, had dignified it.

When she had finished her explanation, she said, "It just seems so pointless—a waste of both of us. It would be different if he was interested in somebody else, or if he disliked me, or anything like that. But I know it's just because he can't let himself go." Then she sat there, feeling foolish, while Valcourt pondered.

"Do you all agree," he said at last, "that this wish of Nicole's is worthy?"

The two men nodded, Spencer without hesitation, Robbie a little less certainly. Charity, still smirking, said, "Of course."

"I, too," said Valcourt. "Then let us see if we can help her . . . bring this man to his senses." Nicole laughed, and the tension broke. "Remember," Valcourt said, one finger raised, "we cannot force–only suggest. Engage his attention in a way that has perhaps escaped him thus far."

"I wouldn't want to force him," she said quietly.

Valcourt nodded with approval. "Tell me, Nicole: Do you know the term *fascination?*"

"I know what the word means," she said uncertainly.

"Not as it is commonly used. I am speaking of a technique long known to the wise. In old times, it was associated with witchcraft, but in reality it is only another facet of natural power, one which everyone attempts to use to some degree, but which few develop enough to be truly effective. Great actors and orators, for instance, whether or not they are aware of it, are in truth applying this ability when they captivate an audience. It is an important component of what we call charisma.

"Now–you must arrange to be alone with this man, in a suitably romantic setting. As your evening progresses, you will begin at some point to *fascinate* him.

195

This is simply a matter of holding his attention and concentrating on your desire. In order to keep his gaze fixed on you, it is useful to employ a visual charm of some sort—a necklace with a pendant of soft-colored stone, or burnished metal, is ideal. Have you such an ornament?"

She nodded. "A beautiful amethyst on a gold chain. It was my grandmother's; she gave it to me because it matched my eyes."

"Perfect. Sit close to him, toy with the necklace to hold his gaze, and concentrate your will upon him. Make him see how desirable you are, both in your physical person and in your heart. If you do this properly, he will be *fascinated,* and your good sense of yourself will be communicated to him directly, in a far more powerful way than mere words or gestures could do. This is, you see, a matter essentially the same as my communication with Lamashtu: contacting the intelligences that inform this man's mind and commanding them to present to him your feelings.

"After that, of course, it is up to him."

She laughed suddenly, blushing. "I'm sorry," she said, putting her hands to her face. "It seems—I don't know—like a trick or something. Like hypnosis."

Valcourt's face was stern. "That is an attitude you must not allow yourself if you expect to liberate your true power. At heart, it is an indulgence, an attempt by certain of your own informing entities to weaken you. Remember, these wish to keep you in bondage and will use every means to dissuade you from gaining control over them.

"No, Nicole, it is not a 'trick.' It is only an intensification of what every person seeks to do in charming a lover. Do you not always wear your best clothes in such a situation, take the greatest care with your appearance, present yourself as attractively as possible? Fascination is nothing but an amplification of this: a presentation of yourself with power. Nor is it merely physical seduction. You are showing him your heart, not your body.

"Finally, remember that the choice is ultimately his. You are in no way forcing him."

In the silence that followed, she tried again to order her confused thoughts and emotions. What Valcourt said seemed perfectly sensible. What was it in her that seemed to shake its head in warning? The voice of weakness, trying to hold her back, just as he warned? She exhaled, then looked at the others, smiling timidly.

"Okay. I'll try it. I mean, what have I got to lose?"

"Speak with strength," Valcourt murmured reprovingly. "Apathy will weaken, even harm you.

"Now, my friends, you will come to understand that ceremonies of any sort are largely for show, a mark of exoteric religion. They impress the common man, who is at heart a spiritual primitive, awed by the trappings of ritual. As you progress in power, you will require such intermediary procedures less and less, and begin to communicate directly with the entities you wish to command.

"But in the early stages, ceremonies are useful for several reasons. They attract the entities' attention, and they provide a focal point for the collective will of the participants.

"Therefore, let us perform a brief and simple ritual for Nicole's success. Next month when we meet, she will report to us whatever results she may have had; and we will take the case of the next member to draw the black stone."

He turned all of the lights off, leaving only the candles, then lit an incense burner. In a few seconds, the room was filled with a harsh but not unpleasant scent: anise, she thought, mixed with what might have been menthol or camphor.

"Rise, then," Valcourt said, "and let us arrange ourselves around Nicole."

They stood, the four of them in a square surrounding her.

"Now join your hands in this way." He demonstrated a peculiar grip of intertwined fingers. It took them a moment to get it right, and though he coached patiently, both his voice and manner had become charged with command. When he was satisfied, he said to her:

"Place your own hands over your heart, and concentrate on the object of your desire."

Eyes closed, hardly breathing, feeling like a complete fool, she nonetheless tried to bring Jesse's face to mind. It came readily, with startling clarity, almost as if she were actually seeing him.

"If you will to aid our sister Nicole in attaining her most worthy desire," she heard Valcourt say, "repeat the words, *I so choose.*"

Haltingly, each spoke the words. Valcourt did not release them. Instead, he began to speak in a language that sounded vaguely to Nicole like the name of her guardian angel: a rhythmic chant of strange, harsh, but flowing syllables. Dim, haunting images that seemed somehow to correspond to the sounds flitted through her mind.

The chant lasted less than half a minute. Then Valcourt disengaged his hands and stepped back, smiling.

"The entities are alerted," he told them. "Now, Nicole, at some point while you are fascinating him, you must distract his attention away from you and breathe on him, without his notice. After that, it is up to you."

Abruptly, he clapped his hands. The door opened, and Alysse appeared to clear away the glasses and tea-cups. Nicole caught a glimpse of Robbie's face. He was staring at nothing, eyes thoughtful.

"Well, my friends," Valcourt said. "I thank you for coming and bid you a safe journey home. Before you go, I must ask you again to keep to yourselves the precise nature of our activities. One of history's great lessons is the suppression of esoteric knowledge by the orthodox, often in a most vicious fashion. The search for that which lies above the ordinary breeds hatred, jealousy, and fear among those who themselves do not dare attempt it. And while there is no longer an Inquisition"–he smiled strangely, baring his teeth–"you will find that even those closest to you are likely to react with suspicion, thus making your progress very difficult.

"Meantime, continue to practice your exercises, and take a moment each time to wish powerfully for Nicole's success. Think on all I have told you; you will find that your confusion will begin to sort itself out. Its source is, after all, the very forces you are learning to command."

He walked them to the door and stood on the porch as they separated to their cars. It was nearly dark now;

the house and fountain were lit by strange, smoky lights. As Nicole opened the Celica's door, still feeling half in a dream, he called her name.

"Power has consequences," he said. "What you make use of, you must be responsible for."

That was her last firm image of the night: the powerful figure with the black eyepatch and robe standing on the shadowed porch.

The next day, before she could decide she was simply insane and lose her nerve, she had marched up to Jesse's and told him firmly that she owed him a dinner for all the time he had spent with Tom Junior, and that it would be a week from Saturday; no excuses were acceptable. Then she had gone back downstairs to her empty apartment to try to catch up on office work—and spend a long evening with the feelings of loneliness, desire, and absurdity warring within her.

And now here she was, dressed in a silk blouse and skirt of a violet color a little lighter than the amethyst, and new, expensive underwear that all together would practically fit in a bottlecap, with just a touch of Joy at the pulse points of her throat and wrists—and the pendant resting between her breasts. During the week, she had managed to keep the matter from her mind, submerging herself in work—except during the moments of magic each night when, alone in her darkened bedroom, she slipped out of her robe and stood in the glow of the window, murmuring the syllables of her guardian angel's name.

At those times, it had not seemed crazy at all.

A light tap came at the door. She breathed deeply and went to answer.

He was wearing clean, faded blue jeans and a light gray button-down oxford cloth shirt, and he carried a large cone of folded green tissue that could only hold flowers. Her heart rose, but when she saw his eyes, kind but distant, she realized that, as usual, he was only being polite. At least if he had been drinking, it did not show.

"Hey," he said. He leaned forward and gave her a brotherly kiss on the cheek; she closed her eyes briefly in exasperation, but was bright-eyed and smiling when he stepped back and held out the flowers.

"For me?" she said, with mock shyness.

"Prettiest girl I know." He strolled inside and stood with his thumbs hooked in his belt, nose twitching. "Smells like rich people's food, Nicole."

Usually his banter kept her off balance and a little chagrined; she suspected it was another distancing technique. She had already decided that tonight, she was going to give it right back.

"Roadkill in wine," she said, and went into the kitchen to get a vase for the flowers. "I don't suppose you want a drink."

"Me?"

She returned with the vase and an unopened bottle of Glenlivet Scotch. His eyebrows rose.

"If you're going to poison yourself, you might as well do it with class," she said. "Pour me one, too, on the rocks."

"Un-uh, no watering this stuff," he said, shaking his head.

201

"You're the expert."

While Jesse uncapped the bottle and poured, she snipped the stems of the roses with a scissors, wondering if he was as aware of her physical closeness as she was of his.

They touched glasses, and she met those maddeningly kind eyes with her own as she sipped the golden Scotch. She hardly ever drank the stuff, and at first it seemed strange and harsh; then the burning subsided into an increasingly sweeter sensation in her mouth and throat. Maybe there was something to it after all.

"Are you starving?" she said.

"I can wait."

"Then come sit a minute."

He finished the liquor in his glass and poured another; she noticed silently that it was bigger than the first. He saw her watching and smiled.

"You know how to show a guy a good time, Nicole."

You ain't seen nothing yet, she thought. She sat at the far end of the couch, giving him plenty of room. He sat as she had expected: one leg pulled up, half-facing her.

"So tell me about work," she said.

"What's to tell? Same old bullshit. Nail them together, stand them up. Nature'll pull them down soon enough. How's the ambulance-chasing scene?"

"Great," she said–teasing with an edge. The closest thing to an argument he had ever allowed had come shortly after they met, when he made clear his contempt for what he called "the lawyer-insurance complex."

"Some clumsy fucker cracks his big toe falling out of a truck because he's half in the bag, and he hires you guys to sue the contractor who put in the sidewalk for ten million bucks so he'll never have to work again, and the lawyers get half of it and Uncle gets most of the rest and the insurance companies just raise their rates and pass it on to everybody else."

She had replied with a heat that had surprised her: "Yeah, and then there are the ones you don't see, who get their arm ripped off or their back crushed by a machine that's malfunctioning because the employer's too cheap to maintain it, and they come to in the hospital and find out they're not just physically ruined, but they've lost their job and pension and whatever else the company can get away with, too. Those people come to us to try to get enough money to keep their kids from starving. We all make mistakes every day. Why should their lives be wrecked because they were unluckier than most of us?" She had paused, then said, "You should talk, Jesse, the kind of work you do. It could be you some day."

His eyes had changed, and she had not been sure whether she should have said what she had. But he had answered only:

"It could at that," and they had dropped it.

"They're crashing and burning all over the city," she said now. "Brisbane was very hot this week—an oil truck explosion and two ironworkers diving off a collapsing scaffold."

"Bet the lawyers were there before they hit the ground."

"Damn right. It's easier to get them to sign contracts when they can't walk away."

He laughed, and she felt herself starting to relax into the game. She almost decided to abandon her project–let the evening take its natural course.

But then he held up his empty glass and said, "Ready?" and after she shook her head–her own drink was hardly touched–and he had poured, she saw with alarm that the bottle was already a good quarter gone.

If she was going to do this, it would have to be soon.

The light outside was fading–she had deliberately set the invitation for eight–and she rose to light the candles on the table. In the process, she unobtrusively set her drink down near his end of the couch. Them she sat a little closer to him.

He began to tell a story–dutifully, she sensed, playing the guest–about something that had happened on a job site earlier in the week. Hardly hearing him, she moved her fingers to her throat with seeming non-chalance, freeing the amethyst and toying with it. It was a beautiful stone, a large oval that glowed a deep, warm violet with the candles' flame. I am absolutely crazy, she thought fleetingly, and steeled herself to concentrate. The amethyst turned and flashed; the candles picked out highlights in the amber Scotch; and Nicole leaned imperceptibly closer, holding his gaze.

You want me, my friend, she thought, like you have never wanted anything before, and you are going to realize it any second now.

With growing amazement, she watched his eyes, fixed on the stone, become puzzled, and heard his words slow. Bracing herself, she said:

"Can you reach my drink?" and pointed past him.

Jesse swiveled. As he stretched to reach it, his back to her, she leaned forward and gently exhaled on the nape of his neck.

He handed her the glass, his gaze returning to the stone. Sipping the warming liquor, she watched his eyes and waited.

Of course, he'd seen the whole thing coming–the invite a week in advance, the kid gone–and when she opened the door, the pretty new outfit and smell of rich cooking came as no surprise.

The Glenlivet, however, he had not expected.

He'd gone to some trouble himself, dressing neatly, keeping the lid on his juice intake. On a whim, he'd even stopped by one of the flower vendors on Nineteenth Avenue and picked up a dozen roses. She was a good lady; she deserved nice treatment. He just hoped she wouldn't take it wrong. Her eyes went bright with pleasure when she saw the flowers, and he smiled in spite of his confirmed suspicion that they had been a tactical error.

It was all very pleasant, no doubt about that: the company of a smart, pretty woman; somebody cooking besides himself; dishes that contained spices other than salt and pepper; even just the opportunity to talk to someone about anything more abstract than lumber and tools. It was the kind of thing that would be easy to get used to—for a while.

But then there you'd be, when that ugly black dog in your mind came sniffing around, lifting his leg on everything good in your life. And there was nothing you could do but go with him, because for some reason you couldn't understand, he had it over on you. Only there'd be somebody else involved, somebody who was going to be extremely unhappy when you starred to do that fade. And there was no explaining it and no changing it. He had done it enough times to know.

Still, this was very pleasant.

He poured another drink, a good stiff one, and returned to the couch, noting with amusement and chagrin that the scene was set: candles lit, Nicole sitting a little closer, leaning forward, fingers calling attention to her cleavage as she played with her necklace. Resignedly, he decided it was time for The Rap.

The way The Rap went down, you kissed a couple of times, then you took her hands and sat back and explained that you really cared for her, but you just didn't feel it would be fair to let this go any further right now because your emotions were all fucked up, and so on—you had to sort of adjust it to the situation. And it was all more or less true and it always worked, because it gave the message that you were concerned about her feelings, which was also true, although the main purpose was to derail the momentum that was gathering.

From there it was fairly cut and dried. You got up, smiling ruefully, and poured another drink, and then maybe stood looking out the window. She'd come to stand beside you, and you'd kiss a couple more times, but it would be okay now; she'd know it wasn't going to happen tonight. Pretty soon she'd be in the kitchen getting dinner on the table and asking you questions to try to figure out the cause of your fucked-upness: Vietnam? a bad love affair?–which translated as her trying to figure out a way around it. And you'd toss the salad or set the table and have a few more drinks while this round of sparring went on, and then you'd eat, and then there would be only one more polite interval until you could plead fatigue and split, leaving her feeling pleasantly confused because you hadn't jumped her even when she'd offered.

After that it was a matter of seeing to it that the situation did not arise again.

He sat, mentally beginning his lead-in: How you getting along without Tommy to take care of you? Tough having him gone, huh. Don't see my own girls much; my ex-wife spits on the floor every time my name comes up. Guess I wasn't much of a husband. Significant pause.

Nicole was gazing at him intently, her eyes dark and soft in the candlelight, her fingers playing with the glowing purple stone. He was not usually much for noticing jewelry, but this caught his attention.

"Pretty," he said. "An amethyst?"

She nodded slowly, her eyes never leaving his face. It should have made him uncomfortable, that kind of gaze–it was just the sort of thing he wanted to avoid–but the stone was like a magnet. Wrong, Jess, he thought distractedly: mistake. He could not seem to break the contact.

Then she said, "Can you reach my drink?" and pointed behind him. Released by her gesture, he turned, and as his fingers touched the glass, there came a sudden, sweet, soft explosion that seemed to fill his head with light.

With astonishing clarity, he began to see a part of his own being that he had long ago hidden away from himself. Like tumblers clicking in an infinite series of locks, layer after layer of disappointment, frustration, violence, anger, and heartache peeled away from the core they had guarded: a core that was unbearably tender but demanded to be touched, that trembled with fear and longing, that had been locked inside a prison of denial for a length of time beyond his recall, but that was suddenly coming free again like a flame of raw need:

Free to fly to, and intertwine with, the counterpart that waited shyly, eyes fixed on his.

Fingers touched, then lips; and some hauntingly distant part of his mind understood for the first time ever this thing that demanded to be expressed with flesh and blood: infinitely precious, powerful, and complex, vastly beyond mere lust—the mysterious union of halves that had been separated in the unknowable past.

As she sank beneath him, it seemed he could hear voices singing a strange, discordant hymn of celebration, in her heart as well as his own.

PART TWO

Enemy of the human race! Source of death!
Robber of life! Twister of justice! Root of evil!
Warp of vices! Seducer of men! Traitor of
nations! Inciter of jealousy! Originator of greed!
Cause of discord! Creator of agony!

The Roman Ritual Of Exorcism

NINE

In the city of Nice, on the long sidewalk called the Promenade des Anglais that fronts the Mediterranean Sea, a dignified couple strolled through the midafternoon, talking quietly with each other. The woman– handsome, strongly built, with gray-streaked black hair and a dark, aquiline face–walked with a slight limp and held firmly to her husband's arm. He was a lean man of perhaps fifty, with sharp, pleasant features that seemed clouded by anxiety or anger. Frequently, he would bend close to hear one of her murmured comments, consider her words, then nod or say something in reply.

To other passersby, they were an affluent married couple discussing a matter of some importance: the marriage of a daughter, perhaps, or the settling of an estate. In fact, the matter that troubled Mélusine and Roger Devarre would have caused most eavesdroppers to decide immediately that the pair was insane.

"He could be anywhere," she said wearily. "Africa, Indochina–thousands of people dying violently every day, and no one pays attention."

"At least we don't have to go back to Germany."

She shrugged. "Until the next one comes along. The point is, it's simply hopeless."

Though Devarre said nothing, he silently agreed. For all they knew, the man they sought–or rather, the spirit of a man who had physically perished nearly seven centuries before–might have taken, by now, an altogether different shape than the one they knew.

"I couldn't stand any more anyway," Mélusine said, tossing her head. "They think we're ghouls."

"One can hardly blame them," her husband pointed out.

"Them" referred to the police of several European nations, whom the Devarres had contacted over the past months, seeking permission to interview the perpetrators of mass or particularly grotesque murders–specifically, those that had involved the shedding of large amounts of blood. Flimsy though the hope had been of locating Guilhem de Courdeval in this way, and though the business itself had been uniformly unpleasant and sometimes sickening, any course of action had seemed preferable to staying home in the village of Saint-Bertrand-sur-Seyre, in the wake of events that had profoundly damaged and nearly destroyed their lives, waiting helplessly to see if anything more would happen-

If Courdeval would return to finish what he had begun.

Devarre, for the first time in his life, had developed migraine headaches. They were rooted in fear for his wife. A physician by training, he had never put any credence in the supernatural–until the night the previous

212

autumn when he had watched the eviscerated corpse of a woman walk toward Mélusine with the very nearly fulfilled intent of murdering her.

Since then, he had turned his intellect to the study of arcana in general–he had learned, among other things, that the practice of necromancy, involving the animation of corpses, was held to have been widespread in past centuries–and to the papers left by the American, John McTell, in particular. Most of the former was nonsense; he saved and organized the occasional bits that had the ring of truth. But McTell's papers included an English translation of much of Courdeval's grimoire, and this produced an unpleasant impression of ruthless honesty in all of the savage details it described.

The only man who might have shed more light on the origins of the mystery, the priest Etien Boudrie, was in a coma that was by all indications permanent. But McTell's papers, together with Mélusine's intuitions and the events themselves of what they had come to call *that night,* allowed them to piece together an account. Courdeval's disembodied spirit, inexplicably quickened after centuries of quiet, had manipulated McTell into performing a ritual that brought about his own possession. The victim whose blood had provided the arcane currency for the ceremony was a young woman named Alysse, whom Mélusine had loved as a daughter. Neither her body nor any sign of McTell had ever been found. While both were still officially listed as missing, the police had determined that the sheer quantity of blood shed–blood that could only have been Alysse's–left no possibility of her having survived.

213

They were correct, she was dead. Mélusine had seen her corpse. But she had not told that to the police, nor that the body had been walking.

To ease the intolerable strain of waiting like tethered bait, Roger Devarre had proposed pursuing the tiny hope that Courdeval, indulging his blood lust, would make a mistake—perhaps through lack of familiarity with the modern world—that might bring him to justice. Devarre had been able to claim professional interest in the psychopathology of the murder cases, purportedly with the aim of writing a book.

As to what to do with Courdeval if they did find him: Devarre had spent considerable time and care constructing a small compartment in the underbody of their Citröen, in which he carried a light, flat 7-mm Beretta automatic. This had sufficed to get the weapon through customs—they were not the sort of people to be subjected to rigorous searches—and in conscious irony, he carried it, concealed in the small of his back, into each police station they entered: prepared to shoot John McTell on sight. In what smacked grimly of a suicide pact, he and Mélusine had agreed that he would destroy McTell's body, even at the price of prison or death. Her task, the far more frightening and difficult one, would be to then send the spirit to rest—this time, forever.

In any case, the process itself had quickly become too unpleasant to bear. The contempt of law enforcement officials—the innuendoes that the Devarres were really nothing but sick curiosity seekers—had in most cases been thinly veiled. The past day, in Munich, they had seen a butcher's apprentice who was suspected of having dismembered and partly consumed upward of six people during the past several months. It was impossible to say which had been worse, the sullen, vicious, mentally deficient butcher or his guardians: smug, heavy-faced men in greatcoats and boots and leather harnesses, for all the world like modern Nazis. Under the commandant's persistent, insinuating questions–"And does this *book* of yours have a publisher, Herr Doktor?"–Devarre had at last declared angrily:

"You're right, I'm not writing any damned book. We're looking for the ghost of a medieval sorcerer." They were gone from Munich within the hour, and he had insisted on stopping in Nice for a few days' rest before returning to their empty house and quiet village, in the hopes that Mélusine's heart would lighten. About himself, he was not much concerned. It was she who was the spirit's enemy.

But she was right: the pretense was over. Devarre recalled with loathing the young butcher's flat, empty eyes, lit only occasionally by cunning. Clearly, the evil that possessed him was of a subhuman, rather than superhuman, kind–nothing like the dangerous, icy brilliance and power that moved Courdeval. And while their list of prospects, gleaned from the newspapers of several nations, grew longer almost daily, their efforts were pebbles flung at the moon.

They had discussed other possibilities: consulting occultists in Paris or London, in another thin hope of aid in locating Courdeval; even leaving Saint-Bertrand and France forever, to live out their remaining years in some obscure spot. But in truth, they both knew well that if he so desired, he would find them wherever they went.

They paused in their walk, gazing out over the pebbled beach, packed shoulder to shoulder with gleaming, bronzed flesh as the holiday season began in earnest. Vendors and renters of *cabanes* were doing a thriving business; the air hummed with talk, laughter, and the sound of radios; and the afternoon's heat seemed heightened by the bare-breasted girls and taut-buttocked young men, sunning themselves in the manner of reptiles and eyeing each other lazily from behind dark glasses.

"So what now?" Devarre said.

She sighed. "Take me home, *mon cher.*"

His mouth opened to protest–he had rented an oceanfront room at the famous Negresco, made reservations for a five-star dinner–but she touched her forefinger to his lips and kissed his check.

"*Je t'adore,*" she said.

He nodded, to himself rather than her, and they turned and began their slow, steady walk back to the hotel to pick up their luggage and car. After twenty-five years, he was still astonished each time she told him all the many things that could not be said–Thank you, I know you're trying to cheer me, but we are both beyond cheering and beyond the illusion of safety, and at home, at least, we stand on familiar ground–all in a few words that seemed outwardly to have nothing to do with the matter at hand.

In the comfort of her own kitchen, Mélusine cleared away the remains of the meal she had prepared–steaks, salad, *pommes frites*–while water heated for coffee. The drive from Nice had taken a little over three hours; the roads were heavily traveled this time of year, and Devarre was a careful driver, even inclined to stodginess–the result of his years of seeing accident victims come into emergency rooms.

It was good to be home. If only she could forget why they had left in the first place.

She took the coffeepot into the parlor, where her husband was sitting on the couch, looking rumpled, paging distractedly through one of several books on the occult that littered the table before him. A feeling close to pity rose in her; the answer, if there was one, would not be found in any book. But at least his new studies kept him occupied–he would not have been able to bear idleness–and so she said nothing. Up until the previous fall–before *that night*–he had devoted much of his considerable energy to painting; while he admitted cheerfully that he was quite untalented, his enthusiasm had been great. The few sketches he had tried since then showed remarkable improvement in technical terms; but a dark, sinister element previously lacking not just in his art but in his character had crept in. With Mélusine's unspoken approval, he had locked away his easels and paints in the spare room of his office, where he now went only as often as was necessary to fulfill his minimal duties as Saint-Bertrand's only physician.

He accepted the coffee with a murmur of thanks. "Join me for a brandy?"

"I think not," she said. "I have letters to write. Are you finding anything interesting?"

"Yes, very much so. Here's a recipe to become the *loup-garou*. One needs only a belt of wolf skin, certain herbs, an ointment made from a dead baby, and a graveyard to prance around in. One must be careful, though: there's a story, recorded as fact, about a hunter who was attacked by such a beast and managed to hack off one of its paws. When he showed it to a friend, they saw that it had turned into a woman's hand, wearing a familiar ring. Sure enough, he returned home to find his wife bandaging the bleeding stump of her arm." He gazed significantly at Mélusine over the tops of his glasses.

"And what happened to the woman?"

"Denounced, tortured, and burned, of course. What else? One is only left to wonder whether the husband was more outraged by her witchery or by her choosing him for a snack."

"Perhaps it was an ultimate expression of love."

"More likely, if there's any truth to the story at all, the whole werewolf business was fabricated by the husband to get rid of a wife he no longer wanted," he said, his thin glaze of humor evaporating. "That seems to have been a common enough motive for many of the witch accusations, in the days before divorce was readily obtainable. Or at least, that's what I would have assumed automatically before—"

There was no need to finish the sentence.

"That's the trouble," he said, gesturing in frustration at the books before him. "One knows it's all hocus-pocus and gibberish. It simply has to be. And yet, when one's seen what you and I have, a whole new level of possibility enters in. We know what Courdeval was capable of; and thus, I have to start wondering: Of all the violence in history I used to dismiss outright as the product of barbaric superstition, of all the thousands who were tormented for witchcraft or sorcery or being in league with the devil—how much of it was real?"

"All or none, it's the same to us," she said. "What we face is real."

She took her coffee and went to the stairs, hearing him mutter, "What happened to the days when I was the practical one in this house?" and climbed, holding the railing, favoring her weaker leg. At the top she paused.

In fact, she had no intention of writing letters. A different motive had underlain her earlier haste to return home. But now that the moment was here, memories stopped her.

For the past days, she had been aware of unrest—a disturbance in an unseen realm to which she mysteriously had access. That access stemmed from a gift that had been hers from birth—a kind of second sight—although since the doings of that night, she had many times thought *curse* was a better word. If she had been an ordinary woman—if she had not tuned in, like a radio receiver, to the evil that was growing around the village last fall—then the lives of herself, her husband, and probably Etien Boudrie would have gone on much as before.

It would be different, Mélusine thought, if she could have prevented Alysse's death—if she could have prevented any of what had been unleashed. But as far as she could tell, her attempt to intervene had only broadened the suffering, costing Boudrie his sanity and making her and her husband's lives miserable. She was still just as helpless as she had been when, before her eyes, Courdeval had commanded the dead to walk.

And now Alysse–for Mélusine was certain that the spirit she sensed was hers–was troubled again, somewhere. She had loved the girl dearly, shared with her a psychic bond stronger than with her own children; and she recognized the faint inner signals, the soundless whispers and little tugs at her consciousness during moments when she was still. She had felt the same stirrings before and after that night, beginning as a sense of the girl's bewilderment as she came under Courdeval's influence; sharpening suddenly into anguish that went on for weeks after her death; and then dimming into an uneasy peace, a sleep too close to the surface, through the next months. But back then, Mélusine had not made the necessary connections until it was too late.

And if it were true–if the girl had been tom again from the sleep that Mélusine wanted to believe she had found–was there anything at all to be done about it? Or was this just more meddling that was likely to cause grief?

Slowly, she limped down the hallway to the attic stairs. She had not touched her aunt Mathilde's amulet since last fall; she had found an endless supply of excuses not to even return to the attic where it was kept. It was impossible to say which had been worse: the terrifying moments in which the disembodied Courdeval had spoken to her through the ancient amulet, or the long, agonizing months since, realizing that if she had been able to decipher the messages and had acted more swiftly and surely, Alysse might have lived.

Three questions Mélusine had asked, three cryptic answers received, before an unleashed wave of menace had sent her stumbling down the stairs:

Come, spirit, why do you trouble us?
Sins of the fathers.
What do you want?
Blood of a flower.
Who are you?
The drowned man.

The first and third remained obscure, but there was no mistaking the second. Alysse, whose name contained the word lily, had indeed forfeited her blood.

And the other two replies? The priest Boudrie had realized something that he had insisted on keeping to himself until he knew more. Therein perhaps lay the puzzle's origins, if not its solution. But with Boudrie effectively dead, what hope was there of knowing?

Only one, and the possibility was faint and desperate: that the restless spirit troubling her now would communicate with her as had Courdeval.

And what, whispered a malicious voice in her mind, if it was really *him* again? She had no idea where, or even who, he might be by now. If he had taken McTell's body, what was to prevent him from taking another? How far did his powers extend? What if this was the beginning of another game of cat and mouse, or another masterful ruse—an attempt to frighten her to madness, perhaps to send her to the realm where Boudrie endured his living death: to put an end to whatever paltry threat she might present to Guilhem de Courdeval, thus virtually assuring his immortal presence on earth—

And sealing her own fate for the rest of time.

Timidly, she reached for the door to the attic stairs. A well of darkness opened before her. She stood, understanding as never before the feelings of those approaching again the object of their fear after having fallen from a height or survived a wreck. Her groping hand found the switch, lighting a single bulb near the center of the room above. The glow was dim, muffled by dust and cobwebs.

But this was madness. Her husband was just downstairs. She had only to explain her plan have him fetch the amulet back down to the parlor, and perform the rite in his presence.

Only she was certain that the presence of another, while benign and comforting, would distract.

Roger will come running if I scream, she reminded herself fiercely, then remembered that last time, she had stood for many seconds, paralyzed by fear, at Courdeval's mercy.

She began to climb.

The tangle of cobwebs had become a jungle, and a sense of shame that she had let the place go so badly cut through her fear, helping her to proceed. She brushed the webs aside, picking her way determinedly through the stored furniture. Her footfalls thumped softly and unevenly on the wooden floor. Through dust-streaked windows, she could see that twilight was fading.

The little wooden box was right where she had left it, resting on a table. It had gathered dust over the months, and she rubbed it quickly with her sleeve until the dark reddish wood shone in the dim light–a gesture that, she realized distantly, was propitiatory. As she opened the lid, she saw that the thin silver chain and amulet lay twisted carelessly just as she had dropped them in her panicked flight. For the better part of a minute, she stared at them. Slowly, nerves tingling with the memory of the current that had jolted her into helpless terror, she touched the chain. It was cool and inert, the amulet a solid weight. Reluctantly, she let her eyes close, trying to feel if something hovered in ambush.

The sense of unrest was clearer now, seeming to focus with the amulet in her fingers–to become more of a discrete presence. She tested and probed, fearful of what might be hiding behind it. But there was only a gentle, distant grief, like the faint fluttering of a moth against a window. Sorrow answered in her own heart, finally outweighing her fear. She inhaled deeply, opened her eyes, and braced her elbows on the table. The amulet hung just above the silver dish that had letters chased around its rim. It twirled slowly. Mélusine waited until it came to rest at the dish's center.

Then she whispered, "Is it you, *chérie?*"

For seconds, nothing happened. The faint scurrying of tiny feet distracted her: mice in the house, more shameful neglect on her part.

Then the tugging began, so faint and soft she could hardly be sure she felt it. A pause; then again, this time unmistakable. The amulet swung to one of the two symbols that divided the dish into poles: the Latin word *ita,* "yes."

Mélusine closed her eyes briefly.

"Where are you?" she breathed.

Slowly, after a pause, the amulet moved. She sensed it was a painful, labored response; it seemed to take minutes before the amulet hung motionless again at the dish's center. The seven letters had spelled *pas dire,* "cannot say"–and Mélusine understood abruptly, almost with panic, that this was not an entity like Courdeval, powerful enough to play games. This spirit was weak, barely sustaining this contact, and able to do so only because it was in great distress. Her questions must be precise. And this time she must be certain to understand.

"How can we help?"

Dragging with perceptibly more effort, the amulet spelled *père,* "father."

Mélusine hissed in frustration. It meant nothing; Alysse was an orphan. Her thoughts whirled, seeking the proper things to ask, as she felt the contact fading. In desperation, she blurted:

"Tell me what I must know!"

With an effort so pained it made her want to cry out, the amulet reached three letters–and then, as cleanly as if the contact had been severed by a knife, it was gone, leaving only the haunting sense of sorrow that had accompanied her for days.

The letters were L-I-V. They meant nothing.

"You fool," she told herself with weary contempt. She had exhausted the spirit's power without having properly prepared. Who knew if it would be able to return with enough force to tell her more?

Father. Liv. What could be made of that?

224

She coiled the chain back in the dish, closed the box, and put it back on a shelf, almost forgetting to be relieved that this time, at least, she had not awakened something that would pursue her down the stairs.

Back on the second-story landing, she switched off the attic light and closed the door, then stood pondering. There was a connection, vague and elusive, flitting in her mind like a bat. *Liv. Father–*

Then she had it: the first message from Courdeval. *Come, spirit, why do you trouble us?*

Sins of the fathers.

Coincidence, possibly–just as it was possible that her subconscious had manufactured the entire experience out of guilt, coupled with the desire to believe that somewhere, in some way, Alysse yet lived.

But Mélusine knew better, knew the difference between wish fulfillment and genuine contact with the world beyond the veil. If her own inner certainty was not enough, there was no denying the grim fulfillment of her earlier visions.

And if there was a connection, a clue that involved a father, how to go about establishing it? To begin with, whose father? Logic indicated that Alysse was the obvious choice, except that her mother had died when she was five and her father was unknown. Or at least, so the girl had been brought up to believe.

But everyone has a father, Mélusine found herself thinking, whether or not they knew him. The question was, did anyone still live who would remember Alysse's?

There was one possibility, a thin one, like all of the others, but it was a place to start. Alysse's aunt and guardian, Amalie Perrin, lived only a few blocks away.

Questioning her would be extremely touchy. It was the old woman's inexplicable illness that had first put Alysse into contact with McTell–an illness that, Mélusine was now certain, had been caused by Courdeval in order to do precisely that–and it was understood, though never voiced, that this had led indirectly to the girl's death. Immediately afterward, Mlle. Perrin had made a full and equally inexplicable recovery. Though there could not in truth be even a shadow of blame, Mélusine knew the poor woman was racked by guilt. She shrugged. The importance of the matter overrode politeness. If the questions produced nothing, then that was that; she could spend the rest of her life wondering what *liv* meant.

A glance at her wristwatch told her it was just after eight, not too late for a visit. Planning, she limped back down the stairs.

Amalie Perrin answered the Devarres' knock with surprise clear upon her face.

"But come in," she said and backed away, gesturing them to chairs. "I'll make tea."

Mélusine caught her husband's resigned expression–sitting in this musty parlor sipping tea was a ritual he had been through too many times during the old woman's illness.

She smiled sweetly at him and said, "That would be lovely."

They sat. The house had changed little in the months since she had last been inside it–visited was not quite the right word–but while then it had been filled with desperate activity, tonight it had a hollowness she could almost touch. Mlle. Perrin, too, was subtly different: one of those women who seemed destined for spinsterhood, she had lived and worked with dignity and energy. But as Mélusine watched her through the open kitchen door, she thought the little woman looked frail, aged, exhausted. To the best of Mélusine's knowledge, she had no idea of what had actually happened to her niece.

She returned with a tray of teacups and lemony cakes. Mélusine watched her husband dutifully accept one of each, and she did the same, shrugging inwardly at the realization that on top of her after-dinner coffee, the caffeine would keep her awake. She had been sleeping poorly anyway.

"You're feeling well?" Devarre said to Mlle. Perrin. "Watching your diet?"

She assured him she was, and for a few minutes the conversation centered around her recovered health. When a pause came, she looked down into her teacup, her shoulders tensed, waiting; Mélusine realized she must have understood immediately that this was not just a friendly visit.

"I have something to ask you which you may not want to answer," she said gently. "It isn't frivolous, or out of curiosity. I can't really explain any more, except that anything you can tell us may be of great help."

"About Alysse?" Mlle Perrin said, without looking up.

"Yes."

Her face lifted, her eyes pained and defiant. "What could help her?"

"Please," Devarre said. "Trust us."

The old woman's gaze shifted from one face to the other, her mouth turned down bitterly. Then her shoulders lifted.

"What is it you want to know?"

"Her father," Mélusine said. "Do you know who he was?"

Mlle. Perrin's mouth tightened. "How could that help?"

"I don't exactly know yet," Mélusine said truthfully.

"I won't have you dragging up dirt for a scandal." Abruptly, Mlle. Perrin stood. Her voice was shrill and accusing. "That's the way of you city people. Here, we only want to let the dead rest."

Mélusine winced at the wearying, half-expected onslaught of peasant suspicion, which could turn instantly and absurdly on the doctor who had nursed her through her sickness without a franc of payment.

"That's just the point," she said. "Alysse is not resting."

"Are you telling me she's alive?" The scorn in the old woman's voice did not mask a sudden note of hope.

Mélusine caught her husband's wry gaze and wished she had phrased the words differently.

"No, mademoiselle," she said. "Alysse is not alive."

"Then how would you know about her—her state?"

The scorn had won out, and Devarre stood too.

228

"She knows," he said, with a hard edge Mélusine rarely heard. "My wife is *clairvoyante,* mademoiselle, you have my word. In any case, before you insult her, I ask you to remember that she treated Alysse as a daughter–and that during your own troubles, we spared no effort to aid you."

For a few seconds, Mélusine thought the flushed, glittering-eyed woman would hiss like a viper and demand they leave her house. But then her hands went to her face, and she sank into her chair. She took out a handkerchief and patted her eyes.

"It's been very hard," she said thickly. "So lonely. The way people look at me–"

Mélusine knelt beside her and touched her knee.

"You're imagining," she said reassuringly, although it was probably true. In a place like Saint-Bertrand, the blame for any disaster had to be attached to someone, with or without reason; and once it was, it remained with that person forever.

For a few moments, Mlle. Perrin sniffled and plied her handkerchief. Then she patted Mélusine's hand, saying, "Sit, my dear," and reached for her tea.

"Very well," she said when she was composed. "Yes, I know who her father was. It's a terrible secret, one I've carried alone since her mother died. You must promise me absolute confidence. Even now, with everyone gone, it would do much damage."

"Of course," Devarre murmured. Mélusine nodded in agreement, leaning forward expectantly. Mlle. Perrin's gaze flicked back and forth, and Mélusine had the sudden sense that the old woman was enjoying the suspense she had created and her role as the center of attention.

"The *curé,*" she said firmly. "Monsieur Boudrie."

Mélusine almost dropped her teacup. Open-mouthed, she turned to her husband and saw her amazement mirrored on his face.

"Etien," she breathed. "Is it possible?"

But of course it was possible. Mile Perrin chattered with animation now, a burst dam of scandal, about the late-night trysts of her younger sister Céleste–Alysse's mother–and the priest, here in this very house, some twenty years before: lovemaking sessions of such violent passion that she, Amalie Perrin, had awakened and listened from her own lonely bed down the hall, half outraged and half jealous at the sacrilege that was taking place beneath her roof. Mélusine realized that pieces of the puzzle were clicking into place. Boudrie's awkward but fierce concern for the girl. His amazement, followed by near panic, when he learned of the malevolent spirit's message, *sins of the father–*

And she remembered Courdeval's own words to her, moments before he walked into the night with Alysse at his side: *At last the sin of a priest and the weakness of a scholar put occasion in my way.*

As if that were a rationale, a license, for the evil Courdeval had brought about.

Mélusine rose, suddenly anxious to be home with her thoughts again, to process this new information into a plan of action.

"Thank you, mademoiselle," she said. "That's very helpful indeed. I assure you, no one else will ever learn this secret from us."

At the door, the old woman's eyes were pleading.

"Have you really . . . been touched by her?"

"I believe so," Mélusine said. "Yes."

"Will it happen again?"

"I don't know."

"If it does, will you tell her something for me?"

It's not like a telephone conversation, Mélusine started to say; but the hope and sadness in the other woman's face stopped her.

"I'll try."

"Tell her I loved her more than I ever let show." She turned away, and as the door closed, Mélusine was sure she heard the sound of weeping.

She looked helplessly at her husband. "Should we stay with her?"

"Let her cry. It will be cathartic. Poor woman! That secret must have been very heavy indeed, especially in light of all that's happened."

They walked arm and arm through the warm night. "I would never have imagined it," he said, "but now that we know, it makes perfect sense. I remember something he said when we thought Amalie was on her deathbed. He seemed inexplicably shaken; I asked if he had been close to her. He got a most peculiar look on his face and muttered, 'To her sister.'"

Mélusine nodded. "I was thinking the same thing– about it making sense, I mean. It would explain why her mother left Saint-Bertrand so suddenly, all those years

231

ago: she was a widow and pregnant, with the child of the village priest, no less."

Neither voiced the obvious sequitur: that it might well explain her suicide, too.

Sins of the fathers. Poor Etien, Mélusine thought. How you must have carried your own burden of guilt and grief through two decades.

"I can hear the wheels whirring in your brain," Devarre said. "Do any next moves suggest themselves?"

Without thinking, without realizing she had even considered the possibility, she said:

"Yes. We have to bring him back."

"Courdeval?" he said, astonished. He stopped, staring at her.

"No," she said. "Etien." And then, as if to explain, "He *has* to come back. She's his daughter."

TEN

"Well, honey, you look terrific," Heather said. Nicole thought she heard a touch of jealousy. "Isn't it wonderful what getting laid can do for a girl?"

"There's a little more to it than that," Nicole said, annoyed. Her life the past three weeks had been like a dream, and she did not welcome intrusions. I was the loner all those years, she reminded herself fiercely. Now it's my turn.

"And the two of you are really thinking about moving?"

Nicole shrugged and said, "We've talked about it." Then she added, with a touch of spite, "Someplace where kids aren't getting ripped up by some maniac every full moon." It had happened again in July, to a young couple who had apparently been necking in a state park near Santa Cruz. Police were finally admitting a pattern.

"Can't blame you for that," Heather said. She took a bite of her sandwich and tucked a gob of mayonnaise into her mouth, rolling her eyes suggestively. "So when do I get to meet him?"

"Whenever you want. Why don't you and Derek come over for dinner one night soon?" Immediately, Nicole regretted her words; the thought of the strained civility she was sure would erupt between Jesse and Heather's yuppie husband, stretched over the course of an evening, was gruesome. But it had to happen sooner or later; there was no way around it.

They were in St. Mary's Square eating deli lunches, surrounded by other financial district employees and old Chinese men playing their endless games of mah-jongg. Half a block over, Grant Street was thronged with tourist traffic. It was early August, and the season was in full swing. Heather sat straight-backed, in a model's pose, frequently tossing her head, the sunlight sparkling off her earrings–obviously conscious of the men nearby–and a dark streak of suspicion cut suddenly into Nicole's contentment. Why was Heather so anxious to meet Jesse? She had never before had a good word to say about him. And while she usually chattered unendingly about her husband, she had said almost nothing about him today. Were things going badly in the marriage? Was she so intrigued at Nicole's rapture with her new lover that, under a veil of wittiness, she was contriving to make a play for him?

Heather glanced at her, and her face went puzzled. "You okay, Nik?" she said, leaning forward a little.

The concern in her eyes softened Nicole's feelings. "Of course," she said, managing a smile.

"You got the damnedest look on your face. I thought I was going to have to pull a Heimlich maneuver."

"I was just thinking about a brief I have to write this afternoon," Nicole lied. "A product liability case. Gives a new meaning to the word dull." She looked at her watch and feigned surprise. "Speaking of which–" They put the remains of their lunches back into the sacks, rose, and started walking.

"Has he quit drinking?" Heather said abruptly. "In the comfort of your lovin' arms?" Her walk was almost a strut, as if she were forever on stage, her audience all of the men in the world. Nicole felt the smoldering surge of suspicion–or was it outright dislike, long harbored and finally admitted?–fan again into flame.

"No," she said. "But he's cut way back." Then, defensively: "Rome wasn't built in a day." Heather said nothing, which irritated her further.

They parted company in the lobby. "Well, I'm happy for you, honey," Heather said, squeezing her arm. "Call me."

In the office, Nicole walked past the secretaries without saying hello, closed the door to her cubicle, and stood at the window. Her anger now seemed silly, even vicious, and she felt her eyes go damp. Heather had her annoying qualities–who didn't?–but had been a good and unfailing friend. Besides which, given her tastes and priorities, the thought of her being attracted to a man like Jesse was simply ludicrous.

Stubbornly, a little at a time, she yielded to the truth: She was already terrified of losing him. For him to fall in love with her had seemed an unachievable dream. What she had not foreseen was that her own feelings would soar completely out of bounds, growing fierce and even violent. He had been with her nearly every evening since the first one, and he seemed everything that she had sensed: kind, but knowing when to be stern; cynical and worldly-wise, but with flashes of boyishness; and possessed of a delicious sense of cruelty, a way of gazing at her through half-closed eyes and saying something that cut to her heart, tore her, enraged her—until the moment came when she would understand that he had put his finger precisely on a part of herself that she disliked. He was father, brother, lover, and friend, and the thought of his leaving literally made her heart beat harder with fear.

But beneath all of that lay a deeper, less pleasant feeling: a sense of guilt over having won his love by means that were not quite proper, as if she had secured a loan on false credit.

She shook her head, confused and a little frightened, her lovely bubble of the past weeks suddenly seeming dangerously thin. She had not tried fascination again; there seemed to be no need. But she continued to evoke her guardian angel secretly each night, and continued to feel that presence grow.

Which unfailingly reminded her that she was, in a strange and mysterious way, indebted to Valcourt—not a comfortable feeling. The hardest part was not being able to confide in anyone. Even without Valcourt's caution of secrecy, how could she tell the person whose approval she needed most—or was it forgiveness?—*I don't know exactly how to say this, but I think I've cast a spell on you.*

Was that true? Or was it just, as she badly wanted to believe, that circumstances had finally been right for them to come together: that he had at last realized what she had sensed all along? That the "spell," like courting her guardian angel, had only increased her natural abilities, as Valcourt maintained? And that her fears stemmed from the enslaving entities in her mind?

The next meeting of the group was tonight.

Distracted, she went to her desk, took out the file for the brief she was supposed to write, and stared at it. The papers could have been written in Martian.

Of course, she could simply choose not to attend the meeting. That would presumably be the end of the matter. Valcourt could find a replacement, perhaps someone more genuinely interested in such knowledge than she, who would have the coveted chance to learn. She had already gotten what she wanted.

But would she keep it?

Was that what his parting words to her had meant?

Power has consequences. What you make use of, you must be responsible for.

Could she afford to take the chance?

Abruptly, her timidity turned to anger, this time at herself. You're retreating back into the same old wishy-washy Nicole, she thought. Here you have this wonderful opportunity that's already paid off in a marvelous way, you've barely scratched the surface, and you can't think about anything but grabbing what you've gained and running to hide. What the hell are you afraid of?

She picked up the papers, gripped them sternly, and forced her attention to the wearyingly self-important batch of evidence about some food processor that had run amok, mangling a woman's fingertips and blending them with several ounces of pureed carrots.

"Tonight, my friends," said Guy-Luc Valcourt, "let us begin by asking Nicole whether our efforts on her behalf last month have borne any fruit." He turned to her inquiringly, hands clasped behind his back. The gazes of the others followed.

Nicole lowered her eyes, feeling her face heating. "Yes," she said. "At least–something happened." Then she raised her head, squared her shoulders, and faced them. "We became lovers. I can't say for certain this was the reason . . ."

"How happy I am for you!" Valcourt said. "There is no need for you to assume that our efforts were entirely responsible for your success. Indeed, they were not. Your own character and desire supplied most of the necessary power; then too, this man was far more attracted to you than he allowed himself to realize. We merely pushed what had already hovered over the edge."

The meeting had begun just as the previous month, with sherry and tea served by the pale, silent Alysse, dressed in a different, but equally antiquated, floor-length gown and scarf, moving with her unhurried, gliding step. Lamashtu watched them lazily from the mantel, curled up beside the glass-encased grimoire. Remembering the cat's performance of the previous month, Nicole wondered again fleetingly if they had all somehow been hypnotized. Lamashtu's tail twitched, and she suddenly had the sense that there was something wrong–something not quite catlike, but almost serpentine–about the motion.

"I offer only a word of caution, Nicole," Valcourt continued. "You must not rest now upon your laurels, as you say. There is no such thing as stasis in this matter; once your power is awakened, it must continue to grow, or it will atrophy, like any other muscle or faculty. Do not fail to perform your exercises, and make an effort to always keep these matters near the forefront of your mind. Soon this will become as natural as breathing.

"Let us all hope for Nicole's continued happiness. Now: Tonight we will plunge immediately into considering the situation of whomever we shall attempt to aid next. Long experience has taught me that this often presents a better forum for discussing more general matters than my own tiresome lecturing, So, let us see what the fates decree!"

Again he took from the cabinet the ancient vase with its grotesque figures, murmuring, "Of course, this time we need but three pebbles." He emptied the stones from the vase, removed one of the white ones, and returned the others. After shaking it, he offered it to Charity. Face tense, she extracted a stone and held it up. It was black.

"A matter that must be pressing," Valcourt said, smiling.

Surreptitiously, Nicole scanned her companions' faces as he replaced the vase. Charity, wearing a cream-colored silk blouse and baggy black pants tucked into knee-high boots, remained obviously tense, lighting a cigarette and examining her nails. Spencer's gaze roved restlessly, as usual. Only Robbie Kinsella, dressed in what Nicole had already come to think of as his uniform—the Hawaiian shirt, khakis, and battered high-top sneakers—met her eye. He grinned and shrugged elaborately.

"Mister Kinsella," Valcourt said. Though his back was turned, his words were sudden and a little sharp, as if he had seen Robbie's gesture. "Can you tell us what event in history took place on Friday, October the thirteenth, in the year thirteen hundred and seven?"

Robbie's face turned startled, then uncomfortable, a student caught goofing off in class. Thirty seconds passed before he admitted, "No."

"The fall of the Knights Templar," Valcourt said, turning to face them. "Seven centuries ago, the king of France and the pope devised a treacherous scheme to destroy the mightiest and noblest order of men the world has ever known. They were fearless in battle and great in knowledge, particularly of the sort you profess to crave. How is it you are not familiar with their history?"

Robbie hung his head, a gesture so boyish Nicole almost laughed aloud, and she saw the corners of Valcourt's mouth twitch. But his voice remained stern.

"Knowledge is built upon the shoulders of those who first earned it, often with immense labor and sometimes at the cost of their lives. If you would call it yours, you have a duty to pay homage to those who went before."

Whether it was his tone or expression, Nicole was not sure—had his accent thickened slightly? But she had the distinct sense that Valcourt had just said something that mattered a great deal to him–that the iron facade of control had slipped a notch. She filed this away among the increasing labyrinth of impressions, questions, and uncertainties–about Jesse, about having shared her inner feelings with people she hardly knew–that was swelling almost daily. *Make an effort to always keep these matters in the forefront of your mind,* Valcourt had said. If anything, her problem was just the opposite. She hoped the bewilderment was only a stage.

"Let us proceed," Valcourt said.

Nicole watched Charity put out her cigarette and could almost see her choosing her words. She guessed that Charity was several years younger than she, perhaps twenty-five. Everything about her–clothing, jewelry, bearing–spoke of money. Though her figure was slender and athletic, her features were somewhat sharp, and she obviously tried to soften them by using, in Nicole's opinion, too much makeup. The effect was, however, striking: an elegant but harsh beauty.

"There's a man in my life, too," she said, still stubbing the cigarette into an ashtray. "Or at least, there was. He's not as nice as yours, Nicole." She dropped the cigarette at last and looked up, her eyes flat and angry. "In fact, he's a real creep. I didn't figure it out until too late, but he's got this sort of specialty, this thing about young women. He's in his forties, very good-looking, has lots of money, and he comes from a wealthy family, so he has access to society–and gets away with lots of shit." She flashed a look at Valcourt. "Pardon my language."

He waved a hand. "I abide by the customs of whatever culture I find myself in."

241

"Talking about him doesn't make me feel very ladylike," she said grimly. "I went out with him for a few months. He had a yacht in Tiburon; we'd go sailing; he'd tell me I was the only woman he'd ever loved, he'd never met anyone like me, he wanted to marry me, all that. Now even I can hardly believe it, but I fell for it.

"Then one day he just stopped calling. When I called him, I'd get nothing but his answering machine. If I tried his office, his secretary would tell me he was away, or out of town; I could almost hear the bitch laughing at me. I finally went to his apartment–shameless, I know, but I was going crazy–and he'd told the doormen not to let me in. You can imagine how *that* made me feel.

"Anyway, that was three months ago. I haven't seen him or talked to him since."

For perhaps thirty seconds, there was silence. Then Valcourt murmured:

"A painful story, to be sure. But alas, a not uncommon one. And given this man's behavior, together with your own anger, I am afraid I do not see much possibility of a reconciliation."

"Oh, no," she said. "That's not what I'm after. I never want to see the son of a bitch again." Her nervous fingers seemed to move of their own accord to take another cigarette from the pack. She held it without lighting it.

"Like I said, he has this specialty I didn't know about until it was all over. He'd meet somebody like me–the younger the better; I was actually pushing the upper end–and start this whirlwind romance until he was sure she'd gone for him. Then he'd lose interest, cut her off, leave town for a while if he had to.

242

"But in the meantime, he'd get her to introduce him to all her girlfriends. And he'd just move right on to whichever one attracted him next. He'd tell the new one that he'd really cared for his ex, but that she'd turned out to be mentally unstable–a deep dark secret he'd uncovered–and he'd act the whole heartbroken part. The new girl would eat it up–I did the same thing, I admit–and by the time she found out what a line of crap it was, he'd be on his way again.

"The worst thing about it was that afterward, while you were dealing with the loss and starting to realize how you'd been had, people you knew would start coming around and telling you how he'd been doing this forever. It was like being the butt of a joke everybody else had been in on all along, laughing behind your back, and then they'd come up and pat your shoulder with that phony sympathy."

She shrugged as if she were shaking something unpleasant off her back, and lit the cigarette. Both Spencer's and Robbie's gazes were averted, Nicole noticed, and they seemed uncomfortable. Sexual guilt, she decided, almost amused.

"And how," Valcourt asked kindly, "may we help?"

She inhaled deeply, shook out the match, and glanced at all of their faces. Nicole caught something far back in Charity's eyes–calculation? A gauging of the effect she was producing? It was gone before she could decide.

"One of the girls I introduced him to is my cousin," Charity said flatly. "She's nineteen. She's not much for brains, but she's beautiful, and so sweet you can hardly

243

believe it. She's like . . . an innocent. She's been in boarding schools all her life–Switzerland, the works–and her parents always watched out for her when she was home. But this summer they let her come to an art school in San Francisco. She didn't know anyone, so I took her to some parties, back when I was still seeing Evan.

"I found out a few weeks ago that she's started seeing him. He's taken her out sailing, playing like an older brother. I called her to try to sound her out, find out how far it's gone; but she got very defensive, and finally she blurted out that he'd warned her I'd probably call and tell her all sorts of lies–the mental instability thing, right?–and I remembered he'd told me the same thing about the girl before me.

"What can I do? He's got her all wired to believe I'm half crazy. Pretty soon she's going to be head over heels in love with him, if she isn't already, and when he disappears, I'm honestly afraid she might kill herself. She's such a"– her voice faltered–"a sweet dope."

When it was clear she was done speaking, Valcourt said, "This information puts the matter in a new light, at least to my mind, and opens several rich areas of discussion for us. Let us pursue these, to see if any appropriate course of action offers itself.

"Here we have a man who goes from woman to woman; courting them with lies and flattery, making promises he has no intention of keeping, until he wins their love–and then cruelly abandons them. Clearly, he suggests a sort of predator–but a very particular sort. He does not destroy his victims outright. Rather, he extracts from them a large quantity of emotion–an unseen, yet undeniably vital, force-and by draining them, by robbing them of this vitality until they are ravaged, he maintains his own vigor. Does this suggest anything to you?"

"A vampire," Robbie said immediately.

"Excellent, my friend," Valcourt murmured. "I retract my earlier jest about your ignorance." It was hard to tell if the remark was intended to be ironic.

"Your conception of the vampire in these times is informed by rather lurid images from books and motion pictures," he went on, leaving Robbie blinking. "In particular, him modeled upon the Wallachian noble known as Vlad Drakula–who was, by the by, a great soldier, although a very cruel man: sometimes from necessity, but often, unhappily, out of mere profligacy; a waste of life and power.

"The sort of vampire who physically sucks blood is only one kind, and primarily an imaginary figure. Far more common, and most real, are what we might call psychic vampires: those who subsist by draining others of emotion, like the man Charity has described.

"Because you do not yet understand the true nature of things, you do not see that blood is only a physical symbol of the deeper, infinitely more powerful life force. This force animates all living things; we may liken it to an electrical current. When it is withdrawn, quickly or slowly, as the case may be, the body is left a spent, empty husk. There are other components of the human being which remain after death–primarily that which we call the spirit–but that is a matter to be discussed another time.

"The psychic vampire, then, seeks to drain his victims of life force, just as his supernatural counterpart seeks actual blood. Though the latter is much more scenic upon a film screen, the former can be just as devastating in the damage he wreaks. It will take each of you but a moment to think of someone you have known in your own life who is recognizable as such a predator to some extent; and in fact, none of us is altogether free of vampiric tendencies, as even the most superficial relationship must involve an ebb and flow of psychic energy.

"But the true vampire is *aware,* on some level, of the real nature of his doings, and he consciously stalks and bleeds his prey. This may be comparatively innocent—a clerk in a shop who takes obsequious pleasure in delaying or harassing you in some petty, uncalled-for way. Or it may be quite serious, even to the point of causing death—as when one drains the finest and strongest emotions, like love, from a victim whose trust one has gained.

"So: We are faced with the awareness of a dangerous predator who stalks the streets of our city, doing very real harm—in many ways, worse than physical—to vulnerable young women. And yet, there is no law in this time and land which can bring him to account. We must ask ourselves, then: Is it our right—perhaps even our duty—to seek to put an end to his rapacious career? If so, by what means might we go about it?

"With those questions, I will leave you to take refreshment. Shall we say, ten minutes?"

He swept from the room. The men got up and moved toward the drink tray. Nicole watched Charity, trying to

246

think of a way to begin a private conversation, to sound out the matter further. There was something about it that struck her as amiss, for no particular reason. Perhaps it seemed a little too neat; or perhaps Charity, despite her name, did not seem the sort to go to a great deal of trouble to spare someone else's emotions. But when Nicole caught her eye, Charity immediately scooped up her purse and stalked out, presumably to find a bathroom. Well, Nicole thought, she was probably just feeling shy and a little silly at having bared her heart: she remembered how she herself had blushed. As for the story's patness, Charity had doubtless rehearsed it many times, knowing there was one chance in three that she would be asked to deliver it.

Spencer and Robbie were talking in low, animated tones. In a moment they, too, left the room. Nicole shrugged at being alone, refilled her sherry glass, then stepped into the dining room and walked to a window. The evening sky was a pale, fading blue, the colors of vegetation muted and soft. So, she thought, now it was vampires.

And why not? In the worldview of a man who took for granted the presence of unseen spirits, who could command a cat to fetch cigarettes, who by all indications had the power to make not just her, but three other reasonably intelligent, sophisticated people believe he could change their lives materially for the better—why should there not be humans who sucked psychic energy the way Dracula sucked blood? The more she thought about it, the less outlandish it seemed. She could remember coming home from work exhausted when it seemed she had done nothing strenuous–but after she plugged in encounters with overbearing colleagues, sullen waiters, hostile taxi drivers, she could imagine that they were all like piranhas, taking chunks out of her vitality. And yes, she could think of several people who seemed to grow almost visibly stronger by demeaning or conning anyone with whom they came into contact.

As she turned from the window, a movement in the driveway caught her gaze. Beyond the fountain stood a dark figure–no, two. When her vision adjusted, she realized they were Valcourt and Alysse. Hands on the girl's shoulders, he seemed to be posing her–oddly, in front of Nicole's car. Yes, now he was stepping back, and he had something in his hand–but not a camera. It looked like a white piece of paper, an index card or envelope.

He held it up and looked at it with apparent satisfaction, then put his arm protectively around the girl's shoulders and started back to the house. Feeling as if she had been spying, Nicole returned to the sitting room. Robbie had come back in, alone, and was sniffling. When he saw her, he grinned sheepishly.

"Nice guy, you get to talking with him," he said, jerking his head toward whatever part of the house Spencer presumably remained in. Nicole suspected he had encountered Charity, and was filling her nose, too. She felt a bit left out but was not really interested, and wondered what Valcourt would think if he knew. Perhaps he did know.

"I gather you're supposed to be the ace student," she said.

Robbie shook his head, looking rueful. "Nailed me to the wall, didn't he? I mean, I'd heard of the Templars, but I didn't know any dates or specifics." His forehead wrinkled. "Have you noticed how when he talks about things that happened hundreds of years ago, it's like he was *there?* Even his voice changes." He glanced at the mantel, where the cat remained, watching them. "I checked out the name Lamashtu," he said, in a lowered voice. "It was a female night demon of the Mesopotamians, very bad news."

She was about to answer with her observation of the cat's tail, when Spencer and Charity came back in together, looking vaguely conspiratorial. Spencer paused by the painting Nicole had noticed on her first visit.

"Wonder what this is worth," he said, sounding somehow defensive. She walked to stand beside him, studying it closely for the first time.

It was impressionistic, the canvas about twenty-four inches wide by sixteen high. A glade in a forest was depicted; deep greens and blues suggested that the hour was dusk. A single figure, clad in a flowing robe of black, was approaching the glade. The dress and supple stance, together with long dark hair, made it clear that it was a woman. While her features were obscured by the artist's style, everything about her indicated reluctance and fear—and yet, fascination. The effect was remarkably powerful, given the sparseness of recognizable detail.

Nicole found herself wondering what the woman was doing alone in the woods at dusk. This was no Gothic novel cover. Was she being pursued? Although her frightened bearing and backward glance made that seem logical, it did not jibe with the unmistakable impression of eagerness. Nicole became increasingly certain that the woman was looking behind her not for fear of pursuit, but for fear of being seen–that she had come to this lonely, gloomy spot at dusk to meet someone, and that this meeting must at all costs be kept secret.

She was wondering what such a meeting's purpose might be when she realized that Spencer was watching her appraisingly.

"You party?" he said.

"No," she said, vaguely offended. "Thanks." Arms folded, she walked back to her chair.

A moment later, Valcourt entered the room. He took his position in the center and waited for them to be settled.

"What, then, is to be done about this unscrupulous man?" he said without preliminary. "Does it fall to us to try to hinder him? If so, does this lie within our power? Suppose I were to suggest that we consider sending him a sort of warning, a signal that his actions are being monitored?" He waited, his single eye inquiring.

"Well, I think we should do something, obviously," Charity declared. Her eyes were bright with cocaine.

Valcourt's gaze moved, next querying Spencer. He shrugged.

"Sure," he said, although not as forcefully. "That's a crummy way to behave."

Robbie nodded in agreement. "Maybe help his karma, too."

"An excellent point," Valcourt said. "In unseen ways, he is damaging himself as well as his victims."

All faces turned to Nicole.

She laughed nervously. "I don't know. Maybe it's because I'm a lawyer–it seems he ought to have a chance to defend himself." She looked at Charity. "I mean, I'm sure you're telling the truth, but so often I get into situations where I hear another side to a story, and it changes everything . . ."

Valcourt's eyebrows rose, and his face went pensive. "Another excellent point."

"It's just like I told you," Charity said heatedly, glaring back at Nicole. "The only other side to the story would be his lies."

Nicole stopped herself from declaring, That's what they all say, sweetie. She turned to Valcourt.

For almost a minute, he considered, hands folded in his sleeves, gaze distant and thoughtful.

"My dear Nicole," he said finally. "Your concern is valid and considerate, and I tell you in advance, this is not a situation of what you call 'majority rule.' We must agree to act wholeheartedly as a group, or we will not act at all.

"Three of you agree that some action should be taken. I will add that I am forced to concur. You are all young, and ignorant of much unseen harshness taking place all around you. I have long been familiar with such creatures as Charity describes. They are despicable, destructive, and smug in the knowledge of their unassailability by law. They possess just enough power to misuse it–and you will come to learn in time that when such misuse is brought to your attention, yes, it is your duty to correct it.

251

"Ah, my friends, I see that you cannot imagine the hideousness of this crime! I have known war and violence beyond your nightmares. I have felt the very talon of death crushing the life force from my body, leaving me broken and helpless as a puppet. Only by a miracle am I with you here today. To think of a gentle young woman having her youth, perhaps her life itself, destroyed wastefully–"

He seemed to collect himself with some effort. Nicole remembered Robbie's words: *Even his voice changes.* War and violence beyond your nightmares. Was that how he had lost the eye? She realized she had never given any real thought to his age, but he could have been in his fifties or even older–able to have participated in any of several wars.

"As for our right to interfere: here we must part company with law, with organized religions, and with all other orthodox systems of thought. These would have us believe that they define right and wrong. This is what adepts know as *exoteric* teaching–teaching for the common people, the masses. But those few who have truly understood the nature of existence have established *esoteric* teachings, which are hidden from the common eyes.

"The basis of these is that the adept must make the decision himself as to the morality of any situation calling for his attention. This is a process that is always laborious and often agonizing. It involves great power but also implies great responsibility. If he acts wisely, he acquires the former; if selfishly or foolishly, he is punished by the latter.

252

"Keep in mind that we are not talking about anything so drastic as a stake through the heart. Rather, it would be a warning, harmless in itself, which would make this man consider before he continued his predatory ways–and which might well benefit him in the final view.

"Four of us have decided, in the best of faith, that we are willing to act. We await with respect the decision of the fifth."

In the tense pause that ensued, none of them looked directly at her, but she could hear the unspoken thought as if it had been shouted: Now that you've gotten what *you* wanted, are you going to back out?

"I suppose," Nicole said weakly. "If you're sure he deserves it."

Valcourt's smile looked almost fierce. "A significant step forward on the path to power. Rise, then, all of you, and come to me."

As in the previous meeting, he dimmed the lights and lit the burner of strangely fragranced incense. This time he instructed Charity to stand in the center of the square they formed, while the others joined hands. Then he gave to her a slender piece of black string, several inches long.

"Last month," he said, "we aided Nicole in attaining the gift of fascination. Now we will demonstrate a minor piece of what has long been called *sympathetic* magic. Since this man's own magic–or more accurately, the force by which he operates–is largely sexual, it is by means of sexuality that we will touch him; thus the term *sympathetic*. Am I correct in assuming, Charity, that he prides himself on his virility?"

Blushing faintly, she nodded.

"And if it failed him for a period of time—let us say a month—he would be concerned?"

"He'd go crazy," she said, grinning.

"We will hope you are speaking metaphorically. If you *will,* then, to aid our sister Charity in attaining her most worthy desire, repeat the words, *I so choose.*"

Reluctantly, Nicole spoke with the others.

"The process we are undertaking is called *ligature.* The thread which Charity holds represents this man's sexual power. Concentrate, Charity, on that image, and link it with him."

For perhaps a minute they held the silence. Nicole stood increasingly aware of an undeniable sense of force rising among them, tempered by a distant amusement as Charity's hands, with seeming unconsciousness, pulled the string taut—and by the lingering sense of doubt, even of regret, about joining in this.

Abruptly, Valcourt said, "Knot it!"

Charity's fingers looped the string and, with sudden viciousness, pulled it tight. Nicole inhaled at the instant sense of the growing power frustrated, even angry. Valcourt was speaking in the strange language again, words that might or might not have been the same as the previous time. He ended with a sharp, strong syllable; with it, the sense of force vanished, leaving her limp and shaky. She sensed from the drooping of Charity's shoulders and the loosening grips on her hands that the others felt it, too.

Valcourt clapped once, smiling. "You are a fine group!" he proclaimed. "There was much power! Let us have a glass of wine, in the hopes that this soon-to-be-chastened man will take our lesson to heart."

Alysse arrived, moving with her unhurried walk, carrying wine and crystal glasses on a tray. Nicole watched her, still uneasy, but smiled when their eyes met, hoping to establish some sort of contact, Without exactly ignoring her, Alysse seemed not to notice—or perhaps for some reason, she was simply not interested in having any dealings with the Americans. Nicole shrugged, trying not to be annoyed; she did not pretend to understand Old World ways. The wine was delicious, Valcourt was jovial and expansive, and they chatted pleasantly for several minutes before moving toward their cars.

"One last matter, my friends," he said on the porch. "Now that we are growing better acquainted, I must ask you for the time being to refrain from seeking one another's company elsewhere than here. I have adopted this practice from past experience, having found that such contact too often leads to erroneous impressions about our work, and even to premature experimentation which can damage yourselves and your fellows. Soon enough, this restriction will be removed; I have no doubt that by then, you will all be the best of friends."

Nicole glanced sidelong at Charity. She doubted it.

As she was getting into her car, she saw the other woman rummage somewhat theatrically through her purse, look around with obvious exasperation, and then hurry back up the steps to where Valcourt was standing—forgotten keys or cigarettes, no doubt. She could see them talking as she pulled away.

She drove slowly along the empty, darkening road toward the freeway. She was still uncomfortable about what they had done, or rather, what they intended to do—where, exactly, did the difference lie?—but then, wasn't it like the police using means not strictly legal to punish or warn criminals they could not otherwise reach? In most circumstances, she agreed that Valcourt was right: it was a good thing there were people around with enough courage to take such responsibility. Feeling better, she squared her shoulders and drove a little faster.

But immediately, she realized that that was only one of the things bothering her. The others were small, almost subliminal, but together they were significant. The strange scene of Valcourt posing Alysse in the driveway, for example, in front of her own car. His occasional odd choice of words, as when he had spoken of Charity's young cousin being destroyed *wastefully*—as if the important factor was not the crime itself, but the use made of the girl. Doubtless he had meant it differently, and it was only clumsiness with the language. Still—

And that painting. Perhaps because it was the only one she had seen in the house—in fact, the only purely decorative touch—it loomed sinister in her imagination.

What *was* that woman doing in that forest glade at dusk?

She merged onto I-280, and with the stream of traffic around her, her worries drifted into a more immediate and normal pattern: How was Tom Junior going to react to coming home and finding that his pal Jesse had moved into his mother's bed?

256

Standing on the porch, Guy-Luc Valcourt watched Nicole climb into her car, even as Charity Haverill affected to discover that she could not find her keys. They were on the table where her purse had rested, surreptitiously placed there by her during the wine-drinking and talk. What she did not realize was that the idea had not been, strictly speaking, her own, but a reaction to his mental suggestion—although, to be sure, a suggestion that was in accordance with her desires.

The time had come for her to be initiated into the true nature of this enterprise.

Behind him, Alysse waited in the hall. "*À chambre*," he murmured. Obediently, she climbed the stairs to her room. Valcourt smiled faintly. During the meeting's intermission, he had conducted a minor but important bit of business: creating a photographic likeness of Alysse posed before Nicole Partrick's car, with the license plate clearly visible.

An image that would find its way to Mélusine Devarre.

It was a most useful invention, this photography. The camera itself had not been necessary; nor were any of the intermediary stages of development. For him, forming images on almost any sort of surface was child's play. But an image impressed on film could be sent anywhere, and it gave no clue of having been produced by other than natural means.

In fact, a dozen more blank photographs were traveling out the driveway this very moment, undetected, in the coat pocket of Spencer Epps. They would record some of the choicer moments of his frolics with his mistress tonight, and then remain in his closet at home.

Until the time was right for them to be discovered by his wife.

As Charity reached the porch, he assumed an inquiring expression.

"I can't find my car keys," she said "May I look?"

"But of course."

She climbed the steps, smiling a bit timidly. Her early desire to revenge herself by using Valcourt as the scapegoat had faded into fascination with him. He would have said she was falling in love, if she were capable of such a thing. But she was definitely capable of desire. The aura of it around her was like musk. Gravely, he offered his arm and led her back into the house.

He had, of course, controlled the outcome of the drawing, just as he had the previous month with Nicole. Their thoughts were like open books to him; it was an easy matter to shape events into a nice escalation of consequences. The ceremonies they had performed, the tidbits of authentic sorcery, were meaningless: like the antics of Lamashtu, they were a distraction, a sop to their primitive sensibilities. It was his own power, dispatched independently, that produced the results.

But that was not important. The critical thing was that they believed in what they did—to get them to acquiesce, first to greed, and finally to harm. Only Nicole worried him. Both her intelligence and her moral depth were greater than he had expected. Next month, the stakes would rise sharply; and it was critical to this entire process that she participate. She must be wooed with utmost care.

But the largest part of that was already accomplished: she had won the love of the man she desired. Faced with the threat of losing him, she would, he was certain, comply.

She would not learn until too late that the love she had gained was an empty bubble: the final nail in the coffin of spiritual agony that was the Adversary's life blood.

The courting of her son–a sprinkling of events designed to raise him to the desired pitch of mental vulnerability–had already begun.

"How weird," Charity said as she walked to the table where the keys lay. "I must have pulled them out of my purse when I was looking for cigarettes. I'm not usually spacy like that." She laughed nervously, toying with the keys, wanting to extend the conversation.

"Clearly," Valcourt said, "you have more important things on your mind."

She nodded, her eyes quickly, almost furtively, meeting his, then slipping away.

"I want to thank you for helping me," she said. "That charm you gave me–there's just no doubt it's working. All these little things I've wanted for a long time are falling into my lap. It's like people are jumping through hoops to please me."

"Little things," he said, "can quickly give way to important ones. For instance, our work tonight. Would you care to watch its result?"

"Watch? Really?" Her face brightened, then went doubtful "I don't even know where he is."

"Come," Valcourt said. "We shall find him."

He took her by the hand, leading her through the empty, shadowed house and up the stairs, feeling her uncertainty mixed with excitement, her wondering if he would attempt the seduction she both desired and feared–

Wondering if he knew that she had lied.

He said nothing to soothe her; the more unrest within her, the more force. She was capable of a great deal of such power, more than any of the others. While she would never acquire any ability to control it, that was to his advantage, as was the fact that most of this power was negative: anger at largely imagined sufferings at the hands of fate, friends, lovers. Most of the insult that was not imagined, she brought on herself. The affair she had described this night was only the most recent in a series of such events, which had ended when the men discovered that beneath her charm she was hard, greedy, and thoroughly self-absorbed. Unwilling to even consider blaming herself, she required an object on which to focus her rage.

This latest man, Evan Phillips, would pay–for his own imagined mistreatment of her and for that of all of the other men before him. It was not just, but it was necessary. Phillips was something of a womanizer, true; but he was also sensible and hardworking, had made her no promises of any kind–certainly not of marriage–and had stopped seeing her only when time had revealed her inner self. The story about his impending seduction of

Charity's cousin was, of course, a complete fabrication. No such person existed. But Valcourt was pleased at the sinister imagination she had shown, and at the fervency of her lying. She was a most useful vessel, filled with dark angry energy and capable of being nurtured into utter ruthlessness.

By the time they reached the third story of the increasingly darker house, her hand was trembling in his; but she held it tightly and had, he knew, no intention of retreat. Her failings did not include cowardice. This part of the house was devoid of both furniture and illumination, except for the remnant of twilight visible through the curtained windows. Their footsteps echoed on the wooden floor, the only sounds besides her harsh, rapid breathing.

Valcourt drew open a door, revealing a final staircase that led through the attic to the cupola. Side by side, they climbed. They passed through a sort of hatch and then stood gazing out over miles of deeply shadowed, tree-covered hills, the distant, widely spaced lights of houses, and the vast sky filled with brightening stars.

He spoke at last: "A fine vantage point, is it not?"

Eyes shining, the night breeze ruffling her hair, she nodded. Her front teeth rested on her lower lip. Amused, Valcourt turned to an object in a comer of the waist-high railing: an oval-shaped piece of dark opaque glass, the size of a serving platter, mounted in a silver frame with a stand. He drew her to it and positioned her in front of it.

"Summon him," he said. "Command him to appear."

He felt with approval the force of her concentration–great when she applied it to gratifying desire. In

261

perhaps one minute, the screen began to glow faintly. Her surprise turned to excitement and a redoubled effort. Dim, swirling images were forming.

"I can't believe I'm doing this," she whispered.

He smiled slightly; of course, she was not.

"You are exceptional," he murmured. "But no more talking. Concentrate! Command him to reveal himself to you, wherever he may be, whatever he may be doing."

He knew perfectly well where the man was and what he was doing. The timing of this little show had required a tiresome coordination of servants, first planting lust in two hearts, then arranging delays to prevent its consummation until now. Evan Phillips and his newest paramour had arrived approximately one hour ago at his apartment—just enough time for drinks, flirtation, the obligatory shyness on her part, and then acquiescence.

The images on the glass sharpened into recognizable figures—like television, he sensed Charity thinking, wild with excitement at her imagined new ability—of a man and a woman, acting out a scene that required no words. He sat naked on the bed, hands clasped between his knees, brooding; she, with bedclothes drawn up over her breasts, touched his back and spoke reassuringly. His hands lifted suddenly from his lap, palms up, and he spoke in pantomime, with obvious chagrin—*I can't understand it; this never happened to me before*—then rose and stalked to where his drink waited on a bureau. The woman watched anxiously, resting on one elbow. Her mouth moved: *Is it me?* Back still turned, he shoot his head.

Charity laughed aloud, a shrill, hysterical neigh, and tossed her head gleefully.

The moment had come.

Valcourt held his open palm before her. In it rested the coiled thread that she had knotted.

"What do you really wish him?" he whispered.

Their eyes met, and then hers gleamed with sudden understanding. She took the thread and, gazing at the screen, picked loose the knot with her long fingernails. The image of Evan Phillips paused with his glass halfway to his lips, and he raised his head as if listening. Charity began to stroke the thread gently. Phillips looked down at himself, with puzzled satisfaction on his face. Grinning, he turned back to the woman in bed, whose eyes widened in surprise. The thread went to Charity's lips. Phillips was moving hurriedly now, climbing into bed, the smiling lass opening her arms.

And then, just as Valcourt had known she would, Charity bit down sharply.

Evan Phillips leaped straight up from the bed, hands cupping his groin, mouth stretched in a howl. The woman half rose, clutching at his thigh, her face tense with concern. Charity shrieked with laughter and again bit the cord. Phillips was rolling on the floor now, curled into a ball. The woman was holding a telephone poised, shouting questions at him.

Charity pulled the cord gently taut again and tantalizingly began to lick it. Slowly, Evan Phillips came uncurled and looked in consternation between his legs. The woman put down the phone and began to edge toward her clothes, her face gone wary. He rose quickly

263

to his feet, held her shoulders, talked to her sooth-ingly–*everything's fine, baby, some sort of cramp*–and she submitted to his kisses, allowing herself to be pushed back to the bed.

They had been interwined for perhaps a minute when the flame of Charity's cigarette lighter pierced the darkness of the cupola. Valcourt watched her lean close to the screen, lips parted, the flame making tiny points of light in her gleaming eyes. Holding the thread by one end, she lowered it slowly over the lighter. It turned to a briefly glowing line of ash. Valcourt watched with interest as Evan Phillips erupted once more from the bed, this time crashing blindly through the apartment, clutching his engorged organ as if trying to tear it from his body.

As the lighter fell from Charity's shaking hands, Valcourt felt the emotions warring within her: joy, fear, shock, doubt, and the naked, evil delight in another's suffering.

There remained only to make her his creature.

Here, McTell's heterosexual proclivities would serve well. He pulled her roughly away from the screen and ripped free the strange modern clothing on her lower body. Her legs wrapped fiercely around him, her nails clawing and teeth biting as he entered her.

Over her shoulder, he watched Evan Phillips run shrieking for the window of his twelfth-floor apartment and burst headfirst through it, plunging into the night sky in a spray of glass and blood, while the horrified woman stood nude in the center of the room. As her hands went to her face and her mouth opened to scream, he allowed the screen to go blank.

264

"You are a sister to me," he whispered harshly into the ear of Charity, writhing upon him impaled, and as her movements quickened, he noted with detached interest that her sobs had changed to a keening sound, like the women of Asia in Courdeval's time had made to mourn their dead.

ELEVEN

Beneath the fattening new moon in a Mediterranean evening sky the color of indigo, Mélusine Devarre played a flashlight beam on the terrain ahead as she limped determinedly up a steep mountainside. Behind her came her husband, carrying in his arms the open-eyed but inert body of the priest Etien Boudrie, whom they had taken from the nursing home in Marseilles for a supposedly brief outing—"Let's face it, this is kidnapping pure and simple," Roger Devarre had remarked as they drove away—earlier that afternoon. On the mountaintop ahead, perhaps half a kilometer further, stood the twelve-century-old fortress of Montsévrain—once home to the band of renegade Templars led by Guilhem de Courdeval. Silent, massive, its crumbled dark stones lit only by the ghostly moonlight, it stood like a fitting monument to the evil its walls had once sheltered.

They had come in darkness to avoid being seen. "Are you sure we wouldn't be better off doing this in, say, a church?" Devarre panted. "Someplace we could drive to?" Though in his months of coma the priest had shrunk to not much more than half his previous bulk, he still weighed a good sixty kilos, and Devarre had not been able to bring himself to carry his friend slung over his shoulder like a sack. He possessed a considerable wiry strength, and by careful exploration and maneuvering, they had been able to drive to within two kilometers of the fortress. But the August night was hot, the terrain rough, and his mind uneasy. The last time he had set foot inside the ruin of Montsévrain was the evening his pleasant, comfortable world had shattered into nightmare.

"I'm going on intuition," Mélusine said, breathing hard, too. Her weak leg was her own burden. "My sense is that Montsévrain is the doorway from which he departed—like someone falling through a hole in the ice on a frozen lake. In order to get out, they must return to that hole." She moved to him and laid a hand on his shoulder. "I know it's very hard work."

"I was joking," he said. "I'll carry him to Lourdes if you think it will help." But each time his gaze fell on Boudrie's drawn face, still wide-eyed with shock after most of a year, he knew the truth: the priest was not going to survive much longer. The nursing sisters kept him alive by spooning pureed food and liquids into his mouth; but soon he would require intravenous feeding. Unlike some life-support patients, he showed no signs of stabilizing, but continued to waste steadily away.

Stopping frequently to rest, they labored on among the muted sounds of their breathing, their footsteps, and the occasional trill of a nightingale from the surrounding forest. The warm night breeze smelled of lavender and pine. At the lip of the brush-choked ravine that guarded the fortress's entrance like a moat, they paused once more. Then Devarre stepped down into the thicket, bent forward to shield Boudrie's face from the whipping, snapping branches, and a minute later stood gasping before the archway's great stones.

Without speaking, Mélusine limped past him into the courtyard. It was the first time that she had set foot inside the fortress. She turned slowly in a circle, her eyes searching the comers of the dark walls while her mind absorbed the emanations of what the stones had once witnessed. She summed this up in a single whispered word:

"Dreadful."

Devarre carried the priest inside and laid him carefully on the spot where he had found him, unconscious, *that night*. Mélusine watched anxiously. She had half hoped that Boudrie would react, even in fear, to his surroundings. Once, and once only, in the many times they had visited the nursing home, she believed she had seen a faint trace of awareness in those staring eyes. But tonight they remained unchanged, mirroring only the moonlight.

Wherever he had gone, it was very far away.

"Show me exactly what happened," she said, hearing the unsteadiness of her own voice. She handed her husband the flashlight.

He directed its beam at a large, flat stone that jutted from the earth some twenty meters ahead, near what appeared to be the rim of a well–but was, she knew, a filled-in dungeon.

His own voice was unusually harsh. "I came through the entrance and found Etien lying here, just as he is now. There was no one else, only a small fire near that stone slab. I checked him, found that he was still alive and outwardly unhurt, but couldn't get any response from him. Then I went to the fire and found that the stone was soaked with blood. A knife was lying at its foot."

He turned back to her, eyes glinting, nostrils slightly flared. "That was when I decided that there was a madman on the loose, you were alone in the house below, and our poor friend here was just going to have to take his chances."

Slowly, she walked toward the stone. It was the size of a small table, and she understood that it had been erected as the foundation of an altar long since pulled down. She could almost hear the shrieks of victims dragged from the dungeon a few meters away, while Courdeval and his black-robed knights chanted fiercely to the dark god they worshipped. Though the stone had been chemically bleached of color since that night, on it remained a faint ragged outline of the stain from the blood its porous surface had soaked up: Alysse's blood.

Hugging herself, shaking her head in protest, she walked back to where her husband waited beside the priest.

"Difficult to imagine," she said, "that a man could be so unrelentingly evil."

Devarre shrugged. "Power is a great lure. Think of all the leaders who have made careers of atrocity. Attila, Genghis Khan, Hitler, Stalin—who was it that said, 'Men

269

are good only when they do not have the strength to be bad'?"

She almost smiled. "I believe that's the first time I've ever heard you philosophize."

"I've had occasion to readjust my thinking over the past months," he said curtly, then added, "At least those men stayed dead."

Her gaze rose to the sky, searching, as if it held an answer. "I suppose," she said, "we'd better get on with it."

"Yes. What exactly are you going to do?"

"I don't really know. I'm still proceeding on feel. But I think–"

"You want to be alone."

She nodded apologetically. "To concentrate."

"I've always wondered what the lights of the Côte d'Azur would look like from this height. I'll be on top of the wall."

"Be careful," she called anxiously, thinking of snakes; her fear of them, which Courdeval had played on, was almost uncontrollable. Slowly, she turned to the inert, staring priest.

So how did one proceed in a situation like this? Strip naked and dance in the moonlight? Wail in forgotten tongues to implore the aid of strange gods? She knelt beside him and gazed down into his face. It was true that she sometimes sensed spirits and had even been contacted by them on occasion. But that was a very different matter than trying to summon some unquantifiable component of consciousness, from an unknown and unimaginable realm of being, of a human who, at least technically, still lived. They did not even know exactly what had happened to Boudrie, but had only Courdeval's mocking words to go on: *The priest is gone, to the realm of lost souls. He chose to play with a pet of mine.* She had made a point of not imagining what the "pet" might have been like. The thought was like a cold finger on her nape, and she could not keep herself from glancing around. For all she knew, Courdeval, in whatever form he was in now, could be watching her at this moment, perhaps with his pet at his side.

Devarre had crossed Boudrie's hands on his chest. She took one of them, holding it firmly in both of hers. It was huge, almost comically disproportionate to his emaciated body, and surprisingly warm. He had been a man of great physical strength, but now with his thinness and whitened hair, cut short by the nursing sisters, he looked old and feeble.

"Etien," she said. "We know the truth, at last, about Alysse. If you're concerned because you broke your vows, you must know it was a lovely sin, and one you've atoned for many times over. If you're guilty because you think it was responsible for her death, that is absurd–only part of Courdeval's manipulation, something he wanted you to believe, to gain power over you.

"And if you're frightened, well, so are Roger and I. But I know you are no stranger to fear. It's no secret in Saint-Bertrand that Etien Boudrie was a lion in the war.

"We need your help, we need your strength. Only you know exactly how this all came about. Only you might possibly help us to locate and combat this man–before we all die, and he inherits the earth.

"Think of us, think of yourself, think of all the innocents who will suffer if he is not stopped. But most of all, think of Alysse. She has come to me in torment. He is using her in some awful way, I am sure, and if he's not checked, it could go on forever.

"Came out, then, from behind your shame, your guilt, your fear—whatever is holding you where you are. Admit your failures and fight again. You no longer have the right to hide: you have a duty, as a man, as a priest, and as a father."

She searched the staring eyes, willing the spark of recognition she had once seen to return to them. There was not so much as a glimmer. She lifted her head and gazed unseeing into the darkness. The faint rustle of the breeze along the weed-grown pavestones was like the sound of whispering voices or dragging robes. Had she imagined that spark, tricked herself, her desire outweighing truth?

Anger rose suddenly—at herself, at him, at the injustice and horror of the whole affair—and she used it, bending close over him and seizing his face with both hands.

"Damn it," she said fiercely, "you have no *right!*" She stared piercingly, deeper, deeper, forcing her will like an arrow into the dark void of his eyes, until the world around her began to slip, as if she was entering sleep—and then the world was gone.

She was in a sort of nightscape, a vast, lowering domain of dimly sensed images that were unlike anything earthly—some moving, some not. There was a need for haste; she could feel the wraiths' awareness of her and hear in her mind their whisperings and pleadings as they turned toward her, desperate to touch a living being, to draw her warmth into their own bloodless shapes. She pressed on, using fury as both sword and shield, but feeling the creep of fear, knowing she could not hold out long. She was fast approaching a barrier, an abyss, which held beyond it what she sought. But even as she started to hurl herself against it, she understood that if she crossed, there could be no return.

With that realization, her will collapsed, and panic surged as the pursuing shadows pressed close, their thin, hungry cries echoing shrilly in her mind, mounting, tearing at her—

Mélusine screamed, her hands clutching at her own face. Then there was whirling, spinning dizziness and nausea.

Finally she was aware again of silence, of the night breeze touching her skin, of the ache in her legs and the rough stones bruising her knees. When she opened her eyes, all was as before. To her left, running footsteps were coming close.

Devarre knelt beside her, his arm around her shoulders.

"All right?" he said, glancing around for an unseen enemy.

She nodded. "I failed," she said simply. "I got close, but couldn't go on."

He squeezed her tightly, then helped her to her feet. "You're the one who's always telling me how powerful such things are." They looked down at Boudrie—he was unchanged—and then, by tacit consent, looked away. "Care to tell me anything about it?" Devarre said.

"Soon."

With forced lightness, he said, "It's hard for a man to admit that he's getting used to his wife screaming."

"I'm sorry. I was surprised, too. I suppose I had a vague idea of what to expect. I just didn't know they were so—hungry."

His mouth tightened, but he said nothing.

She began to pace, arms folded. "So. What now?"

"I suppose we go home and grow old. Or try to."

"I feel like such a fool. If only I could have gone a little further."

"Would another try help?"

She shook her head. "I'm afraid it's simply impossible for me. Someone stronger, perhaps."

"We'll keep looking, then."

She shrugged. Perhaps there were people who could help, but she had not the faintest idea of how to find them.

Devarre turned back to Boudrie and crouched beside him.

"I'm sorry, my friend," he said. "I had hoped with all my heart you would walk home under your own power." With effort, he gathered the priest in his arms and stood.

He had taken perhaps a dozen steps when a faint, hoarse wheeze startled him into almost dropping his burden. He stared down into Boudrie's eyes. They were clearing, beginning to move, and Roger Devarre felt the hairs on his arms lift and separate. The priest's eyes rolled until they found Devarre's face, then spent several seconds focusing.

"Brandy," he whispered.

Mélusine was at his elbow, taking a small silver flask from her handbag. As Devarre supported the priest's head, she held the flask to his lips, watching his eyes light with pleasure.

She looked at her husband, and her face broke into a wide grin.

"I had a premonition," she said.

The August sun began its descent into evening, lighting the westerly windows of the Sunset district like sheets of flame. Jesse Treves sat on Nicole's couch, reading the San Francisco Chronicle, while in the kitchen, she essayed her first Irish stew. On the end table beside him rested a well-watered glass of bourbon which he sipped carefully, at measured intervals.

"Hey, check this out," he said, and rose to lean in the kitchen doorway so she could hear. "Some poor dude up on Russian Hill a couple of nights ago was getting it on with his girlfriend, when all of a sudden he starts grabbing his crank and screaming, and jumps through the window. Twelfth floor."

In the middle of slicing potatoes, she paused. "It says that?"

"Well, not exactly in those words. The deal is, see, they think it was an attack of this rare condition called bang-utot, where a man decides his prick is going to retract into his body and kill him. Found mainly among

275

males of Malaysian extraction, although this individual was a round-eye."

"That's a lovely bit of information" she said. "Thanks for sharing it with me."

"Yeah. I guess it's what you call a human interest story."

She did not reply. After watching her a moment, he tossed the paper on the table, took her shoulders, and turned her around to face him.

"What's going on?" he said. "You've been jumping down my throat every time I opened my mouth today."

"Have I?" she said uncertainly. She held the knife in one hand, a potato in the other. Twisting to set them on the counter, she put her hands on his hips and pulled him close. "I guess I'm nervous," she said into his shoulder. "About things I probably shouldn't be. Tommy coming home, for one."

"What's to worry? We're best buddies, and I'll keep my distance until he gets used to the idea."

She nodded. Voice muffled, she said, "I think what it really is, it just seems too good to be true. When you've been alone so long, you get suspicious that something like this can't last. You know?"

"Hey," he said, pulling back. "It's been twenty years since I looked into a woman's eyes and said 'I love you.' They're going to have to kill me to take it away."

Nicole smiled, her eyes damp. "Are you really ready to leave this town?"

"Hell, yes. Only reason I've been hanging around is I'm too lazy to move. But with an old lady who's got a job, I can perfect laziness to an art. Baby, I can see it all: forty acres of weeds and scrub, a house with blistered paint and a sagging porch, and me lying on it drinking Tree Frog beer, watching you stagger home exhausted from your little country office and put on your apron to start dinner. That's what I call a relationship, man."

She laughed, and he kissed her mockingly and released her. The truth was that he had a pretty good chunk of money in the bank, the result of years of steady work and solitary living. He figured he could afford to set aside ten grand for each of his girls for when they turned twenty-one, and still have enough left over for a down payment on a place and some cushion. Besides which, he'd probably make more money contracting on his own than he was making now.

It seemed, simply, the most sensible thing in the world to get out of the city, find a suitable piece of land somewhere up the coast, build a house on it, and raise Tom Junior and maybe a couple of little brothers or sisters. In fact, it was so remarkable the way his world had changed during the past few weeks that he could not quite get a handle on it. Everything began and ended with this woman with the bewitching eyes, who had infused emotion into the wasteland of his existence like a marvelous, overpowering drug. He had not once drunk more than moderately since their first night—hadn't even felt the urge. The thought of becoming a father again, which until recently would have roused him only to sardonic laughter, now seemed thrilling. Nothing was difficult; the impossible merely required more attention.

"I only wish," he said to her, straight now, "I'd been smart enough to figure this out when we first met. Some kind of fool, huh."

She smiled again but seemed distracted. "One teaspoon black pepper," she read aloud, leaning close to the cookbook.

Later, from her bedroom, Nicole phoned Tom Junior. Tom Senior's wife, Dulcie, answered the phone. True to her name, she was a sweet-natured woman, a pretty, softish blonde who was a little intimidated by Nicole's professional status. Her nervousness communicated itself; she always seemed so anxious to demonstrate that no hostility existed on her part that she would extend the most minor contacts into attempts at intimacy. Nicole invariably came away fatigued; another vampire, she thought, as Dulcie described in detail the events of her week. But she was genuinely fond of Tom Junior, and so Nicole summoned patience and endured.

At last Dulcie relinquished the phone to Tom Junior. "Hi, Mom," he said. "Dad and Dulcie are taking me to Disneyland tomorrow."

His lack of enthusiasm was noticeable even over the telephone.

"Is something wrong?" Nicole said immediately.

"No, I'm fine," he said, again without conviction.

"Tommy," she said, leaning forward intently. "You tell me this second if something's bothering you."

"Well, it's no big deal," he said after another hesitation. "I just had a real weird dream."

Nicole relaxed a little, but said, "Tell me about it."

"It was a couple of nights ago. I'd been feeling kind of creepy anyway when I went to bed. Then I woke up and there was, like, this skull looking in the window. It hung there for a couple of seconds, grinning at me.

"Then it opened its eye. That was the really scary part."

Too many movies, Nicole thought grimly, and started to say, I want to talk to your father; but caught herself. The less she made of it, the better. He would be home in three weeks, and a tighter regimen would begin again.

"The thing is," Tom Junior said, "I'm pretty sure I was awake."

"Lots of times we think we're awake when we're dreaming," Nicole said. "It can be hard to tell."

"Yeah. But I'm pretty sure I was. I mean, after it went away, I went over to the window and looked out. There was nothing else around. It's on the second story."

"Hm." She tapped her fingers on the arm of the couch. "Did you tell your father?"

"No. It didn't seem important in the morning."

"Well, if it happens again, tell him. And if you get scared, you call me right then and there, okay? It doesn't matter what time it is."

"Okay. Thanks, Mom."

That did not seem like much help. Three weeks, she reminded herself.

"Disneyland, huh?" she said. "I guess it's going to seem pretty dull around here when you get back."

"Probably a little," he admitted.

She smiled, and almost said, Well, I'm going to have a surprise for you. But she was not certain how he would react to the news about Jesse. Confusion seemed an all-too-likely response.

By the time they had chatted a few more minutes, he seemed to have brightened.

"Okay, baby," she said. "I can't wait to see you."

"Me, too. Say hi to Jesse."

"Will do. Love you." Reluctantly, she put down the phone.

She rose and walked to the front of the apartment. It was too automatic and too easy to blame her ex for the dream, or for any other disturbance, but she could not suppress the feeling that it would not have happened if Toni Junior had been home.

Jesse was on the couch, watching *The Man Who Knew Too Much*.

"Everything okay?" he said.

"Yes." Then she added, "I think he's ready to come home." She went to the kitchen and poured two glasses of chilled white wine, carried them to the couch, and sat without warning on his lap. "Ever seen this movie before?"

"Maybe five times."

"Are you prepared to consider an alternative suggestion?"

"I can be reasonable."

She held the two long-stemmed glasses up before his face. "Let's take off our clothes and get in bed and drink this stuff real slow."

"My mama didn't raise any stupid sons," he said, and lifted her easily as he stood.

TWELVE

After saying Mass and changing into work clothes, Etien Boudrie waited in the rectory of Saint-Bertrand-sur-Seyre for Mélusine and Roger Devarre to come take him for a drive. They had done this most days during the three weeks since his awakening, and with Mélusine's determined feeding and Roger's helping him to exercise, he had announced himself strong enough to do a bit of exploring.

Although outwardly they were only going for a stroll in the woods, in truth the excursion had an almost humorously grim purpose: to try to find the bones of Guilhem de Courdeval.

It had been a most interesting three weeks. Boudrie was bedridden during much of the first few days, but then began to get up and walk for increasingly longer periods. He also had to be weaned back onto solid food. Devarre had taken care of the business of notifying the nursing home in Marseilles, eliciting a visit from the skeptical, even indignant, doctor who had supervised

Boudrie's care during the months he had spent there comatose.

Devarre had at first maintained that the recovery was simply spontaneous; but the nursing home doctor, perhaps in an effort to save face, then joined forces with the young *curé* who had taken over for Boudrie, and the word miracle, attributable to St. Bertrand du Cians himself, began to be whispered around the village.

At this point, Boudrie and the Devarres agreed quietly that something must be done; and so Devarre admitted to his nursing home colleague that for several months he had been surreptitiously performing a combination of hypnosis and psychotherapy during his visits to Boudrie. The explanation satisfied no one, least of all the ambitious young priest, but the fact that the Devarres were atheists, or at least non-Catholics, tipped the balance, and the matter was dropped.

In the meantime, Boudrie began to resume his clerical duties. To his amazement and chagrin, he discovered that whatever the official position, the villagers were as joyous about his return as if he had borne a halo. The first time he said Mass, old women fell to their knees weeping and kissed the hem of his cassock. The length of the lines waiting outside his traditionally empty confessional made his heart sink. He wanted to shake them, growl that the truth was just the opposite—that if they had any inkling of what had really happened, they would understand that the very reasons for his trouble were rooted in his own vileness.

But as the days passed, be began to discover a more solid explanation for his popularity: his replacement,

283

young Father Tibouchet, had been a martinet on fire with the first enthusiasm of serving God, and he had badgered, bullied, and levied penances that sent the villagers home clutching their hair. Boudrie's return brought back the good old days of two-minute sermons, three-Hail Mary penances, and a priest who could be counted on to share any tasty bit of gossip. He assured himself that this was the true source of his flock's elation, and with mixed feelings, he put the matter out of his mind. Tibouchet went back to the diocesan headquarters in Marseilles with Boudrie's blessings and hints that he would use what influence he could to see that the younger man was assigned to a more active and exciting parish, one befitting a Christian soldier of his enthusiasm.

And now Etien Boudrie sat in the so-familiar room in the little stone house that had been his home for thirty years, with a pot of strong coffee and fresh croissants awaiting his guests. It was strange to be back: good, but different, with the haunting sense that things would never be the same again. Exactly where he had been the past months, he could not say, although he knew it had been all too vivid and real at the time. It was as if a merciful amnesia had intervened at the time of his change from that dreamscape to this one; that whatever had created the rules of this immense cosmic contest–for that, orthodoxy notwithstanding, he was convinced by now it was–had decreed that while one might conceivably travel to such a psycho-spiritual realm, and even be aware of that travel, one could not take the memory of actual experience back and forth. He was inclined to believe that such oblivion was for the best. While he did not think he had actually been in discomfort, he was quite certain that it was not an experience he would want repeated. He had gained something from it–a calm, an absence of fear–but he had lost something too; and he felt that his physical death was not far in the future. He rose and stood before the parlor window, watching as morning came to the village he thought of as his.

Saint-Bertrand had never been a prosperous town, but in the early days of his tenure, faith was strong. Things had changed more in that respect during the past thirty years than in the previous fifteen centuries. Once there had been three priests, and the bells had proudly announced matins and vespers. Saints' days were ob-served by the entire village, with joyous celebrations in the cathedral. But with the waning of faith came a time when the only people who heard Mass on winter morn-ings were ancient, black-clad women wrapped in shawls, like harbingers of the death of the Church. The number of young priests lessened each year.

In those three decades, the Vatican Council had radically altered the liturgy, popes and bishops had come and gone, and the youth of the world had turned their back on the old religion. But Boudrie had remained, like a forgotten exile, sinking deeper and deeper every year, through the dark, dreary months when the tourists vanished and the mistral raged through the Alpes-Maritimes, into the sense of living in a medieval village many days' journey from a real city instead of a short drive or phone call away. Somewhere along the way, his weekly visits to confess to a brother priest in Grasse had gone to biweekly. Later, months often elapsed between trips. From time to time he remembered to marvel at how the years had disappeared in the sweep of routine. It had much to do with his long-ago discovery of what a friend alcohol could be to the lonely.

With grim amusement, he pictured himself as others must, and as he saw himself on those rare occasions when he paid attention to what looked back from his shaving mirror: a thickset, bumbling man with unkempt hair gone white, who since his sickness looked a decade older than his sixty years. His broad jaw and florid nose marked him as a peasant overly fond of the grape. His hands were as big as books, hanging from hamlike arms and bullish shoulders that were only beginning to recover their strength, but that once had lifted the front of a jeep off the ground on a bet–and another time, had carried a badly wounded comrade eleven kilometers over rough, hostile terrain, in darkness, to safety. Etien Boudrie had been seventeen.

He turned and prowled the room, examining the familiar objects he had replaced after Tibouchet's departure: the somewhat lurid portrait of his namesake, St. Etienne, kneeling beneath a savage volley of stones, face aglow with the holy light of forgiveness; a moon-faced Madonna with child; a rosary blessed by His Holiness Pope John XXIII many years before, on one of Boudrie's few journeys to Rome; the shelves of dusty leather tomes containing unbearably ponderous devotional texts of the sort read during mealtimes at monasteries; and, setting it all off, an entirely secular calendar with photos of the Côte d'Azur, most of which exposed a scandalous amount of female flesh. There was

286

also his single keepsake from the war, a German officer's stiletto: the *memento mori* he forced himself to hold, from a night in a village called Vézey-le-Croux, when his own hands had lit a fire that took the lives of nineteen Nazi soldiers billeted in a barn. He thought fleetingly, longingly, of brandy. His thirst for it had been waiting, on his return from his unearthly exile, like a lover.

In the year 1307, so the legend went, among the first of Courdeval's victims—and the man who had indirectly caused the giant Templar's downfall—was a priest of Saint-Bertrand named Larmedieu, literally, "God's tears." Though he had been murdered at the altar—murdered, at least, for all intents and purposes; his body had lived on for some months in a state of shock Boudrie recognized all too well—and had behaved with heroic courage, recording the terror that had struck the village right up until his last hour, no proceedings to canonize him as a martyr had ever been initiated. His body was not even buried in his home churchyard, but in an unknown spot in Avignon, the seat of the Babylonian papacy. The doors of the cathedral of St. Bertrand had been closed for decades, under interdict, as a result of what had taken place. Courdeval's spirit had at last been put down, almost miraculously—until last autumn.

But even before he had learned the truth of the legend, Boudrie had sensed that this curacy was subtly, irrationally tainted. Although to his knowledge he had never done anything to earn the displeasure of his superiors, the uneasy feeling had grown in him over the years that his presence here was no accident.

And though he had sometimes spent days during the dark of winter drinking to stave off the dread that pressed upon him like earth around a coffin, though sometimes it took him an effort that nearly brought him to his knees to perform the simplest priestly duty, and though his hatred for the stupidity, greed, and stubbornness of his flock had led him to rage around the rectory, staggering drunk, shouting, cursing, thundering tirades at imaginary parishioners, he had finally come to know the truth: this was what he was. His rages, like his drinking, took the edge off emotions he might otherwise have directed against his people. As it was, his treatment of them, like his sermons and penances, rarely even approached sternness; and sometimes it was in the depths of his ugliest sieges of depression that he felt the touch of a mysterious love for his fellow sufferers. As if the superiors who had sent him to Saint-Bertrand and left him there thirty years had foreseen it, the village and he had come to a sort of peace that passed all understanding. So for his vices of anger and drink, he forgave himself.

The infinitely more serious problem was that his faith–faith as he had once known it; faith in the good God he had devoted his life to serving–had been eroded away by the events of a single night. He was a man going through motions. The splendid irony lay in the fact that at last he was certain there was indeed a power like that he had always thought of as God. But he was left with questions that smacked of Lucifer's rebellion. Why had God created such misery? It implied a sort of mystical tyranny, a deity who sat back smugly, watching his created beings sweat and bleed and scramble from disappointment to disappointment until they collapsed in final agony–all the while holding a mighty fist poised to smash anyone who dared to be discontent. And if there was a reason beyond the unsatisfactory explanations of orthodoxy, then why were humans kept in such ignorance of it?

Finally, he was certain only that he had been given the chance to play a key role in the incomprehensible cosmic drama: to atone for his own iniquities and perhaps help to save others–

And that he had failed.

And having failed, he was destined to die here as he had lived, in weakness and obscurity, in no long time.

The Devarres arrived a little before nine. They had agreed that it would be best to finish their task early, to avoid the worst of the heat. Boudrie served the coffee and pastries, then said:

"Shall we begin this venture by reviewing once more all the information we have of Courdeval?" They had already filled one another in on their individual experiences of that night. His memory up to the moment of his own undoing remained surprisingly clear. "What else is there, even unimportant little scraps, that we can recall?"

Mélusine and Roger exchanged glances, and she sighed.

"Only one thing, really. I wasn't altogether honest in what I told you about Alysse."

Boudrie's gaze moved to a distant part of the room. He waited.

"While I was alone in the villa," she said, "after I sent Roger to see about you. Nothing happened for most of an hour, except that I got quite frightened. The candles were burning down, and I didn't know where to find more.

"Then two figures arrived: McTell, or so I thought–I recognized him from the photograph in the study–and Alysse. At first, of course, I was overjoyed; McTell was covered with blood, but she seemed safe. When I saw that he was in no immediate danger, I demanded an explanation." She shook her head. "That's when he revealed to me who he really was."

"And Alysse?" Boudrie said quietly.

"It had already happened," Mélusine said. "The blood was hers; he made her take off her scarf and show me the wound. And yet . . . she was walking."

Slowly, feeling very old, Boudrie got out of his chair and paced to a window, hands in the pockets of his overalls. He had known the girl was dead–and had known, too, that her body had not been found.

But he had not imagined that Courdeval, by means of some vile necromancy, had kept her animated.

It was said that he could raise the dead.

His voice soft and even, Boudrie, said, "She's still with him?"

Mélusine was looking down into her coffee cup. She nodded without raising her head.

"I think so. Remember that I told you back then, I was already sensing her spirit being troubled, pushed from her body? Well, she came to me again, only a few weeks ago." Mélusine raised her face, concerned but frank. "She asked for you, Etien. Or rather, she asked for her father."

Without turning, he said, "Then you know." He did not seem surprised.

"We had no desire to pry, Etien," Devarre said. "But it was all we had to go on. We asked Mlle. Perrin. For the record, she was most reluctant; it almost amounted to an interrogation."

Boudrie nodded. When he had seen the little woman, she had seemed timid, almost fearful; probably she thought he knew that she had given away the secret.

"I'll add that I'm quite sure that was how I was able to call you back," Mélusine said.

When he turned again, his face looked so pained and weary that she rose and went to him, took his shoulders, began to speak reassuring words. He embraced her quickly and hushed her.

"I thank you for your kindness, madame; we all must carry our own burdens. Let us continue. Did Alysse communicate anything else?"

"I asked her where she was. She replied that she could not say. I was hoping, of course, to get an idea of where her physical body was, assuming it's with Courdeval and we might locate him. My sense is that she was only recently reawakened and troubled, which would indicate he's making use of her again.

"At any rate, it was a wasted question, one I've kicked myself for many times. I didn't realize how weak she was, already fading. The only other thing I got from her were the letters L-I-V, when I asked what we must know in order to help. Then she was gone."

"*Livre*," Boudrie said suddenly. "Courdeval's book, his grimoire." Could it be that she was trying to tell them it was a point of vulnerability to him, that if they could seize it, they might weaken him? There were other indications to that effect. "The Inquisition maintained that was the key reason they were able to overcome him: he was separated from the grimoire and burned before he could reach it."

"That didn't stop him afterward," Devarre muttered.

"True," Boudrie admitted. "Perhaps as a spirit, he had access to it–at least until he was interred. But you raise a most important point: What are the limits of his power?"

"We know that even as pure spirit, he could send dreams and visions," Mélusine said. "Damage, even kill, by means of them. Cause illness, as with Mlle. Perrin. Obsess, and to a greater or lesser extent, control minds–particularly young or frail people, like Alysse."

And command a familiar spirit whose description was beyond nightmare, Boudrie thought grimly, steeling himself against the memory of the instant when the "pet's" hood had slipped back. It was a sight he hoped with all his heart no eyes would ever see again. He said nothing.

"Obviously, he could take control of a human body," Devarre said, "which he may well have done again."

"I've given some thought to that," said Boudrie. "I doubt it. The process obviously required a great deal of effort on his part, and I'm much mistaken if it wasn't quite risky for him, too. I suspect he would find it far easier to eliminate the three of us. You've found from experience that no one in authority would believe this story. With us gone, he would have nothing more to fear.

"In any case, if we should be so fortunate–or unfortunate–as to find him, we must remember: He was taken once before."

None of them spoke their common thought: Yes, by a small army, who knew where and what he was.

"So," Boudrie said. "Let us try to discover whether the business about the interred bones is true. If it is, perhaps we may assume more."

"And if there's something–attached to them?" Devarre said.

"A magical booby trap?" said Boudrie, smiling icily. He turned to Mélusine.

She shrugged. "I may or may not be able to sense it, but I'll try." Her face went wry. "I've never worked as a miner's canary before."

Weeds had grown up along the driveway to the villa. An almost visible air of desertion hung about the house. From the back seat of the Devarres' Citröen, Boudrie gazed around, remembering the last time he had arrived at this place, not quite a year before, in the same car, with the same two people. But then it had been night, and they had been hurried by fear.

They got out and walked in silence across the drive toward the swimming pool, each absorbed in the impressions left by various objects and events from that night. Here, McTell's BMW had waited, its door left carelessly open–their first confirmation that something was amiss; there, the main door to the darkened house had also been flung wide. Inside the glassed entrance from the patio, Mélusine had stood watching with relief the figures she thought were McTell and Alysse, returning home safely.

The pool itself was empty, the bottom choked with leaves and debris. The water had been procured illegally, during a drought, to fill the pool for the McTells' luxury. If the legend was true, this had begun the whole evil business. But who could have dreamed it? Boudrie felt a stab of pity for McTell and his wife. Certainly, an overwhelming price had been paid for a little bit of greed.

"I suppose we should start at the filter and see if we can trace a pipeline up the mountain," he said. He was going on information he had gleaned from one of the well diggers who had uncovered the spring that for centuries had guarded Courdeval's bones.

"*D'accord,*" said Devarre. He went to the car and got from its trunk two long-handled shovels and a heavy iron crowbar. Mélusine, wearing jeans and a cotton work shirt, had a rucksack with ice water and two powerful flashlights.

They quickly made the agreeable discovery that the well digger had buried the pipeline superficially and with obvious haste, scooping a trench barely deep enough to cover the five-centimeter plastic pipe and then scattering it over with a thin layer of dirt and pine duff. They were able to trace it easily for the first hundred meters; the work became harder as they reached thicker brush and a steeper slope. Devarre was in the lead, probing with the point of his shovel every few meters until it clunked against the plastic, while Boudrie and Mélusine labored, with greater effort, up the hill.

Soon they came to a small grove of unkempt cypresses.

"Not too far now, I think," Boudrie panted. "He described these trees." It was the cypresses that had led the well diggers to suspect a hidden spring and begin dowsing. Both had died mysteriously not long after.

The sun was mounting, and Boudrie had begun to sweat. He squinted up at the mountaintop, to where the ruined fortress overlooked the valley of the river Seyre. Mica sparkled in its bone-colored walls. The sky was like a slate of polished turquoise, the vegetation an emerald mosaic on the rust-colored hillsides that converged into gorges and drying streambeds, sweeping down to the Mediterranean some forty kilometers south. It was postcard-perfect beauty. He could not imagine a more ludicrous mission in such a setting.

"Yes, this must be it," Devarre called. Boudrie took Mélusine's hand and helped her up the final few steep meters to where Devarre stood, pointing with his shovel at where he had uncovered the pipe leading into the mountainside. A couple of minutes' work exposed a precast concrete collection box that also showed signs of a hasty installation: the ground around it was damp beneath the surface. In medieval times, the spring had been one of the main sources of water for the fortress above, probably hauled up the mountain by mules. Dammed over Courdeval's bones, the water had found other channels into the earth, the overflow doubtless disguised by rain during the winter and too minimal to be noticed in the dry season—until the arrival of the well digger.

"The carved stone should be beneath our feet," Boudrie said. "Let's start with that. If we find it, we'll know the man wasn't completely mad."

The brush was easily cleared and tossed aside, the dirt was loose, and only a minute or two passed before Devarre's shovel found the outline of a stone a little more than a meter long and a little less than that wide. When they cleared it off, they saw that it was hand hewn, a rectangle of granite some thirty centimeters thick. With effort, using the crowbar, they turned it over. Boudrie knelt to examine the letters carved into its surface, wiping dirt from them with his sleeve.

"No doubt about it," he said. "It's precisely as in the legend." The characters read:

IN FLUCTIBUS AQUARUM
ACCLINAVIT ME

There followed three crosses in a horizontal line. Then:

QUIESCENTEM NE MOVETO

The first sentence, Boudrie knew, was a deliberate misquote from St. Jerome's vulgate: *He maketh me to lie down in running waters;* the second was a more pointed, *Disturb not that which rests.*

A warning that might have spared a more literate— or less greedy—pair of well diggers' lives.

Boudrie stood. They looked at one another. Then the men attacked the hillside with their shovels.

The dirt had settled from the winter rains, but was still easy digging. From time to time, one of the sweating men would exchange his shovel for the crowbar and spend a minute loosening the impacted rocks. Mélusine watched anxiously, ice water at the ready.

After perhaps fifteen minutes, Devarre drove the point of his shovel through the remaining thin crust into a space. Instinctively, both men stepped back, as if fearing the release of a poisonous gas—although it was not gas they feared. They waited, tense, alert; Boudrie could sense Mélusine straining to *feel* whatever might be there.

After a moment, he said, "Madame?"

She shook her head. "Nothing, at least that I can grasp."

"Good enough for me," Devarre said. He looked inquiringly at the priest, who nodded. Quickly, they widened the hole to its original size, discovering the ragged edges of mortar where the stone had been torn from the earth by the winch of the well diggers' truck.

"The moment of truth," Boudrie said. "May I?"

Mélusine handed him a flashlight. He leaned in, playing the beam down the three or four meters of tunnel he could see before it twisted to the left. The floor was wet to the lip of the opening, and in the distance he could hear the echo of dripping. The tunnel's roof and walls still bore the marks of the tools that had cleared the passageway almost seven centuries ago; and though there had been a few minor cave-ins, a crawling man could still fit, at least as far as he could see. He stepped back, handing the light to Devarre.

"Why don't you let me go?" Devarre said, after he had a look. "I'm skinnier and in better condition. You might get stuck. Then we'd have to bring a winch to haul you out. I'll call out and tell you what I find."

Reluctantly, Boudrie agreed. "It shouldn't be more than a few meters past the turn."

"All right, my love?" Devarre said to his wife. "Do I have your permission?"

Without the flashlight, she leaned into the opening and remained there, silent, for most of a minute. When she emerged, she nodded, her lips tight together.

Holding the light in front of him, Devarre scrambled in. They watched the flicker of the beam on the walls as he crawled on his knees and elbows. In a moment, he made the turn and the light was gone. Boudrie took Mélusine's hand and held it. They waited. A minute passed, and then another. He could fed the sweating of her palm.

He was about to release her and charge in when the beam of light appeared at the tunnel's bend. He saw her eyes close with relief, and exhaled silently himself as Devarre's mud-streaked face came into view.

"Put your doubts to rest," he called. "It's all true." He started to back out of sight, then reappeared and added, "There's plenty of room in the vault."

"Me first," Mélusine declared. Boudrie had not expected this, but he knew better than to argue. He helped her climb into the tunnel and waited decorously until she had passed the turn before he followed.

298

The distance was longer than he had imagined—or perhaps it only seemed that way. The wet stone was hard on his elbows and knees, and in spite of Devarre's assurances, the close walls gave him a scalp-prickling claustrophobia. Mélusine had taken the other light; the daylight behind was blocked by his body. He crawled on in dripping, echoing darkness.

At last he saw ahead a light reflected off the stone interior of a chamber a little smaller than a bank vault, one of the caves that catacombed the countryside. The walls, polished by millennia of dripping water, were smooth as steel, and small stalactites hung like teeth from the roof. Devarre and Mélusine were crouched in a film of water a few centimeters deep, on opposite sides of what the beam of their flashlights played over:

The skeleton of a large man.

In that instant, rage surged in Boudrie with blinding intensity: the hot, fierce lust to have the man who had once surrounded those bones before him right now, so that he could tear the life from Guilhem de Courdeval with his own priestly hands. His fingers dug into the cold, wet stone he knelt on, and he tried to tell himself that his desire for revenge was wrong, tried to pray for charitable thoughts. Nothing within him answered. He rose to a crouch and moved forward to join the others.

"A giant," he murmured, "just as they said." Even stretched out, the skeleton was clearly almost two meters in height, as broad as an ax handle across the shoulders, with a thick, barrel-like rib cage. The face was set in the usual grinning rictus, but this one seemed smug.

And why not, with a man who had gone to his death knowing he would cheat it?

"Have we seen enough?" Devarre said, his voice echoing amid the dripping water. Boudrie nodded and turned to begin the crawl back to sunlight.

Outside, the three of them dabbed with handkerchiefs at the mud on their faces and hands, then sat on the ground, passing the plastic jug of water among them.

"We could try damming them up again," Boudrie finally said without conviction, answering the unspoken question: *Now what?* He looked at Mélusine, one eyebrow raised.

She was shaking her head. "He's gone."

"I suspect you to be right. Well, we can hardly just leave them there. Although given what we know about the man, I can't very well give them a Christian burial, either. We could try a crossroads at midnight, I suppose." His voice trailed off.

"May I make a suggestion?" Devarre said. "I've been scheming in case it turned out this way; analytical habits die hard. My reasoning goes something like this: everything we've found so far leads us to believe that the legend is substantially correct, right down to the matter of the bones being undamaged by fire—not to mention seven centuries of immersion in water. All of which bolsters the belief that there was in fact some sort of . . . magical"—the word came with difficulty from his lips—"protection on them, since they would certainly have charred to some extent, under normal circumstances, when he was burned at the stake.

"Suppose we were to see if they'll bum now. If they don't, we can assume there's still some sort of operative attachment, and see about damming them back up, or acting on them in some other way to try to render him powerless."

"Spiritual blackmail," Boudrie said admiringly.

"Precisely. If they *do* burn, we can probably assume the magic is gone, and with it the attachment to Courdeval."

"And we're back to where we were," Mélusine said.

Devarre shrugged. "True. But we'd know more than we do now, which may one day help us in some way we can't yet see—and at least we'd have solved the problem of what to do with the bones."

Boudrie watched a small lizard emerge from behind a stone, moving in quick, darting movements to take a place in the sun.

"The fire would have to be very hot." he said. "An ordinary fireplace wouldn't suffice."

"I can help there. A friend of mine from medical school is now in the coroner's office in Nice. As you might imagine, holding such a job in such a place, he's very discreet."

"Madame?"

"Yes, I think so," she said. She stood, walked to the edge of the cypress grove, and, with folded arms, looked down over the deserted villa. At her approach the lizard scurried back into hiding. "But there's one more thing we should take into account. We're all aware of the belief that discarded materials from one's body—nail clippings, hair, what have you—contain a sort of essence that can be used magically to affect that person: like fashioning dolls in voodoo, or making love charms that incorporate such things."

"You're saying that tampering with the bones might affect Courdeval?"

"I don't know. I think the magical attachment that could hold him trapped is gone, probably transferred to whatever body he now occupies. As for the other–if something as insignificant as fingernails or shorn hair can conceivably be used to such effect, does it not stand to reason that bones which carried a man for fifty years would maintain some sort of similar bond?"

"I begin to see," Devarre said. "We could be taking a chance on alerting him to our doings."

She shrugged, turning to face them. "He knows perfectly well where we are now. What have we got to lose?"

Spencer Epps was whistling happily as he wheeled the Porsche smoothly up Bay Street toward the Marina. He had just come from three hours at the Jasper Tubbs, time he had spent mainly on the books. Business remained amazing. To Lou's delight, Spencer had taken over control of all finances a month before. He was astonished at how quickly he was learning to hide the steady profits the place continued to haul in–as if he was discovering a long-hidden talent, the thing he was born to do. He had become the soul of industriousness, consulting brokers and investment counselors, studying ways to liquefy and stash assets so that they would be difficult to trace—and easy to recover discreetly from someplace far away.

Tonight, after a stop by the house to shower, change, and pat Yvonne on the ass, he'd hit the bricks again, this time to the Club Tropicana to watch his sweetie dance. Then it was off for dinner and an evening of that pussy he just couldn't seem to get enough of. Maybe it was the money he was making, and the sense of power, of well-being, that went with it; he'd always been horny, but for the past month he'd been acting like a three-balled mountain goat.

In short, he was sitting right on top of the world. True, there remained a long way to go before he could make his move. But he was proceeding carefully, laying the groundwork—the way a smart, strong man would. By the end of the year, he figured to have at least a hundred grand socked away airtight, and if he could make it another year without anybody getting hip, he and Tina were set.

From time to time, he recalled that this remarkable change in his life—not just the money, but the confident, aggressive personality that had emerged with it—had coincided with meeting Valcourt. Whether that in truth had anything to do with his luck, Spencer did not know or much care. But if the man wanted him to mumble some gibberish every night and play games with magic once a month, he'd be delighted to do so. You bet. He'd keep on doing it just as long as things kept going well. Call it superstition.

Until, of course, it was time to split. After that, Valcourt could go fuck himself.

While Spencer was still ninety percent convinced that the magic rap was bullshit, Valcourt did say some interesting things once in a while. The bit about vampires, for instance. The more he'd thought about it, the more he'd started to see Yvonne that way: trying to keep a hold on him with her father's money, sucking the life out of him and getting fat on it, both literally and figuratively. Trying to hold him back from what he deserved to be. She might have been paying the bills, but he'd been carrying her in the other, more important ways: as Valcourt said, with his psychic blood.

That was going to change–soon.

He zipped the Porsche into the driveway and strode up the steps. Yvonne was sitting in a chair facing the door, her hands gripping the arms, wearing one of her tentlike dresses.

"Hi, hon," Spencer said, unknotting his tie as he crossed the room.

Then he realized that she was not watching TV, as he had assumed. The set was off. She was staring, not at it, but at him. Her face was pale and rigid. His gaze moved quickly to what rested in her lap: a stack of photos. Puzzled, disturbed, he stepped closer.

"What are those?" he said.

Slowly, she picked them up between her thumb and forefinger and held them before her.

"Filth," she said, in a cracked, dry voice hardly above a whisper. She leaned forward suddenly and flung them at him. They scattered and fluttered to the floor.

Spencer gave her a hard cool look, then stooped and picked up the nearest one. It took him a second to realize what he was seeing.

When he did, his heart began to thud.

It was in color, extremely clear and sharp. The setting–Tina's apartment–was immediately recognizable, as were the two figures who appeared in the frame. His glance flicked to the several other photos that lay face up on the floor: Tina on her knees and elbows, smiling beatifically into a pillow as Spencer clutched her offered hips, his head back, his mouth open in a cry. Tina with his cock buried to the scrotum in her throat, rolling her eyes wickedly at him. Tina astraddle him like a jockey, her perfect breasts flattening as she reached behind to caress his balls. Tina with a rolled-up bill in her nose, crouched over his belly, snorting a line of coke off his rigid penis. Tina reclining on one elbow, regarding Spencer bemusedly as he grazed between her thighs–

Spencer tried to swallow, but his mouth had gone cotton-ball dry. His pulse was a quick, steady drumbeat in his ears.

"I–" he said. "What–"

Yvonne's face was like a death mask. "I found them in a coat," she said, in the same eerie whisper.

Holding the photo to his chest, Spencer sank into a chair. The whirling in his mind was slowing a little. He was starting to think again. He dropped the photo, leaned forward, put his head in his hands.

"Yvonne," he said in a muffled voice. "I . . . I can't tell you how sorry I am. It just happened, one night when I was drunk. The woman was a whore, it was the only time—"

Yvonne stood, pointing a trembling finger. "I'm going to tell my father," she whispered. "I think I am." She turned and walked heavily out of the room.

Instantly, he was on his knees, grabbing the photos with shaking hands, staring at them in disbelief. Who the fuck had *taken* them? Surely not him or Tina—that much was obvious. He tried to pick out the night, his gaze flicking down the frames. Absurdly, he started to feel aroused. Then he threw them on the chair and paced. It was impossible to tell. There had been many such nights. The question remained, *Who?* Where had the son of a bitch been: behind a two-way mirror? In a closet, or a facing building, with a telephoto lens? And how the hell could they have gotten into his coat?

Unless Tina had set it up.

He stared unseeingly out the window, across the Marina parkway that minutes before had seemed green, busy, happy.

Was it possible? Had she become that impatient about his foot-dragging over the divorce? Impatient enough to do something this crazy, to try to destroy his marriage? How could she not realize how disastrous it would be for both of them?

Because she still thought he was made of money, unlimited and all his. She still had no idea of the true situation. Spencer swallowed against the burning in his throat, the sudden swelling fear that he was being betrayed on all sides.

Cool, Spence, he thought with closed eyes. You are cool. A smart, strong man played priorities, and right now the most significant of those by far was to keep Yvonne off the phone. That would be the end of the show.

He smoothed back his moussed hair with his hands, straightened his shirt, and hurried up the stairs. Yvonne was stretched facedown on the bed, a vast bulk encased in expensive fabric, weeping quietly, her arms clutching a stuffed bear. Spencer closed his eyes. Then he steeled himself, sitting carefully beside her, and touched her shoulder.

"Yvonne," he said. "Honest to God, it was just a mistake. A guy loses his head once in a while. It doesn't mean I love you any less, doesn't mean anything at all. I'll never do it again, I swear."

She sniffled, not moving.

"Yvonne," he said. "Please don't call your father. I understand how you feel, but you and I can handle this. Think of all the trouble it would cause; think of how it would make us both look."

In a ragged, catching voice she said, "Those pictures just . . . slapped me in the face."

He rolled his eyes, felt like tearing his hair. "It was the dumbest mistake I've ever made, a terrible thing. I was drunk, I hardly knew what I was doing. I swear to you, never again."

Her back quivered under his hand. She said nothing.

"Hey, give me a chance, huh?" he said softly. "I love you, Yvonne. I couldn't stand it if we split up." He leaned down and kissed her orangish hair, then stood.

"Where you going?" she said, her voice suddenly sharp.

"Just downstairs," he said soothingly. "I'm not leaving you, honey."

"Spence," she said, and he waited, agonized, in the doorway, while she collapsed again into tears, finally blubbering, "You never do any of those things with *me*."

He fled.

On the kitchen counter he laid out two long lines—*power* lines. Finished, he rinsed his nose and waited while the clear sense of control returned to his mind. A plan was beginning to take shape. It was wild, but worth a try.

The next meeting at Valcourt's was only a few nights away.

Suddenly, Spencer Epps found himself very eager to believe.

THIRTEEN

"Welcome again, my friends," Guy-Luc Valcourt said to the assembled four. "My intuition tells me this will be a most interesting night, so let us proceed without ado. Charity, have you discovered if our efforts last month produced a satisfactory effect?"

She nodded, her eyes flicking around nervously– looking, Nicole thought, as if she were fighting to keep from bursting into either laughter or tears. Her aloof- ness and air of superiority were gone, replaced by something Nicole had no trouble reading. Again and again she saw Charity's gaze linger on Valcourt's face.

"It very definitely worked," Charity said. "Beyond my wildest dreams. I found out through–a mutual acquaintance." She giggled nervously and stole another glance at Valcourt.

If he was aware of this new attention, he did not let it show.

"Excellent," he said. "You see, we are not just playing parlor games, but we are engaged in most serious work.

And if I am not mistaken, we have more of it to do tonight. Shall we see what it might be?"

As Valcourt turned toward the cabinet that held the vase, Spencer Epps cleared his throat. His friendliness of the previous meeting was gone; he seemed wound tight as a spring. Nicole realized that her own fingers were twisting in her lap as she watched him speak.

"Uh, I don't know if this is okay, but I have a real important and pressing problem. I thought maybe, if Robbie didn't mind—"

Valcourt looked inquiringly at Robbie, who answered with a shrug. "Fine with me," he said, leaning back in his chair and clasping his hands behind his head. "My life's not interesting enough for problems." Spencer exhaled with visible relief.

Valcourt said, "Your deep concern must be what warned me that a powerful matter was afoot tonight. By all means, tell us."

Spencer rested his elbows on his thighs and hunched forward.

"I've been married five years," he said, speaking haltingly, as if the words hurt him. "My wife and I have always gotten along fine. I always just sort of assumed I was in love with her.

"Then a few months ago I met this lady, and I fell in love. Really in love. Found out what it was all about." His eyes met Nicole's. They were challenging, defiant—even vaguely threatening. "*You* know what I mean," he said. It was not a question. Reluctantly, she nodded, her own gaze dropping.

310

"We started having an affair, Tina and me," he said. "I know it's wrong in a way, but it's the best thing I've ever had–it's changed my life like I can't believe. I realized I had to get a divorce, that's all there was to it. It wasn't fair to Yvonne, my wife, carrying on like that.

"When I told her, she, like, started to go crazy. I don't mean like mad and throwing things, I mean really crazy: quiet and calm. *Scary.*

"But what's really scary is that her father is in with the mob. She grew up with that whole business of how you can jerk people around by making them afraid. So she started in telling me she was going to call her old man and say I was beating up on her–all kinds of stuff like that. It gets wilder and wilder, the things she's going to accuse me of doing. And she swears she'll have me killed if I try to leave her."

His hands clenched and unclenched; the slender chain around his neck hung loose inside his open collar, catching the candlelight, adding a somehow ludicrous counterpoint to his words.

"I don't know if it's true or not, if she's called and told him anything, or if she ever would. Maybe she's just holding it over me. But a couple of nights ago, we had a really bad fight, and she started telling me about things these guys her father knows have done to people. She might be making it up, but it scares the hell out of me. Every time I turn around, I'm afraid there's going to be a man with a gun, forcing me into a car–that the last thing I'm ever going to see is the bottom of the Bay.

"I think what it comes down to is, she's gone crazy in a particular kind of way. Like, part of her is still totally

311

sane, but another part has flipped out. She could come into this room right now and charm the socks off everybody here. You could never get a shrink to certify her or anything. But when we got back in the car, she'd start whispering that she was going to have my balls cut off.

"I told her I'll give her money, I'll give her anything she wants. All I want is to live my life in peace, with Tina. But Yvonne says she won't let me leave her, ever. Every time I start out the door to work, she grills me. She calls me there twenty times a day and times me from when I leave to when I get back home. It's like the part of her that's flipped out has decided she's going to spend the rest of her life driving *me* crazy, too. The way things are going, it's not going to take very long.

"I mean, I know divorce is rough, and I'm sorry to hurt Yvonne—I love her too, I really do, or at least I loved who she used to be—but let's face it, I'm not going to give up the woman I really love, and whatever chance to be happy I have, to spend the rest of my life being terrorized by—a crazy woman." Spencer spread his hands imploringly, then let them drop to his thighs.

Valcourt paced slowly, hands clasped behind his back, head bowed in thought.

"Truly, a difficult situation," he said. "How deeply troubled even the most outwardly tranquil of lives so often are! Look only a little beneath the surface of the man on the street, my friends, be he rich or poor. More often than we can imagine, we will find tragedy in the wings.

"This is precisely what makes so valuable the work that you are learning to perform. Once again, we are

312

presented with a case no law can touch—and yet, the life of our comrade is rendered miserable, and he may even be in mortal danger from which he cannot defend himself. How are we to proceed?" The question was clearly rhetorical; Valcourt neither looked up nor paused.

"Let us consider potential courses of action. There is some doubt as to the seriousness of this woman's intentions. And yet, there is every possibility that she means real harm, and is capable of fabricating a story, to present to her father or his cohorts, which will bring this harm about. There is no way for us to determine the truth by ordinary means.

"But what is undeniable is that our friend Spencer is living under Damocles's sword, a hellish existence from which there seems to be no escape. The ending of a marriage is indeed a painful thing. But who among us can fault our brothers and sisters"—though he did not look at Nicole, he emphasized the word *sisters* slightly—"for desiring the happiness of love?"

He paused. No one spoke.

"Therefore, I propose this: that we employ another time-honored tradition of 'magic,' and seek to return this woman's malice to her, in whatever degree it is intended." He turned to Spencer. "Is this agreeable to you?"

Spencer's tongue wet his lips. "I don't see that I have much choice," he said.

"Shall we proceed, then?" Valcourt's gaze moved across their faces; apparently he took silence for consent, for he turned again to Spencer and said, "Do you have something of hers?"

"A photo," Spencer said, shrugging. He took it from his wallet. Nicole caught a glimpse of an attractive, if somewhat plump, dark-haired woman.

"Excellent," Valcourt said, moving to light the incense.

Nicole sensed Robbie stirring restlessly beside her, echoing her own unease. This was happening much too fast, without the usual discussion and exploration. She was not at all prepared to accept Spencer's story at face value. How could they be sure he was telling the truth? What if the poor woman was insane? They were convicting her on hearsay.

"Wait," she said timidly. "Spencer, do you really believe your wife would have you hurt? She's probably wild with jealousy; people say things they don't mean when–"

With obvious irritation, Valcourt interrupted her. "Please remember, Nicole, the lessons of our previous meetings. Adepts are not bound by the same petty rules as common men. We have the right, the *duty,* to take such matters into our own hands on occasions such as this, when no alternative of human justice presents itself. This is one of the many manifestations of power."

"But maybe she just needs help."

"When any human being makes a *threat,* with malice accompanying, that person is ultimately responsible for any consequences which might result. This is an absolute law; in time, you will understand it.

"But human justice is inadequate, and cosmic justice slow. We seek to expedite it. If her threat is empty, this action of ours will fall lifeless to the ground, like an

314

arrow that does not reach its mark. Then Spencer may seek other courses of dealing with the matter. At this moment, it is imperative to protect him."

In the tense pause that followed, Valcourt's gaze remained steadily on hers. Finally he smiled, his face relaxing.

"My friends, this matter we are contemplating–the neutralizing of a potentially mortal enemy–is of such a serious nature that I see I must preface it with another: something I ordinarily withhold until much later in a group's development. But you are precocious: The time has come to talk of power.

"Up until now, you have all been proceeding in your studies with only a sketchy awareness of what is in fact taking place. Now I tell you that in order for that awareness to grow–in order for you to strike out on your own and use your gifts without my constant guidance–you must choose the path of power.

"Power offers itself only to the strong. Used properly, it will grow of itself, like a well-nurtured seed. Ignored or neglected, it will die. Intrinsically, it is bound up with choice. You must *will* to accept it, to cultivate it.

"To this end, I offer you tonight a most rare opportunity."

Nicole watched him stalk to the mantel, spring open the glass case that held the grimoire, and take it in both hands. He turned again to face them.

"Here," he said, "is an object in which centuries of tremendous power, of a very special sort, have been concentrated. This book itself is like a dynamo, capable of charging those who understand its use." His voice was deepening and getting harsher, and his accent heavier, just as Nicole had sensed previously when he seemed excited.

"Because you arc all strong, and because the nature of our work has proved so serious so early on, I give you the opportunity for this leap of power, here, tonight. By choosing to accept it, you signify to all the entities in the universe that you are allying yourself with the force this book represents. The change this can bring about within you is beyond your present ability to imagine.

"So. If you will be one of the strong–become like a god compared to your fellow men–then place your left hand upon the cover of this book, above the emblem there emblazoned, and with all your will, say the words, *I so choose*."

Solemnly, he handed the book to Charity. Without hesitation, her gaze fixed on Valcourt's face, she put her hand on the book and spoke the words clearly. Valcourt murmured approval and carried the book to Spencer. Nervously, eyes shifting, Spencer repeated the act.

The book came to Nicole, hovering before her in Valcourt's steady hands.

"But Spencer, it's your *wife*," she said helplessly.

"What are you bitching about?" he lashed out with sudden fury. "Hey, lady, *you're* the one who wanted the love charm."

"Calm, my friends." Valcourt's iron voice rose to fill the room. "Nicole, we must know this minute whether you are with us or not; whether you will aid in our future work–or depart.

"But remember: once the seed of power has begun to grow, as it has already within you, there is no such thing as stasis. Either advance, and increase in strength"–his single-eyed stare held her, piercing, commanding–"or, like a dying plant, *forfeit all you have gained.*"

Her thoughts whirled, hesitation warring with images of Jesse, flicking like a kaleidoscope through her inner vision: his face, grinning, or soft during love-making; the home they had planned; the babies they hoped to raise into strong, beautiful children–

Abruptly, Robbie was on his feet, backing away, a shaking finger pointed at the book.

"*Don't* do it, Nicole!" he burst out. "I see, good God, I finally see what he's doing!" She followed his wide-eyed, frightened stare to Valcourt's face; the older man just watched with patient disdain, still extending the book to Nicole.

"I swear, Nicole, I'm not lying," Robbie said. His voice was lower now, almost pleading. "I can't explain, but it's trouble–I don't mean like with the cops, I mean *trouble.*"

"If you are quite finished," Valcourt said calmly, "I invite you to leave my house."

Robbie looked at Nicole once more, imploringly, then backed out of the room. The front door slammed and, seconds later, the Volkswagen's engine started. Valcourt stood as if carved of stone.

"He–he's gone," Nicole stammered.

"Yes," Valcourt said pleasantly. "A shame, but he is a foolish young man."

"But what was he talking about?"

317

Valcourt sighed. "Poor Mister Kinsella is possessed of a too-vivid imagination, compounded by a rather weak intelligence and the extensive use of mind-altering drugs. I regretted allowing him to join us almost from the first, fearing that something of this nature might occur. Let us say that while he believed he craved knowledge and power, in fact he wanted only the flirtation, the fantasy. Faced with the actuality–and the responsibility it implied–he was forced to confront his own inadequacy, and he denounced me as a means of saving face. Surely you have witnessed such behavior yourself in similar situations.

"Now, come, Nicole. Join us. Time presses." When she still hesitated, his voice turned harder. "Think of all that is at stake for you. Then ask yourself who you choose to believe: Mister Kinsella, or me."

Slowly, she placed her hand on the cover of the book. The leather had a slick, almost greasy feel.

"I so choose," she murmured.

Valcourt smiled broadly. "Ah, my friends!" he exclaimed, lifting the grimoire high into the air. "How happy you make me! It is a great day when three so talented people choose the path of power. The fact that one disturbed man has forsaken it is not a speck of dust by comparison.

"So! Let us immediately carry out our work for this night. Rise and join hands." He returned the book to its place on the mantel and produced a small oval mirror with a silver rim. This he gave to Spencer, positioning him in the center.

"By means of this," Valcourt said, "we will reflect back to her whatever malice she intends you."

Feeling she was in a bad dream, nostrils filled with the strange incense, Nicole watched Spencer hold the photo of his wife up to the mirror, his face excited and frightened. Valcourt chanted the familiar-sounding syllables, this time with an especially harsh intensity. The sense of force rose around them, continuing to climb until it made her dizzy. She spotted Lamashtu crouched on the mantel, watching them with knowing eyes, and sensed the power taking a dark, sinister turn.

Robbie Kinsella pulled out of Valcourt's driveway with his tires squealing. It had suddenly hit him, right at that instant, like a light bulb appearing over a cartoon character's head. This whole group meeting thing, this "development of the psychic gift," was bullshit: a cover.

The business of the grimoire was what had finally flipped the switch. It was a classic bit of Satanism, a reversal of Christian ritual: swearing an oath on an anti-Bible. As if a voice had spoken, he had understood at last that this was no joke or hobby—that they were dealing with things people simply were not meant to tamper with. Which was why they were called Forbidden Arts. Which was why every culture in history either killed practitioners or, if they were too scared of them, bought them off.

There was no doubt that Valcourt possessed genuinely supernormal and frightening powers. He was no quack, and whatever he was up to, it was not good. It was common knowledge that that kind of power could be obtained only by paying a price. Robbie had experienced just enough on psychedelic excursions to have an entirely too clear notion of what it might involve. He hit the gas pedal harder.

He should have put it together earlier, he supposed, but there had not been enough evidence; or maybe he had not been seeing clearly. When he first went to the house and Valcourt asked him what he wanted, Robbie had shrugged and said he didn't care much about money or love or anything like that. What he was really after was to understand the hidden aspects of existence. What had set the whole show up? What ran it? Was there anything to his fascination with the occult, or was it just a fantasy he'd evolved out of an inability to cope with real life?

Valcourt had assured him there was in fact a great deal more going on behind the scenes than even he suspected; had told him about the entities; and had given him a charm to say every night, to train one of those entities to become a sort of informant, a spirit snitch–to explain to Robbie what was going on in the unconscious processes of his own mind.

And son of a bitch if it hadn't worked. It was amazing, like being on the highest, clearest part of a really good mushroom trip all the time. He'd started to understand his own reasons for doing and not doing things, the unknown parts of him that dictated his preferences and lazinesses. The jumble of urges that had always run him around like a sheep started to become a coherent array of inner voices, revealing and explaining themselves to some core being deep inside that listened, evaluated, and acted accordingly. It was like suddenly understanding something important every minute, making the most boring things terrifically interesting. And it had been getting better and better.

The irony was that it was precisely that clarity that had tipped him off to what Valcourt was up to.

And now, he supposed, he was going to lose it. He remembered the man's harsh words to Nicole: *Advance, and increase in strength, or, like a dying plant, forfeit all you have gained.* Unhappily, he shrugged. There was no way he was going to spend another minute in that house.

The real shame was that he had not had a chance to explain to Nicole. He could not have cared less about the other two; Charity was a stuck-up rich bitch, and Spencer a sleazeball, even if he did have some pretty good coke. But Nicole seemed like a good lady, and he felt guilty for abandoning her. He wondered if she had stayed. Probably; she had had no insight like his, and Valcourt was extremely persuasive. He decided to phone her–the hell with Valcourt and his rules; they did not apply to him any more, anyway–and at least tell her what he thought.

He was perhaps a mile up Green Mountain Road, starting to calm down, when the engine coughed, missed, coughed again, and died. He managed to coast the Volks into a turnout, and there spent two or three minutes trying to coax it back into life. It turned over; the gas tank was half full. But it refused to catch. When the battery was worn down to a sluggish whir, he gave up and sank back in the seat. There were no houses, no lights, no driveways in sight; he seemed to be in a patch of forest. He tried the engine once more. The battery started a little stronger, but quickly fell off.

He got out of the car and stood, looking around uneasily, reviewing his options. Maybe one car every fifteen minutes came down this road this time of night; and who was going to pick up a hitchhiker that looked like him? The other group members might come by after the meeting, but they might go the other way, too. Besides, there was no guarantee that they would recognize him. His best bet was to find a house, call the City, and try to get a friend to come down and pick him up. He could deal with the car tomorrow. Right now, he just wanted to be far away from Valcourt's house. Hands in his pockets, he started to walk.

The redwoods and eucalyptus trees seemed sky-high, blocking out the little moonlight that filtered down onto the narrow road. His gaze moved of its own accord from side to side, and he had to stop himself from whistling, like a little kid. It was hard to believe that a place in this part of California could be so lonesome. Rich folks, he supposed; they built their houses way back off the road and kept a good part of the land from being developed. Nobody else had any reason to come here. There were faster and easier ways to get anyplace.

It was pretty in a way, but he had never cared much for lonely places at night. Until he was ten, when his family moved to California, they had lived in the Midwest, on the outskirts of a little town in Indiana. The big, rambling houses were far apart, and to get home from playing with his friends, he'd had to cross through fields and patches of forest—always, it seemed, just at dusk. There was one point in particular that was bad, a belt of trees: hundred-year-old oaks and elms and maples, twisted and sinister, whose branches looked like the fingers of old witches, clutching at him as he went by. Avoiding the place was impossible—it lay between his house and town and was too big to go around—and the path through it was narrow and always dark. Sometimes he would hover for several minutes at the entrance in agonizing fear, then put his head down and run as fast as he could; other times, with a show of bravado, he would force himself to walk stiffly, arms at his sides, all the while feeling the hair prickle on the back of his neck. It made no difference. His child's mind understood with a certainty beyond reason or intellect that *they* were in there waiting to get him. The fact that they never did meant only that they were certain of him in the end and wanted to extend his terror.

Over the course of those years—including numerous instances when he was certain he'd sighted dark, crouching shapes moving among the branches—he'd developed a good idea of what "they" were. Later, as a teenager, he had found a name that fit: ghouls. Not like Victorian graverobbers or psychotics who ate dead flesh, but things that were *un*dead, like vampires. Maybe they were people who had been so bad during life that they were not allowed to rest, or perhaps they had just somehow happened in the scheme of creation, like harpies or trolls. Whatever it was, they were wildly unpretty. They had long, bony fingers, evil faces like rotting corpses, with stringy wisps of hair hanging from naked skulls to their shoulders, and dark tatters of cloth clinging to their bodies. Once they got hold of you, that was it. They'd throw you to the ground, while more and more of them stumbled toward you with their clutching fingers and whispering, rattling cries of triumph and eyes like dark wells into hell itself, and do every terrible thing you could imagine: gouge out your eyeballs, rip away chunks of bleeding flesh and cram them into their rotting, stinking mouths—

He shivered, walking a little faster. Of course, after his family moved and he got older, he had recognized the whole thing for what it was, the sort of dark fantasy all children shared when they were frightened in lonely places. Still, he wondered why he had focused on that particular image rather than more common ones. He supposed he might have seen something in a book or movie when he was too young to remember, or even that it might have something to do with racial memory. It did not much matter.

The odd thing was that while he had not thought about them in years, he'd had a dream about them just a couple of weeks ago—probably triggered by Valcourt, with all his talk about vampires and such—and since then, they had been hovering increasingly in the back of his mind. Grown man that he was, they still made him distinctly uneasy. Several times recently when he'd awakened in the night, he had sheepishly but quickly turned on a light at the thought of one of those faces. And wouldn't that be a hell of a way to go, he thought, the *worst:* to be taken out by creatures of your own imagination—creatures that represented your darkest fears.

He'd been walking for what seemed like five minutes and still hadn't seen a house, a car, or even a light—only the tall stern trees that lined the road, and behind them, a gloomy forest of scrub oak and madrone. The only sound was the scuffing of his sneakers on the asphalt.

Except, of course, for the rustling of small animals in the brush, no doubt spooked by his presence.

That would explain why the noises stopped, suddenly, when he did.

The night was still as death around him. The faint silvery light in the woods was like a fog. Robbie swallowed. Goddamn it, twenty-nine years old and here he was still thinking that clumps of bushes looked like crouched shapes, and imagining that the sounds he'd been hearing were made by something that had to be larger than birds or mice or even possums–

And that they were keeping pace with him, moving when he moved, stopping when he stopped.

Tense, ears straining to hear, he walked another dozen yards. The rustling started again. Then he froze.

The sounds stopped, just a second late.

Very slowly, he turned his head. His gaze searched the gloom in the woods. The limbs of the madrones, repulsively smooth, twisted like the coils of giant snakes, gleaming faintly in the brightening moonlight. Moss hung like dead hair from the branches of the oaks. But the clumps of brush were only that–stands of manzanita and laurel saplings.

Until one of them shifted, lifting its face so the moonlight caught the sheen of the skinless skull, the lank strands of whitish hair, the ferocious protruding teeth. Another shape moved, and then another, and then there were rustling noises all around–behind, ahead, on both sides of the road–and the crouched shapes were stumbling forward, their thin fingers writhing with manic eagerness.

Distantly, Robbie realized that his mouth had opened so wide his jaw hurt. He shut it. Then he began to run with a speed he had not known since childhood, tennis shoes slapping on the pavement like gunshots.

He had made it perhaps thirty yards when he swerved to dodge the shapes that were closing off the road ahead, and a tattered arm snaked out from the brush and tripped him. He hit hard, feeling the gravel bite into his forearms. He rolled and was scrambling to gain his feet when a hand clutched his ankle, and then another, and then yet others.

He flipped onto his back, kicking and lashing his arms, and as the vile, grinning faces closed in and the taloned fingers groped for his eyes, the roar of horror trapped in his chest at last burst free, echoing through his own mind into darkness.

Fifteen minutes later, a pair of Skyline Junior College students on a Honda passed a red Volkswagen Beetle chugging along toward the Crystal Springs Reservoir. The boy driving glanced into the window as it went by, then hit the motorcycle's brakes so hard it nearly spilled.

"What are you doing?" the girl shrieked.

"There's nobody in that thing," he yelled, turning to follow the car.

"You're crazy," she said matter-of-factly. "Come on, I don't want to be late for the movie."

He hesitated. "Come *on*," she said, stoned petulance in her voice. He shrugged and turned the bike again toward San Mateo. But he would have sworn that the moonlight had glinted off an untended steering wheel and empty ragged upholstery in the driver and passenger seats.

Driving home, Spencer Epps was tense and uncertain. The part of the story he had told about Yvonne's father being connected with hit men was made up, granted; he had given a lot of hard thought to figuring an angle that would wash. But the rest of it was all too true. Yvonne had been driving him crazy: hardly willing to let him out of her sight, and never missing a chance to twist the knife about his fall from grace. Worst, with the ax hanging over his head, he was forced to play meek, repentant, and loving—anything to keep her from picking up the phone, as she did approximately once an hour, with the announcement:

"I've made up my mind. I'm going to tell him." He had had to swear he was going to work in order to get to the meeting tonight. Worse, he had only been able to call Tina once, hastily and furtively. The conversation had been filled with the tormenting suspicion that she had planted the photos. He could not bring himself to ask her directly, had only told her that Yvonne had copped—that someone unknown had snitched—and then listened closely for her reaction. She had seemed both anxious and genuinely puzzled. If she was lying, she was smarter, Spencer admitted, than he had given her credit for being.

And now he was nervous because he was not sure just exactly what had gone down tonight. He hadn't been thinking too clearly—had not even rally been sure what he was asking for, except help. When Valcourt brought up the idea of Yvonne's malice being reflected back at her, it had sounded perfect. Maybe she didn't want to have him killed, but she was certainly furious, and certainly capable of ruining his life.

But the question Spencer had not asked himself until now was, What form might that reflected malice take?

Valcourt had not been specific.

A warning, Spencer assumed: something like what they had done to Charity's ex. It had worked, or at least she said it had, and he did not think she had been lying; her eyes had been positively gleaming. That was exactly what Yvonne needed: a warning that would shake her up good.

The next step was to make it clear that he had caused it, and that he could do it again. That would reestablish his control, get things back the way they should be, and eventually ease him out of the marriage with his finances intact. And if he could learn to do it himself, at will—he was beginning to grasp that such a thing could provide him a power even greater than money. His fear gave way to a momentary vision of Yvonne's father, on his knees, begging Spencer for mercy.

But reality came back, and he realized unhappily that it was a thin straw he was clutching at. He still had no actual proof of Valcourt's power. If it did not work, he could see nothing but continuing the increasingly less endurable misery, caught between a jealous wife and a treacherous girlfriend. His coke consumption the past two days had been manic, his drinking heavy. His head ached and his mood was thoroughly foul as he wheeled the Porsche into the driveway and started up the steps to his own little hell on earth. At the door he paused, suddenly aware again, with acute discomfort, of the wish that he had asked Valcourt what to expect. Maybe nothing, he found himself half-hoping. Maybe the spell would fall, as Valcourt had said, like an arrow to the ground.

The TV was on, but Yvonne was not parked in front of it. Her emotional distress had only briefly disturbed her viewing habits, and he suspected that she was secretly enjoying her position of having been wronged. It made her feel like her favorite soap opera wives, all invariably the victims of unfaithful husbands. She was probably learning from the screen how she should behave.

Her grief didn't seem to have affected her appetite at all.

"Yvonne?" he forced himself to call, dutifully playing his penitential role. "Sweetheart?"

"Come on, Raylene," said a hard male voice from the television. "Put down that gun. All we're asking you to do is tell the truth about what happened at the laundromat."

There were no sounds from the kitchen, no running water in the bathroom. A woman's voice with a heavy southern accent quavered:

"If I promise, will y'all let Jim Bob go free?"

Spencer flicked off the set. The house was absolutely still. "Yvonne?" he called again, hearing strain in his own voice. It was conceivable that she had gone out for ice cream or to a friend's, but very unlikely. Yvonne did not like to leave the house alone or on foot, and she kept the pantry well stocked with delicacies. He stepped into the kitchen. The refrigerator kicked on with a buzz, startling him. A few dishes sat on the counter by the sink.

Stomach tense, he walked to the stairs. His unease mounted with each step, as if he were moving into a zone of lingering noxious gas. The bedroom door was wide open, the room as dark as a cave.

"Yvonne?" he whispered. "You asleep?" His fingers found the light switch.

The bedspread was askew, and framed pictures and vials of perfume atop her dresser were knocked over. The bifold door to their walk-in closet hung awry, partly broken from its mounts–

As if someone had come rushing through the room and thrown himself into the closet in a last, desperate attempt to hide.

Or *her*self. Spencer's throat was very dry. "Yvonne?" he managed to say once more.

He forced himself to place one foot in front of the other, across the room to the closet door. He inhaled deeply, then peered around the corner.

Her bulky shape lay half-buried in the tangled pile of clothes that one fist had torn from the rack. Her feet, enclosed in fluffy slippers, were absolutely still. Her face was twisted to the side, and though the light in the closet was dim, he could see one wide-open eye and the corner of her mouth stretched wide in a frozen shriek of terror.

Spencer backed into the center of the room and stood there without moving for perhaps two minutes. Then he sobbed, once, a harsh, choked sound. Brushing his eyes with his sleeve, he hurried to the bathroom, rinsed his face and blew his nose. Methodically, automatically, he took the vial from his pocket and laid out two thick lines on the counter. After he inhaled them, he carefully wiped the area clean.

In the living room, he went to the telephone. As he considered what to say, be was aware that the shock and grief within him were already dissolving into plans for the future of the new Spencer Epps.

Punching the numbers 911, he noticed a strange, faint reddening of his left palm—as if he had unknowingly, and painlessly, burned it.

FOURTEEN

Tuesday morning, Nicole walked into her office, bracing herself for the post-Labor Day season. When she glanced at her desk, she stopped. A copy of the *Chronicle* lay open on it. She had cleared the desktop Friday, as usual. Presumably, one of her colleagues wanted to bring something to her attention. She bent over the paper, scanning it. The page contained a few nondescript news items and several obituaries.

Then a name caught her eye, and she leaned quickly closer.

"Epps, Yvonne W.–in S.F., Sept. 3, 1987; beloved wife of Spencer Epps; devoted daughter of Charlotte and Langdon Winslowe; also survived by many loving aunts, uncles and cousins; aged 32 years–"

Nicole sat down and stared.

Was it possible that there were two Spencer Eppses in San Francisco with wives named Yvonne?

Former wives, she thought dizzily. Dead wives.

For several seconds, she tapped her fingernails on the desk. Then she reached for the phone.

"Wilkes Agency," a brisk female voice said.

"Is Mr. Wilkes in?"

"Not at the moment," the voice said cautiously. "Can I take a message?"

"I'll call back," Nicole said. Holding the button on the receiver down with her thumb, she flipped with her other hand through a Rolodex. She hesitated–it was understood that his unlisted home number was only for emergencies–then dialed.

The phone rang six times before a man's sleepy voice growled, "This better be good."

"Cameron, it's Nicole," she said, hearing her own urgency. "I need a favor, a big one."

"Jesus Christ, lady. You know about my Monday morning hangover."

"I'm sorry, Cam, I would have waited, but this is really important. Besides, it's Tuesday."

"Lost another day," he muttered. "Okay, shoot."

"There's an obit in today's *Chron,* a woman named Yvonne Epps, E-P-P-S. It says she died last Thursday; no information about how. Can you find out what happened?"

"Probably," he said, and she heard curiosity emerging. "You know her?"

"No," Nicole said. "Not exactly. I can't explain yet. But I'll owe you a big one."

She could almost see him shrug. "I'll get back."

He was one of the few people she knew who meant it when he said it. She tore out the obituary, dropped the rest of the newspaper into the wastebasket, and took out her files for the day's cases.

It was just over twenty minutes later when the phone rang.

"Massive coronary seizure, right in her bedroom," Wilkes said. "Apparently it got her near the door, and she stumbled around and fell into the closet. A little strange; she was young, and McCallum in the bod squad told me she had a peculiar look on her face. But she was also terrifically overweight, and there was no evidence of foul play. Okay?"

"Yeah," Nicole said. Her eyes were closed. "Send me a bill."

"Buy me dinner some night," he said. "Now, if that'll do it, I'm going to have two cold beers and go back to bed."

"The look," Nicole said. "On her face. What did McCallum mean?"

"Usually they look surprised, or exhausted from the struggle, or just plain dead. He said this one looked like she'd seen something that scared her right into the arms of Jesus." There was a pause. "You going to tell me what this is all about?"

"Soon," Nicole said. "Thanks again." She put the phone down quietly, got up, and stood helplessly in the center of the room.

Was it conceivable?

But Valcourt had said it was to be only a warning—

Or had he? Had he in fact ever specified that? She had been confused, and had just assumed that it was in the same nature as all that had gone before: essentially harmless.

But she remembered, too, the sinister twist the rising energy seemed to have taken; remembered Valcourt's grimness; remembered that he had ushered them firmly out of the house immediately afterward, with no lingering foe wine and conversation, just as there had been no intermission—as if he had wanted no questions or second thoughts.

Remembered that, driving home, she had not been able to shake the uncomfortable feeling that something had changed significantly.

Remembered that, without sufficient information, not knowing the consequences, against both her instincts and her training, she had agreed to participate.

Dont't do it, Nicole! I see, good God, I finally see what he's doing!

Hands pressed to her head, she paced. She would quit the group, never go back—

Or forfeit all you have gained.

Stay calm, she thought, breathing deeply. Proceed in an orderly fashion, Nicole. You are leaping to any number of completely unwarrantable conclusions. Coincidence does happen. The woman was severely overweight. There was no sign of foul play.

She smoothed her hair and clothes and sat again at her desk.

But what had Robbie realized? She had thought of calling him, but Valcourt's prohibition against contacting the others had held her back—compounded, she admitted, by a faint sense of shame at having stayed after he had left.

Confusion swept in again, and with it came a mocking thought: Nicole Partrick, the girl who prided herself on being tough, strong, and independent, going to pieces as soon as there was a little pressure.

But in truth, there was a lot of pressure. Tom Junior was home. She and Jesse had not slept together in days, but had kept an outward distance, agreeing that it would not have been fair to the boy, after spending time with his father, to thrust him immediately into a potentially threatening situation. The separation was temporary, but it skyrocketed her anxiety that with that distance, Jesse's affection might dim.

Or was the real heart of all of it her guilt over the relationship having been founded on deceit?

She shook off the hovering panic and rook the city phone book from her desk. There were numerous Kinsellas, but only one Robbie. She hesitated, then thought, the hell with Valcourt.

The phone rang and rang.

She put it down and stepped out into the main office. Donna, the receptionist, was typing a letter. When Nicole got to her, she switched off the Selectric and looked up inquiringly.

"Do you know who put the newspaper on my desk?" Nicole said.

Donna frowned, shaking her head. "You and I are the first ones here, and it wasn't me. Could somebody have left it over the weekend?"

"It's today's," Nicole said. She walked slowly back into her office.

A little before midnight, Nicole put down the novel she had been staring at for the past hour and padded quietly down the hall to Tom Junior's room. She stood in the doorway for a moment, then, satisfied that he was sound asleep, she went back to the living room and took her keys from her purse. Though Jesse had long since gone to bed, she had called him earlier and suggested that she come crawl in with him for an hour, an idea he had welcomed with the words, "Thought you'd never ask."

It was not sex she wanted as much as comfort. More and more, she was wondering if she dared to confide in him. But trying to decide how much to tell, how to phrase it and what to leave out was too complicated—and on top of what she had done already, she did not want to lie. She dosed her eyes, shaking her head. Soon, she promised herself, she would decide what to do: things would fall into place. Tonight she wanted only the comfort of those warm arms she had, by fair means or foul, drawn to her.

Her hand was on the doorknob when she heard the cries begin from her son's bedroom. With fear filling her throat, she rushed back down the hall, threw on the light, wrapped her arms around him. After a minute, he was snuffling quietly into her shoulder.

"What?" she said, making her voice stay calm. "Tell me."

Hesitantly, he said, "There were these people with black hoods, and they were, like, singing and they were gonna do something really bad to me." He raised his face, cheeks wet. "I'm sorry for being such a baby, Mom, but it was really scary. A lot worse than that other one."

337

"Hush," she said soothingly. "Even Jesse sometimes wakes up scared."

Tom Junior paused in knuckling his eyes. "He does?"

"Yep," she said. "The important thing to remember is that they're only dreams, and dreams can't hurt you. Just turn on the light, and pretty soon whatever's been scaring you will be gone. Okay?"

"Okay," he said doubtfully. Then, seeing his advantage, he asked, "Could I read for a little while?"

She eyed the clock. It was a school night, but reading was probably the best way to get him back to sleep.

"One half hour," she decreed. "What do you want? I'll get it."

"Conan," he said eagerly.

That's probably what's giving you nightmares, she thought, and was touched with guilt about her own self-righteous assumption that the previous nightmare had been the fault of her ex-husband's laxness. If the dreams continued, she would think about censoring the reading list.

As she took the book from the shelf, it suddenly struck her as odd that something like hooded figures would appear in an eleven-year-old's dream, instead of more common monsters and other tangible images of fright. She put her hand to his forehead, with the thought of fever. It felt cool and normal.

"Want a glass of milk?"

He shook his head. "Did you burn your hand?"

"I don't think so," she said, surprised, and looked.

On her left palm there was a faint but unmistakable reddening of the skin. She touched it with the fingers of her other hand. There was no pain.

"I guess I must have," she said, laughing nervously. "Well, it doesn't hurt."

Back in the living room, she went to a lamp and raised the hand to her face. The mark was shapeless and vague, but definitely there. She shrugged and tried to dismiss it from her thoughts. Doubtless she had burned it slightly while cooking, or scraped it without noticing. No reason to get upset.

Leaving the apartment was out of the question now; she exhaled with frustration. She thought of calling Jesse, but there seemed no point in waking him just to tell him it was back to cold showers for them both.

Time you went to bed, girl, she thought wearily, and walked quietly down the hall to her room, feeling hollow, disappointed—and, remembering Yvonne Epps, a little scared.

How *had* that newspaper gotten on her desk?

As the evening sunlight faded from the Provençal sky, three figures stood in the cypress grove on the slope of Montsévrain. At their feet lay an unusually long coffin made of pine planks, bearing the marks of amateur workmanship. In it was a very large skeleton.

Etien Boudrie, wearing a surplice and purple stole, held a breviary in one hand and a vial of holy water in the other. From time to time, he sprinkled water on the bones or made the Sign of the Cross as he spoke.

"Most glorious Prince of the Heavenly Army, Holy Michael the Archangel, defend us in battle against the princes and powers and rulers of darkness in this world, against the spiritual iniquities of those former angels–"

None of them presumed to know the proper course of action for dealing with Courdeval's bones; Boudrie had finally decided to recite the *Rituale Romanum* over them.

"Humor an old priest," he had said. "It may not be what's called for, but it's all I know."

"As good as anything," Mélusine had agreed. "If anything is any good at all."

They had chosen the late hour on the lesser chance of being interrupted; the two men had crawled into the cave and, with some trouble, wrestled the skeleton out, laying it in the coffin Devarre had built. Then, after washing, Boudrie had robed himself and begun.

As she watched, Mélusine was struck by the power of the priest, by his dignity and force. He was *un homme sérieux,* "a serious man." It was partly his position as emissary of one of the world's mightiest spiritual organizations, a role he exemplified with the certainty of thirty years' tenure.

But largely, it was the man himself. His voice, his figure, his face: all were rough, strong, and absolutely solemn, and she almost blushed to realize, at this strangest of times, that the attraction was to a large extent sexual. She had not once been unfaithful to her husband in their twenty-five years, despite myriad temptations and offers, and she had no intention of starting now; and yet something within her could not help but react physically to Boudrie. Was it simply forbidden fruit, the fact that he was a priest? Or the further spice of knowing that he had once broken his vows in an affair of great passion–had even fathered a child who Mélusine had loved? What was it, that overpowering urge to consummate such an attraction in a sweating frenzy of slipping, sliding flesh? Was it, as some scientists held, merely the body's design for creating strong genetic combinations? Or did it go far deeper, into some ineffable spiritual need to merge inner beings in a tangible way? Certainly, it was vastly more powerful than reason. She wondered if her husband, and even Boudrie himself, sensed her feeling.

"Do not dare further, most cunning Serpent, to deceive the human race, to strike and shake the chosen of God like chaff," Boudrie growled, crossing himself. "Go, Satan! Inventor and master of all falsehood!"

The words rolled on, prayer mixed with threat, until at last the priest sprinkled the water a final time and stepped back. He looked weary, but satisfied in a grim sort of way. For a moment, none of them spoke. Then Boudrie smiled and said:

"Time to join the twentieth century again," and took the stole from around his neck.

"Not quite," said Devarre. He rummaged in a rucksack and came out with a whittled piece of wood perhaps half a meter long, the thickness of a wrist, and sharpened to a point at one end. His other hand held a heavy iron mallet.

Boudrie stared in astonishment. "And what, may I ask, are those?"

341

"Just what they look like," Devarre said. "I've been reading up on all this, and the consensus is that a stake through the heart in such situations is always considered good insurance. There may be no heart per se, but we can imagine."

Boudrie turned to Mélusine. "Is he serious?"

"What can it hurt? It's superstition, true, but after all–" She glanced at the holy water.

Perplexed, the priest looked from one to the other of them, then at the stake, then at the skeleton.

"I suppose you're right," he muttered, "although it seems very strange."

"I hardened the point in fire," Devarre said. "It will go right into the pine." He handed the stake and hammer to Boudrie.

The priest crouched beside the coffin, positioning the stake uncertainly above the skeleton's rib cage. Then he looked up, with obvious chagrin, and said, "But this is absurd."

"Don't be too charitable, Etien," Mélusine said; and then, hardening herself, "He murdered your daughter."

Boudrie's eyebrows rose. When he looked back down at the bones, his face had changed. The stake hovered in his huge hand above the rib cage, while he stared at the grinning skull. Then, with sudden violence, he rammed the stake down through the ribs. With the mallet, he struck three hard, measured blows, to the sound of splintering wood. Then he stood, breathing heavily, and handed the hammer to Devarre.

"Thank you," he said. "That helped."

"To Nice, then?" said Devarre. The clandestine cremation was all arranged.

"Yes," Boudrie said. "I'm most curious."

Devarre produced a hacksaw and quickly took off the protruding top of the stake. Then they closed the coffin lid and the two men gripped its handles, dragging it down the hillside to where a borrowed truck waited. Early tomorrow morning they would return to obliterate all traces of the cave and its guardian stone slab.

"I half expected the holy water to hiss on the bones," Devarre said as they lugged the coffin through the brush.

"Only in the movies," Boudrie panted. "Or at least, so I used to think."

In the small hours of the morning, the man who called himself Guy-Luc Valcourt awoke, immediately and fully, from the two or three hours of light rest he took, sitting upright in an armchair, each night.

Something, somewhere, was amiss.

For several minutes he remained motionless in his dark chamber, attuning himself to the faint, faraway sensation that came to him through a part of his psychic makeup to which most humans were deaf and blind. He had been slightly disturbed for some hours, but the feeling had suddenly intensified.

In some way he could not yet grasp, something that belonged to him was being tampered with.

Abruptly, he rose and stalked through the dark house, past the chamber where Alysse lay like a chaste sleeping beauty, and climbed two at a time the stairs leading to the cupola. There he gripped the railing and thrust his head into the night wind as if he were smelling it, testing each direction, seeking to discover whence the annoyance emanated.

The sense was strongest from the east. He tore the patch from his dead eye, and with all his strength, focused his inner vision: commanding the spirits that rode the night air to bring him news. The distance was great, the effort tremendous. His hands tightened on the railing as if they would crush it. Sweat appeared on his face and neck.

But at last, the faintest whisper reached him. He staggered back, hands clutching the empty air, mouth opening in a choked cry of rage.

His *bones!*

Someone had unearthed the bones of Guilhem de Courdeval, and with deliberate, calculated malice, was burning them! Like a commoner, like garbage!

It was fantastic: an insult not to be borne!

But how was it possible? Only the priest had even known of their existence. The chances of a stranger having stumbled upon them were infinitesimal. It could only mean that the priest walked in the world of men again. And only one person could have brought that about: the Devarre woman.

She had bested him again!

In a fury that filled him like a blood-red mist, he swept back down the stairs to his study. Oh, for the days long gone, for the wild, savage joy of riding down an enemy with swinging sword, before this contemptible need for caution and stealth had arisen! It was almost too high a price to endure. What use was power, what

344

pleasure was there in life, if he was forced to behave like a mouse, to avoid all risk in order to be a useful slave? He had ever been a warrior, leaping into the face of death, thirsting exultantly for danger. But now–

Quickly, he lit candles, then tore the top drawer from the desk and took out the photograph of Alysse, posed in front of Nicole Partrick's car. With icy satisfaction, he held it up and examined it in the flickering light. Nothing he could do–not even murder itself–would cause Mélusine Devarre and Boudrie more anguish than this photograph, and the attendant knowledge that Alysse remained his toy. He had planned to send it after Nicole's compliance was certain: when her gift of her son to the Adversary–and of herself to Valcourt–was a *fait accompli.*

But she was his already, though she did not yet know it. Had she not participated in causing the Epps woman's death? Sworn her oath on the grimoire?

Received the brand of allegiance on her palm?

There was no need to wait, to drag this affair out for months longer. Perhaps two weeks, and the work would be complete. Just enough time for the Frenchmen to receive the photograph and make the journey–their last–to San Francisco.

He took down an envelope and quickly addressed it: Mme. Mélusine Devarre, Poste Générale, Saint-Bertrand-sur-Seyre, Alpes-Maritimes, France; enclosed the photo; sealed and stamped it. Rising, he hesitated once more. Caution warned him to wait until he was absolutely certain, until the thing was done.

To hell with caution! Hurl the gauntlet in their faces! Let them come!

Let them.

"*Viens,*" he hissed. Lamashtu appeared at his ankle. In thick-voiced, archaic French he said, "Post this, and accompany it. Return with them. Alert me when they are one day's journey from here."

The cat shuddered violently as the servant that had controlled it departed; then it crouched on the floor, staring around in bewilderment—only a mere cat again. Valcourt strode to the window in time to see the flicker of the white envelope, held by something unseen, whisk away through the night sky.

To send even a minor entity so far for so long was a costly move and an uncertain one, and doubt assailed him again. These were not ordinary people, this French housewife and priest. Her allies must be even more powerful than he had thought. Both of them had survived encounters with terribly destructive beings. Together, aware of what he was, they might present a real threat. The words to recall the missive hung on his lips.

He turned on his heel and strode into the parlor. There he poured a glass of wine, calming himself. He would see to it that Nicole's confusion and fear were extreme by then, and he knew well that under such circumstances, humans were capable of otherwise inconceivable actions. He would arrange the ceremony to coincide with Mélusine Devarre's arrival, putting him at the absolute height of power. All loose ends would then be tied up within a few hours.

He settled into a chair and sipped the wine, fighting within himself the ominous suspicion that in truth, he was coming to a grudging admiration for this woman who had twice outwitted him.

That some long-ago suppressed and nearly dead part of him wanted to give her a chance.

On his way out of the church after a long, wearying afternoon in the confessional, where, now that the novelty of his return was gone, only two repentant sinners had ventured, Etien Boudrie stopped and turned toward the long disused graveyard. The stone fence that surrounded it lacked the solidity of the cathedral; though the fence was newer by several centuries, it had crumbled to knee height in many places, and the few columns that retained their original shape were still there only because no one had ever bothered to push them over. When he first came to the village three decades ago, Boudrie had tried to requisition repair money from the diocese. He had received instead a terse reply that the fence enhanced the cathedral's picturesque quality.

He stepped inside the cemetery gate and stood, hands in his pockets, a warm breeze rippling the skirt of his cassock—postponing just a little longer the life-reviving decanter of brandy awaiting him in the rectory, which he had not allowed himself to touch until his chores were done. The ancient, worn-away tombstones were barely visible in the dark. In his early days here, he had made a nightly practice of strolling among the graves, trying to imagine lives lived centuries in the past, and meditating on death. Despite his youth at the time, it was something with which he had already come by more than a nodding acquaintance.

But that practice had dwindled and finally ceased, perhaps as the reality of the little world around him sank in. It seemed that he dealt with death of one form or another throughout much of every day—not black and terrifying like the figures that increasingly peopled his dreams, but a dull, ponderous gray. The hill villages were a far cry from the glitter of the Côte d'Azur, although in his heart, he suspected that the forms of living death to be found among the glitter were the worst of all.

The bones of Courdeval had burned to ash. It was comforting to know there was no more power attached to them—but most unpleasant to realize that particular hope of neutralizing him was gone. Burning dead bones was one thing. Facing the living reality was another.

He raised his eyes to the craggy skyline southward, where the massive ruin of Montsévrain capped the highest peak in sight, standing watch over the village like a lonely sentinel of a forgotten age.

Whoever could have imagined it?

He turned and plodded into the rectory. There he exchanged shoes for slippers, washed his hands and face, and went to his small study. Trying not to appear anxious—as if there were someone watching—he uncapped the decanter. It clinked with a tiny tremolo against the glass. Steady, he told himself sharply. This will not do. He sighed aloud with pleasure as the harsh, fragrant liquid burned its way down his throat.

Then the old black rectory telephone rang, startling him. It was not a common thing, especially at this time of evening. Most people who had things to tell him needed to do so in person, to plead his indulgence either with their eyes or through the screen of the confessional.

"Etien," said Roger Devarre. "Would you care to stop by for a drink?"

The priest's practiced ear detected the strain beneath the casualness.

"Something has come up," he said. It was not a question.

Devarre said simply, "Yes."

"Ten minutes," Boudrie said.

Outside, he managed to bully the parish's decrepit 2CV into life, mouthing an automatic prayer of thanks. Although the evening was fine and the walk only a kilometer or so, he could not have enjoyed it. Something was wrong.

When she opened the door, Mélusine said, "Come and sit." And then, accusingly, "Have you eaten?"

Boudrie spread his hands guiltily–since his illness, he had been eating dutifully rather than with appetite, and he frequently neglected the chore–and she exhaled in exasperation.

"We had a roast," she said. "There's plenty left; I'll put it in the oven to warm." Her fussing thinly overlaid the anxiety on her face, and as she started away, he took her arm.

"Please," he said. "What is it?"

Devarre had come into the hallway. He and Mélusine exchanged glances.

"Come, then," she said.

They entered the homey parlor. She took an envelope from the mantel and gave it to him. Boudrie examined it quickly–postmarked San Francisco, no return address, the hand neat and firm, all the French words correctly spelled and accented–then removed the single piece of paper inside.

For perhaps two seconds, he stared without comprehending. Then his heart was jolted as if hit by a live wire. When he looked up, Mélusine's eyes were wet and her husband was standing at a window, hands in his pockets, scowling.

Boudrie walked to a chair and dropped into it.

The worst thing, the piquant touch of cruelty that brought home with devastating force what they were dealing with, was the scarf around Alysse's neck.

"It's a trap, obviously," Devarre finally said. "With the vehicle license number, I mean."

Boudrie nodded, still mute.

"So the question is," Devarre said, "do we walk in like gulls–or wait here like sheep?"

When at last Boudrie spoke, his voice was soft and thick.

"I'll have to get that fool Tibouchet to take over for me again."

FIFTEEN

On the afternoon of September 23, Nicole was, as usual, the last to leave the office. She stepped out onto Kearny Street, walking with her head down and her hands in her pockets. The past days had not been good.

Twice more, Tom Junior had awakened screaming from nightmares about the mysterious black-hooded figures, a scenario that not only remained consistent, but was growing in detail. He described a large stone enclosure that sounded like a castle; strange, tuneless singing; and one man in particular, larger than the rest, whose face was hidden but who held a knife. Nicole had consigned *Conan* to the forbidden list, and hoped that would put an end to it.

In the meantime, she had not dared to leave the apartment at night, and she and Jesse had been limited to quick, almost furtive caresses, like teenagers. Both came away frustrated and on edge. The nightmares had also kept her from explaining to Tom Junior that her friendship with Jesse bad taken a turn. She had even started to wonder if the dreams were rooted in her son's sense that her allegiance was now divided. She had always been entirely his, and she knew that children were not only extremely perceptive to what adults thought was hidden, but that they often reacted in irrational and unintentional ways. *Conan* might be supplying the imagery, but more and more she suspected that *she* might be supplying the momentum.

So, Saturday, she planned to take him for a drive, perhaps to the beach, and gently break the news. It would probably delight him, and she hoped it would quell any disturbance springing from a situation he sensed but was uncertain of.

And she had come to another decision: to call Valcourt and tell him she was no longer comfortable with the direction the group's activities had taken.

The man undeniably possessed remarkable mental powers, and had certainly helped her. But Valcourt himself asserted that what he had taught her had only tipped the balance–that she had merely enhanced what already existed. It followed that what had arisen would continue on its own. As for the death of Yvonne Epps, Nicole assured herself that it was simply impossible they had had anything to do with it. The poor woman was overweight; she had died of a heart attack; the rest was pure coincidence.

Nicole realized that since meeting Valcourt, she had felt herself increasingly under the sword of some unspecified subliminal discomfort–the sense that she was behaving in ways that simply were not *right*. However justifiable it might have seemed at the time, there was no denying that she had shared in the intent to

352

damage others, and her lawyer's mind assured her that this made her in some way guilty of a crime–she almost wanted to say *sin*.

Better late than never, she told herself unhappily. As a first tangible step, she had deliberately stopped saying her chant the night before. Her guardian angel, too, seemed to have changed in a vaguely unpleasant way, from helper to something more like an eavesdropper or spy; and the constantly warring voices in her mind that it brought to her attention seemed increasingly to confuse more than clarify.

No, it had been an interesting education, and it had given her the courage to bring about her own happiness, but it was over. She would thank Valcourt and offer to pay him a reasonable sum. If he refused, that would be that; and if he got angry, she had the weight of the law on her side. Feeling better, she raised her head–

And stopped.

Guy-Luc Valcourt was standing perhaps ten feet in front of her on the sidewalk, facing her, hands clasped before him. It was the first time she had seen him in street clothes, and she noted them automatically in the midst of her shock: an expensive, beautifully cut suit of dark gray wool, a white shirt with a pin collar, a wine-colored silk tie. Except for the patch over his eye, he looked like any other affluent businessman.

"My dear Nicole," he said. "What a pleasure." Smiling, with his usual charm, he walked forward.

"Monsieur Valcourt," she stammered, feeling her courage of the previous moment disappearing like water in burning sand.

353

He saved her from her struggle with what to say next–*How did you know where to find me?* was all that came to her mind, and it seemed both hostile and absurd, even hinting of panic–by asking smoothly:

"Will you join me for a drink?"

"I'm . . . in something of a hurry–"

"I will not take much of your time, I assure you." When she still hesitated, he said, "The information I have to convey to you is very much in your own interest."

Unsure of whether she detected a hint of warning in his tone, she nodded. They began to walk.

"A lovely city, this San Francisco," he murmured. "There is a hint of Old World about it. These quaint little eateries, for example." He gestured at the window of a deli where a row of bratwurst dripped and popped, their skins splitting, over a grill of glowing coals. "Dreadful to think of living humans treated so, is it not? Yet it was a technique the Inquisition did not hesitate to employ. It concurred, you see, with their stated policy of extracting confessions without the shedding of blood."

Again she could think of nothing to say, but she remembered Robbie Kinsella's words: *Have you noticed how when he talks about things that happened hundreds of years ago, it's like he was there?*

As they crossed California Street, she realized with distracted surprise that Valcourt was walking them into the Bank of America building. She glanced at the fifty-odd stories of dark, tinted glass that towered above them.

"What I have to show you is best seen from a high vantage point," he said.

354

The lobby floor was of white tiles overlaid with a huge cross of red carpet. There were shops—a tobacconist, a florist, a travel bureau—and an extensive glassed-in display of Picasso prints and ceramics. They shared the elevator with a couple with cameras and two preteen children, who had to be restrained from randomly pushing buttons. The woman smiled apologetically at Nicole. She tried to smile back, but knew her face must look white and taut. The children quieted when the ascent began. The sense of acceleration was tremendous, and Nicole's ears popped. In perhaps thirty seconds, the light announced the fifty-second floor. Taking Nicole's arm, Valcourt led her into the elegant Carnelian Room, ringed by floor-to-ceiling windows, overlooking the vast grandeur of San Francisco Bay. It was not crowded. They sat at a table far from the bar, in one of the alcoves that the windows formed.

The glass and metal of the city sparkled in the sunlight below them. To the north rose the slender spire of the Transamerica Pyramid, the only taller building. From its base, the diagonal of Columbus Avenue stretched to North Beach. There were rooftop swimming pools and gardens. The Bay itself was a deep green, dotted with triangular white sails, dominated by the great mass of Alcatraz Island with its fortresslike abandoned prison. To the west, the great red arches of the Golden Gate Bridge led to the hillside opulence of Marin County. The sun hung just over the horizon like a great molten globe, dropping into the fog that was beginning to roll into the mouth of the Bay. A waitress came; Valcourt ordered cognac, and she, a Glenlivet Scotch, vaguely aware that she was reaching back to her first night with Jesse for support.

"What," Valcourt said, leaning forward and looking at her intently, "of all that, would you have?" As if to underline his words, to make certain she understood, he swept his arm in a proprietary gesture that seemed to include everything that lay beyond his fingertips.

"I don't understand," she said.

He shrugged. "A lover, that is wonderful. But it is a matter almost of insignificance, compared to what can be yours." He looked amused. "This man, your lifetime through, or any other who might suit you. Wealth beyond your dreams. The power to change history. Youth and beauty far beyond the normal span of years." He sat back, folded his hands on the table, and regarded the world spread out at their feet. "I do not exaggerate," he said quietly. "All these things, I am empowered to give."

She listened in amazement, thinking, *The man is mad.*

"That's very tempting," she said carefully, "but in all honesty, I was about to tell you that I've become uneasy with the group's activities-"

He interrupted curtly. "The group is immaterial. The others are too limited. But you, Nicole: nothing is beyond you—

"Together with your son."

It took an instant for the words to register. Her mouth opened.

He smiled, looking gentle. "I have a confession to make, Nicole. I have understood for some time what you do not: that he possesses your gift in tenfold measure.

356

Nature has forbidden me a son of my own, but I desire an heir, to raise and make strong in this great knowledge."

Faltering, she said, "I don't quite get . . . what you're asking."

"Bring him to me," Valcourt said. "Together, you and I will initiate him. He will start early on his path to power. By the time he comes of age, he will be like a god!"

Abruptly, she almost laughed at the sheer madness of it. But Valcourt's face–solemn, even urgent–steadied her.

"That's just–impossible," she said. "I mean, thank you for offering, but I don't want him to be a god. I want him to be a *boy*."

For an instant, she saw anger flare in his eye. Then he smiled, his charm returning.

"You are in a hurry," he said. "Let us go."

They rode the elevator to the street in silence and walked together back out onto the plaza. There, Valcourt paused beside the giant black glass wedge of the Banker's Heart.

"I have given you much, Nicole," he said. "I ask only to give more. How can you hesitate? I offer power undreamed of, not only for you, but for the one you love most. Think of what this will mean to him in later life. Think of how he could use his great gift to change the world for the better! Accept, and make all mankind glad!"

She turned away and closed her eyes, trying to clear away the buzzing of shock, outrage–and interest?–to give the idea a moment of objective thought. Could she even consider bringing up her son–her *son*–to acquire arcane, mysterious powers? Consider changing Tom Junior from a sweet, dreamy child–

Into a man like Valcourt?

"I'm sorry," she said, turning to face him again. "It's out of the question. He's going to choose his own life. That's the most important thing there is to me."

"On the contrary, Nicole," Valcourt said, "it is not only possible, but absolutely necessary." His voice had taken on a harder tone. "We are near the equinox, when day and night are locked at the height of equal struggle: the moment, the ancients understood well, unmatched for the launching of a neophyte on the path to power. The sun will not pause in its great journey, even for the gods. I have arranged a very special ceremony, to take place tonight."

"Tonight!"

"Tonight."

Shaking her head, she said, "Monsieur Valcourt, I'm afraid you don't understand. That's a firm no."

"It is you, Nicole, who do not understand. You owe me a debt. You must repay it. I will expect you, along with your son, at my home by nine o'clock."

"I don't see any point in continuing this conversation," she said, and turned to go.

"Memory is ever short when it comes to gratitude, Nicole," he called after her. "Perhaps yours requires to be refreshed."

As she hurried away, she could not keep from glancing over her shoulder. He had not moved, was still standing before the sculpture, feet apart, arms folded–

But in those few seconds, oddly, he had put on a pair of dark glasses.

She found her way onto the streetcar with that image persisting in her mind; but the memory it tried to arouse was too distant to grasp.

She sat right behind the driver and sank back.

It had almost been a bizarre sort of marriage proposal. Of course it was preposterous—and yet, a voice in her urged, suppose what he offered was real? What better preparation could she give Tom Junior for his life? A virtual guarantee of the wealth and power everyone else sought, so often ineffectually. Would he not grow into the ability, and was it not his right to decide how to use it? Did her reluctance really stem from her motherly desire to cling?

She leaned forward, face in her hands. What she needed more than ever was someone to confide in; but the understanding she truly craved could come only from her lover. She had still not thought of a way to tell him only part of the story and did not trust herself to tell him all of it.

Memory is short when it comes to gratitude. Perhaps yours requires to be refreshed.

What, exactly, had that meant?

When she raised her head, the driver was watching her in the mirror.

"You okay, lady?" he said over his shoulder.

"Yes," she said. "Just tired. Thank you."

After hesitating on the stairs of her building, she went straight up past her apartment to Jesse's. First and

359

foremost, she needed to be held. When he opened the door, she almost fell into his arms–

Only to pull back immediately in dismay. He reeked of whiskey.

She searched his eyes, and saw with horror that they were just as they had always been before the night of fascination: polite, distant, cynical.

And disinterested.

"You're drunk," she stammered, knowing as she spoke that it came out an accusation.

The skin around his eyes tightened just a little. "We knocked off early," he said, his voice noticeably slurred. "Finished a house; the next slab won't be ready for a couple days. I was bouncing around, and I got to thinking about how good I've been the past couple months." He shrugged, eyes dark, deep, unreadable.

She took his lapels and said, urgently and angrily, "Well, pour the liquor down the drain and start drinking coffee. We need to talk."

Very softly, he said, "Don't ever tell me not to take a drink."

Her hands fell from his shirt. He turned and stalked back into the room.

Nicole closed her eyes, fighting for control. "I didn't mean it like that," she said. "It's just that . . . there's something very important going on that I think I'd better tell you about."

"Sorry, darlin', you're on your own tonight. It's gonna have to keep." He turned back toward her. "I'm feeling really strange, Nicole. It's not just the juice. It's like–I've been walking around in a daze the past couple months, like I hardly know what the fuck I've been doing. I was one thing, one person, for a lot of years, and then bingo! I'm somebody completely different. I'm just now starting to get it. Like all of a sudden, I looked into a mirror."

The fog was rolling up the avenues, thickening with the twilight. He stood there, a darker shape silhouetted against the windows. It was like looking at someone she had once known.

"I think I need a couple of days to myself," he said. "Get drunk, kick it around, touch in with whoever I used to be. Maybe it'll just run its course."

"I can't believe,'" she said, voice trembling, "that you can just back away from me, after . . . after–"

"After what?" he said softly, with a mocking edge. "The gift of your precious pussy?"

She rushed out, her heels clattering on the steps, half imagining that she heard him running after her to pull her into his arms and apologize. But when she stopped at her own door, there was silence above.

She thrust the key into the lock and threw open the door. "Tommy?" she called. There was no answer. "TJ?" again, louder. She walked quickly down the hall, pushing open door after door. The apartment was empty.

She had the telephone in her hand and was starting to dial the police before she caught herself, realizing the absurdity. *How long did you say he's been missing, ma'am?* Her mind raced: Rush out into the street and scream his name? Run back upstairs and beg for Jesse's help?

Then she noticed a small, slender figure on the sidewalk below, wearing a familiar Giants baseball cap and eating a candy bar. She heard the iron gate to the street open and his footsteps on the stairs, and her body sagged. Massaging her temples, she felt an uncontrollable surge of fear and fury. Fists clenched, unable to stop herself, she whirled at the sound of the door opening and screamed:

"Where have you *been?*"

He stared at her, the crumpled candy bar wrapper in his hand, his eyes bewildered and hurt.

"I was hungry," he said.

She hurried to him, knelt, and held him tightly. "I'm sorry, baby," she murmured. "I had a bad day. I don't mean to take it out on you." She stood, managing to smile. "I've got a frozen pizza. I'll doctor it up with hamburger. Okay?"

He nodded, still looking uncertain, but then smiled back.

Over dinner, she questioned him about school and learned that most of his teachers were okay except for a certain Mister Franklin, who gave too much math homework, and that yeah, some of the kids were doing drugs, and that he wanted to try out for Little League this spring but wasn't sure he could make it. She thought fleetingly of her dream house in the country, near a small town that was clean and wholesome and had room for every kid on every team.

But all the while, the image of Jesse's eyes, filled with that cool distance, hung before her like a pair of dark headlights. *It's like I've been walking around in a daze*

362

the past couple months. . . . I was one thing, one person, for a lot of years, and then bingo! I'm somebody completely different. I'm just now starting to get it. Like all of a sudden, I looked into a mirror.

A mirror held up by the same one of Valcourt's "entities" that had created the daze in the first place, at her request?

Memory is ever short when it comes to gratitude, Nicole. Perhaps yours requires to be refreshed.

Was it possible that he had that much control over her life?

As she did the dishes, Tom Junior walked into the kitchen and poured a glass of milk. Abruptly, for no reason, she remembered something that had slipped her notice at the time.

"Tommy? That dream you had at your father's—the one with the skull?"

He nodded, face uncertain.

"Did you say it opened its eyes—or its *eye?*"

"Only one," he said. "I think that's the part that really scared me."

After a moment, she managed to smile and said, "Okay, sorry to bring it up. I was just wondering something."

She finished the dishes, and saw out the window that the fog had thickened with the coming of night. It was going to be a long evening, alone, trying to understand what she had done, what she must do now, all the while straining to hear the footsteps of the man upstairs—*After what? The gift of your precious pussy?*—for whom she had done it.

The clock was nearing nine. Tom Junior was in his room and out of earshot when the telephone rang. Nicole hesitated, certain it would be Jesse, and suddenly not at all sure she was ready to talk to him. In the lull after dinner, she had nearly swallowed her pride and climbed the steps once more with her heart in her hand; but before she could act, she had heard his footsteps pass her door–and then continue on down. The metal gate clanged behind him, and she had watched him walk toward Irving Street, a shadowy figure in the foggy night, not looking back, although he must have known she would see him.

And then she had given in and wept, bitterly, helplessly, trying to convince herself that if she had really won his love by means of a trick, then she did not want it anyway–but knowing that was not true. When the tears subsided, she consoled herself with the hope that Valcourt had had nothing to do with it after all–that the spat was only the first of many inevitable disagreements, a ripple on the pond of honeymoon bliss that could not have continued. Time would tell. The phone rang on, four times, five. She stared out the window, envisioning Jesse calling from a bar, drunkenly contrite, and disgust warred with her anxiety and sorrow. But when it rang the sixth time, she rushed to it.

"Nicole," said a cold, deep voice.

It shook her. In her distress, she had almost forgotten about the earlier part of the evening.

"Monsieur Valcourt–" she said, trying to gear up to be firm, to say, *I thought I made myself clear, please don't call me again.*

"Rest your tongue, woman," he interrupted curtly. "It is for me to speak, and you to listen." His accent was thickened, the words charged with command. "The time for pretense is past: Hear me, and understand well. You have taken what I gave. Now you must give me what I demand in return."

As calmly as she could, trying to make her own voice cold, she said:

"I'm not quite sure what you've really given me. But if there's anything reasonable I can do to pay you back, I'll be happy to. I don't have much money, but–"

"Money," he said contemptuously. "Could money buy you the lover you so craved? Can money yet eradicate your participation–in murder?"

Nicole's breath stopped in her throat.

He laughed harshly, as if he could see her face. "Aye, murder. Can you tell me that you–a lawyer, no less–did not understand the implications of our action? I made them clear enough."

Shaking her head, she tried to speak, to deny, but he spoke again. "At our first meeting, I gave you the name of an entity to do your bidding, and *you gave me your name* in exchange. At that moment, you awakened a great dragon. Then your 'guardian angel' gave you what you desired, strengthening the dragon's hold. Things were well enough with you then, were they not?

"And at the last, you swore a binding oath on my book of power, *of your own free will*–and sealed it by joining in the destruction of a human life–in order to retain what you had already received. You even ignored the warning of the one of your companions not blinded by greed.

"At that moment, the dragon marked you as his own. If you doubt me, you have only to regard your left hand."

The burn Tom Junior had noticed some days before had remained painless and seemed to get neither better nor worse. But as she raised the hand to her face, she saw with horror that at some time in the past hours, it had reddened almost to scarlet–

And had taken on the unmistakable outline of the design on the cover of Valcourt's grimoire.

"You may call that dragon *Adversary,*" Valcourt said, iron-voiced, "and you must henceforth own him master. I am his captain, his bishop, his prince. His is an easy service: obey, and your rewards will be rich. Leave your home at once, and bring your son to me."

"Not for anything," she whispered.

Once more, Guy-Luc Valcourt laughed. This time it was an ugly, menacing sound.

"The dragon devours those who take from him and then seek to cheat him, in ways you would faint to imagine. Death is but the beginning.

"Come to me, *now*. Do not dare to fail!"

The phone clicked. Nicole stood for seconds, staring at it, then, slowly, put it down. It rattled against the cradle with the trembling of her hand.

Had she known? About Yvonne Epps?

Somewhere deep within her, a voice assured her that she had.

You even ignored the warning of the one of your companions not blinded by greed.

She watched her breath form a small patch on the window as she breathed the word, "Murder."

Hugging herself tightly, she turned away and began to pace. Then, insanely, she almost laughed. What should she do now: turn herself in to the police?

The dragon devours those who take from him and then seek to cheat him.

Again she looked at her hand, at the vivid, horrifying brand, and felt a touch of nausea.

Then she heard a muffled sound outside the apartment door.

She waited, tense. It had not been a knock: more like something hitting and sliding down. But Jesse was gone, and she had heard him lock the front gate. No one else could be in the building.

She walked quietly to the door and leaned with her ear against it. Outside, there was silence.

"Who's there?" she said, her voice catching.

Nothing.

She hooked the chain and slowly pulled the door a few inches open. There was no one on the dimly lit landing, but something was lying on the mat. It looked like a pair of shoes.

"Is someone there?" she said. No sound or movement answered. Could Jesse have come back in without her hearing and left the shoes? Possibly with a note, a joking way of trying to apologize?

Quickly, she pushed the door shut, unhooked the chain, grabbed them, and locked herself in again. She gazed at them, puzzled. She was sure they were not Jesse's: a man's black high-top sneakers, worn almost to rubbish, and astonishingly heavy. She parted the flopping canvas top of one and peered inside. It looked like a bizarre sort of doughnut, a fresh red color around the rim with a whitish core.

She was already screaming when she dropped the shoes, and she screamed all the way across the living room to the sink. As she vomited, she was aware of Tom Junior's footsteps hurrying down the hall.

"Don't look," she managed to gasp. "Go back to your room, get your coat, now!"

"But what–"

"*This second!*"

Quickly, she rinsed her face and mouth, then raced down the hall to her bedroom and grabbed her coat and purse. Tom Junior appeared in jeans and T-shirt, holding his jacket, looking frightened. She knelt before him and took his shoulders, speaking in a low but urgent voice.

"Don't ask me any questions, baby. We're going to pretend the building's on fire and get out of here. Okay?"

He nodded, eyes wide.

Holding his hand, she stepped onto the landing. She looked up and down the stairs, then led them to the inside door to the garage. Her groping fingers found the light switch. She stood for several seconds, fearfully scanning the shadowy, feebly lit space. *Hurry,* she thought fiercely.

"Okay, get in the car," she whispered, and opened the door to the street.

Mercifully, there was no traffic on her street. She backed out, turned right at the comer, and stopped at the light, set to turn north on Nineteenth: the opposite direction from Valcourt's home.

In a very small voice, Tom Junior said, "Where we going?"

"Just away for a while." She leaned across the seat to hug him, then put her finger to his lips. "Now hush, I have to think." The fog blurred the shapes of the few pedestrians. Everyone seemed menacing. The light took forever to change, but at last they were moving north toward the Golden Gate Bridge, and her panic relented enough to allow her to think. Just getting away was the priority. She had credit cards and some cash. She did not even want to think about where they might end up, lest Valcourt should pick it out of her mind.

For in the instant of recognizing what had lain on her doormat, what she had picked up in her hands, it was as if a veil had been ripped from before her face: as if her sudden understanding, a gut-level certainty far deeper and more powerful than rationality, had been controlled just as carefully as her previous ignorance–

Controlled by the man in dark glasses who had sat beside her in a restaurant months before, overheard her conversation, stalked her through the city, and even let her see him standing, with macabre humor, beside the so-appropriate giant black heart; who could do all that he boasted, and there was no telling how much more; who had lured and deceived her expertly and thoroughly, by nurturing her self-deception.

369

But the greatest horror was that she had allowed it: had let enter her being as she might let a lover enter her body, this enemy who could be anywhere, and who was capable of anything. *I see, good God, I finally see what he's doing!* She shuddered violently, remembering the heavy weight of the shoes.

But there would be time for pity later—pity for herself and all of the others who had been hurt—time to assess and decide what to do. For now, the only thing that mattered was escape.

She forced herself to stop at a yellow light, thinking, caution; and gripping the wheel tightly, she waited for it to change.

The man who called himself Guy-Luc Valcourt stood in his cupola, facing north into the foggy night, hands clenched around the railing.

"Foolish harlot," he said grimly.

These women! She was prepared not only to give up her lover, but to jeopardize her life, for the sake of her whelp—not even knowing his true intentions. In Courdeval's day, women would sell a child for a loaf of bread. There were always more children.

But it was precisely that—that strength of love—that made the offering so potent. And so necessary. His power had been diminishing steadily. Unease touched him. She was fleeing, and she was determined.

"You will pay," he whispered. Then, with sudden, angry force, he called out the name of her "guardian angel." "Go!" he roared. "Bring her back!"

Valcourt glared into the night mist, following with his will, keeping taut the reins.

Driving through the foggy, dark woods of Golden Gate Park, Nicole concentrated on making it across the bridge with no mistakes. Stay to the left past the Marina turnoff, toll-free this direction, three miles over the bridge itself—and then they would be in Marin, with U.S. Highway 101 wide open ahead and all of San Francisco Bay between them and Valcourt.

Preoccupied, she was not aware that the stirring inside her had even begun, until it had already slipped smoothly around her thoughts like a furtive net.

Stunned, she tried to brake, but the net drew instantly tighter, controlling her actions. She drove on, feeling with horror the familiar presence inside her, the presence she had courted for months—at last revealing its true loathsomeness. It twisted like an intangible serpent, sneering at the futility of her attempt to flee, assuring her that she would never again be free of it—that while believing she had been forcing it to serve her, she had in reality been indebting herself to *it*. The mark on her palm gave a sudden little flare of pain, and her mind echoed with malicious laughter. Then the net tightened again, suddenly, viciously, leaving her helpless.

At Balboa Street she turned right, went around the block, and came back to the Park Presidio. They stopped at the light, blinker on to turn left:

Back the way they had come.

Tom Junior was staring at her. "Mom? Why are we turning around?"

Trapped inside her own mind, Nicole heard her calm, musical voice say:

"I was going to go across the Marina and down 101. But I wasn't really thinking; 280 would be faster."

She could see the confusion in his eyes: wary, sensing something wrong, but not questioning his trust in her.

"How come you're in such a hurry?"

"I'd forgotten all about this appointment, and realized we were late. But it's okay, we'll make it."

He seemed to relax a little. "Where are we going?"

Agonized, she felt herself smile sweetly. *It's not me!* she tried to scream. *Don't listen!*

The net held fast. "It's a surprise," she said, "a really nice one."

The light changed. They turned back south.

Spencer Epps walked into the booming darkness of the Club Tropicana and found a table in his usual part of the room. It was just before nine P.M. He'd done most of a gram of coke in the past couple of hours, and was vibrating so hard as he walked across the floor that he felt he might at any second simply blow up like a grenade, scattering skin, eyeballs, blood, and snot all over the ceiling and walls. The several drinks he had downed did not seem to have helped. For the most part, things had been going amazingly well since Yvonne's funeral. The police had been sympathetic rather than suspicious. Even Yvonne's parents had come up to him and put their arms around him, and Langdon Winslowe himself had said with a cracked voice, "I know how much you loved her. If there's anything we can do–"

Until this afternoon, when Valcourt had called him and told him to come, with Tina, to the house tonight. When Spencer had asked Valcourt why, trying to sound casually curious, the man had said only:

"I wish to know her." His tone made it clear that that was all the answer Spencer was going to get. It had occurred to Spencer that Valcourt might want to make it with her, that this was hidden payment coming due. The idea shook him and excited him at the same time.

But in his guts, he did not think Valcourt was after sex.

He ordered a double Chivas and forced himself to sip slowly while he waited for Tina to appear on the stage. When she spotted him, she gave him a big smile and began to dance as if he were alone in the audience. In the past two weeks, she had just about sucked his cock off, while her hints had gotten less subtle and more frequent. The day before yesterday, it had taken them forty minutes to walk two blocks on Union Square, with Tina stopping like a bank examiner at the window of every jewelry store.

He still had not figured out where those photos had come from.

He watched her writhe on the stage, teasingly unhooking her halter, cupping her breasts, and finally revealing them in all their lovely symmetry. Her eyes batted wickedly, her lips pouted–and for the first time, a voice within him whispered, Is *this* what you want for the rest of your life? A broad who gets off on flashing her zorch at every guy with five bucks and a hard-on? Now that you're rich? Now that you can have beauty *and* class?

The thought caught him flat-footed–stunned him a little. His head was throbbing. He turned away from the stage and ordered another Scotch.

After her set was done, she hurried out of the dressing room, still breathless and smiling.

"Hey, you," she said, slipping into the seat beside him, her hand going automatically to his lap.

He caught it. "I want you to come with me. Tonight. Now."

Her eyes became uncertain. "I can't just leave in the middle of a shift."

"Fuck this place," Spencer said, then realized he had spoken too loudly. He leaned forward, forcing a smile. "You don't have to do this anymore, baby. From now on, you belong to me."

Her face broke into a grin of pure pleasure. "In that case, lover, I sure do. Where we gonna go?"

Spencer felt, with distant surprise, his calm and assurance growing. He could feel the strange red mark he had noticed on his palm several days before. It was not a painful sensation–on the contrary, rather pleasant. It tingled.

"To a party," he said. "A special one."

She laughed, clapping her hands, and for the first time he saw that her teeth were small, sharp, and even–like a cat's.

The first twenty minutes of the drive had been a violent, hidden struggle, but finally, exhausted, Nicole had quieted. Since then, the net in her mind seemed to relax ever so slightly, and a tiny hope was rising within her: a hope she instantly suppressed, fearful that the entity would sense it and renew its vigilance.

Was it possible that if she saved every scrap of energy, there would come an instant when she would be able to break free, force the car off the road, and scream to Tom Junior to run?

They had passed the dark, foggy basin of Crystal Springs Reservoir and were approaching the turnoff for Green Mountain Road. She continued to obey meekly, easing the car down the off-ramp, stopping, beginning the winding journey to Valcourt's house.

It would have to be soon.

She was tensing herself to jerk the wheel, when from outside there came a muted explosion, like a silenced pistol shot, followed by increasingly loud staccato thumping. The back end of the car was listing. It took her a moment to realize what had happened; she had only had a flat tire once before in her life. She closed her eyes on the tears of hope that sprang into them, forcing her racked mind to be still.

It was an unbelievable stroke of luck. Surely someone would stop for a single woman and a child trying to fix a tire. Then would be the time to scream a few short words to alert Tom Junior, to derail this thing: *Get help! I'm not myself!*

She piloted the limping car to the side of the road and turned off the ignition, leaving the headlights on.

"A flat," she said, her voice neutral and controlled. "Guess we'd better see if we can fix it."

"Jesse showed me how once," he said eagerly. She sensed his relief at something concrete to deal with after the strained silence of the drive.

They climbed out. Wisps of fog clung to the branches in the thick woods around them, strangely luminous in the glow of the headlights. A wet breeze moved the mist like shapes through the trees, like a procession of spirits as lost and helpless as her own, whispering forlornly on an endless dark journey. She shivered and opened the trunk, her ears straining for the sound of an approaching vehicle.

Tom Junior had found the jack and was trying to put it together when she heard the hiss of tires on pavement.

"Sounds like somebody's coming," she said. "Let's see if we can get some help." He looked disappointed at surrendering his position of importance, but he walked with her to the side of the road. In her mind, the entity hovered like a suspicious watchdog.

Headlights appeared. She waved her hand, using the motion to quell the excitement washing through her. She could see the car now, a late-model Mercedes sedan—someone affluent, someone she could trust. She closed her eyes, *please stop please stop,* and when it did, she rushed to the driver's window. The car's interior light flicked on.

She was staring into the face of Charity Haverill, lips curved in a faint, knowing smile, and eyes as cold as a snake's.

"Hop in," Charity said. "I'm just going a couple of miles down the road. You can use the phone."

For several long seconds, Nicole fought, but it was useless. "Turn off the lights and lock up, TJ," she said. Slowly, numbly, she climbed into the back seat.

Charity swiveled. Nicole saw all of the antagonism that had hovered between them reflected in the glitter of the other woman's eyes.

"He's *very* angry," Charity said softly, and turned back, leaving Nicole's mind echoing with the malicious laughter of the entity, that had twisted the knife again by allowing her to hope.

SIXTEEN

Across the street from Nicole Partrick's apartment, just before ten P.M., two men and a woman sat in a rented Ford, watching the lighted windows.

They had arrived from Paris that afternoon, but only after several exhausting hours had they succeeded in cutting through red tape and obtaining necessary information, like the tracing of the license plate in the photograph to this address. This had taken considerable influence, and was again a result of Roger Devarre's connections from his Paris days. A former school friend now highly placed in Interpol had accepted without question a story about a runaway teenager, drugs, and a wealthy family in Boudrie's parish who wished to proceed with discretion. He had hesitated at providing weapons, but finally had accepted too Devarre's assurances that they would only be used in the most extreme circumstances, and arranged the loan of two Browning automatics. Boudrie and Devarre now carried the pistols, agreed that they would shoot McTell on sight, and worry about the consequences–and the final laying of Courdeval–afterward.

If, remained several caveats. If he was indeed still McTell. If they ever saw him.

And if the trap they seemed so clearly to be walking into was not sprung so forcefully and unexpectedly that the matter was ended before it ever began.

In fifteen minutes of watching, they had seen no movement in the windows or in and out of the building. But the main garage door was open, the light left on, suggesting that someone might have left in haste–and all three remembered the wide-flung door to McTell's villa that had signaled the beginning of *that night.*

"Well, I can't sense anything," Mélusine finally said. "If there's something waiting that guns are powerless against, we're simply in trouble."

At her own insistence, she walked ahead to the garage, playing the canary again. There was something almost amusing about the three of them crossing the street, she thought fleetingly: herself limping like a hostage through the foggy night, while the two men followed with heads swiveling, pistols held close to their sides.

And if the woman named Nicole Partrick came to the door, seeming genuinely puzzled? They could only show her the photo and request an explanation. It was possible, of course, that Courdeval had chosen the car without her knowledge and that there was no connection. That he had only wanted to lure them to a particular place, perhaps in order to unleash on them something like his "pet."

379

That he might be watching them, about to do so, at this second.

An inside garage door led to the winding stairway.

Slowly, as quietly as possible, they climbed. The apartment door, too, was ajar.

"I don't think there's anyone," Mélusine said softly, "but be careful."

Devarre and Boudrie moved to the door, looked at each other, nodded, and burst through.

The room was empty. They went quickly down the hall, throwing open doors, sweeping the area with their weapons. There was no one.

When they returned, Devarre noticed a pair of battered shoes that had been flung against a wall, out of place in the scrupulously tidy living room. He knelt to examine them. Then he jerked back, exclaiming with horror:

"Good God!" As the other two came toward him, he stopped Mélusine, saying, "You don't need to see this."

Boudrie stared down at the clearly exposed bone and ragged meat of one ankle.

"It looks as if it's been chewed," he said softly.

"Let me look," Mélusine said, stepping around her husband. She gasped, her hands flying to her face.

"I told you," he muttered, his arm going protectively around her.

For almost a minute, none of them moved. "We seem to have come to the right place," Boudrie finally said. "Now what?"

There's nothing to do but wait, Mélusine was about to answer, when the words: "Stay cool," in English, made them all whirl to face the doorway.

A lean man with kinky black hair and a lined face was holding a revolver on them. He looked very controlled and angry, and there was no doubt in Mélusine's mind that he was on the edge of ending all of their lives.

But another instant certainty came too, and as she sensed Devarre and Boudrie starting to raise their guns, she shouted, "No, it's not him!" and threw her arms back to block them. She saw the black-haired man's finger tighten on the trigger, his knee drop to brace himself; but he held, and then the critical instant was past.

"Please," she said in her rusty English. "Let us explain."

The man moved not an inch. "Put down your weapons," he said quietly. She nodded. With obvious reluctance, Devarre and Boudrie stooped to set their pistols on the floor.

"Now sit on the couch," he said, "with your hands on the table."

They sat.

He picked up the pistols and backed away. Then he let the barrel of his own gun drop, but kept it pointed in their direction.

"Talk to me," he said.

Guy-Luc Valcourt entered the parlor, smiling kindly. "So, my friends, I have called for you a garage. They will send a truck along presently, and you will be on your way. I hope you will accept our hospitality in the interim."

381

Nicole sat helplessly in the familiar room, still held by invisible chains. In the presence of Tom Junior, both Valcourt and Charity had affected not to know her. Valcourt's tense excitement was apparent. While the furnishings of the room remained as they had been, the grimoire was gone from the mantel and the shelves of old books emptied, as if the house were about to be vacated.

"You, madame, would doubtless like to freshen up after your hardship. Allow my companion to escort you." Nicole stood, a puppet pulled by invisible strings. "And you, young man, you are doubtless a devotee of the video? Of course. Come with me, then, I have a selection I am sure you will find most entertaining." Tom Junior had been peering in timid fascination at the lavish surroundings and at the strange, powerful man with the accent. Now he looked at Nicole as if to say, Okay, Mom?

Run! she tried to scream, but her lips smiled and her head nodded. Valcourt's arm went around her son's shoulders as the two of them left the room.

"This way," Charity said, her voice gone hard. Sick with fear, Nicole followed her up the stairs.

The halls were lit by candelabras, the candles all black, their flame thick and smoky. They climbed to the third floor, then went through a small door and up a final narrow flight. Charity opened a hatch, and they emerged into the foggy night, in the cupola Nicole had seen from the ground. She gripped the railing with her hands, staring out. It was like being at the prow of a ship that was lost on a black, stormy sea. In every direction, the slate tiles of the roof sloped steeply away to the eaves, glistening and slick with mist. She could catch only

382

glimpses of the ground. It seemed a mile below. Charity leaned against the far railing, watching her, the same mixture of malice and jealousy in her eyes; and Nicole wondered helplessly what she had done to make the other woman such an implacable enemy–wondered when and how the alliance between Charity and Valcourt had come about.

Not more than two minutes had passed when a swift, heavy tread sounded on the stairs. The hatch was thrown open and Valcourt came through, like a dark giant rising from the earth. His benign facade was gone: his face was hard as stone, his mouth a taut line. The entity in her mind squirmed obsequiously, a sensation that nauseated her. Valcourt growled a sentence in the harsh language he had used in their ceremonies. She recognized the syllables of her guardian angel's name.

Then it was gone. She blinked, shaking her head. Her mind was free. But as quickly, she understood that mental restraint was no longer necessary. Now it was her body that was trapped.

Fists clenched, she faced him. "Where is my son?" The words came out a whisper.

"I have told you once tonight," he said harshly. "I will not tell you again. It is for me to talk and you to listen."

He turned away, clasped his hands behind him, and gazed out into the misty dark. When he spoke, his voice was quieter.

"You have incurred a debt, Nicole. It cannot be repaid with money–only in service, in obedience. If you are a willing servant, your bondage will be light, your rewards great." He turned back, fixing her with his one-eyed glare. "Let me explain what your continued lack of cooperation would entail:

"You have already felt the power of the entity you thought to control–you, who know nothing, who were vain and foolish enough to believe you could accomplish what only the strongest and boldest of men have ever dared to attempt. I can summon that entity back at any instant, and leave it with you as long as I choose. For the remainder of your natural life, if it pleases me. I would doubtless tire of you as a plaything for that long a time. But our sister"–be indicated Charity with a sweeping gesture–"would find months, perhaps years, of entertainment." Valcourt let the silence hang while Nicole, with growing horror, searched Charity's face: tense, bloodless, cruel.

"I have liberated the true soul within her, you see," he said, almost gently. "She longs to repay you for your condescension and arrogance. Shall I describe a few of the scenarios she has already envisioned for you, should you become her toy? She thinks, for example, that you would play exquisitely the part of a woman in search of bizarre adventure–say, begging to be defiled by a gang of hoodlums." He paused again, then said, "But such mild entertainment would not satisfy her for long."

Nicole turned away, her stomach twisting. Valcourt waited in silence until she had control of herself again.

"Now let us consider the other alternative. You have offended our master, whom I call Adversary. But he is great in understanding. He knows that the age-old superstitions built around him arc difficult to overcome. You need only to make him an offering, humbly and sincerely, to win his forgiveness. After that, all that I promised you earlier this day will lie within your reach."

"What kind of offering?" she managed to say.

He smiled pityingly. "There is so much you do not understand, Nicole. Life is but a series of heartaches, concealed beneath pretty wrappers, that must one day be ripped away to reveal the ugly truths of disease, calamity, and death. You have it in your power to spare your son this: to send him to the next world still in his purity and innocence, instead of stained with the sins and weariness of time. One quick stroke of your hand, and he will suffer no more."

Nicole stared. "A stroke of my *hand,*" she breathed. "What–?" Abruptly, comprehension dawned: the understanding of what he had been after from the beginning. But in Valcourt's face there was no pity, no tiny spot of softness. Hardly aware of what she was doing, she whirled on Charity and shrieked, "How *can* you? He's a little boy!"

For a second, Charity's face went uncertain, the hardness lost in confusion and guilt. But Valcourt turned too, his forefinger extended.

"Leave us!" he barked. Head bowed, Charity slunk down the stairs.

When he turned back to Nicole, his gaze was ferocious. He pulled from his sleeve a bundle of cloth and thrust it toward her. "Our talk is done. Prepare yourself. I will return within the hour."

As he descended through the hatch, he paused once more. "Remember, Nicole: the boy is no longer yours. You sold him, the moment you received"–he raised his left palm, and for the first time, she saw clearly the deep, smoldering red brand, a precise image of her own–"this. You must repay a life for the life you helped to take. His death can be quick and painless, at your hands." His face twisted. "Or far more . . . protracted, at my own."

The hatch closed. There was a sound as of a bolt being shot.

Slowly, she held up the cloth he had given her and let it unfold.

It was a sleeveless silk gown the color of blood.

The man had told Tom Junior to call him Geeluke, which he supposed was some kind of foreign name; it went along with his accent and strange appearance. For sure he was rich. Tom Junior had never been in a house like this; he'd seen them only on television. It was bigger than the whole building he and his mother lived in. In a way he wished he'd had a chance to show his mom that he could have changed that tire himself, but he was secretly relieved that they hadn't had to depend on it. He might not have gotten the lug nuts tight enough or something.

But mainly, he was just glad they were around some other people. This had been just about the weirdest night of his life. First his mother was screaming at him to get a jacket and rushing them into the car like the building was on fire–he'd seen her late before plenty of times, but she'd never gotten *that* upset–and then all of a sudden it was like she'd taken some kind of dope, all quiet and calm. It had him worried, but what could you do when it was your mom? He supposed everything was okay now—Geeluke had said the guys from the garage would be here soon—but he wished Jesse was around.

The TV set was strange, too, like a thick slab of dark glass on a stand. It must have had a satellite hookup and remote control, because there was no VCR or other equipment he could see, not even any cords. Geeluke had just stood in front of it for a few seconds, then smiled and said:

"You will enjoy this, I think. Your mother will join you soon." But he must have forgotten to turn on the sound; so far the show was silent. Which was okay, because Tom Junior wasn't in much of a mood for a movie anyway; he had mainly pretended interest out of politeness. Besides, whatever was on was starting out pretty dull.

An old woman was talking to a kid about his own age, on the outskirts of a little town. Everything looked like it was a few hundred years old: the old lady was wearing a heavy skirt that dragged on the ground; the boy wore a shirt and breeches of rough cloth; the roofs of the houses in the distance were straw. It was probably some historical drama, and Tom Junior hoped there would be knights and battles. That was almost as good as *Star Wars*.

Now the old woman was looking back over her shoulder toward the village. There was a creepy gleam in her eyes, like she knew she was getting away with something. The picture shifted to what she was looking at: another, younger woman, standing just outside the village, watching. Her hands were clenched, her face white and scared, and she seemed about to run toward the boy. But then, slowly, her hand opened up, and she stared down into a glittering gold coin in her palm. The old woman's eyes looked satisfied now, and she patted the boy on the shoulder, then took his hand and started walking with him away from the village. He looked back at the young woman, afraid, confused; but she was hurrying inside the town's gates, both hands clutching at her skirt.

The scene faded. Tom Junior realized he had been watching very intently, even though there wasn't much action. Even though nothing really scary had happened.

There was something about that look in the old lady's eyes.

Now the picture was coming back on, and it seemed like maybe something good was about to start. There was a castle in the background, way up on top of a mountain, and, sure enough, a couple of knights on horseback riding down the road. Then, out of the twilight, the old lady in black appeared. The boy was gone–

But she was carrying a good-sized sack over her shoulder. It looked heavy, and she was struggling with it. The knights rode down to meet her. One of them took the sack and put it across his saddle; the other tossed her a leather pouch. Clutching it, looking around, she hurried back the way she had come until she blended into the darkness. The knights were riding back up to the castle.

As the scene faded again, Tom Junior was almost certain he saw the sack squirming. He had pretty much decided he didn't like this movie, but he couldn't seem to stop watching. Uncomfortably, he glanced at the door of the room. His mother had been gone a long time.

The scene was inside the castle now, in a huge stone courtyard lit by torches. A fire burned in front of a table covered with a black cloth that had a weird design etched on it in bright red. Now a procession of figures wearing hooded black robes was walking slowly into the courtyard, swaying, as if they were singing. The leader, a man who looked a foot taller than any of the others, was carrying the old lady's sack in his arms.

Something was digging at Tom Junior, some voice of memory whispering deep in his mind. This was not good, not at all. He had seen something like it before, somewhere, and it was very, very bad—so bad that when the leader put the sack on the table and Tom Junior could see that it was very definitely moving, writhing like whatever was in it was trying to get out, and the faint sound of deep male voices singing a strange, tuneless chant came to his ears, he realized all at once that this was exactly the scene that had brought him screaming out of his nightmares.

By the time a knife appeared in the tall man's hand, he was on his feet and backing out of the room.

The house was very quiet. He tiptoed into the room where they had first come in. The lights had been turned off; there were only the flames of several black candles, flickering and throwing jumpy shadows. Heart hammering, he tried to figure out what to do.

How had that TV screen been able to play back his dream?

How come Geeluke was wearing a robe that looked like the ones on the men in the castle?

"Mom?" he said timidly. He had seen her and Charity walking toward the stairs. Geeluke might get mad if he found him wandering around the house, but that was a chance he was going to have to take. It may not have been very grown up, but he wanted his mother, now.

The stairs got darker as they curved up to the second story. Like the room below, the hallway was lit only by black candles.

Tom Junior swallowed. "Mom?" he called again. The house remained silent.

Then he saw, at the far end of the hall, an open door. He started toward it, his sneakers squeaking on the hardwood floor. The hall was very long. It seemed to take an hour to get to the end. Holding his breath, he leaned forward carefully and peeked in.

It was a bedroom, and somebody was asleep in it. Had his mother lain down for a nap? Maybe that was all it was, her acting so strangely; maybe she was just exhausted. He pushed open the door and stepped in. The shape in the bed did not move.

Then he saw, in the dim candlelight, that it was not her. It was a girl, maybe seventeen or eighteen, and really pretty. Her long chestnut hair was spread across the pillow, and her face showed that she was in a deep and peaceful sleep. It seemed a little strange for a girl that age to be in bed so early; even he usually stayed up past ten. But that wasn't the strangest thing. The covers came up to just below her shoulders, which were bare.

So why was she wearing a scarf around her neck?

He was still staring at her, fascinated by her beauty, when he heard a door slam somewhere on the floor above. Abruptly, he realized he had no business being in a strange girl's bedroom, and he hurried back out to the hall, relieved to know that someone was coming.

Then he heard Geeluke's voice, harsh and angry:

"Do you think to betray me?" Immediately there followed the sound of a hard slap and a woman's little shriek.

Tom Junior stopped.

"Forgive me," came Charity's trembling voice. "This is so new–it confuses me. You know I want to prove my love for you."

Geeluke's voice, gentler, said, "You will do as you have promised? Your heart will not fail when blood is spilled?"

Her answer was so faint Tom Junior could hardly hear it. "I swear."

Silently, he tiptoed back toward the bedroom.

"It is well," he heard Geeluke murmur, his strong voice carrying. "Rise, then, and go. See to the boy. He should be in a proper state by now. Charm him, soothe his fears. It is best if he believes he has been delivered from harm–until the last. I have yet a few preparations to make. I will join you soon."

The heavy footsteps began again, and Tom Junior realized with terror that they were coming down the hall toward him. He looked quickly around the room. He would never make it to the closet in time.

He dove beneath the bed.

Holding his breath, scrunched against the wall, he watched the arc of light on the floor widen as the door swept open. He saw the hem of Geeluke's robe, and his sandaled feet. Geeluke stopped and said something in a language Tom Junior thought maybe was French. It sounded like a command.

The bed above him began to move. A few seconds later, another pair of feet came to rest on the floor. They were bare, as were the slim calves above them. For perhaps half a minute, Geeluke neither moved nor spoke. Then he said something else, something soft and thick, almost a sigh.

He opened the closet door and stood before it, then turned back, carrying a dress. Tom Junior could see the bottom: it was as black as Geeluke's robe. There came the soft sound of the gown falling onto the bed. Geeluke spoke once more, again commandingly; and strode out of the room.

Slowly, the slender calves began to move. Torn Junior remained where he was until the sound of Geeluke's footsteps had faded altogether. Then, silent as a mouse, he squirmed on his belly to the edge of the bed. An inch at a time, he moved his face forward to where he could see.

His mouth fell open.

The girl had moved to stand before the mirror on her dresser. She was wearing nothing but the violet-colored scarf. He had never seen a woman nude before, except his mother, who didn't count, and he had never imagined a girl could be as beautiful as this. Slowly, as if she were in a dream, she gathered up her long hair and twisted it into

392

a loose knot, pinning it on top of her head. Torn Junior stared, concern for his mother and his own fear both forgotten in the swell of an excitement he had never before felt.

Then, with the same slow grace, the girl's fingers began to unknot the scarf. As she pulled it loose, she turned toward him, walking to the bed. His gaze traveled up her lovely body, now almost close enough to touch—

And stopped at the jagged purple slice across her throat.

The sound he made was something like a squeak. The girl's gaze came to his face. Her eyes were dark, empty, and she paid no more attention to him than if he were part of the floor. As she leaned forward to take the gown from the bed, the wound separated, clearly showing the severed vessels and muscles within.

Tom Junior hit the hallway at a run, holding back the yell trapped in his chest. He skidded into the banister at the top of the stairs, grabbing it to turn himself. As he shot across the floor downstairs, he heard Charity in the next room, calling anxiously:

"Tommy? Where'd you go?"

Panting, he opened and closed the front door as quietly as he could, then sprinted across the driveway to the shelter of the dark woods. There he crouched, trying to get back his breath. Whatever was going on in there, he wanted to be as far away from it as he could get.

But what about his mother?

Fearfully, he scanned the facade of the house. Most of the windows were dark, the rest lit only by the dim glow of candles. She could be anywhere.

393

And in a place where he had just seen a dead girl putting on a dress, there was no telling what was happening to her.

Maybe this is a dream, he thought. Maybe it's like in those old fairy tales: pinch yourself and you'll wake up. He closed his eyes and dug his fingernails into his arms. It hurt. When he looked up, he was still crouched in a wet, dark thicket, the house still in front of him. He thought briefly about crying, but realized that he was simply too scared.

Then a movement up in the little bell tower on the roof caught his attention. He ducked, watching. Someone was up there, pacing quickly back and forth. It was hard to see, and he stared for almost a minute before the fog parted enough to give him a clear look.

"Mom!" he called, trying to whisper and yell at the same time. She stopped, her gaze searching the woods. He jumped up, waving.

"TJ!" she cried out. She held out her arms, leaning over the railing, and there they stood like two lovers, one on a dock and one on a ship, separated by a slender but impassable distance.

Nicole sagged with relief, her eyes closing–but immediately they flew open again. He was safe, but that safety was a bubble that could burst at any second. She clasped her palms against her temples, forcing herself to concentrate. To send him for help would be useless at best–Valcourt could cause the entity to clamp down on her again, to make her assure anyone who came that all was well, that Valcourt and Charity were their friends, and that Tom Junior had been frightened by something and gone into a fantasy. At worst, it could lure others into a deadly trap.

Others like Jesse.

There was no possibility of explaining, and only one choice. With great effort, she kept her voice calm and barely loud enough for Tom Junior to hear.

"Get to a phone. Call Jesse. Tell him to come get you and then stay with you."

Tom Junior remained where he was, doubt apparent in his posture.

"Now!" she cried. "*Don't* bring anybody back here. I'm all right; I'll come home soon and explain."

Abruptly, she was aware of footsteps pounding up the stairs beneath her.

"Run!" she shrieked, and gave a little sob as he finally turned and sprinted down the driveway into the night.

The hatch door burst open. Valcourt strode up the final steps and gripped her roughly by the shoulders.

"Still you seek to block me!" he growled. "My patience is at an end." He threw her aside and stepped forward. Nicole slammed against the railing with a gasp, but then caught her breath and held it.

He was whistling, a high, mournful sound that did not seem quite human. It made the hair rise on her arms. Electrified with fear, she followed his gaze to the drive below.

A spot darker than the night seemed to be materializing, like a hole that sucked the surrounding blackness into itself. In a few seconds it had formed into a shape, vaguely manlike but half as tall, its face and stubby limbs muffled by a thick robe. Slowly at first, then with increasing urgency, it began to move, bent over, arms outspread, as if sniffing for a scent.

Then, with a suddenness that made Nicole's heart lurch, it dashed off in a gliding, erratic run—in the direction Tom Junior had gone.

Valcourt turned back to her. His face was grim and ugly.

"My pet will return him, never fear. You have only earned yourself a hard death." The mark on her palm flared suddenly, viciously, making her knees buckle.

Gasping, squeezing her hand, she stared at the man before her, and she seemed to see into the implacable cruelty of a heart as hard and black as the sculpture it had amused him to pose beside. As if she was standing on a cliff above a river of time, she saw what he had done to her and to the others and understood the tremendous power that was his to use.

And for the first time she saw that *evil* truly existed: pure, raw, vastly disproportionate in its violence to the petty vices and desires of people like herself: saw that it could never be overcome, only resisted—and that the moment had come, for her, when that resistance could only take one final form.

She rolled over the railing and felt herself sliding, then tumbling down the slick slate tiles to the eave. For a long second, she twisted weightlessly in space, Valcourt's enraged shout in her ears. Then the earth claimed her, with a shock like a blow from a giant fist.

In the instants before the real agony began, as she lay unable to move or breathe, aware of the wet grass

396

against her face and of the twisted angles of her limbs, she realized distantly that the stabbing pain in her palm had vanished.

The man who called himself Guy-Luc Valcourt stood in the foggy darkness, fists raised, howling his fury into the night.

Unhorsed again! And again, by a woman! It was not to be believed!

His hands twisted each other as if they would crush their own bones. He whirled and paced in the tiny enclosure.

All those months of such careful work and planning! Now, of all times, when he had been on the edge of triumph!

And his safety was jeopardized. The Frenchmen were in San Francisco. Through his own arrogance, so grotesque he was not yet able to contemplate it, he was not, after all, prepared.

He inhaled, trying to calm himself. All was not lost; there was, of course, an alternative. But it was a poor and temporary substitute, a propitiation, a sop he had intended to throw to the hungry mouths—nothing like the rich feast he had anticipated with an elation so fierce he could taste it in his mouth like blood.

Patience, he thought: only play the remaining cards surely. The result would require more time and care, but would be the same. First, to salvage advantage out of this defeat. The plan to end the entire nuisance of these Frenchmen at a stroke, in a fiery building, was now void.

But the boy would lead them here, in spite of his mother's warning.

And he, Guy-Luc Valcourt, would arrange for them a surprise.

There was no time to be wasted; Epps and his woman were due within minutes. He issued a harsh command to return the creature known as *celui* to the realm of shadows, stooped to pick up the crimson robe Nicole had thrown on the floor, then strode downstairs and around the side of the house, where her broken body lay on the grass. Her eyes were open, and she was drawing thin, shaky breaths.

He stood over her, letting the robe's hem play across her face.

"A pity you refused to don this," he said. "Now it will serve as your shroud." When he lifted her, she cried out, a shrill, rattling sound. Her eyes stared and her mouth was stretched wide with pain.

The pit he had prepared was half a furlong back in the forest, shielded by brush. In the bottom lay a rotting corpse. It looked half eaten. Its feet were gone. He laid Nicole ungently beside it.

"A measure of my thoughtfulness," he murmured, "to see that you have company in such a lonely spot. You will have yet more before long." He spread the red robe across her. "While you wait, I give you food for thought. You believe you have saved your son, but in truth, he will serve to lure an enemy within my reach. Then I will play with him, as I did with you, until I tire of the game."

He climbed from the pit and left. Consumed by the agony in her bones, Nicole sensed distantly the damp earth and the horrifying stench from the body beside her—whose ravaged, eyeless face she had recognized as that of Robbie Kinsella.

In Nicole's apartment, Jesse Treves crouched on his heels, elbows on knees, the pistol now dangling from his clasped hands, with the barrel pointed at the floor. On the coffee table lay two photographs: of Alysse posed in front of a car, which the Devarres had received in the mail; and of John McTell and his now-dead wife, which Mélusine had taken from McTell's study, along with his papers, that night.

Jesse shook his head and said, "That's Nicole's car, no doubt about it. But I never saw either the girl or the man, and Nicole never said anything that rings a bell."

Boudrie watched him closely, certain that he was telling the truth—beginning, in fact, to find him likable. He was apparently a close friend—or lover, perhaps?—of the Partrick woman, and was clearly most concerned about her—and about her son, of whom they had not been aware until now. The Devarres' glances had confirmed Boudrie's own sense of another ominous underscoring to this whole business.

Because his English was best, Boudrie had acted as spokesman, telling Jesse the agreed-on "starter story": that McTell had, by all indications, gone mad, murdered his wife, and abducted Alysse, the Devarres' daughter; miraculously eluded the authorities; and in a gesture of unfathomable cruelty, sent them the photo.

"Maybe he just picked the car at random," Jesse said, "and it doesn't have anything to do with Nicole. If the guy's nuts–"

"A possibility which we, too, might have accepted," Boudrie said. "But we discovered something in this room only a few minutes ago which, I think you will agree, adds a most sinister element." At his nod, Devarre rose. The movement was abrupt, and Jesse's pistol was instantly steady on his chest.

"*Pardon,*" Devarre murmured, raising his hands. "Perhaps you should come look for yourself."

Warily, Jesse moved toward him. Devarre knelt, keeping his hands in sight, and set the shoes in the open.

Jesse studied them, then blinked and said, "Sweet Jesus."

"If it occurs to you that we brought them ourselves as some sort of ruse," Boudrie said, "I can only promise you that nothing could be further from the truth." He paused, then said, "Have you any idea whose–"

Grimacing, Jesse shook his head. "They're not the kid's, and they're sure not Nicole's."

"We may thank God for that," Boudrie murmured, then mentally added, *I suppose.*

"You think this guy McTell did it?"

"It is the sort of thing we know him to be capable of."

Jesse looked from one to the other of their faces, then exhaled and shoved the revolver into the back pocket of his jeans.

"We had a fight," he said. He hooked his thumbs into his belt and walked to the window. "Nicole and I. Two, three hours ago. I was drunk, and I went out to get

400

drunker. Instead, I started walking it off, I don't know why. Maybe because I knew there was something really bothering her, and I'd acted like a shit.

"I know they were here when I left, her and the kid. Then when I came back, I saw the car gone, the garage door open, and you"–he nodded at Boudrie–"walk past the window. I tiptoed up the stairs and got my gun." He shrugged. "That's honest to Christ all I know."

"Is there anything else familiar about this photo?" Mélusine said, touching the one of Alysse. "Background, perhaps?"

He shook his head. There was nothing else visible but woods.

"Could be anywhere within hundreds of miles." His attention moved to the photo of McTell beside it. "This is him, huh?"

Mélusine sighed. "That is who he was when last we saw him."

Jesse stood, angry again, and said, "What the fuck's that supposed to mean?"

She looked helplessly at Boudrie. Then she shrugged and said in French, "Tell him."

Jesse watched the exchange, wariness in his eyes.

Boudrie exhaled. "If you suspect already that we are mad, my friend," he said, "allow me ten minutes to remove all doubt."

When the expected vehicle arrived at his house, Valcourt perceived that Spencer Epps had made profligate use of his drug through the evening, compounding its effects with drink. This angered him. It would corrode what little willpower the man had, thus vitiating the offering even further. But there was nothing to be done now. At least there would be no more unpleasant surprises.

The girl, Tina, was pretty enough by the standards of the day, although common in demeanor and shallow in spirit, and also steeped in the drug. But Valcourt smiled, maintaining icy control, and led them to the parlor, all along carrying on a conversational patter intended to charm. Tina was cowed, even a little fearful, at the plush surroundings and at the strength of his person. To begin with, she must be put at ease–then carefully played, a mouse to his cat, in order to extract the maximum emotion from her when the moment came.

After a half-hour of too much wine too quickly, she had visibly relaxed. As instructed, Charity had effusively admired her hair and dress, and Valcourt had complimented Epps on his taste in companions.

"Spencer told me it was going to be a really intense party," Tina said. "That you've been teaching, sort of, creative visualization?"

"One could think of it as such," Valcourt agreed, inclining his head.

"Well, thank you for inviting me. Whatever you're doing, it sure has worked for Spence." She glanced at him coquettishly.

"It is I who thank you, for joining us on such short notice. We required a fourth, and female, for sexual balance. Our usual partner was–unavoidably detained." He stood. "But the hour approaches; we must prepare. Will you humor me by donning these robes?" He took them from a box: a hooded black one, like his own, for Epps; sleeveless silk tabards for the women—crimson for Charity, and white for Tina. "Nothing beneath, if you please, and no jewelry. You will find a selection of sandals in the next room." Tina half smiled, in her element, and strutted a little as she and Charity left.

Spencer undressed hastily, with quick, nervous movements, his eyes averted. When he was robed, Valcourt commanded his gaze.

"There was a recent matter of several—delicate— photographs, was there not?"

Spencer stared at him without speaking.

"It was she," Valcourt said, raising his hand to indicate the room where the women were changing. "Under the pretense of affection for you, she in truth desires only your wealth. Thus she sought to hasten the failure of your marriage, caring nothing that it might bring you disaster. Let me assure you, my friend: a lover who has betrayed you once will do so again without hesitation."

Spencer's stunned gaze followed Valcourt's pointing finger toward the door that separated Tina from him.

"Remember," Valcourt said quietly, "what my power has brought you. Serve me, and all that you desire will be yours throughout your life. Remember, too, my protection assures that you cannot be touched by the laws of men. You will never again know fear."

By the time the door began to open, Valcourt saw with satisfaction that Spencer's disbelief had given way to comprehension, and that what remained of judgment was swiftly disappearing beneath a swell of rage.

When the priest was finished talking, nobody said anything for perhaps a minute. Then Jesse walked aimlessly over to one corner of the room and just stood there.

He had almost been about to believe that these people were all right.

His peripheral vision caught Boudrie and Devarre glancing at each other and shrugging. At least they knew how insane it sounded.

Devil worship? That *worked?*

He turned back, shaking his head. "No hard feelings, gentlemen," he said. "I'm afraid my imagination doesn't stretch that far."

"Assuredly, we do not blame you," the priest said. He was an imposing-looking man, Jesse admitted: shrunken, as if he'd been sick, but with a powerful frame and hands, and very impressive eyes. Eyes that measured you, held you accountable. The eyes of a no-bullshit individual.

The eyes of a man who was, nonetheless, patently crazy.

Except for that, all three of them seemed like intelligent, decent people. What did they call it when a pair of crazies made a tacit pact to share some particular mania, like playing Napoleon and Josephine? *Folie à deux,* that was it: one of the few French terms he knew.

"I refused to believe too, *mon ami,*" said the doctor. "If I had listened earlier, then perhaps–" He shrugged again.

"It was all of us," the priest said wearily. "We could not have imagined." Then he turned to Jesse and said, "In any case, please accept our promises that we have not

404

come to do harm. We will leave here as soon as you wish; and if there is anything we can do to help you find your *amie*, we hope you will contact us."

Jesse was about to say, Don't call me, I'll call you, when the telephone rang. He strode across the room and grabbed it.

"Tommy!" he said after a second. "Where are you?"

They waited in tense, strained silence. Boudrie saw the expression on Jesse's face change from relief to anger to something beyond anger.

"Whoa, whoa, slow down," Jesse said. "Think, now: What else did she say?" The effort it cost him to control his voice was apparent. He listened for half a minute longer, then said, "Okay, you do what she told you. Hide in the bushes where you can watch the parking lot, and wait until you see me. Don't go anywhere else and don't talk to anybody. I'll be there in half an hour."

He hung up. His eyes met Boudrie's, and the priest saw the blackness far back that was the mark of a man who was stepping beyond any limit of restraint.

"He's shook," Jesse said. "He's been trying to call me at my place for twenty minutes. He and Nicole broke down and ended up at a house in the woods, south of here. The owner's a one-eyed man named Guy-Luc."

"Guilhem," Devarre said. "An obvious *jeu de mots*."

"There was a girl," Jesse said. He hesitated, then said, "Tommy swears her throat was cut."

Boudrie took a quick step forward, but restrained himself.

"He fled?"

"He's at a rest area on the highway."

"And his mother?" Mélusine said.

"She was still there. She yelled at him to find me but not to go back there. Said she was okay, she'd be home soon." His gaze moved from one to the other of them. "It doesn't sound okay to me. I know this kid. He's got to be wrong about that girl, but he's no liar."

"Let us follow you," Devarre said. "You can see to the boy. We will see to—the rest."

Jesse was on his way to the door. He shook his head, not stopping.

"This one's mine."

Mélusine stepped quickly in front of him, blocking his way.

"Stupid heroics will only get her killed. You have no idea what you face."

"They threw everything in the book at me in Nam, lady."

"Yes? This young dead girl? I have seen her, too: walking."

Jesse hesitated, his face less certain.

"And I," Boudrie said, "killed a score of German soldiers, some with my hands, while you were still at your mother's breast."

For several seconds longer, no one moved or spoke. Then Jesse exhaled.

"I don't have time to argue."

"Our vehicle will seat us all," Devarre said. "I will drive, you may direct." With a hint of irony, he added, "And keep us, how do you say, covered."

Jesse took the two Brownings from his belt and handed them to the other men.

They trotted across the street to the Ford, and accelerated swiftly away from the curb.

"You must understand," Mélusine said, turning in the seat to face Jesse. "There is only one possible reason he would have let the boy escape."

Boudrie nodded. "Bait," he said hoarsely.

Charity and Tina reentered the parlor, giggling and admiring each other's robes.

"Truly, a vision of loveliness," Valcourt murmured. He gave each a black candle to hold, and himself carried his grimoire. Spencer's eyes were flicking back and forth, his hands shaking noticeably. As they stepped onto the porch, Valcourt said, "The night is cool; I apologize for any discomfort. It will not last long."

Some twenty yards behind the house, the grounds ended and the woods, thick with mist, began. Valcourt led them along a twisting path, through gnarled oaks and sinuous madrones. Tina whispered, "Spooky!" with fearful delight.

In a clearing, at the base of a thick oak, stood a small stone altar draped with a black cloth, upon which was emblazoned, in a red that matched Charity's robe, an enlarged replica of the emblem on the grimoire's cover. A silver bowl rested on the altar's center, and behind it, a three-branched candelabra. Valcourt took the candles from the others and placed them in it. Then, standing behind the altar, hands clasped around the grimoire, he faced them.

"We are gathered to do honor to him who is true lord and true friend to man," he said. "He is the fallen star, the son of the morning, the greatest of angels, the tremendous spirit who had courage, before time and the world began, to revolt against a cruel and unjust god. To honor and serve him is the privilege of the chosen few. In return, he rewards his faithful with all they desire.

"Let you who would rise, then, above common men and their false enslaving god, join together in this offering."

He paused to let the words take effect. Tina was still smiling, but her eyes had gone uncertain. Spencer's face was pale and tense; Charity's, eager.

"We welcome our new sister, and thank her for the gift she so willingly provides us. Come to me, my dear." He extended his hand.

Hesitantly, Tina walked around the altar to his side. "Gift?" she said.

"You shall see." He raised her hand, turning her, as in a dance, to face the others; and with a smooth, unhurried motion, he pressed her wrist back against the tree. There was a metallic click. By the time her face could register surprise, he had caught her other wrist and repeated the action, leaving her with hands pinned at shoulder height to the manacles set into the trunk.

He watched with pleasure her shock turn to a timorous smile, the realization that she was being teased. But as she stared at his face, the smile faded. Behind him, he felt an answering fear of a very different sort, emanating in waves from Spencer.

"The gift, my dear," Valcourt said softly, "of your blood."

For long, tense seconds, no one moved or spoke: there were only the drifting wisps of fog, the flickering candles, the mossy twisted limbs of the oak.

Then Tina stammered, "Please let me go. This isn't funny."

"You are quite right," Valcourt said. "It is most eminently serious."

Abruptly, he stepped forward, taking a black-handled dagger from his sleeve. With the same sureness of movement, he slit her robe across the shoulders. She shrieked, and as the garment crumpled at her feet, she strained, white-faced, against the manacles.

"What are you doing?" she gasped. "Give me my clothes!"

"There, there," Valcourt said soothingly. "Modesty does not become a lady of your profession." He turned away, placing the knife on the altar beside the bowl.

"He who provides this great offering to our lord and master," he said, voice harsh and strong, "will grow in favor through the rest of his days." His single-eyed gaze burned with hard, dark fire on Spencer's bloodless face. "Once for all, leave behind the world of puny, common men! You have nothing to fear! Prove your loyalty—and reap your reward!" The scene hung suspended, a silent motionless tableau of the strained faces in the smoky light.

Tongue touching his lips, Spencer stepped forward to the altar.

"*Spencer!*" she screamed, her eyes dark pools of terror. He winced visibly, but his shaking hand grasped the knife.

Valcourt raised the grimoire and began to chant.

"I immolate this victim to thee, O great Master, whose honor, power, and glory are superior to all spirits! I entreat thee to favor us in this adjuration, which I address to thy mighty ministers, Beelzebuth, Ashtaroth, Moloch, Adramelek, Asmodeus, Lilith, Belphegor . . ."

Tina's cries rose shrilly as Spencer approached. Still chanting, Valcourt looked down into Charity's fevered eyes, and pressed a second knife into her hand.

Valcourt moved easily and surely through the dark woods, a corpse hung over each arm like garments. The heads lolled grotesquely, and the limp, hanging hands brushed the ground. Charity remained beside the altar, watching with fear, delight, and amazement the gleeful cavortings of the servants Valcourt called the *hungry mouths,* partaking of the feast: company not ordinarily visible to humans, but which tonight, as a reward for her loyalty, he had opened her eyes to see. She had performed admirably, plunging the dagger into the throat of Spencer Epps as he shrank back in horror from the work of his own hand: the final silencing of the shrieking, struggling woman he had professed to love. Valcourt had noted with dispassion the last comprehension in his dimming eyes as he sank to his knees.

"It is just as I said, is it not?" he had murmured to Spencer Epps. "An iron talon, crushing the life from a husk."

And then he had dipped the silver bowl into the blood that flowed down the woman's lovely breasts and

410

given Charity the drink that sealed their bond. She was in truth a sister, who would be of much use—for a time.

Nicole Partrick was still staring up into the night, and he saw with satisfaction that she had managed to move slightly. Life would remain within her for some hours yet. He would take care that her breathing would not be interfered with. He stepped down into the pit, arranging the two fresh corpses so that an arm of each was thrown across her in a final embrace, their blood leaking onto her breast. Then he smiled down into her pleading eyes and said:

"Farewell. Your lover will be here soon, searching for you. You will likely hear him call your name. Had you served me better, you would stand beside me now in triumph, and return to his embrace this night." He climbed back to the pit's rim and started away.

Then, as if in afterthought, he paused and turned back. "While you say goodbye to light, your keepers for eternity will introduce themselves to you."

A little way farther, alone in the night and surrounded by death, he at last closed his eye and let the surge of newly won strength race through him like hot young blood in his veins. It was not nearly as much as he had hoped; he would have to use it with great care and measure. But there was enough to eliminate the major enemy, now, tonight.

Standing in the misty darkness, he issued a silent command. In seconds, there came a rustling in the brush. The black cat Lamashtu leaped into the crotch of a tree before him. Gripping the grimoire, Valcourt began to chant again, his voice and power rising. The cat crouched motionless, as the minor servant made way for a far more potent one. Slowly, with effort, he summoned the resisting entity: a being without intelligence, but a tremendous black force of hate and fury. At last, barely contained, it yielded. It would strike for him, once.

"The woman," he breathed. "Go!"

Shaking from the strain, he watched the cat leap down from the tree and vanish toward the house. She would be here soon, was already on per way. Her death would crush the will of her husband, and without her as an ally, the priest would be helpless. Killing them would then be a matter of revenge rather than necessity, to be effected at leisure.

And if a taste of disappointment remained in him that he would not have the chance to confront her in person, to explore the strange emotion that had arisen in him, so be it. His chivalry had already brought him too close to disaster. He turned and strode back to where his "sister" waited.

A quarter of an hour later, all was ready: the altar dismantled, the important implements packed, his grimoire safe–and a suitable message left.

There remained only one matter more. At his silent command, the door to the house opened, and a moment later, Alysse moved down the steps. With some surprise, he sensed jealousy flaring in Charity's heart. He turned to her, amused. He had known it was there, smoldering, at his lovely young "niece"; he had not yet revealed the truth to Charity, thinking it might be too much too soon, and frighten her off. But now, there was no more need for secrecy.

"Bring me the girl's scarf," he said.

Charity looked at Alysse, then at him, uncertain; but when he nodded encouragement, she stepped forward and, a little roughly, tugged at the scarf's knot.

A moment later, Guy-Luc Valcourt's laughter echoed through the night, drifting faintly back to the grave that held three dead bodies and one living one: a deep, booming sound of genuine amusement, mingling with the gibbering whispers of the unseen laborers steadily filling the pit.

Nicole lay without blinking, watching earth rise slowly to the level of her face–

Beginning to understand what the hideous voices were saying.

SEVENTEEN

At the rest area, Jesse jumped out of the car and trotted to the center of the parking lot, making sure he was visible beneath the argon lights. As his eyes scanned the nearby shrubbery for movement, the door of a peach-colored XKE opened and a man about his own age stepped out. He had very short hair and a neatly trimmed beard, and was wearing skin-tight blue jeans rolled up above high-topped logger boots. A tiny silver star sparkled in his right car. He smiled knowingly as he approached.

"What are you in such a hurry for?" he said.

Jesse's gaze continued to search the dark line of brush on the hillside.

"Disappear," he said quietly.

The man pouted, striking a pose with one hand on his hip.

"No need to play coy, sailor. You don't come here and hang out in the parking lot unless you're looking for action."

Jesse took the .38 from his back pocket, holding it so it was almost entirely concealed by his hand, and placed the end of the barrel against the smiling lips. Voice still soft, he said:

"You have three seconds to be history."

The man's eyes went the size of quarters. White was visible all around the pupils.

"One," Jesse said.

He had already put it out of his mind by the time the XKE screeched out of the lot. A slender shape was running down the hill. He shoved the pistol back into his pocket and started forward.

"There's our car," Tom Junior said, leaning forward over the front seat to point. Devarre swung the Ford into the turnout and Jesse got out, trotting over to look in the Celica's windows, on the slim chance that Nicole might have found her way back to it.

"Nothing," he said, returning to lean in the Ford's window. "How much farther's the house, Tommy?"

"Maybe a mile," Tom Junior said uncertainly.

"You'll recognize the gate?"

He nodded, eyes frightened. "That's where I saw that . . . thing . . . coming after me," he whispered.

Jesse stood in the darkness, thinking. Nicole had said not to come there, that she would be all right. But it stunk, even if the three Frenchmen *were* crazy. Even if Tommy *had* imagined the girl with the slit throat and the dark creature pursuing him, whose description had made the priest turn away with a venomous hiss. Imagination or not, the boy was scared to death. Was that what Nicole

415

had been trying to warn against: taking him back to the lion's den?

What choice did they have?

He motioned for Boudrie to join him. They walked a few yards away from the car, out of Tom Junior's hearing.

"How about the lady drops us off, takes Tommy and keeps driving?"

Boudrie shook his head. "I would wish that, too. But you see, she is the most valuable of us. She is *clairvoyante,* the one who has some chance to recognize this Courdeval and his traps. Without her, our weapons are nothing."

"Her husband, then."

"He would kill us all before he would leave her side."

Jesse sighed. "Then what do we do with the kid?"

"These are hard words, I know. But if we do not survive this encounter–" His hands came together, and made the sudden motion of breaking a stick. "It is better for the boy to die with us than to be left alone. That monster Courdeval will find him anywhere.

"You do not yet fully believe us, *mon ami.* This is only fair. But that creature the child describes: I myself have encountered it firsthand–just as Madame Devarre has seen the dead young woman who walks." The cold and fog of the night had intensified, but Jesse saw that the priest was sweating. He nodded curtly.

Back in the car, he leaned forward and said to Mélusine, "However this goes down, I want to tell you that I'm sorry about what happened to your daughter."

The Devarres exchanged glances.

"She was not, in truth, their daughter," the priest said. "She was mine."

The iron gate at the entrance to the drive was unlocked. Jesse opened it, then trotted ahead of the car. Devarre followed, headlights out. When he came within sight of the house, Jesse waved them to stop. The drive was empty of vehicles, the windows unlit, and the gurgling of the dark fountain sounded cold and sinister. He stared, wondering how to proceed. Sneak around the back? Kick down the door? He had moved on places at night before, but never a three-story house.

Footsteps sounded behind him. He turned to Boudrie, about to say, Let me go first and check it out, but the priest interrupted him firmly.

"There is no point in stealth. If he is here, he knows perfectly well our whereabouts. To separate would only make it easy for him to deal with us one at a time." The others were coming to join them, with Mélusine holding Tom Junior's hand. "It was a mistake we made last time," Boudrie said.

"One of many," Mélusine murmured.

"You and Tommy stay between us, then," Jesse said. "And not too close." Devarre handed him a flashlight, then went back to guard the rear.

The priest touched Jesse's shoulder. "If by some miracle we see him unprotected," he said quietly, "I intend to kill him on sight. I advise you to do the same."

For the last time, Jesse wondered if he was being sucked into some unimaginable craziness with huge consequences: the murder of innocent people, prison, even his own death.

Then he said, "I walked out on her when she was in trouble."

Boudrie nodded. They started up the steps to the porch.

Carefully, Jesse turned the knob and eased the door forward an inch. It was unlocked. He inhaled deeply, then threw it the rest of the way open and burst through, crouching, sweeping the room with the flashlight beam, pistol following.

Nobody, nothing.

Mélusine stepped in, Tom Junior behind her. The priest and Devarre watched her in silence, and Jesse waited with them.

"I think," she said after a moment, "there is no one."

None of them voiced the obvious: Then where was Nicole?

"Let's get some light," Jesse said.

Devarre walked to a wall and flicked a switch on and off. The house remained dark.

"As I suspected," he said. "It is one of his trademarks."

"There are candles," Boudrie said, pointing with his own flashlight.

"Black," said Mélusine softly. "It is he, all right."

In a moment, the candelabras were filling the room with their smoky light. Mélusine took one, holding it like a torch, and turned to Tom Junior.

"Where did you last see your mother?"

"In that tower on top of the house," he said, pointing at the ceiling.

"*La coupole,*" Boudrie said. "I suppose we should look there first."

They were nearly to the staircase when Mélusine stopped and said, "*Un moment.*" She released Tom Junior's hand and started walking, very slowly, toward the entrance to the next room. Boudrie and Devarre stepped beside her. Jesse could sense her sudden intensity, and a tightening in the knot of fear that held them all. He gripped Tom Junior's shoulder and followed, swiveling at every step to look behind.

The room was a parlor, filled with heavy antique furniture. Above the fireplace was an ornate hardwood mantel, and above that, a gilt-framed mirror.

Even before Mélusine set the candelabra on the mantel, Jesse saw the writing on the mirror. Several words, scribed with obvious care–in blood. His grip on his pistol tightened.

The letters read:

QUID SUB TERRA ET NUNC SPIRAT?

The priest exhaled sharply.

"What does it mean?" Jesse said through his teeth.

Boudrie ignored him, turning instead to Mélusine and speaking a quick, hoarse sentence in French. She shook her head in disbelief.

"God damn it," Jesse said, stepping forward.

Boudrie held up his palm, indicating Tom Junior with his eyes. Jesse let the boy go and walked with the priest to a comer of the room. There Boudrie turned to him, rage mixed with helplessness in his eyes, and was about to speak when there came a faint scratching sound from the doorway. Jesse whirled. His flashlight beam found a black cat, arching itself, rubbing against the jamb.

Tom Junior said excitedly, "A kitty!" and hurried toward it. He stooped and was reaching to scratch the cat's ears when the woman's scream erupted:

"No, get *back!*"

What happened next, Jesse Treves would never be able to reconstruct exactly. In the beat of a heart, the cat swelled before his eyes into something he had no power to describe. It was perhaps the size of a bear, although more fluid than solid, as if made of force rather than matter. It seemed to be composed of parts of many different animals, all of them distorted grotesquely: coarse black fur sprouting through greasy scales, snakelike limbs ending in tremendous curved claws, and a face that, in the brief glimpse he got of it, snarled with such fury and ferocity, such raw, naked evil, that the impact of it literally slammed him back against the wall.

He remembered the creature leaping–not leaping, exactly, but moving somehow with unbelievable swiftness in a way that did not resemble the motion of any animal he had ever seen–toward Mélusine; remembered that even more unbelievably, her husband got in front of her; that there was a terrific ripping sound, clear even above her scream–

And then it was gone. A small, frightened-looking black cat bolted out the door.

420

Slowly, silent now, Mélusine knelt beside her husband. Jesse sucked in his breath.

The man's skull had been crushed, the side of his face and neck simply ripped away. A widening red pool was spreading on the carpet.

She stood, looking at the priest, and said something in French, a quick, harsh sentence. Bondrie nodded dumbly. Then she turned without hesitation to where Tom Junior was standing, round-eyed with horror, and hurried forward.

"Come along, *mon cher*," she said, taking his hand and leading him out. "This is not for you to see."

Jesse looked back to see the priest watching him steadily.

"She will grieve in her own way, in her own time," he said. "As will I."

The savaged corpse lay like accusing evidence that what could not have happened had happened; and as Jesse's gaze was pulled again to it, images from twenty years before, the stuff of his own nightmares, flashed through his mind.

"What was it she said?" he whispered.

"That it was intended for her." Boudrie paused, then said, "With Mélusine gone, you see, you would know only that your *amie* was somewhere nearby, dying, but you would be helpless to find her."

Jesse gripped the priest's arm. "What do you mean? How do you know?"

"The words on the mirror. They say, 'What yet breathes—beneath the earth?'"

Numb with shock, Jesse stared.

421

"You begin to understand not only the power of this man," Boudrie said, "but his nature."

Jesse turned and strode out of the room. Mélusine was standing on the porch, holding Tom Junior's face against her.

"You can find her?" Jesse said.

"I do not know. It may not even be true, his claim. But I will try."

She knelt and took the boy's face in her hands.

"Do you understand what has happened? Your *maman* is hidden from us, in great danger. You must help me find her. Call her with your mind. Tell her you are coming, that she must cry out in her thoughts so we can hear her."

For the longest minutes of his life, Jesse waited, hardly breathing, while the woman knelt motionless, eyes closed, clasping the boy's hands tightly.

Then both of them moved at once, Tom Junior in a sudden little jerk, Mélusine rising swiftly to her feet. With her eyes closed, still silent, she began to walk. Boudrie hurried in front of her, and Jesse joined him, clearing brush and branches from her path as she stepped into the dripping black woods.

It took twenty more endless minutes of stops and starts, turns and circlings, before Mélusine finally cried out, opened her eyes, and began a limping run. Her finger pointed. The two men tore at the vegetation until they uncovered a mound of fresh loose earth.

Jesse dropped to his knees and began to dig like a dog. Boudrie joined him, his huge hands tearing shovel-sized chunks from the earth. The dirt was loose, and in a few more minutes they were crouched in a waist-deep pit.

Then Jesse's hand touched something he recognized as flesh.

Cold flesh.

"She's dead," he whispered, and standing, collapsed against the excavation's side, face buried in his arms.

With half a dozen more swipes, Boudrie uncovered the naked human back that Jesse had touched. He gripped the corpse's extended arm, and with a heave, turned her over. It was a woman, and he noticed distantly that she had once been beautiful, but she had most certainly not been buried alive. Her breast was dark with blood.

He lifted her out, laid her aside, and stooped again, clearing the dirt from another extended arm. In doing so, he exposed a face, also a woman's. Her eyes were closed. He gripped Jesse's arm, pulling him down to look.

"Nicole," Jesse breathed. Quickly, he brushed away crumbs of dirt from the pale, still face.

And cried out when the eyelids fluttered—

Not noticing that Mélusine had turned and limped quietly away, back to where her husband's body lay.

EIGHTEEN

Three days later, deep in the quiet afternoon, Etien Boudrie and Jesse Treves lowered a strange-looking metal cylinder into a hand-dug grave, in an isolated forest clearing not far from the south fork of the Feather River, country Jesse knew well from his backpacking days. He had spent the previous day in his garage constructing the coffin from a length of galvanized metal culvert pipe, welding ends on it so that nothing could disturb the remains. As Mélusine watched, she recalled her husband making a coffin for Courdeval's bones only weeks before. The irony was one she did not care to consider.

Nicole had undergone emergency treatment for several broken bones, including her pelvis; concussion; and attendant shock to internal organs. But nothing, including her spinal column, had been damaged irrevocably. They had manufactured a story about a climbing fall on a camping trip. After she had stabilized, she had been flown to a southern California hospital, ostensibly so that her parents could be close by to care for her.

But really so that if Courdeval was aware that she still lived, she would at least not be within easy striking range. Tom Junior had accompanied her, having solemnly promised Jesse not to breathe a word to anyone else about what bad happened.

After seeing to Nicole, Jesse and Boudrie had returned to the house that same night and accomplished the grim tasks of reclaiming Roger Devarre's body, removing the carpet and cleaning up the blood, and reburying the corpses they had found in the pit. To leave them like that was hateful, but all had agreed there was no alternative at this point.

Mélusine understood that her grief for the gentle man she had loved for twenty-five years was only beginning. But there was no allowance for caving in: it was a simple matter of survival, of war. Instead, she used the torment as a goad to strength, consoling herself that he had died in a magnificent act of courage–and that she would almost certainly join him before long.

And now, she thought, watching Jesse coil one of the ropes they had used to lower the strange casket, a new ally had come, as if to replace him: another actor, stepping from the wings to play out his own part in this tragedy.

Boudrie wiped sweat from his forehead with his wrist, then took his breviary from his pocket.

"I'll keep this short," he muttered. He began to read, his voice edged with bitterness.

When he finished, he reached without pausing for a shovel. Working quickly and in silence, the two men began to fill the hole.

Mélusine turned away and walked with folded arms to the clearing's edge, gazing off at the wooded mountaintops that surrounded them with such cruel loveliness.

On the faint chance that she survived Courdeval's certain third attempt on her life—if by some miracle they overcame him—she would find a way to bring her husband's remains back to France, so that they could be buried together beneath the Provençal twilight he had loved.

If Courdeval won out, it would hardly matter.

Behind her, the sounds changed from the clattering of pebbles hitting metal to the steady thud of dirt on dirt.

ACKNOWLEDGMENTS

Re-releasing these novels has only been possible with great support and expertise on many levels.

Next, After Lucifer owes a particular debt to three classic stories of the supernatural: "Canon Alberic's Scrap-Book" and "Count Magnus" by M. R. James, and "The Book" by Margaret Irwin.

On a more personal level, the major pillars of this undertaking consist of a Gang of Three:

As always, my wife, Kim, has been my mainstay, both for her technical skills and for keeping me relatively sane.

Jason Neal is the genius behind everything from the website and Facebook pages to cover design.

Prof. Lisa Simon has added indispensable advice on editing, content, and shaping the overall process.

We've managed to have a pretty good time together along the way.

My family—who never knew quite what to expect from me, but it definitely wasn't this—have been rock solid, with special thanks to my brother and his wife, Drs. Dan and Barbara McMahon.

Jennifer Rudolph Walsh, at William Morris Endeavor Entertainment, has been my guardian angel for more than a decade. Also at WME, Britton Schey launched the ebooks with swift competence; Claudia Ballard and Eric Zohn retrieved the rights for these new publications; and other colleagues have tirelessly promoted my work.

My terrific editors at HarperCollins, Carl Lennertz and Dan Conaway, along with their colleagues, gave me major support through critical years.

Going back in time to when the books first came out:

Prof. Ted Ahern, of Boston College, kindly provided all Latin translations.

Tom Dunne and Michael Carlisle were the editor and agent who made it happen.

Heartfelt thanks to all of you, and to the many other friends who helped along the way.

NEXT, AFTER LUCIFER

Ancient evil awakens in a rural French village, in the form of a Templar knight who was burned at the stake in the 14th century for practicing black magic. Now it's the 1980s, and his undead spirit, bent on possession of a human body, invades the lives of a wealthy American couple renting a nearby villa. A genuinely frightening story–not recommended for children.

"A well-turned tale of supernatural terror in which lurks one of the best–or worst–monstrous creations to come along in a month of Black Sabbaths." (Houston Chronicle, 1987)

ADVERSARY

A sequel to *Next, After Lucifer,* with the evil Templar, Guilhem de Courdeval, surfacing in San Francisco. He poses as a spiritual teacher and gathers disciples, using a seductive philosophy that quickly fulfills their desires and solves their problems. At first, it all seems inno- cent–until they realize that his true goal is to turn them into servants of evil, and they're in too deep to back out.

"A storyteller of exceptional depth . . . The story blends black magic and mystery within a tight plot. One of the real delights, though, is his talent for describing people and places in few words but rich detail." (Evening News, Norwich, England, 1989)

CAST ANGELS DOWN TO HELL

Baby Selena, conceived and born under sinister circumstances, grows up into a beauty–but she remains shadowed by eerie mystery. The only men she'll take as lovers are loathsome criminals and scum–and they all soon die, raving mad suicides. Still, no one suspects her hellish secret: she's part demon child, cursed to be followed by nightmarish "companions" that feast on the souls of the men she beds. Her human side hates what she's forced to do, and so far she's thwarted the companions by giving them only the rotten meat of corrupt souls. But now they're demanding a goodhearted young doctor who's smitten by her–and her strength to fight them off is exhausted.

"A stylish semisequel to *Next, After Lucifer* (1987) and *Adversary* (1988) . . . Supple, moody prose lends an aura of ancient mystery to the story . . . it's his best yet–a haunting work." (Publishers Weekly, 1990)